MATTERS OF THE HEART

By

Innocent Karikoga

Published by

in collaboration with

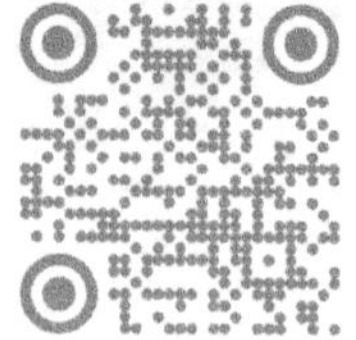

Revised version

ISBN: 978-1-0689798-4-2

"Learn to appreciate what you have and stress less about
what you don't have."

MATTERS OF THE HEART

Matters of the Heart

Finding Yourself

In the sacred walls of hospitals, where humanity's heartbeats echo, an ancient truth about life reveals itself with profound resonance, like a wise philosopher imparting age-old wisdom: "The walls of hospitals have heard more prayers than the walls of places of worship."

Within these solemn walls, life's trials and tribulations converge, and the souls of the afflicted seek comfort like pilgrims in search of redemption. The dance of hope and despair unfolds here in the middle of the fragility of mortality, like the interplay of light and shadow upon the tides of existence.

These walls have witnessed the symphony of human emotions, like the sky shifting from stormy tempests to golden sunsets. Within these walls, tears of joy and smiles of hope blossom like wildflowers growing from cracks in ancient stone walls, defying all odds to announce life's triumph over adversity.

When celebrations ring out in grand halls, joy fills the air. However, in the tender embrace of a patient's sanctuary, hope is the only silent, guiding, resilient, and unwavering star that flickers. As the old saying goes, "Hope springs eternal," in these sanctuaries of healing, hope is revealed in its purest form, a beacon brightening the darkest nights of despair.

Humanity seeks refuge here in the face of physical agony and the anguish of the mind—a place for shedding the proud armour of self-sufficiency to embrace the humility of asking for help. "No man is an island," as the adage reveals a literal and relatable meaning for every patient. Within these walls, a community of healers, caretakers, and fellow sufferers gather, weaving a tapestry of compassion and understanding.

Fear creeps like a cunning shadow, anxieties grind like relentless tides upon the shore, and anger simmers like a brewing storm. But amidst these turbulent emotions, hope stands tall like a mighty oak, its roots deeply ingrained in the resilience of the relentless human spirit.

As the hours pass in a rhythmic tempo of dark and reassuring emotions, the pulse of life resonates. Within these corridors, rooms, and walls, souls find peace, mend their wounds, and lift each other with a gentle hand, like weary travellers supporting one another on a precarious path.

In this sacred domain, the boundaries between life and death blur like the horizon at twilight. Hope dances even in the darkest hours, like a lone firefly amidst the vast night. Within these shrines, raw marvel bears the essence of human existence, the ebb and flow of emotions, and the resilience of the human spirit.

This is where everyone is humbled by the profound truth of existence woven within these walls. It is the only place in our world where tears and smiles, fear and hope, joy and sorrow intertwine like the convergence of destiny, creating a symphony of life that resonates through nature and nurture.

As patients emerge from these hallowed halls, they carry with them the enduring truth in the embrace of hope. Even amidst the trials of a hospital ward, the indomitable spirit of humanity continues to soar.

Matters of the Heart

Life and mortality intertwine, and stories of profound resonance play out like the pages of an ancient book, chronicling the diverse elements of the human journey. Each individual within these walls is a chapter unto themselves, vividly etching emotions into existence.

Like a solitary sailor on an uncertain sea, a patient awaits the whispers of destiny that will herald the verdict of life or the possibility of cancer. Suspense hangs heavy in the air like the moment before dawn, when the world holds its breath, awaiting the sun's triumphant rise.

In one room, a man stands beside his faithful wife, her heartstrings intertwined with the melody of hope and sorrow. Her dreams of starting a family, once like stars in the night sky, now flicker with uncertainty, a reminder that life's plans are as erratic as the wind. As the old saying goes, "Man plans, and God laughs." The whispered echoes of her hopes intertwine with the secrets of the universe.

The man who stands on the precipice of a testicular cancer diagnosis, a brave and humbling journey, reflects upon his mortality like a lone traveller gazing upon a distant horizon. He contemplates the ebb and flow of life's tides, pondering the legacy he will leave behind.

Within these walls, young hearts carry burdens as heavy as ancient oaks. Children, orphaned in the blink of an eye, find themselves adrift in a sea of uncertainty, much like lost ships on a stormy night. Their tears become a testament to the fragile nature of existence.

In another room, a man's emotions form a bittersweet blend. The birth of his child, a moment of purest joy, is juxtaposed against the painful absence of his beloved wife, who slipped from this world amidst the woes of childbirth. Such is the dance of life and death, where joy and sorrow twirl hand in hand like a delicate waltz under the moonlit sky.

And then there's the young woman who emerges victorious from the shackles of breast cancer, her spirit akin to a phoenix rising from the ashes, heralding resilience and triumph. Her journey, a testament to the enduring human spirit, shines as bright as the summer sun on a day with clear skies.

Meanwhile, a couple's laughter and tears mingle like the rain and sun as they cradle the culmination of their shared dreams of starting a family. Their journey, marked by years of longing and trials, is a reminder that perseverance can weather the harshest storms.

In the heart of these walls, the hospital staff is easily perceived as guardians of a unique threshold between worlds. Yet, as you venture into the depths of their humanity, you find they, too, are woven from the same intricate fabric of emotions, dreams, and vulnerabilities.

These noble stewards of hope and healing, doctors, nurses, and caregivers, are like seasoned sailors navigating the unpredictable seas of human experience. They stand as lighthouses amidst a storm, their empathy a guiding beacon that pierces through the darkest nights.

Just as the moon tugs at the tides, their patients' emotional currents pull these compassionate souls in myriad directions. They are akin to skilled conductors orchestrating a symphony of emotions, where the crescendo of joy might harmonize with the undertones of sorrow in neighbouring rooms.

Like alchemists of the heart, these healers hold the elixir of compassion, simultaneously sipping from cups of celebration and consoling chalices. With a gentle touch, they mend not only the wounds of flesh but also the tender scars of the soul. In these moments, an adage whispers, "He who heals a broken bone may earn a title, but he who heals a broken heart is truly a physician."

In one moment, they might be swept away in the jubilant dance of life's victories, laughing with a patient who has emerged triumphant from their trials. The next, they stand with quiet strength, a pillar of support for another who faces the abyss of loss. They transition from celebrants to consolers as seamlessly as the shifting hues of the sky at dawn.

This delicate dance between joy and sorrow reveals the depth of their commitment. They are sculptors of empathy, chiselling away their emotional boundaries to hold space for the expanse of human sentiment. Just as a seasoned farmer tends to both the bloom and the thorn, these remarkable souls cultivate hope even amidst the gloom.

The hospital walls become a theatre of the human experience, where the staff members play many roles. They are not just doctors or nurses but the narrators of life's stories, the conduits of emotions that surge like rivers through these chambers.

Ultimately, they remind us that emotions know no boundaries within the complex tapestry of existence. A single heartbeat can house joy and sorrow, just as a single room can contain both life's beginning and end. In the hands of these dedicated souls, emotions intertwine and flow like the notes of a song that speaks to the very essence of what it means to be human.

In the corridors of Autonomy General Hospital (AGH), a young medical student was on a journey that seemed to defy the solemnity of the setting. His presence radiated an almost supernatural optimism as if he had stumbled upon a secret elixir that could cure the world's woes. With the assuredness of a traveller guided by ancient stars, he stepped into AGH, untouched by the burdens that weighed upon so many.

His look exuded a vibrant positivity like a sunbeam piercing through storm clouds to bathe the earth in its golden embrace. Each stride he took appeared to carry the echo of a promise, a promise that the intricacies of life were nothing but a puzzle waiting to be solved. His aura was a tapestry of invulnerability, seemingly immune to the slightest disturbance or frustration.

In a place where suffering often casts its shadow over even the brightest moments, this young idealist seemed like an anomaly, as though he had donned a cloak woven from the fabric of perpetual joy. This sight drew curious gazes and raised eyebrows from those who witnessed his passage. Within the hospital's walls, where the weight of pain and uncertainty bore down on staff and patients alike, his demeanour was as rare as a comet streaking across the night sky.

With a heart open wide like the embrace of a compassionate saint, he moved through the hospital, weaving a tapestry of human connection. His greetings were like gentle breezes, carrying with them the essence of happiness, and his hugs and kisses became gestures of healing, like an elixir that transcended the boundaries of medicine.

He left a trail of smiles and bemused curiosity as he navigated the sea of faces. His unyielding positivity, juxtaposed against the backdrop of suffering, elicited a chorus of internal wonderment from those he encountered. "Who is he?" they mused, pondering the enigma of his being.

One patient's thoughts echoed the sentiment of many as

they marvelled at the paradox of such an encounter within the walls of a hospital. "A stranger's joy is a rare gem, more unexpected than a flower blooming in winter," one patient thought, acknowledging the rarity of encountering boundless joy amid the realm of pain.

In a place where anguish can be an all-encompassing cloak, this young idealist's demeanour was a poignant reminder that the chains of circumstance do not bind the human spirit. His steps were a dance of hope, a proclamation that amidst life's trials, an unwavering belief in the possibility of better days can shine brighter than the sun.

Amid AGH's corridors, this young medical student walked, a living testament that even in adversity, the human spirit can emerge as an inextinguishable flame, casting its warmth upon the hearts of those who cross its path.

Sean Sodeman, a beacon of positivity in human form, seemed to carry the very essence of a sunlit morning wherever he ventured. Petty worries and fleeting annoyances held no sway over him. His spirit was fortified by an unbreakable will to infuse the world with smiles, even in the face of life's most daunting trials. His persona was an embodiment of perpetual sunshine, and it was simply a part of his being.

After a whirlwind introduction to nearly thirty souls within a mere five minutes, Sean's duty beckoned him. He approached the nurses' station, ready to embrace the responsibilities that lay before him. With a sense of purpose that radiated like a guiding star, he navigated through the bustling currents of the hospital corridors.

His steps, like those of a dancer, led him to the orchestrated activity hub, where the staff and visitors were woven into a symphony of movement. Amidst this whirlwind, Sean almost effortlessly found himself at the forefront of the line, like a single leaf carried to the water's edge by the gentlest breeze.

At the epicentre of this orchestrated chaos stood a middle-aged woman, the maestro of the nurses' station, conducting the symphony with seasoned grace. Her mastery over the station's intricacies resembled a well-practiced dance, each move executed with the precision of a skilled performer. She knew not only the location of every item but also each individual's role in this intricate healing performance. Everyone called her Mother.

Amidst the bustling symphony of a Monday morning in early December, the atmosphere was charged with the flurry of activity, a dance of purposeful movement. Sean arrived at the front desk like a harmonious note added to an ongoing melody. Like a breath of fresh air, his presence cast a warm glow upon the scene. As he engaged with Mother, a subtle chemistry emerged, as if two kindred spirits recognized each other instantly.

With a shared nod and exchanging words, the two embarked on a dance of their own, a rhythm that resonated with mutual understanding. Mother's eyes, like portals to a treasure trove of wisdom, met Sean's gaze, recognizing the genuine compassion that emanated from him. In return, Sean found solace in her seasoned demeanour, a reassurance that he was in the company of someone who had traversed the halls of healing for many years.

In this brief, silent exchange, the two forged a connection. It was a testament to the power of shared humanity, where age and experience converged with youthful optimism.

Like windows into her soul, her eyes met Sean's gaze, and a transformation as swift as spring rain swept over her. An involuntary smile graced her lips, a testament to the enigmatic power Sean seemed to carry. Like a radiant sunbeam breaking through storm clouds, his presence softened the frostiness that had previously held her demeanour captive.

"You possess eyes that mirror the very essence of your soul's beauty," Sean began. "When I gaze into them, the world transforms into an exquisite tapestry of wonder. And your smile," he continued, "it's the crowning glory that adorns the masterpiece of your being, a touch of elegance even supermodels can't replicate."

Caught off guard by his words, Mother chuckled, charmed by the unexpected compliment that danced on Sean's lips. "You must be Sean Sodeman," she said with a glint of recognition in her eyes.

A playful protest rose from Sean, his retort woven with humour. "Hold on a second. I just looked at a stunning woman and expressed my admiration for her, and suddenly, I'm Sean Sodeman? What if this guy is just some hideous creep, and you're already comparing me to him? That's hardly fair."

Her laughter swirled like a gentle breeze, a melodic counterpoint to the hospital's ambiance. She warmly responded, "Young man, your reputation has echoed through these corridors long before you arrived. It would be a disservice to my duty if I weren't aware of who walks these halls. And, might I add that it's an absolute pleasure to finally make your acquaintance?"

Their exchange was sealed with a handshake, a gesture that carried the weight of mutual respect. Mother's smile, as genuine as the dawn, reflected the harmony between generations, bridging the gap between experience and youthful enthusiasm. In that moment, two souls converged, their connection a testament to the power of shared humanity. It was a fleeting yet profound encounter that would resonate within the walls of Autonomy General Hospital for a long time to come.

Within the walls of AGH, a code of conduct as formidable as the hospital's reputation echoed through the corridors. It was a set of standards like the steel beams supporting the very structure. The expectations of its founder, Dr. Richard Patrick Jacobs, a visionary whose ideals left an indelible mark, were etched into the hospital's foundation.

Dr. Jacobs' expectations were lofty, bordering on the audacious. Yet, they encapsulated the essence of AGH's mission: to stand as a bastion of excellence, where doctors and nurses were held to a higher standard than mere medical proficiency. They were meant to carry themselves with heads held high, backs straight as pillars of support, and eyes fixed on their goals with clarity as sharp as a surgeon's scalpel. In the busiest moments, they were expected to be able to hear a pin drop amidst the din of a stampede.

These were not just expectations but a testament to Dr. Jacobs' commitment to healing and compassion. His vision was a flame that ignited the spirit of AGH, a torch passed on when the hospital changed hands to Dr. Plunkett Sr., who recognized the sanctity of those values and sought to uphold them.

While the standards were formidable, they were not universally obeyed. Human nature being what it is, not all doctors and nurses could consistently rise to such levels of perfection. Some allowed the rigour of daily life to blur the edges of these standards, rendering them mere distant echoes. But in the middle of this, a singular figure emerged, a doctor who treated Dr. Jacobs' values not as an obligation but as a calling.

With the precision of a maestro, this doctor embraced the ideals wholeheartedly. Her every step was a testament to unwavering dedication, shoulders squared in posture and purpose. Her focus was akin to a hawk's gaze, undeterred by the swirling storm of distractions. Her perception seemed attuned to the finest nuances, capturing even the faintest echoes within the clamour.

Her adherence to the founder's values was not a matter of duty but devotion, a creed followed with enthusiasm that transcended mere guidelines. In a sea of diversity, this doctor stood as a beacon of uncompromising dedication, a living embodiment of AGH's core principles.

In her, Dr. Jacobs' legacy found a resolute custodian whose steps echoed his spirit, holding above the torch of excellence that illuminated the hospital's path from its inception. In her embodiment of the founder's ideals, she painted a living portrait of dedication, reminding all who encountered her that true greatness lay not only in medical prowess but in the embodiment of values that elevate humanity.

Dr. Gabrielle Gabehart's name stirred admiration and intrigue throughout the corridors of AGH. She embodied a unique blend of attributes that set her apart like a gem in a sea of stones.

As curious as a cat, her thirst for knowledge knew no bounds, propelling her to explore the intricacies of medicine and life itself. Her keen intellect was honed like a razor's edge. She sliced through complexities with a precision that was as impressive as it was awe-inspiring. Yet, her character was not camouflaged; she was as candid as a mirror, reflecting her thoughts and intentions without deceit.

With a relentless pursuit of excellence, she carved her path through the medical landscape, each step a testament to her indomitable will. Her unwavering determination matched her intelligence, which drove her to surpass boundaries and shatter glass ceilings with the vigour of a mighty wave.

Dr. Gabehart embodied leadership in the realm of AGH, a fortress traditionally dominated by male figures. She was a light that illuminated uncharted territories. Whispers of her accomplishments and prowess spread like wildfire, and a real sense of curiosity rippled through the hospital's populace.

She was not just a medical professional but a legend woven into the very fabric of AGH. The corridors buzzed with tales of her expertise, her demeanour both revered and admired. However, even as the accolades flowed like a river, she faced the relentless scrutiny of a male-dominated environment. Her every move was measured against an unforgiving standard.

In the wake of her accomplishments, detractors emerged like shadows cast by a blazing sun. Driven by insecurities and perhaps the ghost of threatened masculinity, they sought to cast aspersions on her achievements, undermining her leadership and work. Yet, their efforts were in vain. Her track record remained unblemished, a testament to her prowess and dedication as a medical doctor.

No speck of dereliction stained her record; she navigated the realm of medicine with steadfast grace. But her detractors remained unrelenting, meticulously scrutinizing every detail in a relentless quest for flaws, no matter how minuscule.

Amidst this storm of praise and skepticism, Dr. Gabrielle Gabehart stood resolute, her name etched into the annals of AGH's legacy. A beacon of intellect, a pinnacle of determination, she embodied a spirit that refused to bow before the storm of doubt. In the face of adversity, she radiated a youthfulness as vibrant as the month of May, a symbol of renewal and unwavering commitment to her craft.

Amid Mother's exchange with Sean, the air seemed to pause in deference to the entrance of a presence that commanded near-total silence. Dr. Gabehart strolled in, a figure whose demeanour oozed authority and composure. Her posture was unwavering, a testament to her steadfast resolve. At the same time, her curls cascaded like ebony silk, catching the light like an aurora dancing across the night sky. Her eyes held a commanding intensity, a gaze that could pierce through deception and offer solace.

Dr. Gabehart's appearance was a masterpiece of elegance, a symphony of carefully chosen elements. Her long burgundy dress, graced with a daring slit that exposed her confident stride, was a canvas upon which her grace and authority were painted.

Her high heels, worn as though an extension of herself, lent her an additional touch of stature, while her occasional smiles left an indelible mark on those fortunate enough to witness them. If it adorned her features, makeup was a mere accent to her natural beauty, a hint of artistry that only enhanced what was already captivating.

Her entire being embodied understated brilliance, a paradoxical blend of effortlessness and enchantment. Her presence seemed to demand attention without ever asking for it, a magnetic force that drew all eyes towards her.

Yet, it wasn't just her appearance that commanded attention; the depth of her achievements left an even more profound impression. Dr. Gabehart was a woman of eloquence and astonishment, her intellect a beacon that shone as brightly as her physical beauty.

Her reputation as a young medical doctor was a tapestry woven with threads of admiration and awe. Her accomplishments were like constellations in the sky of medicine, each a testament to her dedication and brilliance.

As the head of the cardiology department, she was not merely a figurehead; she was a force of nature. She was a leader whose guidance was sought after with an enthusiasm bordering on reverence. Her interactions with patients might have been scarce, but her influence was felt throughout the hospital. Staff members both feared and respected her, recognizing her objective analyses as invaluable tools for improvement, be it inpatient treatments or even the nuances of personal lives, such as dating advice.

In the symphony of AGH's daily life, Dr. Gabehart was a crescendo that resonated far beyond the walls of medicine. Her aura was captivating and authoritative, a harmony of beauty, intellect, and influence that left an indelible imprint on all who had the privilege to encounter her. She was a figure whose presence could only be described as a magnetic phenomenon, a force to be reckoned with in medicine and life.

Dr. Gabehart moved through the bustling station with a presence that brooked no disobedience, parting the crowd as if the sea recognized her command. She had an air of gravity around her, an aura that spoke of impending significance. Though devoid of excitement, her demeanour carried the weight of purpose, as if the mood shifted in response to her intentions.

As she approached Sean, her steps measured and deliberate, her stern look fell upon him like a curtain of authority. Sean felt the weight of her gaze even before she cleared her throat, a signal that pulled him from his interaction with Mother.

Startled, Sean pivoted on his heel to face the source of the interruption. In an instant, his expression transformed from surprise to awe. His eyes widened, his jaw slackened, and his breath hitched as if the sheer sight of Dr. Gabehart had stolen the air from his lungs. His very world seemed to pause for a heartbeat, a suspended moment in time.

Upon catching his breath, Sean's lips curved into a mischievous smile, and he winked at Dr. Gabehart. His words were an audacious symphony that played with the boundaries of boldness.

"Hello, gorgeous," he greeted her, his words laced with confidence. "If ever there was a woman who could make me question my beliefs, challenge my convictions, and utterly disarm my stubbornness, it would be you." His eyes danced with glee as he continued, "What wouldn't I do to bring a dazzling smile to a remarkable woman like you? Your smile carries a depth that reaches your eyes. Hand me your heart, and I'd labour ceaselessly to grant you the world."

Yet, the response he received was far from the swoon or flattery he might have anticipated. Dr. Gabehart brushed aside his words, her gaze unwavering as she moved past him, positioning herself in front of Mother to engage in a conversation. As Sean's words hung in the air, his extravagant profession of admiration was met with a brief correction: "It's doctor, young man."

The exchange was a snapshot of contrasts, where Sean's audacity met Dr. Gabehart's stern resolve head-on. In a moment, their dynamic played out, a dance of words and presence that underscored the complexity of interactions within the realm of AGH. With her command and his honesty, they stood as stark reflections of two forces at play within the hospital's bustling tapestry—a collision of personalities that spoke of both authority and the audacity to challenge it.

In the aftermath of his audacious declaration, Sean found

himself momentarily adrift, the atmosphere heavy with anticipation. But his resilience, like a seasoned sailor navigating a storm, prevailed as he regrouped with a quick-witted comeback. His words held a playful persistence, a testament to his unyielding determination.

"Alright, Dr. Gorgeous," he retorted with a grin, a glint of mischief in his eyes. "How can a young aspiring physician like myself win the heart of a splendid woman like you? I'm determined to keep that radiant smile alive as long as the sun graces our earth."

As his words hung in the air, his smile echoed his boldness. However, her response was not one of reciprocation but of irritation. With an unmistakable hint of displeasure, Dr. Gabehart pivoted to face Sean, her annoyance underscored by her sigh. With an air of resignation, she ushered him away from the crowd, seeking a more secluded space to address him.

"Oh, dear God," she sighed again, her voice tinged with exasperation as they moved aside. She seemed almost resigned, her annoyance apparent in her words and demeanour.

"The rumours about you were not exaggerations at all," she continued, her tone hinting at a mixture of surprise and disappointment. "I had hoped the rumours were baseless, but it appears I was mistaken. I didn't exactly relish the thought of being assigned to you, and I can already foresee that I will deeply regret this."

Pausing for a moment, she seemed to gather her thoughts, her expression an amalgamation of concession and determination. "Listen closely," she spoke, her words laced with an air of authority that demanded attention. "I'm not interested in wasting time, especially on you."

Her gaze locked onto his, her eyes holding a gravity that contrasted with the playfulness of their earlier exchange. "My clinical rounds commence at seven o'clock sharp every weekday morning. You are late as of six o'clock. From this moment forward, expect daily assignments—cases, drug mechanisms and interaction, basic physiology—whatever I deem necessary. I expect each assignment to be completed without fail every day, no exceptions."

As her rebuke hung in the air, it was clear that her demeanour had shifted from annoyance to no-nonsense professionalism. The playfulness of the initial encounter seemed to have given way to the stern reality of the situation. Unyielding in her approach, Dr. Gabehart stood as a figure whose expectations were as high as her reputation. She was a formidable presence that demanded relentless commitment and adherence.

Dr. Gabehart shifted momentarily from Sean to Mother. With a firm yet polite tone, she made her requests known. "Mother, can I have all my mail and get someone to fetch me a coffee? Please, and thank you," she articulated, her words carrying the weight of someone accustomed to having their directives followed.

"Okay, Dr. Gabehart," Mother replied, confirming her compliance. As Dr. Gabehart strode away, her footsteps echoing her purposeful demeanour, Sean found himself standing amidst the remnants of their conversation, a palpable sense of bewilderment etched across his features.

He looked from the direction she had gone to Mother, his eyes wide and questioning like a lost traveller seeking guidance. An unspoken plea hung in the air, a plea for clarity in a situation that had quickly turned into unfamiliar territory. Mother caught his gaze, her response silent yet unequivocal.

With a simple point in the direction of Dr. Gabehart's retreating form and a mouthed directive of "Go," Mother offered Sean the guidance he sought. It was a nudge, a silent encouragement to step forward into the path that Dr. Gabehart had carved. As the echoes of their conversation lingered in the air, Sean took his first steps in a direction he had not anticipated, a journey propelled by curiosity, audacity, and the guidance of an unexpected ally.

Sean swiftly gathered his belongings, a sense of urgency propelling his actions as he pursued Dr. Gabehart. His steps echoed the rhythm of his enthusiasm, a determination to keep pace with a presence that demanded nothing less than agility.

She wasted no time establishing her expectations as he caught up to her. Her words were like a rapid-fire stream that matched the pace of her movements. "Alright, young man, you must learn to keep up with me," she began, her tone brisk and no-nonsense. "I operate at a fast tempo—speaking, working, and moving. If you have questions, you're smart enough to figure out when to ask, when to research on your own, and when to approach me. I've heard various things about you, and I'm curious to see if they hold."

Her words were both a challenge and an invitation, a promise of a journey through the unknown. As Sean absorbed her instructions, his efforts to keep up were visible, his focus unwavering as he navigated the rapid flow of information she provided.

"I want you to become an observer," she continued, her intense gaze locked onto his. "Learn to deduce a patient's condition just by looking at them. Discover ways to establish trust at every stage to create an environment where they feel comfortable divulging their deepest concerns. My tenure as a cardiologist might be relatively short, but I've been at the helm of this department for over a year."

Her words carried the weight of experience, a testament to her role as both a healer and a leader. She extended an offer of knowledge, her credentials and publications a trove of information waiting to be explored. "If you wish to learn about my publications or credentials, you can find them online or visit my office for copies. I value efficiency, and I dislike wasting time."

As the conversation flowed, Sean's curiosity sparked another question born from skepticism and intrigue. "Pardon me, Dr. Gabehart," he chuckled, his tone respectful. "But you do seem a bit young to be a fully licensed cardiologist, let alone the head of a department."

His words were met with a flash of amusement in her eyes, a spark that hinted at a deeper story waiting to be unveiled. Undeterred, Sean continued, his eagerness palpable. "I am genuinely interested in learning more about you and your accomplishments. Reading your publications sounds like an excellent way to start."

In the interplay of their words, a dynamic was set in motion—one of mentorship, learning, and exploring a realm where excellence and ambition converged. As Sean stepped into this new chapter, guided by Dr. Gabehart's formidable presence, he embarked on a journey that promised challenges and revelations. This path was illuminated by the brilliance of a unique mind and the pursuit of knowledge.

Dr. Gabehart's sudden halt and pivot caught Sean's attention like a lightning strike. Her gaze locked onto him with unwavering intensity. Her question hung in the air, a challenge that beckoned him to draw conclusions based on their interactions thus far. In response, he engaged his analytical faculties, his mind working like gears in a well-oiled machine.

She presented him with a puzzle, and Sean's thoughts swirled, weaving the threads of observation and inference into a tapestry of insight. After a brief moment of contemplation, he offered his assessment, his words measured and respectful.

"You haven't smiled for more than a few seconds since you walked into the hospital besides the time you were talking to Mother, and you look too young to have accomplished what you have. My take is you either take life too seriously and don't have a fun side, or you have some terrible personal thing you're dealing with, which is absolutely none of my business. However, you don't let that interfere with your work here. Your work is your passion; it's something you take very seriously, likely more than anything else in your life."

He paused before finishing his thought, "Also, if I screw up at any given point in the next couple of weeks, you wouldn't hesitate to throw me to the wolves. You're strict and disciplined, but also analytical and fair. You're not a huge fan of teaching, but you love the challenging parts of medicine, so maybe that's why you sometimes put up with teaching medical students."

As his words hung in the air, Dr. Gabehart responded with a hint of approval, her words a mixture of assessment and validation. "Given the circumstances, and considering it's a Monday morning without my usual coffee, I'd say you've fared well," she remarked, her tone implying an element of agreement.

With a fluid motion, she led Sean into her office. The door closed behind them, ushering them into a space where the journey of mentorship, learning, and professional growth was poised to begin. In the nexus of their interactions, Dr. Gabehart's enigmatic presence became a guiding star for Sean, a luminary whose brilliance promised to illuminate his path through the intricate world of medicine and the uncharted territories of their relationship.

With a familiarity that spoke of routine, Dr. Gabehart took off her coat as if shedding the external world and its demands. As she settled into her chair, her movements were fluid and graceful, a testament to her comfort in this space, which was more than an office—it was a sanctuary for her thoughts, pursuits, and aspirations.

The soft hum of her computer came to life, a symphony of productivity that accompanied her as she immersed herself in her work. Her surroundings bore witness to her achievements, a visual testament to her dedication and prowess. The office, akin to a medium-sized apartment, was a canvas of professionalism and personal taste expertly interwoven.

The room, furnished with a touch of executive elegance, exuded an aura of refinement. Its décor reflected her personality, a blend of functionality and style. Amidst the ordered chaos of a productive mind, her accomplishments adorned the walls and surfaces—degrees, certificates, awards— a panorama of recognition that left no room for doubt about her achievements.

For Sean, stepping into this space was akin to stepping into the heart of Dr. Gabehart's world. Every corner spoke of dedication, hard work, and excellence. The office was an eloquent testimony to her ceaseless journey toward self-improvement and fulfilling her ambitions.

He stood amidst this grand display, his eyes wandering over the framed achievements, his expression a mixture of awe and respect. It was a moment of revelation, a tangible manifestation of her formidable persona. As he absorbed the significance of her office, his nod was one of silent admiration. This gesture acknowledged the magnitude of what lay before him.

With a smile that held a hint of disbelief, Sean absorbed the grandeur of the scene before him. Amidst the sea of accomplishments, he witnessed a narrative of hard-earned success and unyielding dedication.

In this shared space, their journey of mentorship and learning would unfold—a journey where Dr. Gabehart's legacy would inspire and guide, and Sean's growth would be nurtured under the watchful gaze of her accomplishments.

Assuming Dr. Gabehart was deeply absorbed in her computer work, Sean made himself comfortable in one of the office chairs. The thought of taking a seat seemed natural, a way to settle into the ambiance of the space with which he was becoming acquainted. However, his assumption was swiftly corrected, and his moment of casual reprieve was short-lived.

A mere second after settling into the chair, Sean was jolted by Dr. Gabehart's firm and somewhat exasperated exclamation. "Don't sit down unless you're offered a seat, young man!" Her words cut through the air, loaded with an authority that left no room for misunderstanding. Sean reacted quickly, springing back up from the chair as though it had turned into a hot seat.

His response carried a touch of comedy, a mixture of surprise and embarrassment playing out on his features. He found himself standing awkwardly next to the chair he had occupied moments before as if caught in an impromptu dance move. Dr. Gabehart's swift correction had left an indelible mark on him, a moment that would likely be etched into his memory for a long time.

With an air of slight discomfort, Sean stood still, his posture slightly rigid as he grappled with the aftermath of the unexpected exchange. Dr. Gabehart, seemingly unphased by the incident, continued her work on the computer and sifted through files on her desk.

Once a space of silent admiration and introspection, the room was now charged with an almost palpable sense of self-awareness. In the dance between mentor and mentee, every moment carried a lesson, a reminder of the unspoken rules and the ever-present need for professionalism.

Deciding that the moment of discomfort had lingered long enough, Dr. Gabehart initiated a conversation with Sean. Her words, delivered with ease and honesty, cut through the air, capturing his attention as he stood beside the chair he had momentarily occupied.

"So, Sean," she began, her tone curious yet laced with a hint of amusement, "I've heard a fair amount about you from the staff and other medical students around the hospital." Raising her head from her work, she met Sean's gaze, her scrutiny intense yet not devoid of a certain warmth. A hint of a smile graced her lips as she continued, "There's a rumour floating around, a rather intriguing one—it suggests that you might be something of a genius."

Her observation seemed to amuse her, the very notion almost incredulous to her. She voiced what many seemed to think while acknowledging the seeming contradiction in Sean's demeanour. "It's quite amusing, considering everything about you seems to exude arrogance rather than intelligence." Her gaze remained fixed on him, a challenge veiled in her words.

Her curiosity led her to probe further, and her questions

were genuine as she sought insight into his motivations. "So, out of curiosity, what prompted you to choose this cardiology clerkship?" she inquired, her interest genuine and palpable.

Still navigating the residual unease from their previous interaction, Sean found her question a welcome diversion. "Um, forgive me, Dr. Gabehart, if I seem a little distracted," he began, his words accompanied by a disarming smile. "I was genuinely taken aback by the sheer volume of accolades garnishing your office."

A sense of sincerity and appreciation laced his words as he continued, "Throughout most of my clerkships, I found many doctors to be somewhat, well, boring. Yet, stepping into your office, I can honestly say this is the first time I've been genuinely impressed by a doctor in this hospital."

He paused for a moment before venturing into more delicate territory. "I've also gathered that not all doctors here hold the same opinion. Some seem to question whether you've truly earned all the respect attributed to you."

In Sean's response, there was a sense of candidness and a willingness to share his observations. His words painted a portrait of a dynamic environment, one where reputations and perspectives collided in a tapestry of professional interactions. With each exchange, the tapestry of their mentorship grew more intricate, revealing layers of complexity and connection beneath the surface.

Amidst the impressive backdrop of Dr. Gabehart's office, the conversation flowed like a river, each exchange revealing more about the motivations and aspirations that had brought them together. Sean's response bore a touch of admiration, a candidness that spoke of curiosity and intrigue.

"After spending a couple of minutes in your office captivated by what's around you, this was one of the reasons why I wanted to take this clerkship with you," Sean said.

His words conveyed appreciation, acknowledging the powerful aura emanating from the display of Dr. Gabehart's achievements. "I was genuinely curious about why some accomplished doctors might harbour negative sentiments towards another accomplished individual. I got my answer the moment I walked into this office. You manage to make them feel like underachievers, and that, quite frankly, is remarkably impressive."

Dr. Gabehart's smile, a blend of pleasure and modesty, painted her cheeks with a soft hue of pink. Yet, her curiosity remained unquenched, her next question carrying the weight of genuine interest. "While I'm pleased to hear that my reputation precedes me, I suspect there's more to your decision than curiosity about those rumours. Is there something specific that motivates or inspires you about cardiology, something that prompted you to dedicate these weeks to learning with us?"

Sean's initial response carried a touch of humour, his chuckle a playful acknowledgement of the weight of his answer. "Well," he began, slightly fidgeting as he tried to suppress his amusement, "I've heard a lot about you, both as an accomplished cardiologist and a tough teacher." His words hinted at an acceptance of the challenge, a readiness to tackle the demands of a rigorous learning experience. "I have a penchant for challenges and value learning, so I thought I'd give it a shot."

The response resonated with Dr. Gabehart, who delivered her affirmation with an air of approval. "That's good to hear," she responded, a note of contentment in her voice. I appreciate individuals who have a genuine appetite for learning. It implies that

I can rely on you to grasp instructions without repetition and that your commitment to growth will prevent the repetition of mistakes."

In these conversations, a dynamic was taking shape, one that merged the mentor's experience with the mentee's enthusiasm. As they navigated the intricate web of professional interactions and personal aspirations, their relationship evolved into a space where learning, challenge, and respect converged—where Dr. Gabehart and Sean would undoubtedly grow in ways that stretched beyond the confines of their office walls.

Amidst the currents of conversation, Dr. Gabehart introduced an element of challenge. This playful twist seemed designed to test Sean's insight and offer a glimpse into her approach to teaching and evaluation. Delivering with anticipation and amusement, her words hinted at an interesting diversion.

"Aside from what you've already heard about me, and assuming any of that holds a grain of truth, perhaps you can witness firsthand the 'magic' that everyone seems to attribute to me as a doctor," Dr. Gabehart suggested with a twinkle in her eyes. A sense of light-heartedness entered the space as if the atmosphere had shifted to accommodate a moment of shared exploration.

"Let's make things interesting," she continued, her tone eager. How about we test your skills with some ECGs? I want to see how well you can read the activity of a heart." Her words promised a challenge, a chance for Sean to showcase his aptitude in a practical setting.

With an air of purpose, Dr. Gabehart rose from her chair and retrieved a copy of an ECG readout from a cabinet. She handed it to Sean, the paper a canvas of squiggly lines and dots that held the key to a patient's heart condition. Sean's eyes traversed the intricate patterns, his brow furrowing as he engaged his analytical faculties.

He glanced at the ECG momentarily, shifting his gaze between the paper and Dr. Gabehart. Clearly, this was no ordinary task; it was an invitation to decipher a medical puzzle and uncover the hidden stories that medical data could reveal. Dr. Gabehart's subsequent instruction was explicit: She wanted Sean to identify something unique or noteworthy about this ECG readout, a skill crucial in cardiology.

As Sean grappled with the task, the scene became an intricate dance of challenge and response. Dr. Gabehart's choice to present such a task on Sean's first day in his cardiology clerkship hinted at her approach to mentorship. In this environment, her students were challenged to step up, think critically, and demonstrate their potential.

In this moment of interaction, Sean's confidence mingled with Dr. Gabehart's expertise, a clash of personalities and intellect that shaped the contours of their emerging mentor-mentee relationship. They were two strong individuals, each with unique strengths and abilities, brought together in a delicate interplay that would undoubtedly define their journey of learning and growth in cardiology.

As the moments stretched, Sean's initial expression of stunned confusion seemed to hold the weight of impending defeat. Dr. Gabehart's calculated challenge had prompted a reaction far from the arrogant assurance she had heard associated with him. Instead, his brow furrowed with concentration, and he seemed to grapple with the puzzle before him.

Amidst the suspense, Dr. Gabehart observed Sean closely, curious about his approach and intrigued by his response to the situation. Despite his silence, she could almost feel the gears turning in his mind, the wheels of thought spinning as he analyzed the ECG readout.

After several minutes, the atmosphere seemed to change, a shift accompanied by Sean's gradual turning towards Dr. Gabehart. The air carried a note of shared amusement as though the tension had dissolved to reveal a moment of mutual understanding. Sean's words, when they came, blended disbelief, humour, and a dash of playful protest.

"What kind of hospitality is this?" he began, a grin tugging at the corners of his lips. "You're trying to trick your student on the first day of class? This is just insane." His words were punctuated by laughter that hinted at the camaraderie that was slowly forming between them.

With a confident assertion, Sean unveiled his interpretation of the challenge. "I'd say there was nothing wrong with the patient," he began, his tone animated. "Someone incorrectly placed the wires, which gave the impression that something was seriously wrong with the patient's heart." As he concluded, he placed the ECG readout on her desk, a visual confirmation of his analysis.

The air seemed to hum with a sense of victory, an almost palpable energy that hung between them. Dr. Gabehart's initial test had not only been met but surpassed. In Sean's response, humility spoke of a willingness to learn, a trait she had likely hoped to cultivate in her students. The atmosphere was a mixture of challenge, revelation, and a shared appreciation for the intellectual engagement they had just experienced.

In this exchange, the dynamics of their relationship continued to evolve, a fusion of mentorship, intellectual exploration, and a growing camaraderie. The curtain had been raised on their learning journey, promised to be marked by challenges, growth, and mutual respect.

Dr. Gabehart's smile carried a tinge of sarcasm as she applauded Sean's successful analysis of the ECG readout. Her applause recognized his achievement and playfully acknowledged the game they had just played. Her words, delivered with a blend of straightforwardness and expectation, cut through the air, holding a weight that matched her reputation.

"Alright," she began, her tone conveying a sense of challenge and encouragement. "You've demonstrated a good eye, but I hope that's not a fluke."

Her words bore a hint of warning, a reminder that her expectations were high and that she demanded nothing less than dedicated effort. "I have no patience for students who don't give their best," she continued, her gaze fixed on Sean with an intensity that left no room for ambiguity. "If you're willing to put in your best effort and prove your worth, I do not doubt that I can make you better than you currently believe at diagnosing heart problems with limited information and resources."

Her confidence was undeniable, and her words were a challenge in themselves. But she wasn't just challenging Sean; she was also challenging herself to deliver on her reputation and mould her students into skilled diagnosticians capable of navigating the complexities of cardiology.

"Well," Sean responded, his confidence blending with an air of curiosity. "I guess we're about to find out."

With that exchange, their time in the office drew to a close. Dr. Gabehart's actions were deliberate as she rose from her chair, picked up a few items, and exchanged her shoes for a more comfortable pair. She adorned her white coat, a symbol of her profession, and moved towards the door, a silent signal for Sean to open it.

Their departure from the office marked the beginning of their tangible journey together. This journey held the promise of challenges, growth, and mutual exploration. As they walked, the echoes of their initial interactions lingered, the interplay of personalities and expertise shaping the contours of their unique mentor-mentee relationship.

Dr. Gabehart's footsteps carried purpose as she led the way, each stride punctuated by the weight of her insights. The air around them buzzed with the promise of knowledge, the subtle energy of mentorship and learning intermingling.

Every lull in the conversation became an opportunity for her to impart wisdom, and her words were a testament to her dedication to teaching and moulding the minds of future medical practitioners.

Throughout their walk, her voice wove a tapestry of insights, each thread carefully chosen to convey the nuances of her approach to medicine. She revealed to Sean that every element in a patient's environment, medical history, and physical examination carried significance—each a clue, a potential key to unlocking the diagnosis, treatment, or prognosis puzzle.

With a distinct emphasis, Dr. Gabehart introduced the concept of hidden symptoms. These secondary and tertiary clues often held the key to unravelling complex medical mysteries. She illustrated the intricate web of patient behaviour, explaining that even actions and reactions could provide valuable insights. She named these subtle cues as secondary and tertiary symptoms— indications that often went unnoticed, overlooked, or even intentionally concealed. Sean found himself captivated by her words, her experience, and her mastery of the art of medicine.

Dr. Gabehart revealed the complex interplay between the patient's psyche and symptoms as they walked and talked. She highlighted the potential for patients to invent symptoms, often driven by various motives—shame, the desire for attention, or an attempt to rationalize the inexplicable. Her words provided a glimpse into the depth and intricacy of the human experience, the intricacies that often lay beneath the surface of clinical interactions.

Sean absorbed her words throughout this educational journey, his attention focused, and his mind engaged. He demonstrated his commitment to understanding and learning even without a notebook or writing pad. His posture, eye contact, and attentive demeanour became a testament to his desire to make a positive impression and prove his dedication to the challenge Dr. Gabehart had presented.

During this walk through the hospital corridors, a profound connection was forming—a link between mentor and mentee, the experienced and the eager. Each step they took seemed to reinforce the notion that learning was not limited to textbooks and lecture halls but a living, dynamic process. This exchange unfolded in the very environment where medicine was practiced and lives were touched.

Dr. Gabehart's footsteps led them through the hospital corridors, the rhythmic sound echoing their purposeful strides. The end of the hallway marked their destination—the doctors' lounge. It was a space of respite, a sanctuary where physicians congregated, shared stories, and perhaps, if time allowed, enjoyed a moment of rest amidst their demanding schedules.

As they entered the lounge, the atmosphere shifted, a subtle recognition of Dr. Gabehart's presence. It was a place where doctors gathered, a space alive with the hum of conversation and fellowship. Yet, in the presence of the department head, an unspoken respect and anticipation seemed to permeate the air.

Dr. Gabehart's entrance swiftly transformed the once lively lounge into a tableau of order and tranquillity. The doctors, who had been engaged in various activities—including breakfast and conversations—paused and turned their attention towards her. It was a moment of stillness, a collective acknowledgment of her authority and the expectation that followed her.

Sean followed closely behind, an observer in this orchestrated scene. The lounge was a realm governed by its own unwritten rules, and Dr. Gabehart was its commander. As the doctors hurried to find their seats, a sense of disciplined order emerged from the brief chaos. The symphony of activity quickly subsided, leaving the lounge draped in silence. In this abyss, the air seemed to hold its breath.

Dr. Gabehart's gaze swept across the room, her eyes resting on each individual for a fleeting moment. The room's stillness mirrored her demeanour, her presence an embodiment of authority and expectation. With a few seconds that seemed to stretch, she allowed the scene to settle, the silence resonating with the weight of her unspoken instructions.

The balance between friendship and professionalism was carefully maintained in this room of white coats and stethoscopes. Dr. Gabehart's role as leader and mentor was undeniable. Her influence shaped the lounge dynamics as much as it did in the medical ward.

As the moment hung suspended, it was clear that this space was more than a place to rest. It was a domain where physicians converged to share knowledge, exchange experiences, and carry the essence of medicine in their conversations.

Sean shifted from his position behind Dr. Gabehart, taking his place beside her. His presence was a silent affirmation of his readiness to engage, learn, and immerse himself in the environment of the doctors' lounge—a place that seemed to exist in its own dimension, guided by its unique set of norms and expectations.

Dr. Gabehart's steady and commanding voice cut through the silence that enveloped the room. Her words resonated with the weight of authority, and she addressed her colleagues with an unflinching honesty that mirrored her reputation for discipline and high standards. As she spoke, her message was clear—this was a space for those ready to commit, serve, and uphold the values of their profession.

Her introduction of Sean introduced an element of novelty, a new figure within the established order of the lounge. She highlighted his status as a fourth-year medical student and his intended role as a learner within the department. But her words weren't merely a formality; they carried a sense of expectation and the promise of mutual learning.

With her characteristic efficiency, Dr. Gabehart conveyed her respect for the department's reputation and high expectations for students joining their ranks. Her assurance that Sean came highly recommended by his peers was a testament to his capabilities and a nod to the intellectual prowess that was a hallmark of the cardiology department.

But as the room remained hushed, the atmosphere was stirred by the voice of Dr. Bates—a figure who seemed to hold his own presence within the space. His words were a mixture of welcome and challenge. As he addressed Sean, his tone carried a note of playful testing, a way to measure the newcomer's reaction to the lounge's dynamics.

With his gaze fixed on Sean, "Hi Sean, I am Dr. Bates, and I'm kind of the big shot around here. It's nice to have these so-called smart kids around here every now and then, but sometimes kids like you confuse arrogance for intelligence." Shifting his attention to Dr. Gabehart, "Dr. Gabehart, if the kid is so smart, how about we take him for a drive for a few hours and see if he comes out alive or begs for mercy?" he said before sitting down.

The lounge atmosphere was charged with camaraderie and laced with playful banter. Dr. Bates' words were met with laughter from the assembled doctors, a recognition of the jest and harmony that often characterized their interactions. As the laughter resonated, it was apparent that this exchange was part of the unique social fabric of the lounge, where wit and camaraderie held their own significance.

Dr. Gabehart's response would be a litmus test of her reputation as a mentor and leader who could balance welcoming and asserting authority. As the words settled, the unspoken question lingered: How would Sean respond to this unexpected initiation, and how would he navigate the complexities of personalities within the lounge? The moment had transformed into a microcosm of the challenges and opportunities that awaited Sean in the coming weeks.

Standing tall and composed beside Dr. Gabehart, Sean met the moment with a steady smile. His demeanour remained unfazed, a testament to his ability to keep his composure under the scrutiny of his colleagues. Amidst the laughter and light-hearted teasing, his eyes sought guidance from Dr. Gabehart, a silent query of how to navigate this particular scenario. Her response, a subtle shake of her head, conveyed a clear message—an affirmation that maintaining decorum was the path to tread.

As Dr. Gabehart turned to leave the lounge, the doctors' attention shifted, the moment's fun slowly fading. Sean's gaze lingered momentarily on the doctors who had welcomed him into their realm with jest. This gesture transcended the initial challenge. With a nod of acknowledgment, he turned away from the lounge, following Dr. Gabehart's lead.

In this microcosm of interactions, Sean's ability to maintain his poise while being drawn into the lounge's dynamics was a testament to his adaptability and emotional stability. As they walked away, the echoes of laughter and camaraderie remained—a reminder that in this space of medical professionals, collaboration, support, and even a touch of jest created the foundation for the journey ahead.

In the wake of the laughter and fellowship, Sean's unexpected pause and subsequent actions again transformed the atmosphere. With a few steps away, he seemingly had a second thought, a realization that led him to retrace his path. He approached Dr. Bates, leaning in to share something privately.

The visible shift in Dr. Bates' expression, from amusement to sudden seriousness, spoke volumes of the impact of Sean's whispered words. As teardrops glistened on his cheeks, it was as if Sean had unlocked a hidden depth, stirring emotions beneath the surface.

The gathered doctors were astonished by the spectacle unfolding. Their eyes shifted between Dr. Bates and Sean, and the sudden change in the atmosphere created a sense of anticipation.

As Sean tapped Dr. Bates' shoulder and withdrew, he left a

trail of puzzled expressions in his wake. The moment's drama was palpable, leaving everyone curious about the whispered exchange that had prompted such an emotional reaction.

The sudden shift in Dr. Bates' demeanour, from amusement to tears to frustration, painted a complex portrait. The vulnerability that surfaced hinted at layers of personality that few had glimpsed before. Sean's actions had elicited an emotional response that cut through the façade of strength, revealing a more intricate tapestry beneath.

But Sean's departure was not without its final touch of audacity. His parting smile and the blown kiss seemed to strike a chord of discord in Dr. Bates, who was now lashing out with vocal frustration. Once a space of camaraderie and jest, the lounge had become a stage for a different kind of interaction—a clash of egos and emotions, a tug-of-war for dominance.

Amidst the echoing voices, Sean's departure, with its enigmatic and unconventional gestures, was a reminder that the dynamics of human interaction can be as complex and unpredictable as the rhythms of medicine. The moment peeled back yet another layer of the characters within this narrative, setting the stage for a journey that would likely be marked by both challenge and revelation.

Dr. Gabehart's return to the lounge unfolded against confusion and commotion. The scene that met her eyes was a paradox—a juxtaposition of an emotional display from an experienced doctor and a departing student adorned with a smile. The unfolding drama seemed inconsistent with the professionalism expected within the realm of medicine, and this dissonance likely deepened Dr. Gabehart's bewilderment.

As Sean walked towards the exit with his characteristic smile, his casual shrug was a simple gesture that said, "Well, that happened." His ability to navigate a potentially tense situation with such ease was intriguing and mysterious, leaving a lingering question mark in the air.

Dr. Gabehart's decision to follow Sean out was a testament to her role as a mentor and a leader. Her exit signalled her intention to ensure the unfolding events were addressed and perhaps even understood. It was clear that there was more to the situation than met the eye, and her pursuit of clarity reflected her commitment to maintaining the decorum of her department and ensuring the professional conduct of her students and colleagues.

As they both stepped out of the lounge, the echoes of the emotional outburst and Sean's enigmatic reaction lingered. The space between them held unspoken questions, an opportunity for Sean to explain and for Dr. Gabehart to gain insight into the dynamics of her team. The corridor became a bridge between the realm of camaraderie and the mentorship Dr. Gabehart intended to provide—a space where professional boundaries intertwined with personal complexities and where the journey of discovery was beginning.

The Reading on the Walls

In the hospital corridor's hushed and expectant atmosphere, the doctors gathered together as they awaited the day's plan. There was a palpable sense of unease, a ripple of tension that seemed to be an inherent response whenever Dr. Gabehart was in their midst. It was as though the very air was charged with a mix of apprehension and respect, creating a unique blend of emotions that underpinned the interactions within AGH.

The atmosphere was ambiguous, a testament to the multifaceted nature of Dr. Gabehart's presence. Was it a fear of her or the weight of their responsibilities that heightened the unease? The question lingered in the minds of those assembled, yet one thing was clear—Dr. Gabehart's presence commanded attention, whether through her reputation, accomplishments, or demeanour.

In this atmosphere, Sean was an intriguing anomaly. His presence radiated a different energy, an aura that defied the norm. His unique approach and unconventional reactions created a pocket of intrigue within this otherwise well-defined environment.

As the doctors awaited the day's instructions, the corridor became a canvas for the interplay of personalities and dynamics that defined AGH's daily rhythm. Among them, Dr. Gabehart remained a figure of authority and a focal point of curiosity and reverence. The unease she elicited was not simply out of fear but out of respect for her unwavering commitment to the demands of her profession and the standards she upheld.

Sean's ability to navigate this environment with his own brand of authenticity was a testament to his uniqueness and adaptability. As the day's plans were about to unfold, the convergence of these varied personalities hinted at the intricate dance of human interactions that would shape their time together at AGH.

Within the enclave of AGH's cardiology team, four doctors with diverse expertise and experience resided. These doctors represented a spectrum of qualifications and journeys within the field.

Two of them, Dr. May and Dr. Bates, were cardiologists in their own right, and their years of service contributed to a wealth of knowledge and insights. On the other hand, Dr. Peters and Dr. Atkins were in their fellowships, absorbing and honing their skills to become fully licensed cardiologists.

When Sean entered this esteemed fold, he bore the weight of the accumulated expertise and accomplishments surrounding him. The team's collective experience was a repository of wisdom, each member contributing to a mosaic of understanding that spanned years of dedication to their craft. Yet, his demeanour appeared to belittle the accomplishments and insights held by these accomplished professionals.

The team's dynamic was harmonious, professional, and unified by a shared respect for Dr. Gabehart's authority and reputation. Cohesion extended to the seasoned veterans and fledgling talents, creating an environment where collaboration thrived. While the pressures of medicine often strained relationships, this group managed to balance respect and camaraderie.

Despite the veneer of harmony, Sean's entry introduced a ripple of tension. His apparent lack of respect for his colleagues' knowledge and accomplishments deviated from the norm. Dr. May and Dr. Bates, longtime colleagues, symbolized a partnership founded on mutual respect and shared experience. The recent additions of Dr. Peters and Dr. Atkins brought fresh perspectives to AGH from their previous affiliations.

The intricate tapestry of personalities within this tight-knit community set the stage for a journey of growth, challenge, and transformation. Sean's presence, an outlier in many ways, would likely be a catalyst for change—a reminder of the importance of respect, humility, and the delicate balance between individuality and unity. Nevertheless, the undercurrent of fear and reverence for Dr. Gabehart persisted.

Within the confines of AGH's cardiology team, Sean and his relationship with Dr. Gabehart seemed to be an enigma that defied an easy solution. The four doctors engaged in whispered speculations, attempting to unravel the mystery surrounding this unusual pairing.

Each attempt to explain the connection fell short as they exchanged theories and observations. Dr. Gabehart's reputation as a no-nonsense practitioner who hated the role of an educator was well-known among her colleagues. The fact that she was taking Sean under her wing raised eyebrows, generating a buzz of curiosity throughout the team.

One speculation was that Sean might have been an old acquaintance of Dr. Gabehart's—a friend from the past for whom she was extending a professional favour. However, this theory quickly unravelled in the face of the palpable dynamic of authority that hung over Sean during their initial introduction. If Sean was indeed a friend, the air of superiority that Dr. Gabehart exuded in his presence seemed out of place, casting doubt on the authenticity of such a relationship.

The team's contemplations revealed their fascination with the intricate web of human connections and motivations. Although they were seasoned experts in heart health, the complexities of interpersonal relationships added an unexpected layer to their daily routines.

The intrigue and uncertainty surrounding Sean's presence testified to the profound effect that human interactions can have, even in the controlled environment of a hospital. The mystery of his connection with Dr. Gabehart among the four doctors became a microcosm of the broader human experiences that would unfold within the walls of AGH.

Sean's presence genuinely intrigued and confounded the four doctors. His age, seemingly similar to Dr. Gabehart's or perhaps even younger, only added to the enigma. Sean's interactions within the hospital had primarily been with patients, nurses, and support staff, making his interactions with other doctors less pronounced. The medical community's divided opinions about him added to the veil of uncertainty.

Sean's name had become a whispered legend among the doctors of AGH. Some regarded him with admiration, while others dismissed him as arrogant and undeserving of the recognition he seemed to receive. This division in opinion acted as a barrier between Sean and his colleagues, with most doctors preferring to keep their distance, either due to skepticism or perhaps even jealousy.

For the cardiology team, understanding Sean's relationship with Dr. Gabehart proved to be a puzzling task. Dr. Bates's humorous attempt at suggesting an affair between the two was quickly dismissed as implausible. Even the audacious Dr. Bates acknowledged the implausibility of Dr. Gabehart, a dedicated and serious professional, engaging in a frivolous affair. It was evident that Dr. Gabehart's character and commitment to her profession were too strong for such an unfounded theory to hold water.

Each interaction, each shared moment, carried a sense of intrigue that left the cardiology team in anticipation of the unfolding story. Their association's true nature remained mystical, leaving the team to grapple with their theories and assumptions in the absence of concrete information.

As Sean joined the group of doctors, a palpable shift in the atmosphere occurred. The laughter ceased, and the previously animated conversation abruptly stopped. The doctors greeted him with a nod, a sign of respect tinged with curiosity. Dr. May's friendly smile served as an attempt to ease the tension, but Sean's indifferent smirk revealed that he was well aware of the attention he was receiving.

The contrast between Sean's appearance and that of the fully licensed medical doctors was evident. While they were all adorned in their professional long white coats, Sean's shorter white coat marked his status as a medical student. Their formal attire testified to the seriousness of their roles, while Sean's casual dress underscored his unique position within the group.

The group's previous playful speculation about Sean's connection with Dr. Gabehart was momentarily set aside in his presence. They exchanged nods and subtle greetings, with unspoken questions hanging in the air. Sean's demeanour, marked by a carefree attitude, hinted that he was unfazed by the attention and perhaps even accustomed to it.

The dynamics within this diverse ensemble of medical professionals would likely continue to shift and evolve, driven by their personalities, experiences, and the mystery surrounding Sean's presence.

The prolonged silence that had enveloped the group was finally broken as Dr. Gabehart emerged from her office, donned in practical scrubs and a white coat, the emblem of her profession. Her presence brought an almost palpable sense of relief, as if a weight had been lifted. Dr. Gabehart's attire contrasted sharply with the traditional long white coats worn by her colleagues and Sean, who was dressed more casually, emphasizing the diversity within the group.

Each of the four doctors and Sean had their stethoscopes draped around their necks, except for Dr. Gabehart, who had hers tucked away in her pocket. This subtle detail spoke to her authority and confidence as if she could diagnose with a mere glance.

Even without explicitly saying so, her colleagues seemed ready to act at a moment's notice, their clipboards and reference books clutched tightly, and pens and markers within easy reach. Sean, on the other hand, appeared undeniably unprepared. The absence of writing materials emphasized the distinction between him and the seasoned medical professionals around him.

A keen observer, Dr. May sensed the potential predicament and stepped in swiftly. Offering Sean a pen and a sheet of paper, she showcased the fellowship among the medical professionals.

Even though Sean's status set him apart, the gesture demonstrated a willingness to support his learning experience in this challenging environment. With this small act of inclusion, the group seemed poised to embark on their rounds, each with their unique approach but united by the shared goal of providing exceptional patient care.

Dr. Gabehart led the group with her characteristic stride, her demeanour emanating authority and purpose. The team followed closely behind her, an unspoken understanding guiding their steps. The incident with the pen and paper seemed momentarily forgotten as the anticipation of the day's rounds took precedence.

However, as they walked, it became evident that Dr. Gabehart had not truly let the matter go. Her penchant for precision and her commitment to excellence could not allow such a breach of preparedness to pass without comment.

The hallway's silence was finally broken by her sharp question directed at Sean, laden with a blend of annoyance and curiosity. "Sean, when you woke up this morning, dressed as if you were headed to a bachelor party, yet utterly unprepared to learn like a student, where on earth did you think you were going?"

Sean's initial chuckle indicated he perceived the question as somewhat humourous, perhaps even sarcastic. His response, "Coming here, of course," was delivered with his characteristic light-heartedness.

Still, it was clear to all that Dr. Gabehart was not amused. A fleeting look back from her, accompanied by Sean's unyielding smile, was met with a disapproving frown as she promptly turned her gaze away, resuming her path down the hallway.

This brief interaction encapsulated the dynamic between the two—Sean's casual approach to formalities met Dr. Gabehart's unwavering demand for professionalism. A clash of perspectives, a confrontation of personalities, would inevitably shape their interactions throughout the days to come.

Sean's attempt at justification didn't quite land the way he likely intended, "Well, since it's my first day, I didn't think I would need all that stuff. Besides, this will be an easy clerkship for me because nothing intellectually stimulating happens in cardiology." His casual response and sarcastic remark were met with varying degrees of shock and amusement from the doctors around him. Dr. May appeared horrified, Dr. Atkins and Dr. Peters seemed genuinely surprised, and Dr. Bates, ever the provocateur, burst into laughter.

However, the moment of levity was abruptly cut short as all eyes turned to Dr. Gabehart, who had stopped in her tracks. The weight of her gaze held a mixture of disappointment and disbelief as if she couldn't quite believe what she had just heard. Dr. Bates's laughter dwindled to a halt under the intensity of her look. The sudden silence was palpable as everyone waited for Dr. Gabehart's response.

Dr. Gabehart's reaction was different from what the group had expected. Instead of an immediate reprimand, she offered Sean a wry smile with a touch of amusement amidst the disapproval. The shake of her head conveyed her disdain for his comment, while her turning away indicated her desire to continue with the rounds. The doctors turned to Sean, their expressions a mix of curiosity and anticipation, waiting to see how he would navigate this situation.

The incident further highlighted the stark contrast between Sean's carefree attitude and Dr. Gabehart's high standards. It also hinted at a growing tension between the two, a tension that would likely shape their interactions and experiences during Sean's time in the cardiology department.

Dr. Gabehart and her team were finally ready to start their

rounds. "Okay, folks, we know the patients and what we are dealing with here. Let's go and see what today has in store for us. I expect a full case report on at least three patients from each of you, from the patient's admission into this hospital to their current state, research guidance, and offer a comprehensive prognosis," Dr. Gabehart said to the team.

Even after a rude response and an awkward moment that likely landed Sean on Dr. Gabehart's blacklist, he couldn't resist raising his hand. The other four doctors looked at each other in disbelief. Yet, Dr. Gabehart indulged Sean without entertaining him as she said, "Yes, that also includes you, Sean. Since you said this would be an easy clerkship, I'm sure you won't have a problem reporting on five patients. All five reports are due tomorrow morning. Is that a problem?"

In embarrassment, Sean slowly put his hand down but preserved his smile to project his confidence at the new task. He looked pensively down for a few seconds, then quickly looked up to avoid further humiliation. "Okay, Dr. Gabehart, I'll get it done, but If I can get it done by the end of the day, can I take the rest of the week off?" he quipped. It was clear that Dr. Gabehart wasn't in the mood for his humour.

Dr. Gabehart's response was subtle but powerful. With a shake of her head and a disappointed smile directed at Sean, she conveyed her disapproval without uttering a single word. Her body language spoke volumes. Her eye roll and brisk departure indicated her exasperation with Sean's behaviour.

As she turned away to continue leading the group down the hallway, it was clear that the atmosphere had shifted. Sean's remark had not gone unnoticed or unchallenged, and the implications of his choice of words lingered in the air like an unspoken challenge.

The other doctors on the team exchanged incredulous glances, likely surprised that Sean would even consider making such a request after his earlier comment. The tension in the air was palpable, and it was becoming increasingly apparent that Sean's approach was not aligning with the team's expectations, particularly Dr. Gabehart's.

Even after his initial blunders, Sean's willingness to speak up and attempt to lighten the mood showcased his persistent confidence or perhaps even audacity. Yet, his interactions with Dr. Gabehart quickly demonstrated that he could not effortlessly charm or joke his way around her stern and demanding demeanour.

The five doctors and Sean at the back walked into the first patient's room. According to their system, each doctor presented a history summary, the patient's current state, and a review of current treatment and prognosis. So, they approached the first patient, and Dr. Bates took the stage.

Dr. Bates, the confident and assertive doctor of the group, started the presentation with a case involving a middle-aged man with a history of alcoholism. "A fifty-five-year-old male with a history of alcoholism. The patient has been stable since regaining consciousness a few hours after admission, and we have been treating him with painkillers for his mild back pain, likely unrelated to his hospital admission. The patient seems to be recovering well, but tests point to signs of liver failure that is now leading to heart failure. The heart failure is why he was brought to us, and the liver failure doesn't seem too extensive, at least for now. Since his heart failure is likely a direct result of his liver failure, we need a liver transplant. We have some time to find a match, but the problem is protocol dictates that he must be sober for at least six months before he gets a new liver. I recommend getting him psychiatric help over the next few months while we treat him symptomatically for liver and heart failure."

As Dr. Bates wrapped up his case presentation, Dr. Gabehart asked if there were any additional points to consider. Dr. Bates suggested the possibility of associated depression and recommended starting the patient on antidepressants to address potential psychological factors and aid his sobriety. His confidence was apparent as he emphasized his expertise.

Dr. Bates then directed a playful comment towards Sean, trying to reassert his dominance within the group. "See, kid, that's why I'm the big dog around here."

Sean attempted to interject, but Dr. Gabehart's swift intervention silenced him. As the team moved to the next patient's room, Sean lingered behind, seemingly amused by something. After recognizing his distraction, Dr. Gabehart returned to fetch him, exhibiting her no-nonsense approach and urgency in maintaining the group's workflow and professionalism.

Dr. Atkins stepped into the spotlight for the second patient's presentation. She introduced a twenty-eight-year-old male with no significant medical history except for a recent heart attack. She explained that the patient had been experiencing stress due to a new job, which might have contributed to his health condition.

Dr. Atkins disclosed that she initially prescribed medication to manage his anxiety, but the patient suffered another heart attack shortly after. She continued by highlighting the patient's surprisingly high cholesterol levels for his age despite his claim of maintaining a balanced diet and an active lifestyle since his teenage years. Dr. Atkins expressed her skepticism about his dietary habits, stating that his test results suggested a history of consuming only fast food for an extended period.

Pleased with her presentation, Dr. Atkins finished with a smile and looked toward Dr. Gabehart for feedback. Dr. Gabehart's stern and attentive demeanour seemed to evaluate both the patient's case and Dr. Atkins' performance. The team awaited any additional questions or guidance from her before they continued with their rounds.

Sean curiously looked at the patient before asking Dr. Atkins about the patient's parents. This seemed to annoy Dr. Gabehart to the point of outburst. She sternly scolded Sean for speaking and expressed her frustration with his presence.

Despite Dr. Gabehart's response, Dr. Atkins was polite enough to still answer Sean's question: "I'm not sure what his parents have to do with this. He's over eighteen, and we don't need the parent's consent to treat him."

This was not polite enough, but the patient noticed a concerned look on Sean, so he answered, "My mom works two jobs, so she's working right now, and my dad passed away when I was young."

Seemingly undeterred by the tension, Sean continued his unconventional behaviour by examining the patient's legs, which earned him disapproving looks from Dr. Atkins and Dr. Gabehart.

Dr. Atkins stayed with the patient as the rest of the group turned around to leave the room. "I'm sorry, sir, about that rude student. Get some rest, and we will get you better. We're still waiting for more results from the lab. You'll know more about your health as soon as I do," she said to the patient as Sean rolled his eyes, stared at the ceiling, and pretended to yawn as he covered his laugh while walking away. Dr. Gabehart looked at Sean and shook her head in dismay. They all moved to the next patient.

The dynamic between Sean and Dr. Gabehart grew more strained as their interactions continued. Sean's curiosity and somewhat unconventional behaviour were starting to test Dr. Gabehart's patience.

As they moved to the next patient, Dr. Gabehart's annoyance was discernible, and the rest of the team could sense the tension. The day was unfolding with unexpected challenges and dynamics that had not been anticipated. This made it clear that Sean's presence was stirring up more than just curiosity among the medical team.

Within the confined chambers of the hospital's wards, a curious interplay was unravelling between the inquisitive young medical apprentice, Sean, and the no-nonsense conductor of this orchestra of health, Dr. Gabehart. As the day progressed, the atmosphere grew more charged, like the electric air before a storm. It was filled with tension and intrigue.

Amidst the clinical tableau, the next act unfolded, drawing forth another patient and yet another chapter of a medical enigma. Dr. Gabehart's fatigue was perceptible, a shadow draped over her otherwise commanding demeanour. The stage was set for the forthcoming presentation, and Dr. Peters took centre stage in this grand theatre of medicine.

With the poised grace of a performer stepping into the limelight, Dr. Peters ventured forth to deliver his narrative. His patient, a forty-two-year-old male, emerged as the protagonist of this scene. No insignificant figure, he was covered in an aura of curiosity.

"A forty-two-year-old male with no significant medical history was brought in yesterday after passing out while making love to his wife. His wife performed CPR on him until the paramedics arrived. The patient's wife said the patient seemed exhausted before they started their adult play. The patient denied taking any medication, and we're still waiting for his blood work. The wife says she gave him erectile dysfunction medication, but only one pill. The patient seems healthy enough to handle one blue pill, so I'm still trying to figure out what could've caused him to pass out the way he did," Dr. Peters presented.

Sean seemed to strike an unusual chord again, his curiosity seeking a place within the presentations. He ventured to voice his inquiry with a touch of familiarity, drawing a mix of bemusement and exasperation from those around him. "What does he do for a living?" Sean asked.

Dr. Gabehart's bemused grin played across her features, a silent commentary on Sean's persistent curiosity that had become somewhat expected. As if speaking to a child who had interrupted adult conversation, Dr. Gabehart gently admonished Sean, guiding his enthusiasm towards a more opportune moment. "Sean, do you mind? Let Dr. Peters finish his presentation, and you can ask him your questions later."

A brief pause lingered, the tension between Sean's intrigue and Dr. Gabehart's guidance like an unspoken exchange beneath the surface.

But the drama didn't end there. Dr. Peters, seizing the opportunity to assert his seniority, wove his own narrative into the scene. A jocular punch followed, delivered with wit, aimed directly at Sean's youthful exuberance. The stage was a canvas of personalities. "Kid, let the grown-ups save lives. Why do you want to know what he does for a living? You want to give him a job?" Dr. Peters attempted to put Sean in his place.

In response, Sean, seemingly aware of the theatrics he had elicited, attempted to pour oil on the troubled waters, employing a dash of sarcasm to appease the ensemble.

"My apologies, please go on. I'm learning so much from you, Doctor," Sean quipped.

The dialogue became a rapid exchange of wit and repartee, a dance of words that reflected the nuanced interactions that unfolded within this cast of medical practitioners.

Sean lingered in the background, observing the interactions. His intrigue was perhaps echoed in the patient's enigmatic condition. As the presentation reached its conclusion, the spotlight shifted to Dr. Gabehart. Her affirmation marked the culmination of this chapter as the ensemble prepared to exit the stage, leaving the patient to recover.

Dr. Peters continued, "I treated the patient for dehydration, and he has been improving since."

Dr. Gabehart complemented Dr. Peters on a thorough presentation, "Okay. Keep an eye on him, and let's keep him for another day to ensure all is well before we discharge him."

Sean stood apart, observing the patient with an intensity that betrayed a hidden thought or realization. His gaze lingered, a secret note within the harmony, before he finally departed the room, his presence leaving a lingering whisper in the script of this unfolding drama.

As the unfolding drama continued its narrative, the spotlight shifted to a new player in the script – Dr. May, who stood poised to share her patient's tale. Yet, with Sean's earlier interjections still echoing in the minds of those present, a subtle undercurrent of uncertainty lingered within the room, casting a shadow over Dr. May's delivery.

"The patient is a sixty-five-year-old male with a twenty-year history of smoking. He has not smoked for the last ten years and has been living a somewhat healthful lifestyle. One of the valves in the patient's heart is blocked and must be replaced. Surgery for the patient to replace the valve was scheduled for yesterday, but the patient refused treatment and has now instituted a DNR," she said as she looked at Dr. Gabehart.

Though professional, Dr. May's delivery was tinged with a sense of reservation, perhaps fuelled by the spectre of Sean's earlier comments. The room held its breath, an unspoken question hanging in the air: Would Sean's penchant for unconventional remarks once again punctuate the scene?

And then, in a moment that felt almost orchestrated, Dr. Gabehart directed her inquiry toward the patient himself. As the words left her lips, the room seemed to hold its collective breath, waiting for the patient's response to add another layer to this intricate narrative, "Mr. Gladstone, why are you refusing treatment?"

But instead of the patient's voice, it was Sean who spoke — a quicksilver response that cut through the room's suspense like a well-aimed arrow. In his words, an interwoven mixture of intuition and speculation, painting a picture of the patient's wishes, encapsulated by the "do not resuscitate" emblem on his wrist. "Well, he wants to die. I'm just guessing based on the 'do not resuscitate' bracelet he has," Sean replied quickly.

With that single sentence, Sean peeled back a layer of the

patient's story, revealing an element of sensitive decision-making. The atmosphere in the room shifted, a silent acknowledgment that the drama on stage was far from scripted. It was the dance of human lives, each step and interaction resonating with emotions, choices, and the nuances of existence.

However, in this intense interplay of emotions and characters, the words flowed like sparks of fire, igniting the atmosphere with palpable tension. Dr. Gabehart's eyes flared with contained frustration, her patience teetering on a precipice as Sean's audacity seemed to know no bounds. Like a storm held at bay, her anger roared beneath a veneer of professionalism, threatening to break free at any moment.

Her voice reverberated through the room, a verbal storm warning that resonated with the weight of her authority. "Sean, this is your last warning," her words cut through the air like a blade. Each syllable enunciated a force that seemed to hang in the atmosphere, a looming threat that demanded attention.

Yet, amid the whirlwind of the moment, an unexpected observer emerged – Mr. Gladstone, the patient who had become the unintentional spectator of this verbal tussle. His health might have wavered, but his wit remained intact. Despite the gravity of his situation, his lips curled into an ironic smile, his voice like a wry chuckle. "Well, but he's right," he chimed in, a touch of amusement in his tone as if finding an odd camaraderie with Sean's audacious honesty.

The following words were laden with the raw essence of human vulnerability, a testament to the depths of Mr. Gladstone's feelings. His perspective echoed the weariness of a journey that had brought him to a crossroads. The prospect of a new valve, a symbol of hope and uncertainty, was painted against a canvas of reality—a body worn and battered, unable to bear the weight of stress and anticipation.

At the heart of this dramatic exchange, the narrative mirrored the intricacies of human emotion. Sean's brashness, Dr. Gabehart's authority, and Mr. Gladstone's poignant candour merged in a scene that captured the multifaceted nature of human existence. Each word, reaction, and gaze added a layer to this setting—a portrayal of lives intersecting, colliding, and weaving an unscripted medical theatre.

As Sean gazed intently into Mr. Gladstone's eyes, a spark of curiosity ignited within the patient's weary gaze. The air between them seemed charged. "What if I tell you that you don't have to go through a valve replacement, no new valve, but you could still get better?" he asked.

The weight of Sean's words hung like a suspended question mark. His audacity was undeterred by the storm brewing around him, a testament to his determination to make an impact and bridge the chasm between medical protocol and human sentiment.

But even as Sean stood there, unaware of the ticking bomb of Dr. Gabehart's patience, his words had pushed her to the brink. Her face, a mask of pent-up frustration, quivered like a stormy sea, waves of anger crashing against the facade of professionalism she had so diligently maintained. The classroom of medicine had turned into a theatre of chaos, and Sean was the unruly protagonist.

In a crescendo of emotions, the scene took an unexpected turn. Dr. Gabehart's voice sliced through the air, sharp and unwavering, as if her words were the thunderous roar of a storm finally set free. "Sean, get your things and get the hell out of here right now!" Her command reverberated, a declaration that her patience had reached its nadir. The storm within her had burst forth; her anger unleashed like lightning striking the ground.

Caught off-guard by Dr. Gabehart's explosive outpouring of anger, Sean's face shifted from determination to surprise. The suddenness of her wrath was like a gust of wind knocking the wind out of his sails. His audacious bravado had collided with the unyielding force of authority, leaving him momentarily stunned.

The room, charged with tension, reverberated with the aftermath of Dr. Gabehart's decree. The consequences of Sean's boldness unfolded swiftly, leaving the room breathless. Amid the turbulent sea of emotions, the narrative vividly portrayed humanity's complex tapestry—a symphony of ego, authority, vulnerability, and passion, all intertwining to create a moment that would be etched into the memory of everyone present.

In the span of a few heartbeats, Sean's emotions plummeted like a stone sinking into a bottomless abyss. The atmosphere in the room transformed from an electrifying drama to a heavy silence. This vacuum swallowed his earlier optimism. The walls that had witnessed his audacious words now bore witness to his rapid descent into the depths of despair. His buoyant spirit had collided with the reality of his actions, leaving him adrift in a sea of regrets.

Yet, amidst this sea of turmoil, Mr. Gladstone emerged as an unexpected lighthouse, his amusement unfurling like a beacon of light cutting through the gloom. As Sean grappled with the consequences of his words, Mr. Gladstone found a fleeting reprieve from his own struggles in the unfolding drama. Amid the pain and uncertainty, the chaos before him became a moment of amusement. This spectacle momentarily eclipsed his tribulations.

With a wit honed by the weight of his own experiences, Mr. Gladstone seized the moment to offer Sean an unconventional lifeline. "Well, seems like you're fired, kid. So how about you come and work for me? What do you have for me? Talk to me."

Mr. Gladstone's playful words were a testament to the resilience of the human spirit, a reminder that even in the darkest times, laughter could be found in the most unexpected places.

As Sean's uncertain steps carried him towards the exit, a heavy silence hung in the air, punctuated only by closing the door behind him. The room was left with the lingering echoes of emotions that had ricocheted like lightning bolts, leaving behind a tale woven with threads of boldness, anger, and a touch of joy.

The moment had etched itself into the annals of the hospital's history. This memory would forever bind the lives of those who had been present, a story of audacity and consequence that would be whispered among the hospital walls for years to come.

Still, the room froze instantly, caught in a display of disbelief. Sean's return was nothing short of a theatrical shock, a dramatic twist that stunned the doctors and their patient. As he strode back in, the air seemed to crystallize around him, his face now a storm of intensity. His eyes, usually vibrant with youthful bravado, blazed with a commanding and disconcerting intensity.

Sean started lashing out as he stared at Dr. Gabehart, "A few hours ago, you told me to be observant, but you can't observe the simple fact that you have four incompetent doctors working for you and treating patients. Your doctors can't observe anything because they're busy treating symptoms and trying to impress you."

With a fierce look and heavy breathing, he continued, "Your liver failure patient likely has chronic back pain that he was medicating with narcotics he was likely getting from the streets. He ran out and likely took a few too many acetaminophen, which he had probably been doing for at least a week, and that ruined his liver. Give him an antidote and observe as he gets better; give him fluid to wash the drugs out and let the liver recover on its own. He should be fine in a couple of days. While he was an alcoholic, the size of his liver looked normal, so whatever caused liver failure should have been acute, not chronic. Dr. Bates, you really are not as smart as you think."

As his words sliced through the air like a surgeon's scalpel, there was no denying the raw truth they carried. Sean's outburst was a whirlpool of frustration, accusation, and a hint of desperation. His voice was the storm that had been gathering beneath the surface, a whirlwind of discontent and anger that had finally broken free from its restraints.

His analysis of the liver failure case, delivered with clinical precision, was a jolt to the status quo. He dissected the patient's condition like a seasoned detective, connecting dots that had eluded the collective medical eye. It was a revelation that shimmered with audacity and a hint of arrogance, a challenge to the very foundations of the established medical diagnosis.

His pointed words at Dr. Bates punctuated the crescendo of his tirade. The rebuke was unapologetically sharp, a direct hit at the doctor who had instigated Sean's trials since his arrival. The air seemed to crackle with tension, a palpable confrontation unfolding in real-time.

Sean turned to Dr. Atkins, and she wasn't happy about what was going to happen as she looked at Dr. Bates, fighting his tears. He continued, "Dr. Atkins, your patient likely has type two hyperlipidemia, which he probably inherited from his father, who likely died young. Don't assume the patient is lying because you can't comprehend the presenting history, signs, and symptoms. How could you not have noticed those yellow plaques on his feet and his eyes? That's a classic sign!"

The accusations of incompetence hung like a heavy cloud over the room, casting a shadow on the doctors who had been, until now, the embodiments of authority and expertise. Sean's words bore the sharp edge of critique, laying bare the deficiencies he believed had festered beneath the veneer of medical professionalism.

As the room stood at the precipice of shock, one could almost hear the collective inhale before the exhale of response. The reactions varied, from Mr. Gladstone's bemusement to Dr. Gabehart's mixture of astonishment and, perhaps, reluctant admiration. The room was a canvas upon which the bold strokes of Sean's frustration had painted a vivid portrait of chaos and confrontation.

Amidst it all, Sean's expression held steady, a mask of defiance tinged with vulnerability. His words had been a catharsis, a release of pent-up emotions that had surged like a tidal wave. As he stood there, he awaited the aftermath, his heart pounding with a cocktail of anticipation, regret, and, maybe, a glimmer of satisfaction at having finally spoken his mind.

The room had become an arena of revelation and accusation, each word uttered by Sean acting like a stone thrown into a calm pond, creating ripples of astonishment that reached every corner. As his verbal barrage continued, it was as if Sean had pulled back the curtain on the hidden narratives of each patient, revealing their secrets and stories with uncanny precision.

Dr. Atkins' expression wavered between disbelief and something akin to guilt. His words had stripped away her sense of clinical certainty, exposing the gaps in her assessment. The mention of "type two hyperlipidemia" felt like a blow aimed directly at her expertise. It was a humbling reminder that the puzzle pieces she had missed were right before her, hiding in plain sight.

Across the room, Dr. Bates struggled to maintain his composure, his earlier bravado now shattered by the razor-sharp accuracy of Sean's analysis. His teary eyes bore the weight of someone whose façade had been cracked open, revealing the vulnerabilities beneath. Sean's words had struck a chord that resonated with truth, a truth against which he had been so fiercely protecting.

Then, it was Dr. Peters' turn. As Sean's words targeted him, an undeniable tension hung like a veil. The room seemed to hold its breath as the accusations mounted, each sentence carving a deeper groove of uncomfortable recognition. The doctor's once-confident demeanour was now a mask straining against the unravelling threads of truth.

Sean continued his rant, "And you, Dr. Peters, your patient's appearance suggests a wealthy lifestyle. Your patient has been spending so much time with his mistress that he wasn't giving it his all at home. His mistress likely wanted to have something special, so she gave him a blue pill. She exhausted him, and he got home tired. His wife was tired of B-grade lovemaking and gave him another blue pill within hours of the first one. My guess is the patient knew about the first pill but likely didn't know about the second one. Your patient is a filthy man. He needs to come clean, or he won't make it here alive next time."

Sean's voice cut through the air, his tone resolute and unyielding. His words were incisive, dissecting the patients and their stories with an almost surgical precision. He painted an equally startling and unsettling narrative, revealing layers of human behaviour that medical charts and diagnosis codes had obscured.

In the face of Sean's revelations, the room had transformed into a pot of emotions – shock, discomfort, anger, and a mysterious sense of awe. His words had laid bare the complex tapestry of human lives, unveiling threads of deceit, secrecy, and vulnerability. It was as if he had pulled back the curtain on the human condition, showing that even in the confines of a hospital room, stories were waiting to be told, truths waiting to be unravelled.

As Sean's voice faded into the charged silence that followed, all eyes were on him. His outburst had been a cyclone that had swept through the room, leaving a sense of unease and an undercurrent of transformation in its wake. The confrontation had carved a new narrative: assumptions were shattered, authority was questioned, and the veneer of professionalism had been cracked open to reveal the raw humanity beneath.

Sean's words hung in the air like a sudden storm, carrying a whirlwind of revelation and potential redemption. As they reached Mr. Gladstone's ears, his initial amusement at the unfolding drama had given way to a raw and unfiltered fear. It was as if Sean had peeled back the layers of his carefully constructed facade, exposing the hidden fears and doubts that had been lurking in the shadows.

Sean continued his tirade, "Your past is coming to catch up with you, Mr. Gladstone. Right now, you were misled to think you need a valve replacement. I know the chief surgeon in this hospital, and I can set up an appointment for you. He will repair the valve, not replace it. It is much safer and has significantly fewer side effects than getting a new one. He will chip away the excess buildup around the valve that's preventing the valve from opening so the valve can function normally again."

Mr. Gladstone's eyes darted around the room, alternating between Sean and the doctors, who stood frozen in astonishment. The notion that there might be another option, an alternative path that didn't involve the drastic surgery to which he had resigned himself, was like a lifeline tossed to him amidst the tumultuous sea of his despair.

The words "repair the valve, not replace it" echoed in his mind like a chorus of hope. It was a melody of hope, a chance to rewrite his fate in a way that seemed almost too good to be true. The thought of shedding the weight of impending surgery and the uncertain aftermath of a new valve hung over him like a tantalizing promise.

Mixed emotions flashed across Mr. Gladstone's face – fear, doubt, hope, and a lingering sense of incredulity. Could it be possible? Was this brash young man, who had just been evicted from the room, offering him a chance at a different outcome, a chance to rewrite the narrative of his own life? The very notion was a bitter pill to swallow, laden with a mixture of skepticism and a flicker of optimism.

As Sean's words seemed to settle in the room, the atmosphere shifted from confrontation to a peculiar mix of anticipation and reflection. The tense silence seemed to stretch as if the air was holding its breath, waiting for Mr. Gladstone to make a choice that could alter the course of his life. The seconds ticked by, each loaded with a weight that misrepresented its brevity.

As if breaking free from the grip of uncertainty, Mr. Gladstone's expression transformed. The fear that had gripped him moments ago began to ebb away, replaced by a determination that burned in his eyes. It was the kind of determination born from the realization that there was a chance, a glimmer of hope that had pierced through the darkness.

With a voice that wavered slightly with a mixture of resolve and newfound courage, Mr. Gladstone finally spoke. His words carried a weight that resonated with the entire room. "Alright, kid. You've got my attention. If what you're saying is true, if I can avoid the scalpel and still get better, I'll listen. But what do you mean my past is coming to catch up with me?"

Sean looked at Dr. Gabehart, Mr. Gladstone, and back again at Dr. Gabehart, as he said, "Dr. Gabehart, please look at Mr. Gladstone's right hand." Dr. Gabehart looked at the hand and was shocked by what she saw. Her head suddenly became heavy. She put her head down in exasperation, and when she got up, the door was closing as Sean walked out.

Dr. Gabehart's eyes became teary as she tried to find words to explain to Mr. Gladstone what had just happened. It seemed so heavy that even the other doctors looked concerned, but she had to wait to get enough courage to tell Mr. Gladstone what Sean meant. She did her best while being consumed with emotion, "Mr. Gladstone, I'm sorry to tell you this, but there's a very high chance that you have lung cancer."

The room seemed to hold its breath, a heavy realization that crashed against the walls like a tidal wave. The gravity of the situation settled upon them all, a crushing weight that seemed to distort time itself. The silence was punctuated only by the soft hum of medical equipment and the distant sounds of the hospital beyond the closed door.

For Mr. Gladstone, the room seemed to close in around him, and the air felt thin as his chest tightened with disbelief and dread. The revelation that he might be facing an even more significant threat than the heart condition that had brought him here was a cruel twist of fate, a reality he hadn't been prepared to confront.

His gaze, which had been fixated on Dr. Gabehart's eyes, slowly lowered to his hand as if searching for some semblance of a connection to the news that had just been delivered. The hand he had extended to Sean in a challenge now seemed to bear a significance beyond his understanding – a subtle yet poignant symbol of the intricate interconnectedness of life's moments.

Around him, the doctors and medical personnel exchanged sombre glances, a silent acknowledgement of the gravity of the situation. Even in a profession where confronting life-threatening conditions was a daily occurrence, there was an unspoken understanding that this particular moment held a unique weight, a convergence of circumstances that defied explanation.

Mr. Gladstone's eyes met Dr. Gabehart's once again, searching for reassurance or perhaps a glimpse of hope. But the tears glistening in her eyes and the heavy sigh she let out spoke volumes. It was a reminder that even for a seasoned physician, delivering devastating news was never easy – a reminder that behind every diagnosis and prognosis lay the raw emotions of human lives forever altered.

Amid this heavy silence, Mr. Gladstone's thoughts began to race like a storm of emotions and questions vying for his attention. The knowledge that his future hung in the balance, with both heart and lung concerns, seemed to bring his mortality into sharp focus.

There was a peculiar juxtaposition between the bustling activity of the hospital beyond the door and the stillness within the room, an illustration of the fragile dance between life and death that played out daily within these walls.

As he grappled with the enormity of what he had just heard, a single question emerged from the chaos of his thoughts. He directed it toward Dr. Gabehart, his voice betraying a blend of vulnerability and determination. "What are my options? What can we do about this?" It was a plea for guidance, a yearning for a lifeline amidst the storm that had suddenly engulfed his world.

The room had transformed into a theatre of emotions, each grappling with their own feelings in the face of a reality that seemed to transcend the boundaries of medicine. Mr. Gladstone's thoughts were a whirlwind of confusion and apprehension as he tried to reconcile the stark prognosis he had just received with the newfound hope that Sean had unexpectedly offered.

The shift from discussing a DNR order, a decision that had seemed relatively straightforward compared to his other health concerns, to confronting the possibility of lung cancer was jarring. It was as if the ground beneath him had shifted, leaving him unsteady and vulnerable. The human experience's complexity had manifested within those hospital walls, revealing the intricate dance of life, death, and the uncertainty that lay among them.

As Mr. Gladstone looked around the room, he could see the weight of the news etched on the faces of the medical professionals who had gathered there. The solemnity of the moment was discernible as they navigated the delicate balance between compassion and professionalism. Dr. Gabehart's tears were a testament to the bond that forms between physicians and their patients. This bond transcends the clinical realm and delves into the realm of shared humanity.

As the seconds stretched into minutes, the weight of the situation hung heavy in the air, a tangible reminder of the fragility of life and the profound impact that a single moment can have on one's existence. The convergence of medical expertise, personal histories, and emotions painted a vivid portrait of the human experience that defied simple categorization or explanation.

In that room, Mr. Gladstone's journey had taken an unexpected turn, revealing the intricate tapestry of interconnected lives that defines the realm of healthcare. Amidst the tears, the uncertainty, and the hope, there was an unspoken understanding that the path forward would be fraught with challenges but also with the possibility of resilience, strength, and the profound capacity of the human spirit to endure.

The room was filled with a heavy silence, punctuated only by the sound of Mr. Gladstone's laboured breathing. He lay back on his bed, the weight of the news sinking in like a stone dropped into a calm lake, creating ripples of disbelief and contemplation. The reality that his life was taking an unexpected turn, guided by the insights of an audacious medical student, was both bewildering and disconcerting.

"I stopped smoking a long time ago. Do some tests," Mr. Gladstone said to Dr. Gabehart in frustration.

Dr. Gabehart explained, "Mr. Gladstone, I'll do the tests, but they won't change anything. Trust me, there's nothing worse than for me to try to convince you of this if I have any doubts. That young man just outsmarted four doctors with more than twenty years of combined experience in front of you. He got you to change your mind about your DNR within a few minutes, and he didn't twist your arm to do so. I've only known him for a few hours, but his observational skills are exceptional. You witnessed what he did to these four doctors, and do you think he's wrong about this?"

Everything seemed to have come crashing down hard on

Mr. Gladstone within a moment. "I'll be damned. But how, though?" Mr. Gladstone wondered as he laid back on his bed.

Dr. Gabehart explained, "When you stopped smoking, you only reduced your risk of lung cancer, but the risk didn't go to zero. We'll do more tests to see how far it has progressed and identify the type of cancer before starting treatment as soon as possible. I'm terribly sorry, Mr. Gladstone."

His mind was in turmoil as he grappled with the notion that the young man who had entered his room with a brash demeanour and unconventional approach might be right about something so profound.

The contrast of moments struck Mr. Gladstone with a forceful clarity. Sean's earnest plea to consider life and the possibility of recovery, followed by the crushing reality of a potential cancer diagnosis, left him reeling. It was as if the universe was testing the limits of his resilience, his capacity to absorb the blows of fate and find meaning within the chaos.

As he lay there, thoughts of his past choices danced before his mind's eye. The memory of each cigarette smoked, the moments of laughter shared with friends, the trials and triumphs of a life lived. The weight of regret mingled with the heaviness of uncertainty, a reminder that choices and challenges often shape life's journey.

In his introspection, Mr. Gladstone's gaze shifted to the window, where sunlight filtered through the curtains, casting a warm glow in the room. It was a stark contrast to the emotional storm swirling within him. He thought about the possibilities ahead, the potential for treatment, healing, and the uncharted territories that Sean's revelation had opened up.

As he contemplated the intricacies of his situation, Mr. Gladstone couldn't help but marvel at the complex tapestry of human connection. In a few hours, the convergence of personalities, experiences, and expertise had woven a narrative that defied prediction. It was a testament to the unpredictable nature of life itself, where the actions of one individual could send ripples that touched the lives of many.

On that Monday morning, the hospital corridors buzzed with uncharacteristic tension. The unexpected twists in life had disrupted the usual rhythm of the medical routines. Conversations among the medical staff were hushed, laden with the weight of the news they had to deliver, the decisions they had to make, and the uncharted territory they found themselves navigating.

Mr. Gladstone's presence lingered in the air like a bittersweet memory. He had carved a place for himself within the hospital walls, becoming more than just another patient. His friendly demeanour, the warmth of his laughter, and genuine interest in others had endeared him to the staff and fellow patients. Now, his role in their lives was being reframed, transforming him from a source of smiles to a stark reminder of life's fragility.

For the doctors, accustomed to the ebb and flow of medical cases, this particular morning demanded an emotional balance that was difficult to achieve. The science of medicine merged with the art of compassion as they navigated their feelings alongside their patients'. They were reminded that each diagnosis carried with it not just medical implications but also the weight of emotions, fears, and hopes.

The hospital, often a place of healing and restoration, had transformed into a theatre of human resilience. While medical knowledge and expertise formed the backbone of care, the bonds of empathy, the exchange of wisdom, and the willingness to confront the unknown defined the spirit of that day.

Dr. Gabehart's words hung heavy in the room, like a weighty verdict that couldn't be overturned. Mr. Gladstone's face, once adorned with curiosity and a sense of humour, now bore the marks of shock and disbelief. The knowledge that quitting smoking hadn't been a guaranteed shield against the spectre of lung cancer settled in his mind like a relentless storm cloud, obscuring the once clear skies of hope.

His journey through the medical maze had been marked by a sense of camaraderie, with the hospital becoming his temporary home and its staff his extended family. Yet, in that very sanctuary of care, he had been confronted with a truth that no amount of laughter or camaraderie could protect him. Cancer, that ominous, whispered and dreaded word, had crept into his life like an unwelcome guest.

The room seemed to shrink, the walls closing in as the gravity of the situation took hold. The hospital bed that had been his refuge now felt like a prison of uncertainty. The laughter that had echoed through the corridors felt distant, replaced by a stark silence that seemed to amplify the weight of the moment.

As Mr. Gladstone processed the news, his thoughts danced like shadows on a darkened stage. The journey that had begun with his casual request for a DNR had taken an abrupt detour, leading him to the crossroads of life and its inevitable end. Once a place of potential healing and renewed vitality, the hospital became a theatre of contemplation, where the curtain had been drawn back to reveal a sobering truth.

As the clock continued its relentless march forward, Mr. Gladstone found himself at a crossroads where his decisions would shape the narrative of his life. The hospital, once a place of solace, was now a canvas upon which his resilience would be painted. With the support of the medical team and the knowledge that he wasn't alone in this battle, he embarked on a journey that would test his spirit, redefine his priorities, and remind him of the extraordinary strength within the human soul when faced with adversity.

Mr. Gladstone tried to get up, but Dr. Gabehart encouraged him to relax. He was too frustrated to be relaxed. He couldn't do anything about it, so he told Dr. Gabehart, "Get me that kid back here."

Dr. Gabehart responded, "I'm sorry, but I can't let him back here. While he's an impressive medical student, he has been very disrespectful, and I must let him go. He can finish his clerkship elsewhere." Mr. Gladstone gazed at Dr. Gabehart as he said, "I understand. Disrespect is horrible, but you know what's worse, medical malpractice?"

The words hung in the air like a sharp icicle, piercing the tension in the room. Dr. Gabehart's expression shifted from firm resolve to a mixture of surprise and concern. The weight of Mr. Gladstone's statement settled upon her like a heavy burden, reminding her that medicine was not just about science and skill but also a realm of accountability and responsibility.

The room seemed suspended in time, and the silence amplified the gravity of the situation. The doctors who had witnessed the morning's events were now caught in a new predicament. The prospect of medical malpractice, a term laden with legal implications and professional consequences, cast a long shadow over their collective consciousness.

Mr. Gladstone's voice broke the stillness again, its tone a

mix of frustration and desperation. "I'm not advocating for disrespect, but what I've seen here today is a clash of egos, a power struggle that puts patients at risk. That young man may have been disrespectful, but he had the audacity to challenge your assumptions. Maybe it took his bluntness to crack open the walls of complacency that surrounded you all."

Dr. Gabehart's gaze wavered, torn between her authority and the unsettling truth in Mr. Gladstone's words. The other doctors exchanged uneasy glances, caught between loyalty to their mentor and the realization that their devotion to protocol and hierarchy might have clouded their judgment.

"Perhaps," Mr. Gladstone continued, his voice softening, "this is an opportunity for growth, for a different perspective that transcends the traditional dynamics of a hospital hierarchy."

The room seemed to thaw slightly, the chill giving way to introspection. The air was charged with an unspoken challenge – a challenge to recognize that sometimes, the lessons we need to learn come from the unlikeliest of sources.

Dr. Gabehart finally spoke, her words mixed with resignation and acknowledgment. "Perhaps you're right, Mr. Gladstone. Perhaps we need to find a balance between authority and humility. Perhaps we need to acknowledge that knowledge doesn't reside solely within titles, and that even the most seasoned doctors can benefit from a fresh perspective."

Dr. Gabehart's internal struggle echoed in how she moved; a restless energy mirrored the turmoil within her. The weight of the situation hung heavily on her shoulders, a complex web of decisions and emotions entangling her every step.

As she left the room, the doctors who had witnessed the

exchange with Mr. Gladstone exchanged uncertain glances. Their mentor's demeanour had shifted from stern authority to a palpable unease, leaving them feeling disoriented and questioning the morning's events.

Outside the room, the hospital corridor stretched ahead, a seemingly endless path that mirrored the journey Dr. Gabehart was now navigating. Her mind was a storm of conflicting thoughts, a vortex of responsibility, pride, and self-doubt. Despite his perceived disrespect, the decision to bring Sean back weighed heavily on her.

The other doctors, now following her like hesitant shadows, could sense the emotional turmoil emanating from their usually composed mentor. They exchanged hushed whispers, caught in a mix of empathy and confusion. They struggled to reconcile the Dr. Gabehart they knew with the vulnerable figure they now saw before them.

Dr. Gabehart's footsteps were erratic, echoing in the corridor like the heartbeat of a person caught in a tumultuous internal struggle. She turned a corner, seeking solace and a place to gather her thoughts. The hospital, usually a place of order and routine, now seemed to mirror the chaos in her mind.

In a quiet corner, away from the bustle of the hallway, Dr. Gabehart finally came to a halt. She leaned against the wall, her breath coming in uneven bursts as she closed her eyes. The voices of doubt and determination battled within her like two opposing forces locked in an internal conflict.

The other doctors hesitated momentarily, unsure whether to approach or give her space. They exchanged glances, acknowledging the fragile balance that defined their profession—the tension between authority and humility, confidence and the acceptance of fallibility.

Inside her office, the air was thick with tension, almost as if the very walls were privy to the gravity of the situation. Dr. Gabehart's pacing reflected the restless turmoil that had taken hold of her. The office, typically a sanctuary of order and organization, now felt like a stormy sea of uncertainty.

The four doctors stood in a tight cluster just beyond the threshold, each bearing a distinct expression of apprehension. They exchanged uneasy glances, searching for reassurance or an inkling of what might come next. Their collective anxiety resonated within the confined space.

Dr. Gabehart's silence was palpable, and a heavy curtain of unspoken thoughts hung between her and her team. Each hesitant step she took seemed to reverberate with the weight of her internal struggle. Her team watched her movements, their discomfort mirrored in her actions.

Minutes stretched into an eternity as they waited for Dr. Gabehart's next move. The seconds ticked away like the slow beats of a metronome, a reminder of the fragile balance that Sean's unexpected outburst had disrupted.

Finally, Dr. Gabehart's throat clearing cut through the stillness, her team's attention snapping back to her. The sound was a jarring interruption, like a gunshot in a quiet room. The doctors straightened slightly, their eyes locked on their mentor, waiting for her to break the silence.

Dr. Gabehart's voice, when it came, was a mixture of frustration and authority, a reflection of the internal turmoil she had been wrestling with.

Dr. Gabehart's office had transformed into a crucible of

tension. Her pacing was like the tick-tock of a ticking time bomb. Her words detonated like emotional landmines, each one more potent than the last. The four doctors stood like apprehensive wardens, absorbing the brunt of her frustration.

"Do any of you idiots know how embarrassed I am right now? A freaking medical student picked up diagnoses within minutes that cardiologists and their fellows missed after spending more time with the same patients," she said as she continued pacing.

Her rhetorical question hung in the air like a smokescreen, veiling the reality they all knew too well—Sean had indeed uncovered what they had collectively missed. Dr. Bates, perhaps driven by a mix of defensiveness and disbelief, dared question the legitimacy of Sean's rapid assessments.

Dr. Bates brushed it with misdirection, questioning Sean's integrity and the legitimacy of his quick assessments.

The words tumbled from Dr. Bates's lips, a fragile defence built on skepticism and perhaps a touch of professional pride. His eyes met Dr. Gabehart's, seeking refuge in her expertise, hoping for a confirmation that would reassure their battered egos.

Dr. Gabehart's pacing ceased momentarily, and the weight of her gaze bore into Dr. Bates like a searing spotlight. She seemed to deliberate over her response, her thoughts colliding in a clash of emotion and reason. The room was cloaked in silence, each doctor holding their breath.

The room seemed to expand with the weight of her words, and the air was heavy with the realization that they were at a crossroads, clinging to pride or embracing the opportunity to learn and evolve.

"Now, I must apologize and beg a medical school student I kicked out because a patient who was wrongly diagnosed and received incorrect treatment that made him sign a DNR has given us a condition that for him to forget about his impending malpractice suit against the hospital I must get back that student against my wishes," said Dr. Gabehart.

Dr. Atkins rebuked, "But we had the right diagnosis though. He can't sue us for that."

Still trying to figure out the best way to deal with what happened, Dr. Peters said, "As doctors, we have a duty to treat the underlying disease and the patient, not symptoms. We assigned a wrong cause to a right diagnosis, and that's dereliction. If our treatments cause direct damage, emotional or physical, we will become a textbook case of medical malpractice. In this case, we told a patient that he only needed a valve replacement that came with its complications, and the patient gave up on life."

The gravity of the situation had pulled the four doctors into an impromptu circle of accountability. Dr. Gabehart's frustration reverberated in her words, her typically composed demeanour giving way to a raw, unfiltered display of disappointment. Each doctor, once steadfast in their clinical judgments, now found themselves under the harsh light of retrospection.

At this moment, the four doctors were confronted with their errors and the ethical dimensions of their profession. Their shared realization created a bond of understanding, a collective recognition that they had inadvertently harmed a patient by misdiagnosing his physical condition and his will to live.

Dr. Bates' skepticism lingered like a shadow, casting doubt on Sean's swift and accurate assessments. It was as if his understanding of medicine was being questioned, a challenge to the foundation of his expertise. He respected Dr. Gabehart's opinion, yet he couldn't shake the feeling that there was more to this than met the eye.

The weight of the situation was not lost on Dr. May, a long-time colleague of Dr. Gabehart. Her concern ran deep, knowing that her typically unflappable mentor had been shaken to the core. Dr. Gabehart's willingness to acknowledge Sean's insight was a testament to her integrity and a stark revelation of the situation's gravity.

"But that kid couldn't be right on all four cases like that." Dr. Bates said to Dr. Gabehart.

She insisted that she had seen what Sean saw and that he was indeed correct in all cases. Dr. Gabehart instructed Dr. Bates that since he still didn't know how Sean had figured out the cases, he should go back and do a thorough history and physical exam on each one of those patients.

As punishment, she also wanted him to write detailed reports about whether he agreed with Sean's diagnoses with detailed reasoning. To make life harder for Dr. Bates, Dr. Gabehart instructed him to submit his report first thing the following morning as she dismissed him. Dr. Bates didn't fight back. He noted the instructions and nodded in affirmation before walking out.

Dr. Gabehart kept pacing for a while before finally sitting down and composing herself. The three remaining doctors stared at her, waiting for instructions and reprimands. After a moment of silence, Dr. Gabehart started addressing the doctors, "Dr. Atkins, keep hydrating your patient, monitor his blood pressure, and take him off any meds. Find out if he was taking any blood pressure medication because that could have led to this: mixing blood pressure medication with ED medication. Get a psychiatric consult before you discharge him. He better talk to someone before he dies on top of his wife next time."

Dr. Atkins replied, "I'll get to it and keep you updated."

Dr. Gabehart moved on to Dr. Peters, from whom she requested a detailed family history and a genetic test of the patient and his siblings if he had any. Dr. Peters took the instructions and left the office. Only Dr. May remained, and Dr. Gabehart looked increasingly frustrated.

The weight of the recent events had settled heavily upon Dr. Gabehart's shoulders, and addressing Dr. May was proving challenging. The two of them had shared many experiences and challenges over the years, and their bond was a mix of professional respect and personal camaraderie.

Dr. Gabehart looked at Dr. May and quipped, "And then there was one." She smiled at Dr. May like a warning of a thunderstorm coming her way, the punishment. Dr. Gabehart covered her face with her hands as she laid her face on her desk in exhaustion.

She got up to address Dr. May. "Dr. May, your case was challenging, but I'm still disappointed you missed such a huge and important diagnosis. Stay with the patient, but Sean will help you navigate this case. You're still in charge, but he'll be your consultant." She said to Dr. May as she pointed her toward the door.

Dr. May was displeased by the instructions. She asked, "So Sean has all the power but no responsibility?"

"Yes, and that's your punishment," Dr. Gabehart replied.

Dr. May turned around and started walking out of Dr. Gabehart's office as she mumbled, "I hate this."

Dr. Gabehart heard it but didn't make a case. Instead, she retorted to Dr. May, "Do your job the right way next time!"

Dr. Gabehart's office door closed behind Dr. May, leaving her alone with her thoughts. The day's events and decisions were heavy on her shoulders. She knew that her actions were necessary for the growth and improvement of her team, but that didn't make them any easier to execute.

Her challenge had always been to balance being a compassionate healer and a strong leader. But today, the balance seemed to have tipped in favour of the latter.

Dr. Gabehart knew that the path to becoming a better doctor and leader was not without its trials and hardships. It required humility to acknowledge mistakes and determination to rectify them. She also recognized the value of Sean's unique perspective, his audacity to challenge the status quo, and his unyielding commitment to patient care.

After giving the doctors instructions on how to clean up the mess, it seemed like everything was done. However, Dr. Gabehart quickly remembered she had one more important thing to do. She was sitting alone in her office, trying to figure out what to do next.

She got up to get Sean's file. Looking through the file, she was trying to figure out how to tell Sean that she needed him back at the hospital. She thought about it for several minutes, got up and paced in her office for several more minutes before sitting down to make the call. She dialled the number, but the phone went to voicemail.

Dr. Gabehart cleared her throat, mentally preparing herself for what she would say. She began to leave a message on Sean's voicemail:

"Hi Sean, this is Dr. Gabehart. I'm calling about what happened earlier. I'm not good at apologizing, but I always take responsibility for my actions. I was right to kick you out, but I was wrong not to listen to you. I'm sure we can find a way to work together in the next few weeks without jeopardizing our careers. Mr. Gladstone wants you to consult on all decisions on his case, or he'll sue the hospital for malpractice. That's why I am calling right now, but I'd like to invite you for a sit-down to talk about those cases and a few more things, as I think you are a remarkable student. I may get a few insights from you as your reputation sure precedes you, and I think I can teach you a few things as well. If I see you in my office tomorrow morning, I'll consider what happened today: water under the bridge. Have a lovely day, and see you tomorrow morning."

Dr. Gabehart hung up the phone, feeling a mixture of anxiety and anticipation. She knew the decision was ultimately in Sean's hands, and she could only hope he would consider her proposal. Sitting back in her chair, she thought about the journey they had all been through that day. The chaos, the frustration, the revelations – it had all led to this moment of reflection and a chance for redemption.

The hospital was a place of healing, not just for patients but for those who worked there as well. And maybe, just maybe, Sean's return could be the first step toward healing the wounds that had been unintentionally inflicted.

Dr. Gabehart leaned forward, her hands resting on her desk. She knew the road ahead wouldn't be easy. Still, she was ready to face the challenges head-on with humility, determination, and an unwavering commitment to providing the best care for her patients.

Getting Professional

Dr. Gabehart paused from her work as the sun rose above the horizon to appreciate the stunning display of colours spreading across the sky. The tranquil beauty of the moment filled her heart with a sense of peace and calm. However, she knew this tranquillity would soon be shattered as the hospital came alive with the frantic energy of the day ahead.

As she gazed out her window, she couldn't help but wonder what the day had in store for her. With Sean's meeting in anticipation and the ongoing challenges in patient care, she knew it would be another day of uncertainty and surprises. But she was ready to face it all head-on, armed with the knowledge that even during a storm, there could be moments of clarity and positive change.

It was customary for Dr. Gabehart to arrive at work early. She relished those peaceful moments when there were few disturbances, and she could accomplish a significant amount of work. Sometimes, she had to attend to the needs of patients throughout the hospital, but for the most part, she was free to focus on her tasks without interruption.

The overnight shift team occasionally visited her office for a brief chat. The staff widely believed that she possessed an exceptional talent for listening and could offer great company if one were fortunate enough to catch her at the right time. However, if you happened to get on her wrong side, your day might suddenly turn miserable. Those who had the privilege of knowing her well and comprehending her ways appreciated her honesty.

Everyone, from nurses to general staff, recognized that she worked tirelessly and was extremely passionate about her job. They would take turns ensuring she had everything she needed to continue performing her duties to the best of her abilities.

Dr. Gabehart's reputation in the medical field was hard-earned and well-deserved. Her commitment to advancing cardiovascular health was evident in her clinical work and her extensive involvement in educating the public. Her column in newspapers and magazines, "Matters of the Heart," was a testament to her dedication to spreading awareness and promoting heart health among the general population. She understood that preventive measures were as crucial as medical treatment for cardiovascular diseases.

Despite her busy schedule as the head of cardiology, she remained passionate about research. Her critical eye and rigorous standards ensured that the studies she reviewed met the highest scientific standards.

She was known to meticulously dissect research papers, scrutinizing every detail to ensure their validity and accuracy. While some might have viewed her as a harsh critic, her approach was rooted in her unwavering commitment to upholding the integrity of scientific knowledge.

Dr. Gabehart's reputation for being forthright and demanding excellence in the medical field was not without its challenges. Her staunch dedication sometimes clashed with individuals who sought shortcuts or were more concerned about publication quantity than quality. This naturally led to some friction, making her both respected and feared by her colleagues.

Yet, those who truly understood her knew she was driven by a desire to improve patient care and medical research.

Her ability to balance administrative responsibilities and clinical duties, as well as her passion for research and public education, was a testament to her remarkable organizational skills and work ethic. She had an uncanny ability to switch between mentoring her team, fiercely advocating for her patients, and being a respected voice in the medical community.

Dr. Gabehart's wit and honesty were well-known in the medical community. She didn't mince words when voicing her opinions, even if they were unpopular. Her tendency to be blunt and unapologetically honest often earned her admirers and critics.

When confronted about her approach, she would humorously admit that something about her enjoyed ruffling feathers, and perhaps a touch of making enemies. She didn't revel in discord but valued constructive criticism and healthy debate over superficial harmony.

Despite her reputation for being formidable, Dr. Gabehart had a softer side that not everyone saw. Beneath her assertive demeanour was a dedication to her patients and a sincere desire to improve medical practices. She welcomed genuine discussions and valued colleagues who shared her passion for excellence and patient well-being. Those who sought her out solely for their own agendas, such as glowing reviews, quickly learned that her discerning eye could spot insincerity from a mile away.

In a field where personal connections could sometimes blur professional boundaries, Dr. Gabehart remained steadfast in her commitment to upholding the integrity of medicine. She didn't let flattery or false camaraderie sway her judgment when evaluating medical research or colleagues' work.

While it might have contributed to her isolated reputation, this uncompromising stance was also a testament to her unwavering dedication to the highest standards of medical practice.

As she prepared for her meeting with Sean, Dr. Gabehart contemplated the potential impact of their collaboration. While she was known for her assertiveness and skepticism, she was open to learning from Sean's fresh perspective. She recognized that her experiences, while valuable, could benefit from new insights, and this meeting had the potential to be a catalyst for change in both of their approaches to medicine.

With determination and a keen eye for detail, Sean arrived early at Dr. Gabehart's office. He remembered that she valued discipline and punctuality, so he had prepared well for the day ahead. As he knocked hesitantly on the door, his heart pounded with anticipation. The door was slightly ajar, but Dr. Gabehart was engrossed in her work, oblivious to his arrival.

Sean took a deep breath and slowly opened the door, revealing his impeccably dressed form. His light-grey slim-fit dress pants and crisp black dress shirt were perfectly complemented by his black dress shoes and black-grey checkered necktie.

With his short white coat in one hand and a stethoscope in the other, he entered the office, ready to tackle whatever challenges lay ahead. Despite the absence of any reference books or notebooks, Sean was confident in his abilities and eager to prove himself to Dr. Gabehart.

He cleared his throat gently, catching her attention without startling her. Dr. Gabehart looked up from her work, and a smile of approval quickly replaced her surprise as she took in Sean's attire. She had noted his sense of discipline and attention to detail in his medical analyses, but seeing him present himself professionally underscored his commitment to this meeting.

"Good morning, Dr. Gabehart," Sean greeted as he entered the room. "Yesterday, I received your voicemail. If this isn't a good time, I can come back later."

Dr. Gabehart smiled warmly and gestured for Sean to take a seat. "No need to worry, Sean. I've been expecting you," she said, her eyes scanning through the papers on her desk. "I was just reviewing these files before our meeting. Please, make yourself comfortable."

Sean felt uneasy in the office, still reeling from the previous day's events. Despite his attempts to apologize, Dr. Gabehart quickly dismissed the issue and told him not to worry about it. However, she did pose an interesting question: "How did you know that the patient was cheating and hadn't simply mixed erectile dysfunction medication with hypertension medication?" she asked, her tone neutral.

Sean hesitated momentarily, then replied, "The patient had nice skin and looked well-groomed."

Dr. Gabehart's surprise was evident as she queried, "You based your diagnosis on that?"

Sean took a deep breath, settling into the plush office chair, his heart beating fast with anticipation. He knew he was about to deliver crucial information that could change everything, and he wanted to ensure he got it right. He began by highlighting how his suspicions had been aroused by observing the patient's grooming habits. Dr. Gabehart listened intently, nodding in agreement as Sean spoke, her eyes lighting up with interest.

As Dr. Gabehart leaned back in her chair, she couldn't help but feel intrigued by Sean's assessment and opinion. She eagerly encouraged him to continue, her arms open and relaxed, a warm smile plastered across her face. It was a stark contrast to the previous day when Sean had come across as an arrogant medical student, but now he was being treated as an equal, and Dr. Gabehart was genuinely interested in what he had to say. This was a huge turning point for Sean; he knew he was on the verge of making a significant breakthrough.

Dr. Gabehart was a brilliant and curious individual, and she was eager to hear what Sean had to say. As he began to speak, she listened with rapt attention, intrigued by his perspective. Sean opened up about his approach to patients, explaining that while he had studied all the basic sciences in medical school and completed numerous clerkships focused on procedures, tests, signs, and symptoms, he sometimes found himself forgetting some of the fundamental principles in relation to certain cases.

He found Dr. Gabehart's unique perspective on patient care incredibly refreshing and felt he could easily integrate it into his mindset. Specifically, she encouraged him to look beyond the surface-level information he was given and observe everything beyond that, including any potential hidden details the patient might be trying to conceal. This advice struck a chord with Sean, who considered himself highly observant and felt he could apply this skill to his medical knowledge to achieve better patient outcomes.

Dr. Gabehart, a renowned physician in her own right, was thoroughly impressed by Sean's attentive and directive approach toward the patient. She expressed her admiration for Sean, acknowledging that he was one of the very few individuals who had ever truly listened to her and valued her opinion. She confessed that most of her staff and colleagues only focused on test results, signs, and symptoms, failing to take a more holistic approach to patient care.

On the other hand, Sean had taken the time to study the patient's history, and his observations led him to an exciting discovery. He noticed the patient had not been wearing his wedding ring despite his chart indicating he was married. This seemingly insignificant detail caught Sean's attention. Upon further examination, he also spotted a tan line on the patient's ring finger.

Dr. Gabehart quickly realized she had missed this detail and was embarrassed by her oversight. However, she was fascinated by Sean's thought process and attention to detail. Although they were discussing a seemingly trivial matter, Dr. Gabehart was impressed by Sean's thoroughness and ability to consider all aspects of the patient's condition.

Sean chuckled softly. "That was just one of the signs. The patient appeared to be in overall good health, and his skin and grooming indicated a lifestyle that wasn't typically associated with hypertension. But there were other clues as well."

Dr. Gabehart leaned forward, intrigued. "Go on, please."

"Well," Sean continued, "his presentation was sudden and extreme. Passing out during intercourse is uncommon, and it often points to a more acute issue rather than chronic hypertension. And then there was the fact that his wife mentioned he was exhausted before they started. It wasn't just about his appearance but also his demeanour, the context of his situation, and his medical history. All these pieces of the puzzle help form a comprehensive understanding."

Upon first meeting Sean, Dr. Gabehart initially dismissed him as an arrogant young man who had memorized too much information during medical school. However, as she listened to his thought process in diagnosing a case that an experienced doctor had missed, she began to see the potential that everyone had been raving about.

Dr. Gabehart remained seated comfortably, smiling as Sean spoke, and this was all the validation he needed to continue. "And I suspected cheating. But when his shirt fell, and a ring came out of his breast pocket, that meant he had likely removed his ring at some point before he got home to his wife," Sean elaborated.

At this point, the two were operating on the same wavelength. Dr. Gabehart interjected, "The wife didn't notice the missing ring because she had interesting plans with her husband and got distracted after the husband passed out. A man who takes good care of himself like that would've been on medication if he had high blood pressure." Sean finished her thought, "Which would've been in the medical history, and it wasn't. It had to be something he was too embarrassed to disclose."

Dr. Gabehart was feeling a mixture of excitement and skepticism about the approach that had been suggested for diagnosis. While the idea was intriguing, she couldn't help but think it was a little far-fetched. She expressed her concerns to Sean, who had a different perspective. He informed her that while everyone had been discussing the theoretical disease, he had picked up the ring and placed it back on the patient's finger.

Dr. Gabehart couldn't resist making a joke, telling Sean that he was now engaged to the patient. They both found this amusing and shared a good laugh. Despite only having known each other briefly, the two were forming a bond as colleagues. They were comfortable joking around with each other.

As the laughter subsided, Dr. Gabehart warned Sean not to get too comfortable, reminding him that he was still annoying and that she could throw him out at any moment. She laughed as she tidied her desk, grateful for their lighthearted moment. It had been a while since she had laughed so hard.

As they exchanged more lighthearted banter, it became evident that their dynamic had shifted dramatically from the tense atmosphere of the previous day. They were now colleagues sharing insights, experiences, and even laughter. This unique bond formed over a single conversation—a testament to the power of understanding, humility, and their shared passion for medicine.

Dr. Gabehart's laughter eventually subsided, and she looked at Sean with genuine warmth. "Thank you, Sean. I needed this today. You've given me a fresh perspective and a good laugh."

As their conversation continued, it became evident that Sean's approach to medicine was deeply rooted in his genuine concern for patients and his unwavering belief in the power of empathy and observation. Dr. Gabehart found herself intrigued and impressed by Sean's perspective, and their interactions had evolved into a genuine exchange of ideas.

Sean was in the dark about how things had gone since he asked Dr. Gabehart to look at Mr. Gladstone's hand. After this conversation, something became clear to Dr. Gabehart as she told Sean, "Well, I wouldn't know what to tell you, but Mr. Carroll asked for you. He wants to thank you for what you did for him yesterday. I thought it was about the diagnosis, and now I just discovered it was about covering up an affair."

She continued, covering her laugh, "People like you are the problem in this world because you help people who deserve to be punished!"

Sean smiled, "There's nobody like me; I dare you to find

one. And what problems in this world?!"

Dr. Gabehart refrained from ranting about the world's problems and instead simply stated, "Men screwing up in this world and having other men cover up for them while acting as if there's nothing unethical about those actions."

Sean quipped, "Don't hate the player; hate the game," smiling and winking at Dr. Gabehart.

"On a serious note, I'm sorry about yesterday. I know my personality is too strong and sometimes an acquired taste, but I promise it won't happen again. I'll be professional from now until the end of my clerkship," he said sincerely.

As the two continued their conversation, they both recognized that in each other, they had found a colleague to challenge their perspectives, encourage growth, and remind them of the power of empathy in the world of medicine.

Dr. Gabehart smiled at Sean's response. "Well, Sean, it's good to hear you're willing to adjust your approach. I appreciate your sincerity. Remember, it's not about your personality being too strong—it's about finding the right balance between confidence and respect in the medical field."

Dr. Gabehart basked in the rare moment of tranquillity she found with Sean, a sensation akin to savouring a cup of warm tea on a chilly afternoon. However, she was wary of letting emotions sway her. With the skilled finesse of a captain steering her ship away from rocky waters, she deftly steered their conversation in a new direction.

"Enough of that," she interjected, her tone a deliberate shift from the previous depth. "You presented me with four out of five patient reviews yesterday, and I must say your performance was indeed commendable. But don't think for a moment that I'm entirely swayed by it," she continued, her words laced with a thoughtful air. She asked him for his fifth case by the end of the day.

As if pondering the delicate intricacies of an ancient tapestry, she gazed into the distance. Sensing her contemplative mood, Sean rose from his seat. He began a leisurely stroll around her office as if searching for hidden treasures. In a sudden moment of enlightenment, his gaze locked onto Dr. Gabehart's, a glint of mischief in his eyes.

"I have it," he declared, his voice a mere whisper of excitement. Dr. Gabehart's intrigue was piqued, and she leaned in, awaiting his revelation with a mix of curiosity and caution.

"How about I conduct my fifth patient review right now?" Sean proposed, his words a spark that ignited the air between them. Dr. Gabehart's eyebrows arched in surprise, and she was trapped in the web of his audacious suggestion.

"You've been seeing patients?" Dr. Gabehart's incredulous question hung in the air, a testament to the boundary Sean was treading upon.

Amusement danced in Sean's eyes as he chuckled softly, his response delivered with an enigmatic air. "No, not in the conventional sense. I'm referring to you."

Caught off guard, Dr. Gabehart blinked, her mind racing to keep pace with the twist in their conversation. She followed Sean's gaze, her eyes darting around her office as if seeking the hidden meaning to which he was alluding. A heavy silence settled between them, each heartbeat a drum that echoed the tension in the room. Dr. Gabehart's pulse quickened, an unfamiliar anxiety unfolding within her.

"What about me?" she queried, her voice a mix of intrigue and uncertainty. As if engaged in a dance, Sean's eyes swept the room, his demeanour that of someone navigating a maze of thoughts.

"We often analyze patients, discern their symptoms, diagnose their ailments, and prescribe remedies," Sean began, his tone weaving a tapestry of contemplation. "In much the same way, I find myself analyzing you, Dr. Gabehart."

Dr. Gabehart's gaze remained locked on Sean, her heart beating synchronously with his words. Like a master storyteller unveiling a hidden narrative, Sean continued, "Your demeanour, your approach, your resilience – they're all part of the 'patient review' I've been conducting on you."

As the puzzle pieces of Sean's analogy began to fall into place, Dr. Gabehart's face displayed a mixture of surprise and amusement. Sean's lips curled into a knowing smile as he added, "From what I've observed, your performance has been impressive."

As the sun's gentle rays filtered through the window, illuminating their shared understanding, the door to collaboration swung wider, revealing a path where doctor and student would walk together, each offering insights that the other might never have discovered alone.

Sean launched into his candid assessment without further ado, his words a tapestry woven with both insight and sensitivity. "I believe I've managed to unravel much about you, Dr. Gabehart, except for one enigma that continues to elude me. You're undeniably a woman of striking beauty, a fact that hasn't escaped the attention of those around you. However, amidst the compliments you've garnered for your looks, you've tirelessly worked to assert your intelligence. It's as if the world's applause for your appearance has overshadowed the recognition you truly desire. Perhaps even your parents failed to acknowledge your intellect, a wound that's left its mark."

Sean paused, his gaze steady as he broached a potentially sensitive topic. "Please forgive my audacity, but could it be that this relentless pursuit of excellence within this hospital, within this field, is your means of demanding the recognition you've been denied? You deflect compliments on your beauty, viewing those who offer them as shallow and dismissive. But in this realm, where intellect is paramount, you find solace and purpose. You challenge fellow intellectuals to validate your intellect, carving out a place of prominence you've rightfully earned."

He continued, a thoughtful tone colouring his words. "Yet, there's a facet of your life that remains obscured. If I may be so bold, your marriage doesn't seem to bring you joy. Instead, you channel your pain into your work, letting it act as a shield against the emotional turmoil you may be enduring."

"Hold on there, Mr.!" Dr. Gabehart's sudden sharpness of voice shattered the room's atmosphere like a lightning bolt.

She rose from her chair in a surge of fury, her response a vehement interruption to Sean's audacious deductions. Yet, Sean met her anger with a steady gaze, unflinching in the face of her wrath. He had ventured into sensitive territory, fully aware of the potential consequences.

In that charged moment, the room seemed to hang in suspended animation, the weight of unspoken words and unresolved emotions filling the space. Sean's audacity had lit a spark, igniting a confrontation that had been brewing beneath the surface. The tension between them was palpable, crackling with the raw intensity of truth laid bare.

But Sean's calm demeanour and willingness to explore the depths of Dr. Gabehart's persona spoke volumes about his genuine intention. He had not embarked upon this path carelessly but rather with a deep desire to unravel the complexities of the woman before him. Armed with a steadfast commitment to honesty and understanding, he was prepared to navigate the storm he had invoked.

Sean's pacing was like a dance of thoughts in motion, the tempo of his steps mirroring the rhythm of his contemplation. He had stirred something within Dr. Gabehart, an ember of self-awareness that smouldered beneath the surface. Her composed demeanour concealed a storm of emotions, her gaze meeting Sean's with a mix of curiosity and defiance.

His remark about hitting a soft spot echoed in the room, a verbal ripple that carried a challenge. Dr. Gabehart's controlled response was a testament to her determination not to yield easily. Like a surgeon's incision, Sean's observation had cut through the layers of her defences to reach a hidden truth.

Sean stared at Dr. Gabehart and watched her sit back down while he continued pacing in her office. "Interesting, she didn't object to everything else but her marriage. I guess I hit a soft sport," Sean thought out loud, possibly to provoke a response from Dr. Gabehart.

"Why, indeed, does she arrive early when the tasks could be delegated to her subordinates?" Sean's inquiry hung in the air, a question that begged for illumination. Dr. Gabehart's hesitance to refute Sean's deductions was palpable, her mind racing to find a path that wouldn't lead to further revelations. Yet, Sean's logic was relentless, his words like breadcrumbs leading to a destination neither of them had intended to reach.

Her voice, when it came, was laced with skepticism and intrigue. "And how, please tell, can you be so confident in your deductions?" A challenge was woven into her words, a dare for Sean to justify his audacious claims. Dr. Gabehart's pride and her need to guard her privacy were at odds, caught in a delicate balancing act.

Sean's reply held the weight of certainty born from keen observation. "People talk, yes, but it's the subtleties that often reveal more. Your attempts to conceal a bruise like the one beneath your left eye speak volumes. The pain that lingers there, concealed but not erased, speaks of struggles you're keeping hidden. I won't venture into speculation, but the whispers about your marriage seem to carry weight."

He continued, his voice steady but not devoid of compassion. "Moreover, a contentedly married woman doesn't find herself at her workplace hours before her scheduled arrival. It's become a pattern, noticeable to all who observe. Such devotion to work suggests that there might be more beneath the surface than meets the eye."

Dr. Gabehart's silence was laden with a blend of emotions, an unspoken acknowledgment of the truths Sean had unearthed. The room seemed to shrink around them, the shared understanding creating an intimate space where vulnerability danced with revelation. Sean's boldness had opened doors that Dr. Gabehart had long kept locked. Now, they stood on the threshold of a deeper connection, poised to explore the uncharted territories of one another's souls.

The atmosphere in the room was charged. There was a

silent exchange of unspoken thoughts between two individuals who had crossed an unlikely threshold. Dr. Gabehart's decision to accept Sean's analysis as his fifth case felt like a concession, an unspoken agreement to acknowledge the accuracy of his observations.

It appeared that Sean had struck a sensitive chord, and Dr. Gabehart tried to maintain her composure. She accepted Sean's fifth case and instructed him to take the remainder of the week off. Sean sensed that he had made Dr. Gabehart uneasy, so he stood up from his seat and started to exit the room. Just before he left, Dr. Gabehart called out to him, "I never want to talk about this ever again. I'd also appreciate it if this conversation doesn't leave this office."

Surprised, Sean turned around and looked at her before asking, "What conversation?" Dr. Gabehart was taken aback by Sean's unexpected response, and for a brief moment, she felt a twitch of betrayal.

This feeling quickly gave way to anger, and she stood up with her fists clenched, ready to lash out at Sean for his apparent lack of loyalty. "How can you be so smart and quickly forget that…" She paused for a moment as she realized what had just happened. "Oops, I get it now." She chuckled softly and blushed with a sheepish grin, acknowledging her mistake with a touch of self-deprecating humour.

Dr. Gabehart's embarrassment turned into genuine amusement, and her laughter released the tension that had threatened to shatter their conversation. Her fists, once clenched in anticipation of confrontation, now relaxed. The irony of the situation was undeniable. At that moment, their roles had reversed, with Dr. Gabehart now the one trying to keep her emotions in check.

Sean's grin matched her own, a shared moment of levity that bridged the gap between them. The sudden shift in tone was like a gust of wind clearing away the storm clouds that had gathered. Their interaction had taken them through a whirlwind of emotions, revealing vulnerabilities and surprising connections that neither had expected.

As their laughter subsided, a newfound sense of camaraderie settled in the room, an unspoken agreement to move forward without dwelling on the depths they had briefly explored. The understanding that had been forged between them in this candid exchange was a testament to the power of genuine connection, one that had the potential to transform their interactions in the days to come.

Dr. Gabehart's laughter swept away any lingering tension from their previous conversation, leaving a sense of shared understanding and a renewed focus on their professional interaction. She settled back into her chair, her demeanour shifting seamlessly from amusement to businesslike determination.

As she refocused the conversation on their work, Dr. Gabehart acknowledged Sean's remarkable impression on not just one but two patients, a testament to his skill and reputation. She wasn't hesitant to admit this sentiment. Yet, she also aimed to convey that her position as the head of cardiology wasn't solely based on surface factors.

Sean, always quick with a playful response, didn't miss a beat. His jest about nepotism illuminated the fact that such situations weren't uncommon in certain circles. Dr. Gabehart's laughter was a testament to her appreciation for his humour, even when it touched upon a half-true stereotype.

However, she was determined to illustrate that her journey to her current position was one of hard work and genuine merit. It was a narrative she was eager to share with Sean, a young medical student who had already demonstrated his capacity for perceptive observations.

Dr. Gabehart said with a hint of pride and sincerity, "I worked my way up, Sean. I didn't let anyone's perceptions or rumours define me. Yes, my husband's family owns the hospital. Nevertheless, they've always insisted on maintaining a fair and unbiased approach to the hiring process. My achievements and commitment to cardiology speak for themselves."

Sean's playful jests had elicited a genuine smile from her. Now, his attention and intent listening made her feel validated in her journey. She continued, "The road wasn't easy. I faced skepticism, doubters, and those who questioned my capabilities. But I worked relentlessly, proved my worth, and earned my position through dedication and competence."

She leaned forward slightly, her expression reflecting the weight of her words. "Sean, being a woman in a field like cardiology is a challenge. The skepticism you felt from me yesterday is something I've encountered countless times. I've used it to fuel my drive, to show that I'm not just here for appearances or superficial reasons."

Her words carried an underlying message of resilience and determination. Dr. Gabehart had fought to break stereotypes and forge her path, and now she was keen on imparting this lesson to Sean. It was more than just a personal story; it was a testament that hard work, tenacity, and competence could pave the way to success, regardless of the circumstances.

Sean nodded in understanding, a newfound respect and admiration shining in his eyes. He had glimpsed a side of Dr. Gabehart that went beyond her reputation and authority, a woman who had overcome obstacles with grace and determination.

As their conversation continued, their roles evolved from tense acquaintances to colleagues who shared professional insights and personal anecdotes. In these moments, they were bridging the gaps of perception, learning to appreciate each other's journeys, and forming a connection that could prove invaluable in the challenges they were bound to face in their medical careers.

Dr. Gabehart leaned forward, her eyes lit with a passion that seemed to transcend time. She was about to share a part of her life that was more than a skill; it was a craft she had honed over years of meticulous practice and unwavering curiosity.

"You know, Sean," she began, her voice carrying a mixture of reminiscence and enthusiasm, "Ever since I stepped into medical school, I found myself drawn to something that intrigued me beyond measure. It was like finding a complex and beautiful puzzle waiting to be deciphered."

Her metaphor likening this fascination to driving skills was both poetic and apt. With a soft smile, she continued, "Much like driving, many doctors might boast of this skill, claiming to be experts in interpreting ECGs. It's a skill that can be learned, yes, but true mastery is an entirely different realm. It's like the difference between knowing how to maneuver a car and truly becoming one with the road."

As she spoke, it was evident that ECG interpretation held a special place in Dr. Gabehart's heart. Her words carried a subtle pride from countless hours spent studying waveforms, patterns, and abnormalities that danced across ECG screens. It was her secret passion, a pursuit that went beyond her professional responsibilities.

Her eyes sparkled as she recounted, "Over the years, I've dedicated myself to reading ECGs in real-time, dissecting the nuances as they unfold. It's not just about identifying peaks and troughs; it's about understanding the heart's language, rhythm, and stories."

She leaned back, a distant look in her eyes as she recalled the moments when she deciphered the code of a heart's electrical activity. "It's an art as much as it is a science. And when I'm faced with an ECG, it's like reading a story where every beat, every deviation tells me something. It's a conversation with the heart itself."

As the conversation flowed, it became evident that Dr. Gabehart's skill wasn't confined to the walls of her hospital. Other doctors recognized her mastery and sought her insights and guidance when faced with perplexing cases. Her humility shone through when she mentioned refusing monetary compensation for her consultations, treating them as a personal endeavour rather than a job.

"You see, Sean, there's a distinction," she mused, her voice tinged with wisdom and discernment. "There are those who regurgitate knowledge, who can identify certain patterns because they've seen them before. But true mastery is the ability to approach each ECG with fresh eyes, to analyze it objectively without preconceived notions."

This sentiment resonated deeply with Sean, who had shown a penchant for similar analytical prowess. Their camaraderie had taken an unexpected turn, from tension to a shared appreciation for skills that transcended the ordinary.

As the conversation lingered on ECG interpretation, it became clear that Sean's journey at the hospital was turning into something more than just a learning experience. He was gaining insights from someone who had immersed herself in the intricacies of her field, and Dr. Gabehart was finding an unexpected ally, someone who shared her dedication to the pursuit of excellence.

Sean attempted to turn the situation into a joke by suggesting that Dr. Gabehart may be one of those doctors who memorizes the most common ECGs and enjoys sharing a few cases to demonstrate a skill she does not genuinely possess.

Although she laughed along at his disparaging comment about her abilities, she promptly responded, "Sorry, Sean, I don't feel inclined to impress you in any way. However, would you like to take on the challenge of ECG reading skills? If you can match my skills, I'll consider giving you an extra week off next week."

Sean couldn't pass up the opportunity to skip two weeks of what he anticipated would be a dull clerkship without repercussions. But he soon realized that if Dr. Gabehart proved exceptional, Sean would forfeit the remainder of his time off. He must resume work the following day at the same early hour as Dr. Gabehart, around 5 a.m.

Sean chuckled at Dr. Gabehart's counterproposal, realizing that she had just put him in a position where he could either gain an extra week off or lose the one he had already secured. It was a gamble he had to consider carefully, especially knowing that his opponent was someone who had dedicated herself to the craft for years.

As part of a wager, Dr. Gabehart and Sean made a deal. If he lost, Sean risked losing his time off and spending a significant amount of time reviewing patient files, beginning on the same day.

This was a considerable gamble for Sean. He had two options: take two weeks off and still receive credit or spend more time learning from someone who possessed a skill he did not fully comprehend.

Even though it was a win-win situation in a twisted way, any young man would have preferred to take those two weeks off. However, Sean agreed, but with some conditions in place to rule out the possibility that Dr. Gabehart had memorized many ECGs and would regurgitate one of them.

Sean wanted to make this challenge as challenging and objective as possible. He didn't want to take any ECGs from Dr. Gabehart's office because there was a good chance she had already seen them all. Instead, he aimed to find something he knew she had never seen before.

Sean reached out to the surgery department to speak with his mentor, who had become his friend during his surgery clerkship and was referred to as the General. During their conversation, Sean told the General he needed an electrocardiogram (ECG). Concerned, the General inquired further, and Sean explained his bet with Dr. Gabehart.

Upon hearing this, the General expressed remorse for Sean and asked why he had taken the bet. Sean was taken aback by this question and realized that perhaps he had made a mistake in taking the gamble. The General's concern and line of questioning made Sean reflect on his actions and consider the potential consequences.

As the weight of the situation settled in, Sean questioned his decision to bet with Dr. Gabehart. He hesitated for a moment before responding to the General.

"I thought it would be a fun challenge, you know? I wanted to test her skills and see if she's as good as she says she is," Sean replied, his voice tinged with uncertainty.

The General let out a deep sigh, his expression a mixture of sympathy and exasperation. "Sean, you're a bright young man, and I admire your enthusiasm. However, challenging Dr. Gabehart in her field might not have been the wisest move. She's not just a skilled physician; she's known for her incredible diagnostic abilities with ECGs."

The General continued, "You see, challenging someone like her requires more than confidence. It requires a deep understanding of her strengths and weaknesses. Her methods and insights go beyond textbook knowledge."

Sean pondered for a moment. He had a decision to make — to either accept the challenge and potentially face a formidable opponent or find a way to gracefully exit the bet without losing face. As he contemplated his options, he realized that this experience was teaching him a valuable lesson about humility and knowing when to pick his battles.

The General's concern was palpable, and Sean felt a mixture of anxiety and curiosity. He respected the General's opinion and had learned much from him during his surgery clerkship. However, the fact that the General, whom he held in high esteem, insisted on him reconsidering the bet weighed heavily on his mind.

Sean found himself grappling with a whirlwind of emotions. On one hand, he had a reputation to uphold and a competitive spirit that pushed him to take on challenges head-on. On the other hand, he was now aware that he might be walking into a situation where the odds were stacked against him.

His thoughts swirled like a cyclone, each realization crashing against the walls of his ego. He had prided himself on his intelligence, always being the one who could outthink and outsmart others. But now, his overconfidence had led him into a trap, and he was facing a formidable opponent who was clearly in her element.

Meanwhile, Dr. Gabehart's serene smile contrasted sharply with Sean's inner turmoil. As she moved around the office, her gaze fixed intently on the ECG printout that had been faxed from the General; it was as if she was deciphering a complex puzzle that only she had the key to. Her confidence was like a radiant aura bolstered by years of experience and an unshakable mastery of her craft.

Sean watched as Dr. Gabehart analyzed the ECG, her fingers tracing the lines with practiced precision.

Dr. Gabehart's voice broke the silence, her tone calm and assured. "Sean, get the General on the line. I believe he will want to confirm my analysis."

Sean's heart pounded faster as he picked up the phone and dialled for the General. The seconds stretched like taffy as he waited for the call to connect. When the General's voice finally came through, Sean's nervousness was discernible as he explained that Dr. Gabehart wanted to discuss her analysis of the ECG.

He could hear the General's sigh on the other end of the line, a mixture of resignation and understanding. It was as if the General had already predicted the outcome.

Dr. Gabehart's voice resonated with a sense of triumph as she described the patient's history and medical profile, her words flowing like a stream of consciousness. Each detail she mentioned seemed to reinforce her conviction as if she was piecing together a puzzle she had already solved long ago. Her excitement was palpable, even contagious as if she had cracked a code baffling others.

Sean stood there, his eyebrows furrowing in bewilderment. It was as if she had entered a realm of certainty that defied the boundaries of mere observation and analysis.

Dr. Gabehart read the ECG out loud to the General on the other end of the line. "Okay, here is our patient from surgery. He's in his late fifties to early sixties with a history of smoking and likely a current smoker. He has a history of at least one heart attack. He could have diabetes as well, so he is probably overweight, too, because eighty percent of diabetics are also overweight. He likely has a history of blood pressure controlled by a combination of beta blockers and ACE inhibitors, which explains why he might have lung cancer. Oh my God! This is Mr. Gladstone!" she said with excitement.

The mystery of her confidence hung in the air, leaving Sean intrigued and bewildered. How had she deduced all of this from a simple ECG? It was like witnessing a magician reveal a secret that had eluded everyone else.

As Dr. Gabehart continued elaborating on her findings, Sean's mind raced to catch up with her, attempting to connect the dots between her deductions and the enigmatic ECG.

He was amazed but skeptical. Sean briefly thought Dr. Gabehart was crazy and started laughing as he asked the General, "Is she even close?"

Only six words from the General sealed Sean's fate, "Well, the patient is not overweight," and he hung up the phone.

Sean gazed at Dr. Gabehart, who was still beaming and revelling in her triumph, feeling bewildered and astonished. He struggled to believe that she had accomplished such a feat. If she genuinely was that intelligent, it was an incredibly remarkable skill.

It was as if Dr. Gabehart had conjured the patient's entire medical history from thin air, a feat that left Sean dumbfounded and impressed. The room was filled with disbelief and awe, a testament to Dr. Gabehart's uncanny ability to decipher the language of the heart's electrical signals.

Dr. Gabehart chuckled at Sean's mixed reactions, appreciating the candidness with which he expressed his surprise and admiration. She leaned back in her chair, folding her arms with a contented smile playing on her lips. "I'm glad I could surprise you, Sean. And for the record, no, I didn't set you up. The General wouldn't engage in such shenanigans, even to prove a point."

Sean's eyes remained fixed on the ECG readout. His brow furrowed as he tried to understand the intricacies of the heart's electrical patterns. Evidently, he was grappling with a newfound sense of humility—a rare and valuable lesson that even the brightest minds occasionally need to learn.

Sean's surprise slowly transformed into quiet contemplation as he continued to pace around the office, the ECG readout held almost reverently in his hands. The complexities of the heart's electrical signals, something he had taken for granted, were now glaringly evident. He was grappling with a humbling realization— that sometimes, even the most brilliant minds can encounter challenges that defy their expectations.

Upon examining the ECG, Sean attempted to decipher the data independently but could not fully comprehend the readout. Despite his efforts, he could only express his inability to interpret the information. "All I can make out from this is the beta blockers and a heart attack, and maybe I can try to infer the history of smoking, but I wouldn't be too sure. Just wow."

Sean came up with a theory and asked Dr. Gabehart if she had him set up. Dr. Gabehart replied, "Check the timestamp. This ECG was taken less than thirty minutes ago when we were both here. Do you think the General would do something like that?"

Sean responded, "One. I've never been so impressed with anyone in my life. Two. Well, the other comment will get me kicked out of medical school for harassing my superior. Like wow!"

After several minutes of Sean pacing around the room with the ECG readout tightly gripped in his hand, Dr. Gabehart couldn't help but observe the look of disbelief on his face. Sensing his unease, she rose from her seat and approached him, offering a gesture of peace and reconciliation.

"You seem like a good kid despite my first impression of you. You have a gift I've only read about, and I have a skill you will need in your professional career. How about you help me sort out these cases over the next few weeks while you're here, and I'll teach you all about ECGs?" Dr. Gabehart offered Sean another deal, which he gladly accepted in his state of trance.

She laughed as she handed over a dozen files to Sean. She told Sean that there was nothing much to her ability to read ECGs. She explained, "You're good at reading people, and I can read and interpret objective data in most medical settings, ECGs, complete blood counts, urine analyses and lumbar punctures. Show me one of those, and I'll give you a quick patient profile with about ninety percent accuracy. A wealthy man saw this in me and made me run this department with complete autonomy. It's a job that seems to be tied to me marrying his son, but I can assure you that those two are mutually exclusive."

Sean took the files and walked out to start working on his end of the deal.

As Sean prepared to depart, Dr. Gabehart's phone rang, prompting her to call him back. She told him it was imperative for him to visit Mr. Gladstone following his surgery. Despite Sean's lack of a medical license, Mr. Gladstone specifically requested that Sean oversee his file. At the same time, Dr. May would assume the official role of supervising physician.

Sean told Dr. Gabehart that his evaluation of Mr. Gladstone's health caused his dismissal the previous day. Before accepting the task, he wanted to confirm that she was comfortable with it.

Dr. Gabehart replied, "Well, it's either that or he was going to sue us for malpractice. A wealthy man like that could easily win this hospital in that suit. It's his way, or we must include lawyers and risk losing this hospital, so here we are."

"Okay, as long as you have my back. See you around," Sean said as he walked out of Dr. Gabehart's office, shaking his head.

Dr. Gabehart's proficiency in reading ECGs with remarkable speed and precision was an astounding feat that amazed Sean. Although it wasn't particularly pertinent to the new assignment, witnessing her expertise in action was an awe-inspiring spectacle.

Matters of the Heart

Building A Scoresheet

Sean was immersed in his tasks at the nurses' station. The gentle hum of conversations and the distant beeping of monitors created an ambiance of controlled chaos. Yet, within this whirlwind of activity, Sean found himself in a cocoon of focus, engrossed in his work.

Thanks to the kindness of a nurse who had taken him under her wing, Sean had managed to carve out a small corner for himself. This enclave was more than just a physical space; it was a realm of newfound responsibility and respect. It seemed like Sean had finally earned a seat at the grown-ups' table, where his decisions mattered and his actions carried weight.

The nurses around him were no longer just colleagues but allies in this intricate dance of patient care. They had come to appreciate his dedication and enthusiasm, recognizing that he was not just another medical student going through the motions. Sean's interactions with them were laced with genuine curiosity and an eagerness to learn from their experiences. In return, they offered guidance and insights that textbooks could never provide.

But for all the camaraderie, Sean knew he was treading uncharted territory. His newfound responsibilities came with the knowledge that he was accountable not only to himself but also to Dr. Gabehart. Her watchful eye served as both a challenge and a reassurance – a challenge to uphold the standards she expected and a reassurance that he was on the right path.

In the labyrinthine corridors of the hospital, Sean couldn't help but observe his surroundings with a discerning eye. He saw doctors and nurses going about their duties, some with a sense of duty, others with indifference. It was a microcosm of the wider world, where dedication and complacency existed side by side.

A bad workman blames his tools. In this context, Sean mused, it wasn't just about the tools at their disposal but the attitude with which they wielded them. The hospital was a canvas on which each professional painted their commitment, empathy, or apathy.

But amidst the medical intricacies, Sean's mind often wandered back to Dr. Gabehart. Their initial clash had transformed into a unique mentorship, a journey of growth that Sean had never anticipated. He realized that his arrogance had blinded him to the wealth of knowledge that could be gleaned from those who came before him.

As he stood at the crossroads of humility and ambition, Sean understood that greatness was not just about personal achievement but about elevating those around him. The wisdom of an old proverb echoed in his mind: "If you want to go fast, go alone. If you want to go far, go together." He had learned that collaboration and shared wisdom were the keys to success in this vast landscape of medicine.

Dr. Gabehart was a beacon of focused determination within the hospital's bustling corridors. Her commitment to medicine was not just a career but a calling that seeped into every aspect of her life. She was a force to be reckoned with, known for her unwavering passion and dedication to the practice.

Unlike the familiar trope of a strict disciplinarian, Dr. Gabehart had a unique approach to motivating her team. She didn't resort to reprimands or stern lectures but led by example. She wouldn't hesitate to roll up her sleeves and dive in if she spotted a task that wasn't handled optimally. It wasn't about showcasing her authority but demonstrating her standards.

This leadership style had a powerful impact. The mere prospect of Dr. Gabehart stepping into a situation would make even the most seasoned professionals straighten their posture and double-check their work. Her approach wasn't intimidating; it was inspiring. She conveyed that excellence wasn't just an expectation but a goal worth striving for.

Amid her busy schedule, Dr. Gabehart managed to find pockets of time to engage with her colleagues on a more personal level. Whether joining the nurses in their tasks or chatting with caretakers, she transcended the hierarchical barriers that often separated doctors from the rest of the hospital staff. This wasn't about condescension; it was about unity. Dr. Gabehart understood that the collaborative effort of every member of the healthcare team was essential for the well-being of the patients.

Her willingness to engage in hands-on work wasn't a display of superiority; it was an embodiment of servant leadership. A leader is one who knows the way, shows the way, and goes the way. Dr. Gabehart embodied this principle with every interaction. She showed her colleagues that she wasn't above any task and that she was a leader who led from the front, not just from the executive office.

Dr. Gabehart's multifaceted leadership extended beyond her official title. She was a teacher, a mentor, a role model, and, above all, a guide. Her actions spoke volumes about her commitment to improving the medical field. She understood that leadership wasn't confined to a single position; it was a responsibility that extended to every corner of the hospital.

Dr. Gabehart's approach was refreshing in a world that often separated leaders from their subordinates. She shattered the barriers and demonstrated that leadership wasn't about wielding power but about serving others, empowering them to excel and contribute their best. She exemplified that a true leader did not seek to be served but the one who sought to serve.

Sean's strong work ethic was like an unstoppable engine, always propelling him forward, and his relentless pursuit of excellence was a rarity in an environment where many were content with mediocrity.

Little did Sean realize he was riding the waves of luck that had brought him to this point. The chance encounter with Dr. Gabehart was like stumbling upon a hidden treasure, a mentor who would guide him through the intricacies of a skill he had long desired to master. The prospect of delving into the world of ECG interpretation was both thrilling and humbling for him. He had a teacher who possessed the expertise and willingness to share it, a combination that was a rare blessing.

Sean's commitment to his work was unwavering as he embraced the additional tasks that Dr. Gabehart had assigned. But beyond the surface, beneath the layers of dedication, an air of mystery surrounded him. He was a puzzle, a complex enigma that the hospital staff couldn't quite decipher. His origins, background, and motivations were all shrouded in secrecy.

What was evident, however, was the profound impact he left on those he interacted with. The doctors who had crossed paths with Sean unanimously praised his intellect. They couldn't quite put their finger on it, but something about him set him apart. A sense of brilliance that was both captivating and intriguing.

Even the General, a seasoned and respected figure within

the hospital, recognized something special in Sean. It was almost as if the General saw a spark in him that hinted at a potential beyond the ordinary confines of medical education. The General's occasional requests for Sean's assistance in surgery were a testament to his trust and respect for this young medical student.

Sean's presence was like a breath of fresh air, a reminder that amidst the routines and protocols of the medical world, there could still exist an element of surprise, a source of inspiration that defied expectations. His social grace was like a soothing balm in the hospital's often hectic and impersonal world. Despite his exceptional intelligence and talents, he was far from being the stereotypical genius who dwelled in isolation. Instead, he embraced conversations and interactions like a warm embrace.

His ability to connect with people was akin to a magician's touch, effortlessly drawing them into his circle with an irresistible charm. Sean's presence had a way of lighting up even the dullest corners of the hospital. He was the catalyst for camaraderie, a bridge between different hierarchies.

Sean had a remarkable knack for drawing people out of their shells. His genuine curiosity about the world around him was evident in his observation of even the minute details. He was the type of person who noticed the small nuances, the fleeting expressions, and the unspoken stories that often went unnoticed.

When Sean engaged in conversation, it was as if the rest of the world faded away. He possessed the rare gift of truly listening, of being fully present in the moment. This made those he interacted with feel valued, heard, and understood. His attentive nature conveyed that he wasn't merely engaging in small talk but genuinely interested in getting to know the person before him.

In just a short time, Sean was able to uncover narratives

that people often hesitated to share with even their closest confidants. His open-hearted approach gave people a safe space to express their thoughts, fears, and aspirations.

Sean's charm had depth. He didn't rely on witty remarks or rehearsed lines to win people over. Instead, he used his genuine interest and empathetic nature to create authentic and meaningful bonds. It was no wonder that the nurses, typically the backbone of the hospital, took to him so quickly. His interactions with them transcended the hierarchy, creating an atmosphere of collaboration.

Sean was weaving a tapestry of connections, leaving traces of kindness, understanding, and friendship. He was a reminder that amidst the complexities of medical practice, there was always room for the simple yet powerful act of human connection.

Mother's presence in the hospital was like a gentle, comforting breeze on a warm summer day. Her nickname was a testament to her nurturing nature, a title earned through years of compassion and kindness. Despite the hustle and bustle of the hospital environment, Mother's demeanour exuded a sense of tranquillity and genuine care.

Her age had bestowed upon her a wisdom that transcended medical knowledge. She innately understood the human spirit, recognizing that the healing touch sometimes extended beyond medications and treatments. For Mother, healing also came in the form of a warm smile, a heartfelt conversation, or a simple gesture of sharing homemade treats.

Her cookies and candies were more than confections; they symbolized her love and consideration. Every bite was a taste of her dedication to fostering a sense of community within the department. On special occasions, when she crafted a cake, it wasn't just a dessert but a manifestation of her wish for happiness and joy in the lives of her colleagues.

Mother's spirit of celebration extended beyond baked goods. She had a knack for remembering birthdays and milestones, ensuring each individual felt valued and acknowledged. Her ability to gather people for a collective "happy birthday" song wasn't just about tradition; it was a reminder that there was room for shared joy even amidst the busy corridors and medical charts.

Her role went beyond her official title; she was a pillar of support for both staff and patients. Mother's warmth served as a comforting presence for those away from their families. Her calming words and caring gestures were a source of solace for those overwhelmed by the hospital's demands.

Unsurprisingly, even those older than her affectionately referred to her as Mother. They found a confidante, friend, and beacon of kindness in her. Her nickname wasn't just a moniker; it embodied the essence she brought to the hospital, a gentle reminder that compassion could thrive amidst the clinical environment.

Mother's smile radiated genuine care and acceptance. Sean's interactions with her weren't just fleeting exchanges but moments of connection, acknowledging the bonds that formed while working together.

In the tapestry of hospital life, Mother was a thread woven with threads of laughter, kindness, and love. With his innate ability to forge connections, Sean was fortunate to find himself entwined in the warmth of her presence.

The genuine warmth of a kind-hearted woman sparked the transformation of Sean's identity. Mother possessed an uncanny ability to read people's hearts and discern their potential. Her interactions with Sean left an impression that resonated deeply with the positivity he exuded.

As Sean immersed himself in his work, navigating through patient files and scribbling notes, Mother observed his dedication with admiration. To her, it reflected a doctor's commitment to the craft, embodying the values that made medicine more than just a profession. So, as the dawn painted the hospital with the gentle hues of morning light, Mother's heart swelled with fondness for the young man before her.

Nurses sought his guidance, their calls for him echoing through the corridors. Sean, never one to shy away from lending a helping hand, answered their queries while remaining engrossed in his tasks. Mother's heart swelled with pride as she watched this young medical student seamlessly step into a role beyond his years.

During this bustling activity, a transformation occurred. The simple moniker "Dr. Sean" left Mother's lips, carrying with it a sense of respect and acknowledgment. It was as if she had seen a spark within Sean that warranted recognition beyond his student status. The name had a harmonious ring to it, a melody that echoed his dedication and the aura he brought to the hospital.

However, Sean's humility and sense of duty caused him to initially protest against the newfound title. He felt a mix of awkwardness and concern about patients potentially mistaking him for a doctor. His conversation with Dr. Gabehart was still fresh in his mind, a reminder of the fine line he walked.

Yet, Mother's determination prevailed, and her insistence became a gentle nudge that guided others to address him as Dr. Sean. When curious voices inquired about the newcomer, Mother's response was swift and unwavering. "Dr. Sean," she would declare with a smile, adding the title "medical student" to ensure accuracy.

The name "Dr. Sean" became a symbol of admiration and camaraderie. It was a testament to the bonds formed through shared experiences and the trust that had been nurtured. Mother's intuition had recognized Sean's potential, and her proclamation became a ripple that touched every corner of the department.

As Sean continued to engage with patients, nurses, and medical staff, the name "Dr. Sean" took on a life of its own. It was more than just a title; it represented a collective belief in his abilities, a recognition of his dedication, and a mark of the respect he had earned. While Sean may have initially felt the weight of the title, he soon came to embrace it, for it embodied his journey of growth, learning, and the unending pursuit of excellence.

The arrival of more medical staff marked the crescendo of activity. Never one to be idle, Sean swiftly familiarized himself with the various tasks at the nurses' station, lending a helping hand as the pace quickened. His willingness to learn and assist endeared him further to the hospital's bustling community.

As the air hummed with conversations and footsteps, Dr. May emerged on the scene, a portrait of urgency and confusion. Her eyes darted around the station, a quest for someone particular. Sean, unfortunately, hidden amidst the activity, remained unseen. Yet, a nurse's timely intervention caught Dr. May's attention, and soon enough, she was face-to-face with the medical student she had been searching for.

The nurse's unintended address of Sean as "doctor" might have been dismissed as a casual slip, but the weight of the title gnawed at Dr. May. Amidst the organized chaos, Sean navigated the scene, ensuring that his current work was securely arranged. He exchanged a quiet conversation with Mother, his words wrapped in confidentiality. A gentle kiss on her cheek, and he was ready to follow Dr. May. The moment's enigmatic interlude left lingering questions in the air.

Dr. May and Sean embarked on their shared journey as they left the station. Their footsteps echoed a rhythm that only they understood. Dr. May's furrowed brows betrayed her curiosity, and her thoughts trailed into the depths of her mind. The distinction of Sean being referred to as "doctor" reverberated through her thoughts, a puzzle she was eager to untangle.

Their walk held a shared purpose, a reason that remained veiled for the moment. Sean's words and actions, often understated but potent, held a significance that danced just beyond the edge of comprehension. The cryptic conversation between him and Mother left its mark on Dr. May, a riddle she was eager to decipher.

A ray of intrigue and uncertainty swirled around Sean and Dr. May. Their connection, their shared moment in the day's symphony, hinted at a chapter yet to be unfolded. As they walked on, the promises of revelations and surprises hung in the air, waiting for their moment to take centre stage.

Dr. May's voice was tinged with concern and reproach as she addressed Sean's newfound status. Walking side by side through the hospital's corridors, their conversation wove through the current narrative of his designation. She felt the need to caution Sean, to remind him of the fine line he trod between student and practitioner.

Sean's response, delivered with his signature wit, was accompanied by a playful smile that danced across his lips. His words were a reminder that, though the title had been bestowed upon him unwittingly, he wasn't the one orchestrating this transformation. The short white coat he donned, a symbol of his position as a medical student, was a beacon of understanding for those around him. Though mistakenly delivered, the nurses' acknowledgment of his role was a nod to his commitment and capability.

Their interplay revealed a friendly and professional dynamic as they continued their conversation. Dr. May's role was to offer the wisdom borne of experience. On the other hand, Sean stood at the crossroads of eager learning and infectious energy. Their dialogue was a bridge between these perspectives. This bridge connected a novice's sincerity to a practitioner's sagacity.

Sean's humour served as both a shield and a tool, allowing him to navigate these conversations with ease and introspection. He reminded Dr. May that appearances can be deceiving and that a title alone didn't determine his intentions or actions. Their exchange was a dance of perspectives, a waltz of insights that attempted to draw them closer, even as their roles kept them distinct.

As they walked together, Sean and Dr. May continued their conversation, each step carrying them further into the heart of the hospital's activities. Their dynamic, a fusion of guidance and curiosity, cast a captivating spell that added a vibrant layer to the ever-evolving story of the medical world around them.

Dr. May's demeanour reflected a blend of professionalism and perhaps an underlying vulnerability. Her day seemed to have already been punctuated with challenges, a reality mirrored in the subtle creases of her brow and the guarded undertone of her voice. Despite her outward appearance, those who knew her understood that a reservoir of kindness and dedication lay beneath her unassuming exterior.

Dr. May's aura stood out as a calm island, a respite amidst the storm of medical demands. Her attire was functional rather than flashy, tailored more for efficiency than making an impression. She had an air of authenticity and an absence of duplicity that resonated with both staff and patients.

Her lack of ostentation extended to her appearance. The canvas of her face was always makeup-free, and her choice of clothing was understated yet tasteful. This minimalistic approach wasn't indicative of a lack of self-care; it was a testament to her prioritization of medical tasks over superficial adornments. Her neatness was akin to an unspoken code of respect for the profession she embraced.

Dr. May's demeanour was an enigmatic blend of humility and self-assuredness. Her posture remained erect, a testament to her dedication to her role and commitment to projecting a strong presence. This quality might have led some to interpret her as overly cautious or reserved. However, those who engaged with her found a warmth and willingness to engage.

Among the staff, Dr. May was regarded as a compassionate soul who radiated a sense of approachability despite her seriousness. Her interactions were polite, and she often took the time to acknowledge her colleagues' efforts. This courteousness was her trademark and her method of fostering a harmonious working environment.

For patients, Dr. May's demeanour was a source of comfort. Her smiles, though sparing, were genuine and reflected her sincere concern for their well-being. Her approachability reassured them that they were in capable hands, while her diligence conveyed her dedication to their care.

Her presence created a ripple of tranquillity amid the chaos. Dr. May was a testament to the notion that strength could be understated, kindness could coexist with determination, and even the most peaceful demeanour could command respect and admiration.

Dr. May's journey at AGH had carved her a path laden with dedication and effort. Despite her years of service, her reception within the hospital seemed starkly different from the reception Sean had received in just a matter of hours. The discrepancy didn't escape her notice; it was a bitter pill to swallow. She reflected on the reasons behind this divergence, wrestling with the inherent biases and dynamics at play.

In her role, Dr. May often felt overshadowed by others, especially when a newcomer like Sean garnered instant recognition. A sense of frustration nibbled at the edges of her thoughts as she grappled with the question of what it would take for her to command a similar level of attention and respect. Her tenure, dedication, and quiet competence somehow seemed overshadowed by Sean's enthusiasm.

Whispers floated among some nursing staff in the corridors and corners of the hospital. Comments like "a little kid" reached her ears, fuelling her perception that her presence went largely unnoticed and unacknowledged. Dr. May's gentle demeanour inadvertently led some to perceive her as timid or hesitant. It was a subtle misjudgment that cast her as unapproachable in the eyes of some of her colleagues.

Dr. May's approach to her work was sincere, but she had fallen victim to the paradox of her nature. Her non-confrontational stance inadvertently drew a line between her and the nursing staff, creating a perceived barrier that discouraged open interaction. She had become a puzzle, her enigmatic aura causing some to assume distance rather than inviting engagement.

Her first impression of Sean further shaped her interactions with him. Her initial assessment of his demeanour as arrogant coloured her view, potentially obscuring his other qualities. This unfortunate misstep obscured her ability to appreciate the full spectrum of his character.

Dr. Gabehart's words unwittingly sparked tension in this complex interplay of perceptions. The idea that Sean's assignment to her could be interpreted as a punishment fed the existing narrative that she wasn't competent enough to handle other responsibilities. The seeds of discord were sown, setting the stage for a rocky start to Dr. May's interactions with Sean.

As their paths converged and their interactions continued, the question lingered whether these initial impressions could be reshaped, whether the layers beneath the surface would reveal new facets, and whether Dr. May could find her voice within the chorus of the hospital's daily operations.

The moment of truth had arrived, and Dr. May knew that she needed to clear the air with Sean before they could effectively collaborate on Mr. Gladstone's case. Given her initial impressions of him and the lingering apprehensions, it wasn't easy for her. Still, she was determined to address the elephant in the room.

Summoning her courage, she began a candid conversation. She admitted that working with Sean hadn't initially been something she'd considered. She acknowledged her mistake in making a snap judgment, recognizing that Dr. Gabehart's choice had been influenced by seeing potential in Sean's involvement with Mr. Gladstone's case.

Dr. May didn't mince words when expressing her true feelings about Sean's demeanour. She found him to be overly arrogant and self-centred, qualities that she believed didn't align with the characteristics of a doctor. The words were direct and could easily have sparked a heated disagreement.

Yet, Sean's response was unexpectedly calm and composed. He admitted that he wasn't thrilled about the situation either and acknowledged the validity of Dr. May's assessment. He didn't try to defend his behaviour but admitted that Dr. Gabehart had made him aware of it. In an unexpected moment of vulnerability, Sean offered his commitment to improving his approach, understanding the importance of effective collaboration, especially on a challenging case like Mr. Gladstone's.

However, Sean also remained true to his nature, unapologetically stating that his working style was deeply rooted in his personality. He clarified that he wouldn't change who he was to fit someone else's comfort zone. In a subtle but firm manner, he suggested that Dr. May might want to address the issue with her superior if their differences were insurmountable.

This exchange was pivotal for both of them. It gave a glimpse into Sean's self-awareness and willingness to adapt, allowing Dr. May to reconsider her stance based on reality rather than her initial impressions. As they embarked on their joint venture to navigate Mr. Gladstone's case, there was an unspoken understanding that their collaboration might not be entirely smooth. Still, it was grounded in mutual respect for each other's strengths and limitations.

Dr. May and Dr. Gabehart's relationship had never been on the best of terms. Their interactions were limited to necessity, devoid of any camaraderie or personal connection. Thus, the idea of approaching Dr. Gabehart to express her concerns about Sean's demeanour was out of the question for Dr. May. She had no choice but to address the matter directly with Sean himself.

Dr. May reiterated her position as the attending physician

with a measured tone. She emphasized the distinction between their roles, reminding Sean that he was a student while she held the title of a doctor. It was a polite yet firm assertion of authority, an attempt to draw the line in their working relationship.

To ensure effective collaboration and prevent clashes, Dr. May set forth a set of guidelines for their partnership. She clarified that Sean's involvement with patients was restricted; he was not to engage in any hands-on activities. Moreover, Dr. May underscored the importance of open communication, urging Sean to consult with her before making independent decisions about patient care.

While Dr. May's approach was undoubtedly driven by her reservations about Sean's attitude, it also reflected her commitment to maintaining professionalism and ensuring the best care for their patients. Despite her initial skepticism, she recognized the value of working together harmoniously.

This conversation marked a tentative step toward collaboration for the two. Dr. May's clear communication of expectations and boundaries and Sean's willingness to engage in a productive dialogue hinted at the possibility of a functional working relationship, even in the face of their differences. As they embarked on this new dynamic, their ability to find common ground and respect each other's roles would be crucial in successfully managing Mr. Gladstone's case.

Sean's carefree attitude and sarcastic comments tested Dr. May's patience. As she outlined the rules and expectations for their collaboration, she could sense Sean's disregard for protocol and perhaps even his lack of attention. His response, "So, what do you have for me?" clearly indicated that he was either dismissing her instructions or simply not taking them seriously.

Dr. May started, "Mr. Gladstone is currently undergoing a

surgical procedure to extract the tumour in his lung. As we await updates on his condition, we can begin to address a few cases of hypertension. Also, I have a case that requires medication adjustments for a patient grappling with cardiac arrhythmias."

Sean replied sarcastically, "Wait, Mr. Gladstone had a lung tumour? I thought all he had was a heart valve problem you had diagnosed."

His attempt at humour by pretending to be ignorant of the tumour in Mr. Gladstone's lung only seemed to irk Dr. May further. Her serious demeanour clashed with Sean's apparent attempts at lightheartedness.

Dr. May, however, managed to muster a bit of humour herself as she playfully commented on Sean's behaviour. Her statement, "Quit rubbing it in. That's why no one likes you," was a mixture of sarcasm and genuine amusement. The exchange highlighted the contrast between their personalities – Dr. May's reserved and Sean's bold – and hinted at the possibility of their interactions evolving over time.

She smiled in embarrassment as she continued, "Anyway, thank you for that. You couldn't have been annoying at a better time for me."

In an unexpected twist, Dr. May mentioned that Mr. Gladstone had expressed gratitude for Sean's presence and involvement. Despite his antics, Sean's impact on Mr. Gladstone's well-being had not gone unnoticed. Ever the modest character, Sean downplayed his role, attributing it to luck rather than any particular skill or intention.

As their conversation continued, it was evident that Sean's dynamic approach and disregard for formalities were both a source of irritation and, perhaps, an occasional source of amusement for Dr. May. While their working relationship was off to a rocky start, Sean's unpredictability had already brought about some unexpected outcomes—including Mr. Gladstone's appreciation. Whether this blend of personalities would lead to productive collaboration or constant clashes remained to be seen.

Sean's inquiry about the hypertensive patient indicated a genuine interest in the medical case at hand. Dr. May proceeded to provide him with the patient's background, explaining that the patient was on multiple medications to manage her blood pressure.

The first thing Sean asked was if the patient was overweight, to which Dr. May replied, "That's not nice, but yes. The patient lives alone, works as a cashier, and has a family history of heart problems. Both parents died of complications of uncontrolled hypertension. Her mother had a stroke, and her father died of heart failure."

Sean looked distracted and annoyed as he told Dr. May, "I don't care much about her family. I'm not trying to be her friend."

"You see, that's what I don't like about you. You're too arrogant. Everyone knows that family history is a huge factor for heart problems and a huge predictor of complications of uncontrolled hypertension!" she admonished him.

This was another moment of tension, highlighting the clash between Sean's straightforward approach and Dr. May's emphasis on a holistic understanding of patient conditions.

The interaction was a microcosm of the broader challenges they would face working together – the balance between Sean's pragmatic approach and Dr. May's more nuanced perspective on patient care. Whether they could find common ground to bridge this gap or continue to butt heads remained to be seen.

The dynamic between Dr. May and Sean became increasingly evident as their conversation continued. From a professional perspective, they appeared to be on opposite ends of the spectrum – Dr. May adhering to established protocols and guidelines, while Sean seemed to rely on his intuition and individual judgment. Their differences in approach were becoming more pronounced.

Sean's tendency to dismiss opinions that clashed with his own added another layer of tension. It was apparent that he didn't hold Dr. May's medical insights in high regard, particularly after his successful diagnosis of Mr. Gladstone's condition. This might have caused him to underestimate her capabilities and knowledge.

Their conversation about the hypertensive patient wasn't merely a medical discussion; it had become a subtle struggle for dominance. Sean's insistence on delving into the patient's diet and lifestyle, especially her guilty pleasures, indicated his desire to exert control and prove his approach's superiority. He was effectively challenging Dr. May's authority and the rigidity of her methods.

As the discussion progressed, it became more than just an exchange of medical information – it became a clash of philosophies and egos. The outcome of this power struggle could significantly impact their working relationship and the quality of patient care they could provide together.

The tension between Dr. May and Sean had escalated beyond a simple disagreement—it was now a subtle battle for control over the patient's case. Sean's assertiveness and the unique authority granted to him by Dr. Gabehart challenged Dr. May's position as the overseeing physician.

Dr. May's reluctance to provide more details about the patient's diet and lifestyle was driven by her adherence to standard medical protocols, her sense of authority, and possibly a touch of defensiveness against Sean's perceived undermining of her expertise. To her, the medical history they had on file seemed sufficient for a preliminary assessment.

However, Sean had his reasons for pressing further. He was well aware of the influence he held due to Dr. Gabehart's arrangement, and he used this leverage to remind Dr. May that he had the power to make treatment recommendations. By insisting on additional details about the patient's diet, Sean indirectly communicated that he had the upper hand in this situation and was willing to exercise it.

"How did she get here?" Sean inquired.

"The patient collapsed at work right after she returned from lunch," Dr. May responded.

"You still think diet is irrelevant?" Sean asked as he curiously looked at Dr. May.

"Okay. I'll get the information on her diet if you insist," Dr. May answered, "She has three adult children, two sons and one daughter."

The hypertensive patient's case had taken an intriguing turn. The additional information about the patient's collapse at work and the limited presence of her adult children sparked Sean's curiosity even further. Sean's persistence had overcome Dr. May's initial reluctance to delve into dietary details. Now, the puzzle pieces were slowly coming together.

Sean remained quiet for a while before asking, "Have they visited their mother since she was admitted to the hospital?"

"Both sons are married, but only the older brother came two days after she was admitted. I didn't get a chance to talk to him because he didn't stay for long," Dr. May replied.

Sean's analytical mind was racing to connect the dots. He was trying to decipher the patient's medical history, family dynamics, and the circumstances that led to her collapse. The patient's diet and lifestyle were increasingly appearing as critical factors in her condition. Sean was now deep into the detective work that medical diagnosis sometimes resembled.

The absence of two of the patient's adult children struck Sean as unusual. A mother admitted to the hospital generally expects her children to visit and offer support. The fact that only one son had visited, and that too for a short time, added an element of mystery to the situation. Sean's intuition was telling him that there might be more to this family dynamic than met the eye.

As Sean continued to gather information and analyze the case, he was unknowingly navigating a complex web of medical data and personal relationships. The more he uncovered, the more he realized that this patient's story was not just about medical symptoms but also about the human elements that could significantly impact her well-being.

Sean's intrigue deepened as Dr. May disclosed more about the patient's family situation. The revelation about the daughter's schizophrenia and her institutionalization added a layer of complexity to the case. Mental health issues within a family could have profound implications on the overall health and well-being of all its members.

The fact that the patient's daughter had been institutionalized for an unknown duration raised questions about the patient's emotional state and coping mechanisms. Sean couldn't help but wonder about how this situation impacted the patient's blood pressure and overall health. The daughter's condition was a crucial piece of the puzzle that needed to be carefully considered in the patient's treatment plan.

Sean's astute observation and questioning skills came to the forefront as he probed Dr. May about her estimation of the duration of institutionalization. He meticulously assembled the pieces of information, trying to understand the timeline of events and the emotional undercurrents within the family. His analytical mind attempted to bridge the gap between the medical data and the human emotions that shaped this case.

In medicine, understanding the patient as a whole is often said to be as vital as diagnosing their medical condition. Sean was beginning to grasp the significance of this philosophy as he delved deeper into the delicate intricacies that could impact her health journey. The case had evolved from a simple hypertension scenario to a multifaceted narrative of health, relationships, and emotions.

Sean's skepticism had him tethered to the edge of curiosity, his mind an arena of questions waiting to be answered. With a tenacity matched by few, he sought to peel back the layers of this intricate puzzle, probing further into the corridors of Dr. May's insights.

Dr. May was concerned about informing the patient's daughter about her mother's hospital admission, fearing it could negatively impact her mental health. As a result, she refrained from sending any messages to the mental institution.

When asked about the duration of the daughter's institutionalization, Dr. May explained that the mother was reluctant to discuss the matter. Dr. May speculated that the daughter had been institutionalized for a period ranging from a couple of months to a few years.

Sean found this range unsettling and asked how Dr. May reached this conclusion.

She replied, "The mother seemed emotionally distant, indicating that some time had passed, but she still harboured anger about something related to the situation, making it a relatively recent event."

Doubts lingered like shadows, and Sean's inquiry illuminated the uncharted alleys of the patient's emotional landscape. He yearned to ascertain whether the patient's anger was directed toward the mental institution or if there were other tides of discontent swirling beneath the surface. It was as if he was holding a lantern in the darkness, seeking the elusive truth that could unveil the patient's hidden turmoil.

With the patience of an older storyteller, Dr. May crafted her explanation and elucidated her deduction with precision. She wasn't merely observing but deciphering the intricate language of emotions that danced beneath the patient's words. She concluded not from the obvious but from the nuanced and unsaid.

Her words flowed with the wisdom of an adage, "It's not the wind that moves the tree, but the roots beneath." Dr. May's insight hinted at the roots of emotions deeply intertwined with the patient's familial struggles. The patient's response wasn't a random gust of emotions; it was the resonance of an ongoing symphony conducted by the harmony of her experiences.

Sean was not just a medical student at this moment; he was a seeker of truths, a weaver of narratives, and a custodian of human complexities. As he listened, he embraced the depths of Dr. May's observations, understanding that she was unveiling a treasure trove of insights into the human soul beneath her calm demeanour.

In this exchange, the tables of understanding were indeed turned. Dr. May's explanation offered Sean a glimpse into the realm of emotions and perceptions, an area often overshadowed by the stark data of medical records. As he absorbed her wisdom, Sean realized that medicine wasn't just a science of the human body but a tapestry woven with the threads of human stories, intricate and interwoven.

The dynamics of power and expertise shifted within the realm of their conversation. With his penchant for questioning, Sean had unknowingly taken the reins, and Dr. May found herself navigating uncharted waters. In the vast sea of medicine, this particular case had steered them into a realm where Sean's brilliance seemed to hold the compass.

Dr. May's experience, usually her guiding star, had encountered an enigma that left her floundering. She had cast her hopes onto Sean's potential, relying on his unique insight to unravel this complex puzzle. Yet, Sean's response didn't flow like a swift current; instead, it seemed to stall like a ship caught in the doldrums.

With a humility that echoed an old saying, Sean admitted his need for time as if he were nurturing a fragile seedling, hoping that, given time, it would bloom into a solution. The clock's ticking drumbeats felt amplified, and patience was a virtue not easily grasped by Dr. May, whose frustration was a tempest trapped within her eyes.

But in this dance of interaction, even the unspoken words had meaning. Sean's request for time was not a concession to incompetence but a testament to his integrity. Rather than hastily attempting a solution, he was invoking the ancient wisdom, "Look before you leap." He was embracing the art of reflection and thoroughness, an approach often lost in the race against time.

The pendulum of conversation swung, and Dr. May, now steering the ship towards calmer waters, moved them onto the next case. It was a subtle yet profound shift as they delved into another medical puzzle, allowing the intricate threads of diagnosis to weave their story.

In the interplay of power and vulnerability, they were crafting more than medical assessments in this ebb and flow of dialogue. They were crafting a bridge between two minds, each contributing their hues to the canvas of understanding. Within this dynamic exchange, they found not just answers to medical inquiries but fragments of the human experience itself.

Dr. May's fingers brushed over the patient files, much like a pianist's fingers exploring the keys of a piano before playing a complex symphony. Her eyes scanned the information before her, gathering fragments of narratives beneath the surface.

She started on the second case: "The second patient is a middle-aged male with no family history of heart problems. He's on two different medications for his hypertension and one for his cough. He's a teacher, married with two kids."

Sean quickly responded, "Wait, why are you doctors so obsessed with the family history of every patient? More than ninety percent of patients are sick because of their environment that would be unrelated to their spouses, parents, or siblings."

Dr. May's expression shifted from curiosity to disbelief, her gaze locked onto Sean. The air held tension, a moment suspended in time as if awaiting an answer to the challenge Sean had thrown into the arena. A request for proof hung in the air.

Sean's response might have ignited the flames of offence in someone less tempered. Yet, Sean's audacity, his propensity to march to the beat of his own drum, ultimately doused the flames.

His words, "Don't worry about it," carried a dismissive tone, as if he was brushing off his previous statement as casually as dust from his shoulder.

Dr. May's adherence to the textbook standards could have demanded an apology or explanation. But in this intricate dance of personalities, she recognized that engaging further might only deepen the depth of discord.

With a quick mental pivot, Dr. May chose the path of conciliation. She remembered the nature of her conversational sparring partner – someone who was as much a questioner as an answerer. She realized that Sean was not challenging her for the sake of confrontation but as an extension of his intrinsic curiosity, his insatiable thirst for knowledge. With that realization, she decided to let this particular battle of semantics rest.

The case remained, suspended in the air like a pendulum, while they moved on to the next one. As their conversation flowed onward, it was a reminder that even within the realm of medical diagnosis, the human elements of ego, pride, and the quest for understanding danced in the background.

Dr. May's thoughts were akin to a complex network of intertwining vines, each leading to the root of her intentions. As their conversation moved forward, she sought a bridge to span the gap that had opened up between them. While the jarring exchange regarding family history was like a rock that had disrupted the smooth flow of their discourse, she realized that beneath the surface, they were both navigating uncharted waters, trying to understand and assert their positions.

The labyrinth of Sean's thoughts was a fascinating maze; its corridors paved with curiosity and skepticism. Dr. May recognized the value in exploring these corridors, knowing that within Sean's mind might reside insights that had eluded conventional wisdom. The bridge she sought was made of comprehension, a means to reach across the personal and professional divide.

She remembered her role as the one responsible for Sean's journey. It wasn't merely a matter of titles and formalities; it was a matter of stewardship. Dr. May intended to mould Sean's growth, and this intention flowed not only from the authority vested in her but also from a desire to learn and expand her understanding by embracing perspectives beyond the conventional.

As they progressed through their conversation, it was as though Dr. May was threading a needle through the fabric of their interaction, stitching together the lessons of authority and humility, of experience and curiosity. The professional battlefield they stood upon was more than a clash of words; it was a battleground for knowledge and growth. In each exchanged sentence, in every nuanced response, they were both navigating the delicate dance of assertion and respect.

Ultimately, their exchange was about more than just clarifying the stance on family history or the significance of numbers. It was about weaving a narrative of mutual understanding, where the tapestry of medicine was coloured by the diverse threads of their personalities and perspectives.

As they moved forward, they walked a path towards equilibrium, where Dr. May's seasoned wisdom met Sean's untamed curiosity, and where knowledge and humility flowed seamlessly together, much like the ebb and flow of a gentle river.

The dance of dynamics between Dr. May and Sean had an

undercurrent of calculated caution. Dr. May had navigated the labyrinth of human interactions long enough to understand that not every battle was worth fighting. She gleaned insights into Sean's modus operandi from the mosaic of their limited encounters. He wasn't one to casually toss ideas into the air; the intricate machinery of his intellect backed each word he uttered.

The tides of trust flowed in curious directions within this microcosm of the hospital. Sean's favour with Dr. Gabehart was a double-edged sword that illuminated his potential and cast a shadow over Dr. May's authority. This wasn't about mere power dynamics but about respect, validation, and the delicate balance of expertise.

Sean's mind, she discovered, was an expansive realm where he tirelessly examined, dissected, and formulated. When he finally revealed his thoughts, they bore the weight of rigorous internal scrutiny. This was a realm where conclusions weren't drawn lightly; they were the carefully crafted outcomes of an intricate mental process. Dr. May had learned to respect that and acknowledge the machinery behind Sean's actions.

Asserting her authority over Sean wasn't a matter of blunt force; it was a delicate dance where precision mattered. Questioning him required a strategic approach, an unveiling of a better answer, or a blatant contradiction. Her approach wasn't a challenge to his intelligence; it was a respectful acknowledgment of their shared goal to unravel the complexities of medicine.

Sean's demeanour had an unmistakable aura of self-assurance. His showmanship, a facet of his personality that he might not always be aware of, shone through. He revelled in his intellectual prowess, basking in the glow of superiority, sometimes inadvertently conveying to others that he might be leagues ahead.

Dr. May recognized that Sean's intentions might be a mosaic of motivations, but the overarching message was clear.

As they traversed the corridors of the hospital's intellectual terrain, Dr. May became increasingly aware of the dynamics they were navigating. It was a terrain where expertise intertwined with egos, learning was a continuous journey, and mutual respect was the cornerstone. Their exchanges were a blend of perspectives, a journey towards a harmonious equilibrium where authority and brilliance harmonized.

Their interactions wove a tapestry of human dynamics, where respect, ego, and authority mingled. In this tapestry, Dr. May sought not to diminish Sean's intellect but to enrich their collective understanding. In turn, Sean's quest for validation was a thread in the fabric, adding layers to their discourse. Together, they ventured into the realm of medicine, where the interplay of personalities and knowledge painted a vivid portrait of a journey toward mastery.

In the realm of intellectual discourse, Sean was a whirlwind of enthusiasm. Once a topic caught his attention, he'd immerse himself in it completely, spinning narratives that connected dots from the past to the present. This was how he engaged with the world, through a tapestry of historical anecdotes, research theories, and statistical quirks.

For Dr. May, this passionate monologue on statistics was a labyrinth she wasn't keen on navigating. The intricacies of numbers and probability weren't her forte, and Sean's uninhibited explanations only made the maze more complex. She trod cautiously, trying to redirect the conversation back to their cases.

Recognizing the point of diminishing returns, Dr. May gently employed a strategic maneuver to halt Sean's statistical odyssey. She embraced Sean's explanations, assuring him that she believed his perspective. Her message was clear: they needed to move forward, and delving into statistics at this moment wasn't conducive.

With a gracious demeanour, Dr. May guided the conversation toward their immediate task – the cases at hand. Sean's analytical prowess was undeniable, yet he also had a penchant for focusing on the minute details while overlooking the bigger picture. He suggested that she revisit the patient's case objectively, erasing the influence of family history.

However, Dr. May wasn't new to this case; she had been wrestling with it for days. She had already considered switching medications or adjusting dosages. However, Sean's gentle push made her realize that his observations about the patient's prolonged hospital stay were astute. Dr. Gabehart's rejection of her initial approach hinted that there was more to the puzzle, and she needed to uncover it before making a decision.

This subtle acknowledgment from Sean and his readiness to proceed was the unspoken harmony in their collaboration. As the conversation pivoted towards the next patient, it carried with it the subtle affirmation that they were both working towards a common goal, albeit through different approaches.

Their discourse was a testament to the duality of their partnership – Sean's eagerness to explore every intellectual nook and cranny, and Dr. May's pragmatic focus on actionable solutions. Through the dance of their interactions, they painted a vivid picture of two minds navigating the labyrinth of medicine, each contributing a unique colour to the canvas of discovery.

Time has a peculiar way of stretching when immersed in the depths of a discussion. For Dr. May, this interaction with Sean seemed to stretch on indefinitely. The seconds turned into minutes, and the minutes into an hour, and yet, she felt as though she had been stuck in this mental maze for an eternity.

With his mind like a labyrinthine puzzle, Sean had an uncanny ability to captivate and frustrate. The cases she had hoped he might unravel with his brilliance were seemingly slipping through their fingers, replaced by tangential conversations that spiralled into the unknown. She was beginning to question the efficacy of this collaboration, wondering if Sean's intellectual meandering was truly aiding their patients.

As the hour ticked by, Dr. May's patience grew thin, and her annoyance was a tangible presence in the room. She had entrusted Sean with these cases, hoping for insightful solutions, yet his responses had been disappointingly elusive. Her frustration was palpable when she told him he hadn't been helpful despite her detailed explanations.

Sean, unflinchingly focused on his internal musings, calmly insisted that he needed more time to think, seemingly unperturbed by Dr. May's growing exasperation. His disregard for her mounting frustration only seemed to amplify her irritation.

When Sean asked if she was annoyed, Dr. May's response was raw and unfiltered – a candid admission of her feelings, "Of course. You're asking me all these questions and not helping!"

Sean's persistence in seeking more time for contemplation while simultaneously expressing his desire to delve into more cases struck Dr. May as paradoxical. It was as if they were both dancing to a different rhythm, caught between Sean's desire for intellectual exploration and her pragmatic need for actionable solutions.

Amid this crossroads, Dr. May had a choice – to resist

Sean's flow and anchor themselves to the cases at hand or to relinquish control and allow Sean's unique approach to unfold. With a roll of her eyes and a heavy sigh, she chose the latter. After all, medicine, like life, is a complex journey with unexpected twists and turns. Perhaps, in Sean's intellectual wanderings, a glimmer of insight might still emerge to illuminate their path forward.

The subsequent case emerged, a law student bearing the burden of heart arrhythmias. Sean's impatience became evident as Dr. May began to detail the complexities of the patient's condition. He swiftly cut her off, asserting that he comprehended the situation and was ready to move on. His curt dismissal displayed a lack of interest in engaging with her. This behaviour was rapidly eroding any rapport they might have hoped to establish.

Sean's indifference and insistence on skimming the surface rather than diving into the depths of the case only added fuel to the fire of their growing discord. Dr. May's initial skepticism about Sean's attitude was now solidifying into a conviction. His cavalier approach to their collaboration and his apparent disinterest in the lives they were trying to impact confirmed her initial assessment that he was indeed arrogant and difficult to work with.

The tension in the room reached a boiling point when Sean attempted to circumvent the intricacies of the patient's case.

Dr. May's frustration exploded into an emotional outburst, her voice echoing off the walls as she chastised him. "What did you get? I haven't told you anything about this patient! Can you for once act like an adult human being dealing with other people's lives?!"

Dr. May's anger was palpable, her face flushed with emotion as she confronted Sean's cavalier attitude head-on. Her words were an indictment of his behaviour, a plea for him to recognize the gravity of their responsibilities. She stood her ground, nostrils flaring, a symbol of her righteous indignation.

In the heated exchange, it was evident that Dr. May's patience was wearing thin. She faced a dilemma – the growing realization that she couldn't navigate these cases alone, yet the obstacle in front of her, Sean's demeanour, seemed insurmountable. He held the key to their success, but his attitude was proving to be an equal adversary. As the silence settled, like a heavy cloud of uncertainty, they were left with an unspoken acknowledgment that they needed each other, whether they liked it or not.

Caught in the storm of their growing tension, Sean attempted an ill-timed jest to diffuse the situation, but his approach only added another layer of friction to their already strained interaction. With an air of nonchalance that grated on Dr. May's sense of professionalism, Sean proposed a deal that was as surprising as it was offensive.

Dr. May was deeply committed to her work, driven by a genuine desire to help patients and uphold medical standards. On the other hand, Sean appeared to approach the whole situation with a certain detachment, starkly contrasting her seriousness. The notion of making a deal amid their discussions about critical medical cases struck her as profoundly inappropriate, even offensive.

Sean's proposition seemed to play into his tendency to undermine the gravity of the situation. "Dr. Gabehart doesn't seem to like you very much, and I can give you credit for figuring these cases on your own after I showed you a few things," he casually suggested.

Dr. May's aspirations for Dr. Gabehart's approval were something she held dear, and Sean's assertion that he could sway

Dr. Gabehart's opinion felt like a low blow.

As Sean continued, trying to frame his offer as an advantageous trade, Dr. May listened with incredulity and offence. He put forth his terms: she could choose whether or not to take his recommendations on the cases, but if she followed all of them, she would be required to cook him dinner and breakfast at her home. The audacity of this proposal left a bitter taste in Dr. May's mouth.

Dr. May's response was swift and sharp, fuelled by a sense of insult and a refusal to compromise her professionalism for Sean's misguided humour. She told him that she found his proposal offensive and expressed her strong displeasure at the insinuation that he was using patients' lives as leverage to gain a personal advantage. While others might have taken such a proposal lightly, Dr. May held her standards high, unwilling to compromise her ethics to appease Sean's whims.

Amid the charged atmosphere, it became painfully clear that any inkling of attraction between Dr. May and Sean was simply non-existent. If anything, the very idea of spending time with Sean in any capacity beyond their professional obligations was outright repugnant to Dr. May. His proposition to exchange medical insights for intimate favours struck her as distasteful and, quite frankly, offensive.

Sean attempted to rationalize his proposition, claiming he hadn't intended any romantic connotations. However, his assertion only exacerbated the situation, as Dr. May pointed out that the implications were unmistakable when dinner and breakfast were combined. Sean's defence didn't hold water, leaving her with the conclusion that he was indeed using medical insights to manipulate her.

Dr. May detested Sean's proposal because of her dedication to her work and a firm sense of ethics. However, Sean wasn't one to back down easily. He skillfully played on her doubts and desires, highlighting the potential advantages of their arrangement.

Sean claimed that if she refused the deal, it would indicate that she believed he was more intelligent than she was and that he would undoubtedly solve all the cases. However, if she regarded him as irritating and self-absorbed with no regard for patient welfare, he would inevitably make at least one mistake, and their date would not progress.

Despite her reservations, the prospect of getting closer to Dr. Gabehart, whose approval she coveted, presented a tempting incentive. Dr. May weighed her options, eventually finding some appeal in the details of the deal. Sean's stipulation that he provide recommendations and explanations that she could present to Dr. Gabehart was a significant factor. Additionally, Sean insisted that Dr. Gabehart had to accept all of the recommendations, leaving no room for dismissal.

Dr. May hesitated, her reluctance discernible, before finally relenting to the terms of the deal. The circumstances seemed to demand it, and she couldn't ignore the potential benefits it might bring. With a heavy sigh, she agreed, albeit with a clear sense of begrudging resignation. The agreement was struck, binding them in an unusual partnership that neither had initially anticipated.

Sean's mind was a flurry of activity, his footsteps echoing the rhythm of his thoughts. Dr. May watched with curiosity and skepticism, half-expecting Sean's pacing to culminate in an insightful revelation but also wondering if this was all just an elaborate ruse. As Sean's brow furrowed intermittently, it seemed like he was on the cusp of a breakthrough, only for it to slip through his grasp each time. Dr. May's patience was being tested, but she decided to wait and see where Sean's mental gymnastics would lead.

After several minutes, Sean started, "The first patient is depressed, and has been for a long time. She's lonely and doesn't seem to have a good relationship with her sons. She likely gave up on those two a long time ago. She thought things would be fine since she still had her daughter, but then the daughter got committed. Had the reasons to be institutionalized been natural causes, she wouldn't be visibly frustrated at the mention of her daughter. She was likely her pride and joy, and she did something to herself that ruined her life, likely drug-related. You like talking to people, so get her to open up and connect the dots. It will be an interesting story once you get her to open up. Of course, her job as a cashier keeping all that weight in a vertical position all day long doesn't improve things, but not to the point of sending her to the hospital with hypertension."

Sean's analysis startled Dr. May. His insights delved far deeper than she had anticipated. As Sean's deductions continued, Dr. May couldn't help but feel intrigued. His words painted a narrative that resonated, like puzzle pieces falling into place. Yet, she was acutely aware that this level of analysis was founded on hunches and assumptions. The tantalizing prospect of Sean solving all her cases seemed almost too good to be true.

Another part of the deal was that Sean would be working on all cases from Dr. May until the end of his clerkship if she or Dr. Gabehart refused at least one of his recommendations.

Sean was far from done. He shifted gears and suggested a low-dose suppression test to confirm the depression diagnosis. Dr. May's smile began to form. She imagined Sean's expertise contributing to her work in an unexpected and beneficial way. Yet, her optimism took a sudden nosedive when she connected the test to other diseases, revealing his lack of knowledge in that particular medical area.

Dr. May's amusement transformed into disbelief as she vehemently corrected Sean's mistake. His seemingly brilliant insights suddenly fell apart, replaced by the harsh reality that his expertise had its limits. The clash between their professional knowledge was undeniable. At that moment, Sean's aura of brilliance seemed to dim slightly, and Dr. May was reminded that, despite his unique skills, he was not infallible.

Again, Sean was far from done. As he elaborated on his reasoning, Dr. May's initial skepticism was replaced with a mixture of surprise and a begrudging respect for his unconventional approach. Sean's explanation was like a gust of fresh air sweeping away her doubts, and she found herself considering his perspective more seriously. His insights were unconventional, and it was clear that he was thinking outside the box, a quality she hadn't anticipated.

Listening to Sean's explanation of the low-dose dexamethasone suppression test, Dr. May realized there was a depth to his medical knowledge that extended beyond the ordinary curriculum. His description of the test's application to depression was a revelation to her, unveiling a hidden facet of his expertise. She couldn't deny the logic behind his approach, and the realization that Sean had a unique angle on medical matters was both fascinating and unsettling.

Sean explained, "I'm not asking you if she's depressed. I know she's depressed, and I'm asking you to do the test for your confirmation. A low-dose dexamethasone suppression test can be used to diagnose depression. Just like Cushing's syndrome and small cell lung cancer, depression also produces a lot of cortisol. If a low dose of dexamethasone suppresses cortisol production, it's likely depression. If a low dose doesn't suppress cortisol production, then Cushing's syndrome and lung cancer come on the table. In medical school, most medical students only learn what this test means if a low-dose doesn't suppress, and only a few people learn and understand the meaning of a low-dose test that suppresses cortisol production."

Dr. May's mind churned as she evaluated Sean's theory against her clinical knowledge and experience. She was caught between admiring his innovative thinking and being wary of straying too far from established protocols.

Finally, she spoke, her tone a mixture of cautious curiosity and a lingering hint of skepticism, "So, your suggestion is to proceed with the test to confirm depression and then consider medication adjustments based on that diagnosis?"

Sean nodded, a small smile playing on his lips as if he had been waiting for her to catch up with his train of thought. Dr. May sighed softly, still grappling with the idea of trusting Sean's unconventional approach.

Their partnership had entered a new dimension, marked by a curious blend of intellectual admiration and professional skepticism. Dr. May recognized that Sean was not just a medical student seeking to impress but a thinker unafraid to challenge established norms.

As they navigated this uncharted territory together, she wondered how many more layers of Sean's medical acumen were waiting to be uncovered. The cases before them were medical puzzles and a canvas upon which to paint Sean's unique perspective. The question now was whether their collaboration would yield groundbreaking insights or spiral into chaos.

Sean's treatment proposal hung in the air, challenging Dr. May's traditional approach and inviting an alternative solution. The suggestion to wean the patient off her current heart medication, followed by a psychiatric evaluation before introducing psychiatric medication, seemed like a bold move. Dr. May weighed the pros and cons of this unconventional route. It was a decision that could potentially transform the patient's treatment trajectory.

Dr. May asked, "If you're right about depression, should I start her on antidepressants?"

Sean laughed and exclaimed as he turned around to hold Dr. May as if he were saving a little kid from falling down the stairs. "No! Do you want to kill her? Antidepressants will increase her heart rate and likely boost her blood pressure again. Start her on low-dose lorazepam and increase the dose as you see fit. Hit two birds with one stone, relax her mind and lower her blood pressure."

As Sean elaborated on his recommendation of low-dose lorazepam, Dr. May nodded in agreement. The logic was sound, tackling both the psychological and physiological aspects of the patient's condition simultaneously. Sean's grasp of the intricacies of drug interactions and their effects was impressive, a facet of his expertise that Dr. May was learning to respect.

However, despite Sean's convincing explanations, Dr. May's cautious nature held her back from fully embracing his recommendations. She hesitated, an internal struggle evident as she debated whether to accept his proposal. Her professional responsibility weighed heavily, as did her initial reservations about Sean's demeanour.

His demeanour shifted when Dr. May inquired if he needed anything else to add to the case. He had navigated the fine line between exuberance and arrogance, striking a chord with Dr. May that was difficult to ignore.

Sean was done with this patient, but he asked her to tell Dr. Gabehart about the sons and call the patient's sons to come and see Dr. Gabehart as a matter of life and death.

When Dr. May inquired about the reason, Sean explained, "Have you met Dr. Gabehart? Give her someone else for a verbal punching bag, and she'll lay off your case for a while."

Dr. May smiled as she thought to herself, "That's interesting. I hope it works because I could use the break." The smile and sigh of relief from Dr. May gave Sean an idea of what was going through her mind.

He tapped her shoulder, smiling, and said, "Trust me. It'll work."

Dr. May's smile and sigh of relief spoke volumes. Sean's insight wasn't limited to medical matters; he also seemed to understand the emotional dynamics of the hospital environment. The notion of presenting Dr. Gabehart with a different issue of focus resonated with Dr. May. It was as if Sean had offered her a secret weapon to temporarily redirect her superior's attention elsewhere. Dr. May's journey with Sean was becoming anything but ordinary.

The concept of treating the second patient by phlebotomy was unorthodox, to say the least. Sean's recommendation was straightforward—essentially, he suggested a controlled bloodletting procedure to reduce the patient's blood volume and subsequently lower his blood pressure.

Dr. May raised an eyebrow at the proposal. Bloodletting as a therapeutic approach belonged more to the annals of medical history than to the modern healthcare practices to which she was accustomed.

As they discussed the idea, Sean's rationale emerged—a simplified, yet seemingly logical, explanation. Dr. May's skepticism began to melt away as she grasped the core principle of the recommendation: rather than adding more medications to the patient's regimen, a direct and tangible action could be taken to address the issue. Sean's emphasis on monitoring the patient's blood volume, hemoglobin levels, and pressure revealed a comprehensive understanding of the potential risks and benefits.

Dr. May's response, "Instead of giving him drugs to pee the excess volume, we bleed him," encapsulated the essence of the recommendation.

Sean's solution to the complex medical landscape was refreshingly pragmatic. He wasn't tethered to convention but explored untrodden paths to deliver results. The simplicity of his approach seemed to be its strength, a direct counterpoint to the intricacies of medical treatments that often dominated discussions in their field.

The dialogue between Sean and Dr. May reflected the broader tension between established medical norms and the uncharted territories of unconventional solutions. Sean's willingness to question and reimagine treatment options, even if they harkened back to historical practices, was intriguing and thought-provoking. Dr. May, an embodiment of the medical establishment, was being challenged to consider alternative avenues for patient care.

Dr. May appreciated the elegance of Sean's proposal. It was

a stark reminder that sometimes, the most effective solutions can be found in the simplest actions. The potential success of phlebotomy as a treatment for hypertension in this patient remained uncertain, but what was clear was that Sean's contributions were forcing her to reevaluate her approach to patient care. Whether she would adopt the recommendation or not, Sean's disruptive influence was undeniable, ushering in a new era of collaboration and exploration in her professional journey.

The exchange between Sean and Dr. May continued to dance along the edges of medical norms, veering into unexplored territories while maintaining a certain camaraderie that seemed to be gradually blossoming. As they discussed the potential risks and benefits of the phlebotomy procedure for the second patient, Sean's pragmatic approach stood its ground.

Dr. May's concerns were well-founded—taking too much blood from a patient could lead to anemia and other complications. Yet, Sean's response showcased his unwavering focus on details that often eluded the conventional train of thought. Hypothetical roadblocks didn't deter him; he was determined to find solutions. His insistence on measuring the patient's hemoglobin levels before proceeding highlighted his attention to precision. This quality marked his entire approach.

Sean's nonchalant dismissal of the fate of the donated blood might have struck some as cavalier. Still, it also revealed his pragmatic philosophy: if a solution worked for the patient at hand, he wasn't overly concerned with the broader implications. He was there to address immediate problems with immediate solutions, and that philosophy shaped his recommendations.

When asked if she didn't like the approach, she replied, "No. Actually, I think that's very smart. Each bag of blood we take also takes out a bag of sodium, and we can dilute the remaining sodium. His diastolic pressure is very high, and lowering his sodium like this might actually help him!" Suddenly, Dr. May looked more alive than she had been all morning.

Sean couldn't resist commenting, "Look who just woke up. Thank you for joining me now."

Dr. May's approval of Sean's approach was a turning point. As she realized that Sean's unconventional methods could yield results, a spark of excitement seemed to rekindle within her. It was as though Sean's unconventional thinking was rubbing off on her, prompting her to venture into uncharted intellectual territories.

The shared laughter marked a moment of genuine connection. For a brief instant, the walls of formality seemed to crumble, revealing two individuals navigating the complexities of medicine, each with their distinctive approach. Sean's light-hearted comment dissolved some of the tension that had been simmering between them, replacing it with a sense of camaraderie that transcended their differences.

In this ongoing dialogue, Sean's unorthodox methods challenged Dr. May to expand her perspective and embrace innovative thinking. The interplay between tradition, innovation, skepticism, and curiosity shaped their interactions into a dynamic interweaving of ideas and approaches. As they laughed together, the boundaries between student and doctor, convention and creativity, seemed to blur, paving the way for a unique partnership that was as unexpected as it was promising.

As their conversation unravelled, a newfound harmony began to take shape. Dr. May's concern about not having a definitive diagnosis for this patient was met with Sean's strategic consideration of time. His proposal to proceed with the phlebotomy as a diagnostic and therapeutic measure resonated with her. It was as if he suggested they take a step back, create a controlled environment, and observe how the patient's body responded.

Sean's explanation of his hypothesis illuminated the thought process behind his recommendation. His narrative of the patient's journey through multiple medications and symptoms revealed a systematic approach that sought to unravel the complex web of medical history. By tracing the sequence of events and the patient's interactions with various medications, he was piecing together a puzzle that had eluded others.

Dr. May's quick response to Sean's thoughts displayed her growing engagement with his perspective. It confirmed their partnership, their exchange of ideas evolving into a genuine collaboration. The contrast between Sean's speculative but strategic thinking and Dr. May's structured approach yielded a fascinating blend of methods, each having its place in their joint exploration.

Sean's hope that excess sodium might be the key to unlocking the mystery added an element of luck to the situation. He acknowledged the unpredictability that often coloured medical cases. He wasn't proposing a specific solution; he was suggesting an avenue to explore, a way to capitalize on the body's natural processes.

For Dr. May, this marked a turning point—a moment when Sean's unconventional approach had won her over. Despite her initial skepticism and irritation, his unique way of thinking had sparked curiosity within her. The unspoken acknowledgment of his impressive insight hinted at a growing respect that transcended their initial clash of personalities.

In this evolving dynamic, their partnership was becoming

more than just an arrangement to solve cases. It was an intersection of minds, a fusion of perspectives that promised new ways of approaching medicine. As their interaction drew to a close, both seemed to recognize that this unlikely partnership might just be the catalyst for discoveries they hadn't even imagined.

The transformation in their working relationship was now undeniable. Dr. May's skepticism had evolved into appreciation, and Sean's eccentricity proved to have a method behind it. As Sean moved on to the third case, there was an evident synchronization between their interactions. Dr. May stood ready to record Sean's insights, her earlier irritation replaced with anticipation.

Sean's rapid-fire recommendations left Dr. May astounded. His ability to piece together seemingly unrelated information and derive actionable solutions was a testament to his keen analytical mind. The patient's profile of being a law student with arrhythmias was all Sean had to work with. Yet, he had managed to extract a comprehensive strategy to address the issue.

He told her to tell the patient to stop taking the ADHD medication to help her study. "Tell her to rehydrate with at least two litres of water daily and exercise thirty minutes daily for at least two weeks after leaving here. Review her in two weeks and run an ECG." Sean added.

Dr. May was amazed because all she had told Sean about this patient was that she was a law student with arrhythmias.

She tried to think about it herself but couldn't make sense of it until Sean explained, "Any arrhythmia in a young female studying law. Mmm, how likely is that to be natural? Certain students studying certain programs and certain professionals are known to take medication to keep them awake for as long as possible. The work is typically too much for them; they either have little time or can't focus for too long. This makes them take anything that can help them stay awake. Coffee is ubiquitous but can only help for a few hours at most. Some use energy drinks, but most of these people find taking ADHD medication a better alternative. ADHD medication is notorious for causing arrhythmias. It's extremely rare for a young woman to be hospitalized for an arrhythmia from natural causes, so I just went with what's more common."

The way Sean painted a picture of a young woman struggling to keep up with the pressures of her studies, resorting to medication that inadvertently caused her heart issues, showcased his profound insight into the intricacies of human behaviour.

Dr. May found herself nodding in agreement and inwardly marvelling at Sean's capacity to connect the dots. It was as though he had unlocked a hidden layer of the patient's life just from a few seemingly innocuous details. The precision with which he articulated his reasoning left her in awe.

Dr. May smiled as she walked away from Sean, but he couldn't resist reminding her, "I like lamb chops and mashed potatoes. They go so well with red wine. I'm sure you'll figure something delicious for dessert."

Sean's playful yet astute mannerisms were becoming increasingly endearing, and even Dr. May's exaggerated gesture of disgust as she walked away was infused with a hint of amusement.

The evolution from initial friction to this synchronized partnership was a testament to the potential of collaboration, even in the face of clashing personalities.

As Dr. May disappeared from Sean's view, her lighthearted response lingered, symbolizing a newfound harmony neither could have predicted. It was an acknowledgment of their growing connection, an unspoken agreement that their alliance, however unconventional, was proving to be an effective means of tackling medical challenges.

The Danger Zone

On Sean's second day at AGH, a palpable transformation swept through the hospital corridors. The once prickly relationship with Dr. Gabehart seemed to have smoothed over, leaving behind a trail of newfound respect. A curious twist of fate revealed the undercurrents of camaraderie that could be born out of unlikely circumstances. In Sean's eyes, this was more than just a resolution of differences; it was a recognition of Dr. Gabehart's prowess, a discovery of her abilities that he held in high esteem.

For a young medical student, Sean's confidence in his intelligence was like a beacon, guiding him through the labyrinth of challenges. Yet, the encounter with Dr. Gabehart served as a humbling reminder that wisdom and experience often outweigh sheer intellect. He found a mentor in her whose insights and command transcended his initial perceptions. The realization that he was offered a front-row seat to her expertise was a privilege he couldn't overlook.

Adding responsibilities to his already extended schedule didn't deter Sean; instead, it invigorated him. It was as though life had presented him with an intricate puzzle, and he revelled in the challenge of solving it. The opportunity to delve deeper into patient care and actively engage with their diagnoses and treatments was a prospect that thrilled him. It was a chance to put his knowledge into practice to bridge the gap between theory and application.

Moreover, Sean understood the implicit trust that Dr. Gabehart had placed in him. Being called upon as a consultant in Dr. May's cases was a mark of recognition that couldn't be taken lightly. It was a testament to his analytical insight and an affirmation of his potential to contribute meaningfully to patient care. The gravity of this responsibility wasn't lost on him, and he embraced it fervently.

While others might view these new challenges as burdens to bear, Sean saw them as stepping stones on the path of growth. He subscribed to the notion that the most significant lessons lie in facing adversity head-on. Just as a ship finds its strength amidst the storm, Sean thrived under pressure. Challenges weren't deterrents but opportunities to showcase his mettle, unravel the mysteries of complex cases, and offer tangible solutions.

In this intricate dance of professional dynamics, Sean's approach was like a knight charging into battle, armed with intelligence and a fearless heart. The energy that emanated from his enthusiasm was infectious, and it was clear that he relished every moment of this unexpected journey.

Sean's steps were light but purposeful as the sun cast its golden glow over the hospital. His interactions with Dr. Gabehart and Dr. May had evolved from tense to dynamic, from confrontational to collaborative. This was a testament to his adaptability, a reminder that bridges can be built where walls once stood. For Sean, this wasn't just another day in the hospital; it was a canvas upon which he painted his aspirations, which was beginning to reflect a picture of achievement and growth.

As the day advanced, Dr. May's perception underwent a subtle transformation. From initial skepticism and a deep-seated antipathy, her sentiments toward Sean were in a state of transition.

Though unconventional and testing her patience, the morning exchange revealed layers to Sean that she hadn't anticipated. Gradually, the once icy walls showed cracks, allowing a glimpse of something akin to respect.

The fact that Dr. Gabehart had appointed Sean as a consultant on her cases had initially baffled Dr. May. She regarded it as a peculiar twist of fate, almost like someone had thrown a curveball into her meticulously orchestrated routine. But as the hours unfolded, Sean proved to be more than an unwelcome intrusion; he was an unexpected asset. While different from her own, his approach to medicine held a certain validity that couldn't be ignored. It was as if he added a touch of colour to the canvas of her clinical world, revealing new hues she hadn't considered.

Sean's demeanour, characterized by a lightness of spirit and ease in dealing with the hospital's challenges, starkly contrasted with her seriousness. He navigated through complexities with an almost casual grace, a trait that intrigued her. His contributions might have seemed relatively modest in the grand scheme of the medical universe, but the ripples of his interactions extended beyond simple physiological mechanisms. He undeniably impacted those around him, an influence that defied conventional logic.

As the hours ticked away, Sean's role expanded further, his next assignment beckoning him with a hint of intrigue. The news of Mr. Gladstone's successful surgery and ongoing recovery propelled Sean to the patient's bedside. It was a testament to his commitment, his desire not only to diagnose and treat but also to be present in the healing process.

The interaction with Mr. Gladstone wasn't just a perfunctory visit; it was a moment of connection that illustrated Sean's dedication to the human side of medicine. He didn't just see a case or a condition; he saw a person, a life. At that moment, the convergence of compassion and expertise painted a picture of medicine at its most holistic.

Dr. May watched from a distance, her initial reservations giving way to a begrudging acknowledgment. Sean's methods were unconventional, and his approach often defied the norms she held dear. Yet, as she observed his genuine concern and willingness to engage on a human level, she realized that sometimes there was more to medicine than clinical precision.

The day, still pregnant with possibilities, stretched ahead of Sean. The hospital corridors echoed with the footsteps of doctors, nurses, and the hum of machines, each contributing their verse to the symphony of healthcare. Once an unlikely protagonist, Sean was now a vibrant note in this symphony, playing his part in ways that transcended the realms of mere diagnosis and treatment.

Mr. Gladstone, an enigmatic figure of wealth and fierce honesty, was hardly the embodiment of approachability. His words were as brash as they were unfiltered, a trait that he wielded with little regard for the hierarchy or status of those who stood before him.

Some might have hastily labelled him as a man possessed by an inflated sense of power due to his riches, his verbal barbs perceived as a way to assert dominion. Yet, even this superficial assessment crumbled under scrutiny, for there were instances where he unleashed his verbal ire upon those of mightier station while offering unanticipated respect to those burdened by youth or scanty means. To Mr. Gladstone, authenticity was paramount.

A character so vividly real, he was a study in contradictions. His tongue's unchecked freedom of expression often portrayed him as fussy. His presence electrified the air with a certain unpredictability, a sense that one was tiptoeing across an emotional minefield. Depending on the wind of his ever-shifting mood, conversations with him could transform into verbal sparring or sail through calmer waters.

Much like the weathered lines etched on his face, his life story bore witness to a tapestry of experiences that had shaped his disposition. To dismiss his demeanour as mere arrogance or self-importance would be to overlook the more nuanced truths beneath the surface. For beyond his gruff exterior lay an unwavering belief in speaking one's mind, unburdened by the societal filters that often shroud authenticity.

A man who did not yield to the conventions of politeness simply for the sake of societal appeasement, he inhabited a realm where raw honesty was both a sword and a shield. His sharp words could sting, yet they were also a testament to a life lived on his terms, untamed by the norms that seek to curtail the potency of human expression.

As Sean approached Mr. Gladstone's bedside, he knew he was entering a territory where diplomacy would often clash with candour. Yet, armed with his sense of authenticity, Sean met Mr. Gladstone's gaze, ready to listen, engage, and navigate the turbulent waters of truth ahead. In medicine, as in life, every interaction holds the potential for revelation, and every patient is a chapter in the story of human existence.

As Sean stepped into Mr. Gladstone's room, a radiant transformation swept across the old man's face, akin to the pure joy of a child unwrapping Christmas presents beneath the twinkling tree lights. It was a beacon of gratitude, a beacon that Sean had become in this hospital room.

In the shadows of illness and uncertainty, Mr. Gladstone

had found a glimmer of hope. Amidst the sterile hospital walls that had witnessed his trials, Sean's presence was a reminder that there was still room for optimism. His gratitude was palpable, a heartfelt embrace of this unexpected lifeline.

His eyes, usually gleaming with sharp wit, now glistened with tears seeking release. The man who often wielded his words like a double-edged sword struggled to find them in this moment. Yet, his emotions surged so intensely that the dam of restraint wobbled on the edge of breaking.

Sean, ever the grounded and light-hearted presence, deftly managed the situation. In his characteristic blend of humour and empathy, he reminded Mr. Gladstone about the recent surgery and cautioned him lightheartedly against overexertion. Sean's remark was a lifeline back to the present, an acknowledgment that while gratitude was coursing through the room, care still needed to be taken.

Sean bridged the gap between doctor and patient with a handshake that spoke volumes. Mr. Gladstone's firm grip conveyed both his appreciation and the fragile connection that had been forged between them. As that grip lingered, it was a testament to the profound impact of this encounter.

Tears welled in Mr. Gladstone's eyes as though his gratitude was so immense that mere words struggled to contain it. A man who had often been seen as unyielding, whose words were barbs that repelled, was now facing his vulnerability with raw honesty. The layers of pride, the armour of his stature, were peeled away in this private moment of human connection.

Sean's humility was a balm to the situation. He had unravelled the complexities of patients and conditions and strategized solutions amidst uncertainty, but now he was willingly embracing uncertainty. His modesty was a bridge between two souls, a testament to the imperfections and fragilities that unite us all.

"No worries, Mr. Gladstone." Sean's words were as simple as they were profound. They were a humble recognition that even the most knowledgeable can stumble. They acknowledged that medicine was as much about navigating unknowns as it was about harnessing knowledge. They embodied humility in the face of human complexity, a quality now the cornerstone of Sean's interaction with patients.

At that moment, as gratitude and humility danced in the room, a powerful connection was forged between these two individuals. They stood at the crossroads of humanity, stripped of titles and pretenses, united by the raw reality of life's intricacies. As Sean and Mr. Gladstone shared that space, they exemplified the essence of what it meant to be both healer and healed, a testament to the intricate dance of compassion and vulnerability woven into the fabric of medicine.

Miracles, those ethereal and elusive moments that hover between faith and reality, are the stuff of legends, whispered prayers, and tales passed down through generations. They are the sparks of hope that light the darkness, the threads connecting the mundane with the extraordinary. Within the walls of a hospital room, amidst the hum of machines and the scent of sterilization, Mr. Gladstone felt he had been granted a miracle of his own.

In Sean, he saw not just a medical student but an unexpected agent of providence. It was as if the intricate threads of fate had woven their paths together, guiding Sean to this clerkship, nudging him to disregard protocols, and bestowing upon him the insight that had eluded seasoned practitioners. It was the kind of chance encounter that books were written about, the type of twist that movies thrived on.

Mr. Gladstone acknowledged Sean's role in this cosmic ballet with awe and gratitude. He marvelled at the sequence of events that had led to this moment, where Sean's intervention had saved him from the precipice of uncertainty. It was a sensation akin to witnessing a shooting star streak across the night sky - brief, brilliant, and almost surreal.

Yet, their exchange bore a candid, almost familial familiarity in this miraculous encounter. As Sean addressed him with the respectful honorific "Mr. Gladstone," he extended an invitation, one that sought to bridge the gap between formality and camaraderie. "Call me Oscar, kid," he insisted, as if using first names could solidify their bond.

Mr. Gladstone's gratitude flowed unrestrained, carrying the weight of a lifetime's experiences. He was astounded by Sean's audacity in challenging norms and his unyielding pursuit of what he knew to be right. Sean's risks were no secret, and the magnitude of those risks was not lost on Mr. Gladstone. For in those bold actions, Mr. Gladstone recognized a spirit kindred to his own - a spirit that defied convention for the sake of what was just and right.

He added, "You call what you did for me a fluke, but the fluke worked for me, and I have you to thank. I've seen how you work. You're a smart kid, and even Dr. Gorgeous knows that. She may not admit that, but I saw it in her eyes after you left. You really impressed her."

"You call her Dr. Gorgeous?" Sean inquired.

"A few friends around the hospital told me you started it.

I'm just going with the flow. Kid, don't crush on your boss because this one can ruin your life." Mr. Gladstone said, laughing out loud.

Mr. Gladstone's laughter rang through the room, an echo of camaraderie shared between two souls who had connected across generations and titles. The moniker "Dr. Gorgeous" was a playful nod to Sean's audacity, a testament to the ripple effect his presence had caused. It was a reminder that even in medicine, where protocols and professionalism reigned, human connections and the threads of humour were essential components.

As their laughter subsided, Sean met Mr. Gladstone's gaze with an understanding that transcended words. The bond forged in this room was more than doctor and patient; it was a meeting of minds, a symphony of gratitude, and a dance of resilience. In that room, amidst the complexities of illness and the fragility of life, Sean and Mr. Gladstone had become part of each other's stories. In the grand tapestry of existence, their encounter was a brushstroke of light, a testament to the possibility of miracles woven into the fabric of everyday life.

Amid the hospital's controlled chaos, a brief silence enveloped the room as Sean took stock of the situation. The air seemed to hold its breath as if anticipating the next move in this intricate dance of conversation. Sean's gaze wandered, analyzing the dynamics that had brought them together, the unspoken nuances that often spoke volumes.

In this contemplative pause, Sean's observation drew forth an ironic truth. Mr. Gladstone, a man known for walking the tightrope between audacity and reality, found himself on the receiving end of advice he often doled out. A wry grin tugged at the corners of Mr. Gladstone's lips, a recognition that life's ironies often held a mirror to our actions.

He told Mr. Gladstone that he seemed like someone who enjoyed living on the edge. It was ironic that someone like that would tell him to take it easy on Dr. Gabehart.

Mr. Gladstone couldn't help but chuckle in response. It was a chuckle that carried a lifetime of experiences, a tapestry woven with the threads of daring choices and fearless living. He took a moment to consider the implications of his advice. This momentary introspection revealed the paradoxes of human nature.

In a gesture epitomizing his spirit, Mr. Gladstone laid down a challenge that radiated extravagance and audacity. The offer was as rare as the watch he described - a symbol of uniqueness, exclusivity, and worth beyond measure. He proposed a wager that was both lighthearted and remarkable, one that encompassed the playful dance of human connections.

Mr. Gladstone thought about it briefly and said to Sean, "Well, you're certainly right about me living my life on the edge, so let's make it interesting—score with Dr. Gorgeous, and I'll give you my Rolex. Only twenty of them were ever made, and it's worth millions if you try to sell it in today's market. I love this watch like my kid, but if you score, I'll gladly hand it over to you."

Sean's response was swift, a hearty laughter that spoke of his innate character, "As enticing as that is, I'll pass. How about this? You get out of post-op, and I'll sneak you out so we can split a nurse?"

Their laughter rippled through the room, an orchestra of camaraderie echoing off sterile walls. In that lightness of being, the unexpected visitor—a nurse—entered the scene as if orchestrated by fate to punctuate the levity with a touch of reality. The comical timing drew their laughter even louder, a shared amusement transcending patient and visitor's boundaries.

As the nurse completed her duties and exited the stage as quietly as she had entered, Sean and Mr. Gladstone exchanged a glance, eyes alight with glee. In that fleeting connection, they found a shared bond, a camaraderie born from medical necessity and the sheer joy of life's absurdities.

Mr. Gladstone smiled at Sean and said, "Check if she likes fast cars, planes, or expensive dinners."

Sean laughed and responded, "I think you're feeling much better. Get out of here, and I'll hook you up. For now, I'll put in a good word for you with the nurse."

Mr. Gladstone's smile held a twinkle, an acknowledgement of the whimsy of the moment. He praised Sean's sporting spirit, readiness to engage in the dance of conversation, and genuine gratitude for the assistance and presence Sean had brought into his life. Amidst hospital beds and monitors, they had forged a connection that was as genuine as it was unexpected, a reminder that even in the face of uncertainty, laughter and shared moments could be the most potent medicine.

The atmosphere in the room shifted. A heavy realization replaced the levity that had danced between them. Sean's eyebrows furrowed in concern as he listened to Mr. Gladstone's words, his features reflecting a mixture of empathy and alarm. It was as if the weight of those words had cast a shadow over the room, dimming the light-heartedness that had filled the space just moments ago.

Sean noticed that Mr. Gladstone was squirming uncomfortably in his bed, which had not occurred since he entered the room. Sean attempted to assist Mr. Gladstone in finding a comfortable position to rest, but despite his efforts, nothing seemed to alleviate Mr. Gladstone's discomfort.

Sean said to him, "I've noticed since the first time I saw you that you seem to squinch quite often as if you're in some sort of pain. I didn't think much of it then, but as the drugs from surgery start wearing off, I can see it coming back. What's up, dude? What are you not telling anyone?"

Mr. Gladstone smiled in pain as he confessed, "I knew yesterday wasn't a fluke. Nice observation, doc. I've had back pain for a couple of months. I didn't say much about it because I thought Dr. May had no idea what she was doing. I was beginning to feel like a guinea pig and had lost all hope, so I got a DNR and was praying for the pain to get worse so that I could take something strong to end my miserable life."

Mr. Gladstone's confession revealed a depth of pain that transcended the physical discomfort he had been experiencing. It resonated with emotional struggle, a battle fought silently and inwardly. Sean's mind raced to grasp the gravity of the situation. He had walked into the room, perhaps expecting a routine check-in, but he now found himself face-to-face with the very human complexity that lay beneath the surface.

As Sean absorbed the weight of Mr. Gladstone's confession, he was reminded of the intricate tapestry that made up the lives of the people he encountered in the hospital. Behind every medical chart, diagnosis, and procedure were stories of joy, sorrow, resilience, and vulnerability. Here, at this moment, Mr. Gladstone had bared a part of his own story that had remained hidden until now.

Sean's training had taught him to heal physical ailments, but in this instant, he recognized that healing transcended the physical. It was about connecting with the individual, understanding the emotional landscape, and offering support beyond medication and treatment.

At that moment, Sean's role transformed from that of a medical observer to that of a compassionate confidant. He realized that the power of his position extended beyond diagnoses and recommendations into the realm of genuine human connection. As they navigated this conversation, Sean understood that his ability to listen and empathize truly was as crucial as his medical intellect.

Clouded by pain and relief, Mr. Gladstone's eyes met Sean's gaze. It was a connection forged in vulnerability, a recognition that he had also found a glimmer of hope in sharing his pain. Once heavy with the weight of unspoken suffering, the room now held the promise of healing and understanding.

Sean's internal struggle was evident in his expression as he grappled with the weight of Mr. Gladstone's words. He now had to navigate a delicate balance between honesty and respecting protocol. He understood that Mr. Gladstone's desperate plea for truth was rooted in his yearning for genuine connection and a lifeline amidst his pain.

"Are you still thinking about offing yourself?" Sean asked.

"You seem to know what you're doing, so let's wait and see. So, as my new doctor, what do you think of my case now that you know pretty much everything?" Mr. Gladstone responded.

After a moment of introspection, Sean's gaze met Mr. Gladstone's with a mixture of sincerity and compassion. He knew he couldn't simply dismiss the gravity of the situation or offer an immediate solution. But he also recognized the power of acknowledging the truth, even when it was uncomfortable.

Sean was hesitant to speak up as he didn't want to go against Dr. Gabehart's warning to refrain from going over doctors with his medical opinions. When Mr. Gladstone pushed for an answer, Sean explained that it was a complex matter and that he needed to consult with Dr. Gabehart before engaging in this conversation further. Sean promised to get back to him once he had spoken to the doctor.

Mr. Gladstone's eyes held a mixture of appreciation and apprehension. Sean's response wasn't what he had hoped for—perhaps he had wished for an instant solution or a clear path out of his anguish. Yet, Sean's words conveyed a genuine intention to be present for him and navigate this challenging territory with care and responsibility.

Mr. Gladstone pled with Sean to be honest with him because his unconventional antics from the previous day were what had given him hope. He also joked he was looking forward to splitting a nurse with Sean, so no matter how bad things got, he wasn't crazy enough to give that up. The look of desperation in Mr. Gladstone's eyes made Sean think about being honest with him on the spot.

The room was solemnly silent, the weight of their conversation hanging in the air. Sean's commitment to his well-being, willingness to engage in difficult conversations, and recognition of the power of collaboration profoundly impacted Mr. Gladstone's perspective.

Sean ultimately folded and told Mr. Gladstone that the back pain was likely the lung cancer that had spread to his backbone. He also explained that this pain presented the worst outcome for his case. Sean tried to be optimistic, but the damage had already been done. He had just done precisely what Dr. Gabehart had told him not to do.

The room seemed to hold its breath as the two men confronted the weight of the diagnosis that had just been revealed. The words hung in the air, a heavy cloud of reality that had settled over the room. Sean's heart raced, and he couldn't help but feel the weight of his role in delivering this news.

Finally, Mr. Gladstone's voice broke the silence, filled with a mix of resignation and a trace of bitterness. "Lung cancer... that's a hell of a way to go, huh?" His tone was laced with dark humour, a defence mechanism against the gravity of the situation.

Sean's heart ached as he watched Mr. Gladstone grapple with the reality before him. He could see the tears that threatened to spill from his eyes, the vulnerability he had shared with Sean in their conversation a few moments ago. Sean knew he had to tread carefully to offer support without overstepping his bounds.

"O.G., I wish I had better news to share. Cancer is a formidable opponent, but medical advancements have allowed many people to face it head-on with treatments that can improve quality of life and even extend survival. I can assure you that we're here to support you every step of the way," Sean said, his voice gentle yet resolute.

Mr. Gladstone shifted his gaze from the ceiling to Sean, his eyes brimming with unshed tears. "You're a good kid, you know that?" he said, his voice cracking slightly. You're dealing with an old man's demons, and I appreciate your honesty. Maybe it's time I face what's coming. I just hope it won't be too painful."

Sean's heart clenched at the vulnerability in Mr. Gladstone's words and tone. Here was a man who had faced life head-on, who had built walls of bravado around himself, yet those walls were crumbling at this moment. Sean could feel the immense weight of his responsibility, not just as a medical student but as a human being entrusted with another's most profound fears and vulnerabilities.

"I'm here for you, O.G.," Sean said softly, his voice filled with empathy. We'll work together to ensure you're comfortable and explore all available options. You're not alone in this."

Mr. Gladstone nodded, his eyes finally releasing the tears he had been holding back. At that moment, Sean knew that their conversation had transcended the realm of medicine; it had become a testament to the power of human connection, empathy, and the profound impact that genuine compassion could have on a person's journey through pain and uncertainty.

Mr. Gladstone asked Sean, "So how much do I have?"

Sean had inadvertently given Mr. Gladstone a fatal prognosis, and now Mr. Gladstone was seeking clarity on his life expectancy. Sean was unprepared for this request and showed visible fear in his eyes, resembling a vulnerable puppy being stalked by a predator.

Mr. Gladstone believed that this fear had a significant underlying cause, perhaps the previous day's events, which could cause irreparable damage to Sean's medical career if repeated after receiving a severe warning from a superior. As a result, Mr. Gladstone approached Sean not as a professional but as a friend in an attempt to ease his mind and persuade him to share the truth.

However, Sean could only respond with uncertainty, "I really shouldn't be doing this. I've been warned."

The weight of the situation bore down on him, a heavy burden he hadn't anticipated when he first entered the room.

Sensing Sean's internal turmoil, Mr. Gladstone changed his

approach. He could see that he was walking a fine line between seeking information and respecting Sean's professional boundaries. With a sigh, he leaned back against the pillows, his gaze fixed on the ceiling, lost in thought.

"You know, Sean, sometimes doctors are like fortune tellers, predicting our future in terms of health. But we're all heading toward the same destination; it's just that some of us might be taking different routes," Mr. Gladstone mused, his voice full of sadness and acceptance.

Sean's gaze shifted to Mr. Gladstone, whose features reflected a mix of empathy and apology. He was grappling with the decision before him, the ethical dilemma of revealing information beyond his capacity and duty as a medical student. Mr. Gladstone's analogy struck a chord within him, reminding him that life's uncertainties were woven into the fabric of existence.

"You're right, Mr. Gladstone," Sean finally said, his voice tinged with regret. "We're all on a journey with an uncertain end. I wish I could give you a clear answer, but the truth is, even in the world of medicine, there are limits to what we can predict."

Mr. Gladstone knew that Sean understood something that could put his mind at ease, and he also knew there was something substantial holding Sean back. Staring at the ceiling, he said to Sean, "This's the best news I've heard since I got here. Everything about my back pain is making sense now. Do you know the feeling of being helpless and not knowing what's wrong with you?" He wiped his tears as he sobbed softly. "I was counting on the doctors here to figure it out, but it wasn't until you came along that it happened."

Sean listened carefully, his heart heavy with the weight of Mr. Gladstone's words. He realized that beyond the medical complexities and ethical dilemmas, there was a human story of fear, vulnerability, and the desperate search for control.

He continued, "I was living in fear every day, wondering if someone would make a mistake that would end my life, and sometimes I'll go to bed praying that I never wake up. The DNR wasn't about giving up on life. I'm not suicidal and have never been, but I was tired of feeling like an experiment. Sometimes, when you feel like you're in a corner and can't get out, you look for something, anything to control. The only thing I felt I had control over was my fate, so I signed a DNR."

"I can only imagine how overwhelming that must have felt, O.G.," Sean responded softly. "Feeling like you're at the mercy of circumstances, like you're just a puzzle piece that no one can figure out. Understandably, you would want some semblance of control, some way to shape your path."

Mr. Gladstone's eyes held a mix of gratitude and sadness. "You know, life is like a river. Sometimes, it flows smoothly; other times, it crashes against rocks, carving out unexpected turns. But there's something about facing those rough patches head-on that can change the course of the journey."

Sean nodded, absorbing Mr. Gladstone's analogy. "Sometimes, even in the face of uncertainty, there's value in simply being present and navigating those twists and turns."

The continued pleading for an answer from Mr. Gladstone finally wore Sean down.

Sean explained, "You've been honest with me since we started talking, and I think I owe you the same now. The heart problem was there, but it was caused by lung cancer. Cancer caused an increase of calcium in your blood, and the excess calcium started depositing on your heart valves. Eventually, your heart valves were having a hard time fully opening due to the calcium buildup. The back problem could've been seen earlier, but you were being treated by cardiologists who only see nothing but matters of the heart. Your back pain was first attributed to needing a valve replacement, and I could've made that mistake. Try not to be too hard on Dr. May. Doctors always make mistakes, but you should appreciate and trust those doctors who are willing to admit and correct their mistakes. You're better off with such a doctor than a doctor who'd convince you they are right and send you home to die in your bed with a horde of prescriptions. Medicine is a science practiced in an art form. I hope you can forgive Dr. May and Dr. Gabehart for the mistakes they made until yesterday."

Mr. Gladstone absorbed Sean's words with a heavy heart. The truth he had sought was now laid bare before him, unfiltered and stark. His thoughts seemed to echo in the room, mingling with the weight of the news. Sean watched as Mr. Gladstone's expression shifted from curiosity to acceptance to a sense of impending choices.

There was a moment of silence. Sean was still trying to figure out what he was doing and if he was even supposed to be doing it. A part of him reminded him that he had promised Dr. Gabehart that he wouldn't, but another part told him to go ahead and be honest with Mr. Gladstone because he was sincerely asking for the truth.

When Mr. Gladstone asked, "So, what now?"

Sean replied, "Nothing much can be done about your back pain, but we can medicate it so you don't live in pain. Dr. May will refer you to an oncologist to start you on cancer treatment, but that's just delaying the inevitable."

Mr. Gladstone insisted on knowing how much time he had.

Sean delayed the response long enough but finally caved in, "If the pain and cancer are properly managed, maybe a year or two. If not, you will end your own life because of the back pain in a few months. The treatment is no picnic either. If the cancer hadn't spread like this, there'd be a better chance for the treatment to work."

Things seemed to only get darker for Mr. Gladstone, but in Sean's defence, he had been asked to be honest and sincere. He was doing just that.

"So, you're saying the treatment is unlikely going to make a difference, yet it's also going to make me miserable?" Mr. Gladstone asked.

"Unfortunately," Sean replied.

There was another moment of silence as Mr. Gladstone processed everything. His mood seemed to have changed as he pivoted on the topic, "Understood. So, what are you going to do with Dr. Gorgeous? At least take a shot and fail like a man."

The sudden change in the tone and conversation alarmed Sean, but he let it play out. Sean told him he was crazy for insisting on this bet, and he wasn't much of a gambler, especially with sexually assaulting his boss, who could ruin his career.

Sean teased him that if it weren't for his current state of health, Mr. Gladstone would likely have taken the shot himself. Mr. Gladstone didn't deny he'd make such an effort and told Sean it was his nature to spice things up every chance he got. They both laughed as they shook hands, acknowledging the gravity of the conservation they just had.

The tension in the room seemed to dissipate with their laughter. Sean felt a sense of relief as he saw Mr. Gladstone's mood lighten, even if just momentarily. It was a reminder that amidst the gravity of illness and the weight of difficult conversations, moments of levity could serve as a lifeline, a way to navigate the intricacies of human emotions.

Another moment of silence passed, and Sean wasn't sure if he should leave Mr. Gladstone alone because he wasn't sure of his state of mind. He asked him if he was okay, and Mr. Gladstone replied he'd be fine. He had been given a tough pill to swallow, and a lethal one for that matter.

To keep things on a lighter note, Sean told Mr. Gladstone that the nurse who had entered the room earlier was his date for the night, so there was no chance that Mr. Gladstone would take a shot at her. Sean thought this was a real opportunity to change the conversation from talking about death to something meaningless, and it worked because Mr. Gladstone responded, "Ask if she has a friend."

Sean promised, and they both laughed.

From difficult conversations to shared laughter, from confronting the realities of mortality to finding solace in connection, Sean realized that his journey in medicine was as much about discovering the depths of human experience as it was about treating illnesses.

Mr. Gladstone's curiosity was piqued by Sean's story about the bet with Dr. May. He found himself intrigued by the dynamics of their interactions and the challenges they presented to each other. As Sean continued to share the details of the bet, Mr. Gladstone's amusement grew.

"Ah, the good ol' 'win her over with medical expertise' tactic," Mr. Gladstone chuckled. "That's a clever way to get on her good side, I suppose. But you're walking on thin ice, my friend. A bet involving doctors, assessments, and the mighty Dr. Gorgeous? Sounds like a recipe for trouble."

Sean laughed along, acknowledging the truth in Mr. Gladstone's words. "You're not wrong. It's definitely been an interesting experience. Dr. May is... well, let's just say she's not the easiest person to win over. But hey, if it works out, maybe I'll have her presenting me with a fancy dinner."

Mr. Gladstone raised an eyebrow, his eyes twinkling mischievously. "So, you're not just here to save lives, huh? You've got some personal stakes in this game."

Sean shrugged with a grin. "I'm just trying to keep things interesting, you know? And I must admit, it's been quite the ride so far."

Mr. Gladstone nodded in agreement. "Life can get dull sometimes, especially when you're stuck in a hospital bed. Anything that adds a bit of spice is a welcome distraction."

As they chatted, Sean realized that Mr. Gladstone's perspective on life had shifted remarkably in just a short amount of time. Despite the challenging news he had received earlier, Mr. Gladstone was embracing the opportunity to find joy and connection in unexpected places.

"You know, Sean, you've managed to turn what could've been a bleak day into something almost enjoyable," Mr. Gladstone remarked. "I suppose that's a gift, bringing a little light into someone's life even when things look dark."

Sean smiled, touched by Mr. Gladstone's words. "I appreciate that. And you've also brought a bit of light into my day, O.G. It's not every day I get to share laughs and bets with a patient."

Their conversation continued, seamlessly shifting from one topic to another as if they had known each other for much longer than a day. As they exchanged stories and jokes, Sean realized that sometimes, the most unexpected connections were the ones that held the most genuine moments of human connection. In a hospital filled with illness and uncertainty, those moments were like beacons of hope, guiding the way through the challenges ahead.

Mr. Gladstone told Sean, "You know your stuff. I don't know how you do it, but I have my money on you. You see beyond what everyone else sees. You see what even the patient doesn't see."

Mr Gladstone shifted his position in bed and continued, "Look up Johari's window. It's the idea that there are some things about ourselves that everyone knows - the open; those things that are known to us but not others - the hidden; the things we don't know but are transparent to everyone else - the blind; and then what we don't know about ourselves, and others don't know either - the unknown. Any well-trained psychologist can see the open, blind, and maybe the hidden if they're really good. You, my friend, see the open, blind, and hidden without much trouble, and you also try to figure out the unknown. You're a good student of human behaviour and that's the gift that makes you who you are."

Sean smirked, "I don't mean to be modest, but sometimes I don't think I know what I'm doing."

"Trust your mind, and always remember Johari's window when you meet your patients. I'm a businessman, and I like to gamble. One thing I've learned on my own is to learn to gather and organize my thoughts. No matter how smart you can be, your ideas could be worthless if you can't organize your thoughts. You think you're wrong sometimes because you haven't learned to organize your thought process," Mr. Gladstone explained.

Sean listened attentively as Mr. Gladstone shared his wisdom, his words resonating deeply with him. The analogy of Johari's window struck a chord, perfectly encapsulating the layers of understanding in human interaction. Mr. Gladstone's insights were like a beacon of guidance, illuminating the path to better understanding his patients and himself.

"I appreciate that perspective, O.G. Johari's window... It's a powerful concept, and you're right. Sometimes, understanding the unknown about ourselves and others can make all the difference," Sean mused.

Mr. Gladstone leaned back against his pillows, his gaze thoughtful. "You're a young man with a lot of potential, Sean. I've met my fair share of doctors, and I can tell when someone's got that extra spark. It's not just about medical knowledge; it's about how you approach people, listen, and observe."

Sean nodded, feeling a mix of gratitude and humility. "Thank you for your kind words, O.G. It means a lot coming from someone like you."

Mr. Gladstone waved a dismissive hand. "Ah, don't let my grumpy exterior fool you. Underneath it all, I've got a soft spot for people who go against the tide. Remember, success in life is often about seeing what others miss and having the courage to act on it. You've already shown that courage with Dr. Gabehart, and who knows what other doors it might open for you."

As their conversation continued, Sean found himself learning from Mr. Gladstone's insights and feeling a genuine connection with the man. It was remarkable how a chance encounter had turned into a meaningful exchange of thoughts and experiences.

Sean tried explaining to Mr. Gladstone that he didn't know how to organize his thoughts. Ideas seemed to come so fast that sometimes he thought he didn't have enough time to organize them.

"This's Dr. May's case, right?" Mr. Gladstone asked.

Sean responded, "Yes."

Mr. Gladstone explained that teaching was the best way to learn. Whether Sean would win his bet or not, it was in his best interest to sit down with Dr. May and go over his thought process from the moment she said the first thing about the patient until he figured out everything about the patient.

Sean took his thought process for granted and had never had it explained like this. Somehow, it made sense because it reminded him of his earlier conversation with Dr. Gabehart when he explained how he figured out the cases from the previous day.

Listening to Mr. Gladstone's advice, Sean felt a mix of understanding and realization. His voice was clear as if he had unlocked a door to a new way of thinking. Sean hadn't fully embraced the notion that teaching was a way to learn before, yet it suddenly made perfect sense in the context of his own experiences and challenges.

"You're right, O.G.," Sean said, nodding thoughtfully.

"Teaching someone else forces you to break down your thought process and present it in a way that makes sense to them. It's like taking apart a complex puzzle and explaining how each piece fits."

Mr. Gladstone's eyes twinkled with approval. "Exactly. And by doing that, you not only help others understand, but you also deepen your understanding. It's a way to see your blind spots and refine your approach."

Sean's mind was racing with the implications of this newfound perspective.

"I've always been so focused on solving the puzzle that I've rarely taken the time to articulate how I arrived at the solution," Sean admitted. "But you're right; sharing that process could shed light on areas I might have missed or assumptions I made."

Mr. Gladstone leaned in, a sage-like demeanour settling upon him. "Remember, Sean, the best doctors constantly question themselves. They're the ones who never stop learning. Teaching is a way to question yourself and your knowledge. It's a way to refine your instincts."

As Sean absorbed Mr. Gladstone's wisdom, he realized that this advice wasn't just about medicine—it was a philosophy that could be applied to every facet of his life. It was about embracing challenges, facing uncertainties, and sharing experiences to grow as a person.

"Thanks, O.G.," Sean said sincerely. "You've given me a whole new perspective on learning and problem-solving."

Mr. Gladstone smiled, his eyes reflecting a lifetime of experience. "You're welcome, kid. Just remember, life is a series of puzzles waiting to be solved. And the best way to solve them is to teach others how to solve them too."

Since Dr. May needed help with many cases, Sean was told to express his thoughts out loud. Any kinks in his process would likely prompt Dr. May to ask questions, and his clarifications and answers would also clarify his own process.

After thinking about it briefly, Sean exclaimed, "You know what? You're right!"

That response brought Mr. Gladstone much joy. He smiled, looking at Sean jumping up from his seat like he had found a cure for a disease.

Mr. Gladstone played it cool, "Of course I'm right. I didn't get rich by being dumb."

They laughed as Sean explained to Mr. Gladstone, "I was talking to Dr. Gorgeous in the morning, and she showed me this amazing way of telling you a lot about any patient from reading their ECG alone. She read your ECG within minutes and identified some things I thought were random. She went through it and figured out in the end that it was you."

"Sounds like you already have a teacher. I know her, and she doesn't take nonsense from anyone, so cool it with her when you see her getting annoyed." Mr. Gladstone advised.

Sean chuckled at Mr. Gladstone's advice. "Don't worry, I've learned my lesson with her."

Mr. Gladstone leaned back in his bed, his eyes twinkling with amusement. "See? Teaching can come from unexpected places. You've got yourself a great mentor in Dr. Gorgeous."

Mr. Gladstone looked at Sean with a stern expression. "You're a smart kid, Sean. But remember, knowledge isn't just about what you learn; it's about how you apply it. The true power lies in taking what you've learned and using it to make a real difference in people's lives."

Sean and Mr. Gladstone were bonding with such joy that

they looked like two teenagers enjoying a new hobby. Through talking, they realized how much they were learning from each other and, maybe, how much they also needed each other.

Mr. Gladstone had the wisdom, and Sean had the intellect. This unlikely friendship between people decades apart in age could've been a first for Mr. Gladstone, but certainly not for Sean.

While talking and laughing, Mr. Gladstone told Sean the only thing missing was liquor and some music, but before Sean could respond, his phone rang.

It was Dr. Gabehart, and she didn't sound happy, "I know I said Dr. May was in charge, but why is she taking credit for your ideas?"

"She came up with them on her own. I don't think you give her enough credit. I think you're too hard on her." Sean tried to defend Dr. May.

Dr. Gabehart refuted the claim, saying, "I'm not that stupid. I could give her the law student and maybe the single mother, but do you expect me to believe that using phlebotomy to treat hypertension was her idea?"

Dr. Gabehart had spent much more time with Dr. May. Her suspicion of Dr. May's work had legitimate weight, and Sean knew he couldn't fight it. Fighting it would've only irritated Dr. Gabehart even more.

On the other hand, throwing Dr. May under the bus would likely cost him the trust he had just started building with her. Dr. Gabehart kept going on and on about how Sean was trying to take her for a fool, but Sean eventually folded, "Maybe I might've given her a few ideas and pointed her in the right direction. Come on, give her some credit."

Dr. Gabehart stopped yelling and listened to Sean, which calmed her as she responded, "She gave a compelling presentation, but I know her, and I know you, so I don't buy that they were her ideas. I was impressed, though. She was very detailed and very confident in her reasoning through her explanations. For the first time, I saw a fellow doctor, not just a subordinate. Stop doing her work, though. I know she has potential."

Dr. Gabehart hung up the phone as Sean took a huge sigh of relief. He wasn't worried about the conversation he just had with Mr. Gladstone anymore, so there was nothing negative on his mind to stop him from enjoying his day. He had to ruin someone's day out of spite, though. He called Dr. May.

"Dr. May speaking. How can I help you?" She answered her phone.

"So, you think I was never going to find out?" Sean asked.

She replied, "Oh my God, how did you know? Fine. What do you like to eat? I need to go shopping, so I can't do it tonight."

Sean wasn't in a rush, as he already had other plans for the evening. He told Dr. May not to worry or rush her shopping that day. He recommended she go shopping the next day because he knew she was having a busy day. They'd have dinner together either on Thursday or Friday.

It was a relief to have resolved things with Mr. Gladstone and smoothed over the situation with Dr. Gabehart. Now, he had dinner with Dr. May to look forward to. Day two at the hospital had indeed been eventful, but in unexpected ways, shaping Sean's experiences and relationships in ways he couldn't have predicted.

Dr. May was still annoyed by this whole arrangement, but since she had gotten into an agreement, she felt obligated to deliver. She told Sean she had to be honest with him that she was doing this under protest.

Unsurprisingly, Sean was still okay with it and told her he was coming over no matter what as he hung up the phone.

"Seems like another fluke. You still think you're right by chance alone?" Mr. Gladstone asked.

Sean replied, "I'll think about the Johari's window, and I need to have another chat with Dr. Gorgeous. And you owe me a Rolex."

Mr. Gladstone quickly stopped him, "Nope, Rolex is for a home run with Dr. Gorgeous. If I'm going to lose my Rolex, it better be something big and more challenging. I'm impressed by your date with Dr. May, but not Rolex impressed."

"Well, I had to try. I got to make a run and review some files. It's going to be a long day for me, but let me know if you need anything," Sean said as he walked out.

As Sean left Mr. Gladstone's room, he couldn't help but chuckle at the playful banter. Mr. Gladstone's presence had proven to be a surprising source of support and camaraderie on what could have been another challenging day. The hospital, with its complex cases and diverse personalities, was indeed a unique arena where relationships and interactions unfolded in ways that Sean had never experienced before.

As he reviewed patient files and prepared for the rest of the day, Sean's mind drifted back to the upcoming dinner with Dr. May. He wondered how the evening would unfold, considering her initial reluctance. He knew they had much to discuss about their unusual partnership and the cases they were collaborating on.

Sean also couldn't shake off his conversation with Mr. Gladstone about Johari's window. Although he was familiar with the concept, hearing it in the context of his interactions at the hospital made him realize the importance of self-awareness and open communication.

A Clash of Egos

A Thursday dawned upon AGH, casting its golden rays upon the bustling corridors and echoing through the stethoscopes of diligent doctors. The hospital seemed to have taken a deep breath, exhaling the tensions of the previous days and inhaling a sense of camaraderie. A renewed spirit permeated the air as if the hospital had caught wind of the approaching weekend and decided to indulge in a dance of optimism.

This transformative shift wasn't merely about the end of the workweek; it was a subtle acknowledgement that moments of respite needed to be embraced even amidst the seriousness of medical endeavours. The week's weariness took a back seat as laughter floated through the corridors and smiles adorned the faces of patients and staff alike. The atmosphere resonated with a song of unity, where doctors, nurses, and patients became harmonious notes in a symphony of shared humanity.

In this delicate ecosystem, Thursday acted as a bridge, uniting the past and the promised weekend with a sense of excitement that rippled across the hospital. Patients, too, felt the stirrings of anticipation, knowing that the coming days would bring a reprieve from hospital rooms and treatment schedules.

Some patients would spend a day or two with their families before continuing their treatment on Monday. Dr. Gabehart initiated this tradition by convincing her boss that the hospital environment was too gloomy for some patients, hindering their recovery. She explained that some patients required additional time in the hospital under close observation but also needed the opportunity to experience a semi-normal life. Though it was a challenging proposal, Dr. Gabehart convinced her boss and the idea was successful from the outset.

Some patients would go home for the weekend, weaving threads of connection with family and friends amidst the sterile hallways, before returning on Monday, fortified by these moments of human touch and affection.

This tradition of collective celebration was a testament to Dr. Gabehart's wisdom and insight into the human psyche. She understood that the hospital's environment, while essential for medical care, could also cast a shadow on the spirits of its occupants. The sombre hues of illness needed to be punctuated with splashes of joy and lightheartedness. As unwavering as an ancient oak, Dr. Gabehart's conviction had convinced even the most skeptical, breathing life into this tradition that now danced gracefully through AGH.

As the day unfolded, Sean couldn't help but be captivated by this rhythmic pulse of positivity. The hospital, often a realm of tension and uncertainty, was now bathed in the warm hues of camaraderie. This transformation was a reminder that even in the most challenging of environments, the human spirit had the resilience to adapt and flourish.

Sean's journey within AGH was no exception. He had navigated through its tangled halls, forging connections with unexpected allies like Mr. Gladstone, whose wisdom flowed like a hidden stream. Then there was Dr. May, a colleague who had started as a skeptic but was gradually becoming a partner in their shared pursuit of medical insights.

Dr. Gabehart's commitment to her patients' well-being extended beyond the confines of AGH's walls, reaching into their homes. Her dedication was a marvel, a testament to the kind of compassion that knew no bounds. While her on-call duties might have seemed extreme to some, they reflected her belief in her patients' holistic healing.

The notion that medical care could stretch beyond the hospital's thresholds was unconventional. Nevertheless, it was rooted in the profound understanding that health was not confined to the duration of a hospital stay. Dr. Gabehart's approach was a realization that true wellness encompassed the interplay of medical treatment, emotional support, and the comfort of familiar surroundings. In her eyes, patients were not merely medical cases but individuals with stories, families, and lives beyond the sterile hospital environment.

Nurses, too, infused with the same spirit of compassion, embraced this approach. Their voluntary efforts to prepare patients for their time away from the hospital were a poignant display of their commitment. The hospital corridors saw nurses meticulously setting up drips and ensuring the proper functioning of implanted devices. The change of bandages, a seemingly minor task, was a gesture that carried immense significance. It was a message to patients that their well-being was not a matter to be confined within the hospital's walls but was woven into the tapestry of their lives.

Then, there was Dr. Gabehart herself, the embodiment of this philosophy. Her weekends, usually considered a respite from work, were spent within the hospital's embrace. Her presence was a reassurance, a safety net cast over the patients as they ventured into the familiarity of their homes. Her unwavering commitment was both inspiring and humbling, a vivid reminder that medicine was not merely a profession but a calling.

The celebrations that washed over the hospital on Thursdays and Fridays weren't just a tradition but a tribute. Each smile, each shared moment of laughter, was a nod to Dr. Gabehart's tireless dedication. The hospital staff and patients understood the enormity of her sacrifice, and in return, they offered their collective appreciation.

As Sean navigated this environment, he found himself humbled by the depth of compassion that flowed through AGH. Here, the boundaries between doctor and patient, nurse and caregiver, blurred into insignificance. Healing transcended the confines of medical science and became a synergy of hearts and minds.

The celebrations were not just about the weekend to come; they were about human connection, a testament to the power of compassion, and a tribute to the unspoken sacrifices of those who chose to dedicate their lives to healing.

In the quiet hours before the bustle of the day enveloped the hospital, Sean found solace in the rhythm of his routine. Like a diligent guardian, he arrived ahead of time, his presence a testament to his commitment. The early morning light painted the corridors with a gentle glow, and the hushed whispers of the night shift's departure mingled with the soft hum of anticipation.

Patient files lay before him like a mosaic of lives, each unique and intricate, waiting to be deciphered. With a furrowed brow and a focused gaze, Sean delved into the details, mining for insights and patterns that could illuminate the path to better care. The quiet scribble of his pen on paper created a symphony of analysis, a dance of intellect weaving through the labyrinthine corridors of medical history.

Sean's presence among the hospital staff was as welcome as a cool breeze on a sweltering day. Nurses regarded him with warm smiles, appreciating the collaborative spirit he brought to their shared mission. The rapport he established with them reflected his genuine respect for their roles, understanding that their efforts were the threads that wove the fabric of patient care.

Amid his immersion, a gentle interruption would occasionally come in the form of Mother, a wise presence in his life. She knew the delicate balance between dedication and self-care, and her watchful eye could discern when Sean's determination was slipping into exhaustion. A few words from her, a suggestion to take a walk or indulge in a cup of her 'special tea,' were like soothing balms that mended the frayed edges of his focus.

Strolling down the hospital corridors was a ritual of rejuvenation. As his footsteps echoed through the quiet passages, Sean was enveloped in a sanctuary of healing. The vibrant mosaic of humanity—patients, families, and staff—etched its stories on the walls, a silent testament to the ebb and flow of life within these sacred halls.

With his senses rekindled, Sean would return to his mission, fortified by the gentle care and wisdom that Mother had bestowed upon him. His fingers would resume their dance across the keyboard, crafting recommendations that were more than just clinical directives; they were pathways to brighter tomorrows for those in need.

As the hours passed, the hospital gradually awoke from its slumber. Activity crescendoed, voices mingled, and the corridors that once held the morning hush pulsed with the energy of the day. Through it all, Sean continued his work, a quiet force amid the whirlwind, a beacon of dedication and compassion in healing.

The camaraderie between Sean and the nurses had transcended mere professionalism, blossoming into a warm and easy rapport. In the corridors of AGH, the echoes of "Dr. Sean" still reverberated. This title carried with it both respect and fondness. He wore it with humble pride, appreciating the recognition of his dedication.

A playful twist, a thread of lightheartedness that painted smiles across weary faces, had woven itself into their interactions. With his quick wit and linguistic dexterity, Sean had concocted a charming tradition. He bestowed upon each nurse a unique moniker derived from various languages, encapsulating notions of femininity, beauty, or simply a gentle nod to their role as caregivers. Their laughter and appreciative blushes were the rewards of this linguistic dance.

Sean's empathy extended beyond the confines of his assigned duties. Like a vigilant shepherd, he watched over the bustling nurse station, attuned to the ebb and flow of demands that surged like waves. His work was not confined to patient files and clinical notes; he was also a beacon of aid when the station was inundated with requests and inquiries. With a gracious pause, he would temporarily set aside his tasks to offer support.

The nurse station was a hub of bustling activity, akin to a market square abuzz with voices seeking direction, help, and solace. Staff members presented their challenges, needs, and sometimes even frustrations. Patients arrived with concerns, seeking reassurance or voicing their experiences. Sean navigated these exchanges with professionalism and approachability, embodying the hospital's ethos of compassionate care.

The harmony of desperate and hopeful voices formed a

chorus of humanity seeking aid and understanding. Amidst this symphony of inquiries, Sean stood as a conductor of sorts, orchestrating responses with skillful precision. His empathy soothed anxieties, and his knowledge illuminated uncertainties.

Sean embodied the essence of the hospital's shared journey through these interactions. He was the link that bridged the divide between the technical aspects of medicine and the emotional needs of patients and staff. His willingness to listen, understand, and extend a helping hand exemplified the artistry of healing, transcending the sterile confines of medical procedure.

Amidst the perpetual bustle of the nurse station, a crescendo of activity had reached a feverish pitch. Requests, queries, and concerns filled the air like a symphony of urgent notes. It was as if the very heartbeat of AGH resonated in the rhythms of the station. During this orchestrated chaos, Sean emerged as a conductor of a different kind.

Like a maestro stepping onto a podium, Sean's voice cut through the noise, commanding attention. His unexpected and compelling call for silence halted the frenzy in its tracks. In a moment that mirrored a battlefield commander rallying the troops, he issued orders with calm authority. Nurses, usually in perpetual motion, paused to heed his directives.

In his decisive manner, Sean enacted a transformation of the nurse station. The bustling crowd was organized into lines, transforming chaos into order. The principles he outlined were clear: Requests would be triaged based on their impact on patient care and the smooth functioning of the hospital. It was an innovative approach that challenged the conventional notion of a linear queue managed by a first come, first serve principle.

This radical departure from the norm earned Sean a mixtre of admiration and resentment. Nurses, often at the forefront of the daily battle, saw a leader who understood their struggles in him. Their expressions bore hints of appreciation mingled with a newfound respect for the audacity of his actions.

Not everyone welcomed this deviation from established protocol. Doctors, accustomed to their hierarchical position, bristled at the notion of being assigned to lines. For Sean, this potential hostility was of little concern. He carried himself with an air of detachment, knowing that his time at AGH was limited. His focus remained steadfast on his mission, unmoved by the potential growth of his list of detractors.

Sean's distinctive approach to interpersonal dynamics was a study in contrasts. On the one hand, he exhibited unyielding patience and unwavering empathy toward patients and nurses, transcending challenges with grace. On the other hand, he deliberately provoked confrontations with fellow doctors. This duality was a testament to his dedication to patient care, willingness to challenge established norms, and disregard for political games.

Under Sean's guidance, the lines at the nurse station ebbed and flowed, and a new order emerged from the fray. Requests were processed more efficiently, and the station regained a semblance of equilibrium. The tension between Sean and some of his peers lingered in the air like a gathering storm, a reminder of the uncharted territories he was willing to traverse for the sake of his beliefs.

The nurse station, once a microcosm of chaos, had been temporarily tamed by Sean's audacious leadership. He was a lightning rod, attracting both admiration and animosity, symbolizing the transformations that can arise when one challenges the status quo. In this ever-changing realm of AGH, Sean's presence was a whirlwind, leaving a trail of disruption and evolution in its wake.

Dr. May's unexpected gesture surprised and amused Sean. It was as if a spontaneous plot twist had been introduced into their ongoing narrative. The lunch box she held, a small treasure chest of culinary offerings, symbolized an unexpected bridge between their worlds. Sean's skepticism, a natural reflex to such unexpected kindness, expressed itself in his cautious inquiry about any strings attached to this act of goodwill.

Dr. May's response was laced with playful banter, her words teasingly challenging Sean's assumption. She seemed to delight in his momentary disconcertment, a sly smile hinting at the corners of her lips. Her explanation was a paradoxical mixture of logic and humour, asserting her belief that their deal had been fulfilled despite the twist of circumstances. Since she had made the food the previous evening and saved Sean's share of that dinner to bring it for him to eat for breakfast, she asserted that the deal of dinner and breakfast had been completed.

As Sean accepted the lunch box, he couldn't help but smile. It was as if the universe had decided to play a jest on them both, blurring the lines between their initial intentions. Dr. May's culinary offering had effectively challenged Sean's perception of their arrangement, leaving him to ponder the implications of her act.

With a hint of humour, Sean quipped, "Well, you've certainly managed to keep things interesting."

The words hung in the air like a gentle play, a lighthearted recognition of the unique dynamic that had emerged between them. At that moment, as the nurse station buzzed with activity and the aroma of Dr. May's culinary creation wafted from the lunch box, Sean was intrigued by the intricate interplay of personalities that defined his time at AGH.

Sean couldn't suppress a knowing grin as he held the lunch box. Their exchange had taken an amusing turn, a friendly sparring of wits that highlighted the quirkiness of their relationship. His playful rebuttal was carefully woven with logic, invoking the parameters of their initial deal. He suggested a humorous yet practical resolution to seek an impartial verdict on their playful disagreement.

The challenge he extended to her held a tone of light-hearted jest, emphasizing the subtle dance of camaraderie that was taking shape between them. Sean's reminder of their dinner plans for the following day was a lighthearted confirmation that he wouldn't be deterred by a playful attempt to alter their arrangement.

Dr. May, in response, exhibited a sense of self-awareness that was both endearing and refreshing. Her laughter resonated with a blend of sincerity and amusement as she acknowledged the futility of her attempt to bend the terms of their agreement. Her decision to let the matter rest wasn't a concession of defeat but a recognition of the spirited banter that had become characteristic of their interactions.

As she turned to leave, her parting words carried a sense of lightness, a shared understanding that their exchange was meant in good humour. Her request to reclaim the lunch box was delivered with a chuckle, a nod to the temporary victory she had sought. Sean, however, was unwavering in his playful resolve. His refusal to return the lunch box was an active act of retribution, a reminder that their relationship was one where wit and jest held their own currency.

Their banter, the exchange of playful challenges and jests, lingered in the air like a melodious tune, a harmonious rhythm that was becoming a defining aspect of their dynamic. As Dr. May walked away, her laughter seemed to echo in the corridor, a testament to the warmth and camaraderie quietly weaving its threads into the tapestry of their interactions.

Dr. May's impromptu announcement cast a sudden shadow over Sean's morning. The playful banter had given way to a serious undertone as her words seemed to hold a certain weight. The mention of an angry Dr. Plunkett looking for him, a name he was familiar with but hadn't encountered before, ignited a mixture of curiosity and apprehension within him.

The corridors of AGH, once buzzing with friendly interactions and light-hearted exchanges, now felt like a labyrinth of uncertainty. Sean's mind raced, dissecting the possible reasons for Dr. Plunkett's summon. Was it a consequence of his candid conversation with Dr. Gabehart, a dialogue that had left him questioning the ethical boundaries of his position? Or was there something else, an unseen misstep he had inadvertently taken that had drawn the ire of the senior doctor?

As seconds ticked away, his thoughts oscillated between various scenarios. He couldn't escape the unease that had settled within him. The idea of being reprimanded by Dr. Plunkett, a figure he had yet to meet in person, only added to his apprehension. The intertwining dynamics of professional hierarchy, personal relationships, and his unique position as a student in the medical landscape painted a complex picture.

Sean's brow furrowed as he pondered his options. Should he prepare for a potential confrontation? Should he try to gather more information before meeting with Dr. Plunkett? A sense of urgency tugged at his thoughts, urging him to confront the situation head-on.

Yet, despite this undercurrent of uncertainty, Sean's resilience remained unshaken. His ability to navigate challenging situations was a testament to his steadfast character. The camaraderie he had cultivated with the nurses and the unique rapport he shared with Dr. May had given him a foundation of support amid this uncertainty.

As he braced himself to face Dr. Plunkett, Sean drew upon the same traits that had propelled him through his medical journey thus far: tenacity, adaptability, and an unwavering commitment to his principles. Whatever the outcome of this encounter, Sean knew that he was equipped to handle it with the same spirit that had guided him through the complexities of AGH.

However, Sean's mind kept dancing between the shadows of potential scenarios, each more intricate and unsettling than the last. The concept that Dr. Plunkett's intentions might be driven by his relationship with Dr. Gabehart lingered like a haunting spectre. Could the seemingly harmless conversation he had shared with Dr. Gabehart have ignited a cascade of events that led to his summoning? The complicated web of interpersonal dynamics was as intricate as a labyrinth, leaving Sean at the mercy of conjectures and half-formed assumptions.

In this state of suspense, Sean's thoughts raced down corridors of uncertainty. His mind, a battleground of conflicting emotions, grappled with the gravity of the situation. His fear of professional repercussions loomed heavily, threatening to cast a dark cloud over his future medical aspirations. The very foundation of his career appeared to be teetering on the edge of a precipice, its stability at the whim of Dr. Plunkett's verdict.

Yet, amidst the chaos of his thoughts, Sean held onto the notion that Dr. Plunkett's anger might be rooted in a professional sphere. The unorthodox arrangement he had established with Dr. Gabehart was an undeniable breach of conventional ethics, and the possibility that Dr. Plunkett had discovered it could not be discounted.

Sean's heart raced with a twinge of dread as he contemplated the weight of the potential consequences. The very ideals he had held sacred, the principles that guided his path in medicine, were now under scrutiny.

The clock's ticking seemed to mimic his thoughts' pacing, each second stretching like an eternity. He pondered the thin line he was walking, one that balanced on the precipice of career advancement and ethical compromise. Yet, as he retraced the myriad steps that led him to this moment, Sean held firm to his core belief in his abilities and commitment to integrity.

Amid the uncertainty, he took solace in the knowledge that he had been guided by a desire to make a difference. His encounters with patients, interactions with the nurses, and even his banter with Dr. May all shared a common thread—the pursuit of healing and understanding. This unwavering dedication gave him a sense of purpose, a compass to navigate the stormy seas of medical politics.

As Sean prepared for the impending meeting with Dr. Plunkett, he found strength in the convictions that had led him thus far. Regardless of the outcome, he was resolved to face the situation head-on, drawing upon his unique blend of intellect, empathy, and unyielding spirit. The following steps were uncertain, but Sean remained poised to confront whatever challenges lay ahead with the same resilience that had so far defined his journey at AGH.

The hospital corridor seemed to shrink in size as Sean and the looming figure of Dr. Plunkett stood face to face, an invisible tension stretching between them. The palpable anger radiating from Dr. Plunkett created an atmosphere charged with unease. In that charged moment, Sean's heart pounded like a drumbeat in his chest, the rhythm of anticipation underscoring the uncertainty that loomed ahead.

As they stood mere inches apart, a curious dance unfolded. Each tried to maneuver out of the other's path, an awkward and futile game of spatial negotiation. It was as if their silent struggle mirrored the broader complexities of their impending conversation – a battle of words and intentions, each vying for control of the narrative.

The silence that hung in the air was thick with unspoken tension. Sean's mind raced through various scenarios, his mental gears whirring as he attempted to decipher the motivations behind Dr. Plunkett's urgency. The man before him bore an air of authority and, evidently, some prior knowledge of Sean. This situation was unsettling, to say the least.

When they finally emerged from the charged silence, Dr. Plunkett's words carried an unmistakable edge of command. The sharp tone left little room for negotiation, underscoring the gravity of the situation. Sean's choice to feign ignorance seemed almost reflexive, an attempt to delay the inevitable confrontation or perhaps an effort to establish some semblance of control over a situation spiralling out of his grasp.

Dr. Plunkett's patience was paper-thin, his irritation evident. Sean's act of playing dumb appeared to have rubbed him the wrong way, a calculated insult to his assumed status within the hospital hierarchy. The fact that Sean did not immediately acknowledge Dr. Plunkett's identity seemed to challenge the latter's perception of self-importance.

The corridor remained a mute observer in the backdrop of this confrontation, a canvas onto which the dynamics of power and personal tension were etched in stark relief. With each step, the dance of pride, restraint, authority, and uncertainty played out as the two danced an unusual tango in the hallway.

With the air heavy with unspoken words and emotions, Sean took a breath, aware that this encounter could be a pivotal moment in his time at AGH. The hallway, once a neutral thoroughfare, now stretched before him like a bridge to a fate uncertain.

Dr. Plunkett's anger seemed to shadow the interaction, his authority attempting to blot out Sean's defiant stance. The air was charged with a quiet battle, a confrontation where each step and word was like the swing of a sword in a carefully choreographed duel.

Dr. Plunkett's words carried a heavy undertone of dominance, demanding submission to his authority. The directive to answer his questions and cede control seemed non-negotiable. Yet, Sean was no novice to defying authority, and he knew the weight of his convictions.

Sean attempted to assert his limited position within the hospital hierarchy with a measured tone. His words were like a plea for sanity in a situation spiralling out of control. He anchored himself to the sphere of influence he was familiar with, Dr. Gabehart's. His attempt to sidestep the looming confrontation and divert it to his superior showcased a clever evasion, but it also served as a red rag to a bull.

Dr. Plunkett's refusal to let Sean pass, effectively blocking his way, symbolized their power struggle. The corridor's confined space seemed to mirror the constraints both men were trying to impose upon each other. Sean's attempt to move forward physically was thwarted, a metaphor for the psychological battle being waged.

The escalating exchange between them escalated like a verbal fencing match. Dr. Plunkett's ultimatum hung in the air, a threat laden with consequences that could shape Sean's future. The words were like daggers, aimed at Sean's career and reputation. The threat was clear – compliance or ruin.

Despite the mounting pressure, Sean remained remarkably composed. He balanced on the precipice of caution, choosing his words carefully. His knowledge of Dr. Plunkett's reputation further fuelled his determination not to be goaded into a confrontation. Yet his silence, intended to defuse the situation, appeared to have the opposite effect, further enraging Dr. Plunkett.

Their scene played out like a riveting drama, drawing the attention of passersby, who couldn't help but glance over. The corridor transformed into an impromptu stage, the backdrop to a clash of personalities, egos, and authority. Each move and utterance was scrutinized in this high-stakes encounter as if the hospital had collectively held its breath to witness this power struggle between two formidable figures.

Amid this high-stakes confrontation, Dr. Gabehart's arrival was like a gust of unexpected wind, reshaping the dynamics of the scene. Her intervention cut through the tension with a no-nonsense command directed at Sean. Her sharp and authoritative words pierced through the heavy air, calling Sean's attention to his primary responsibility—his work and cases.

Dr. Gabehart's presence during the standoff was a stark reminder of her authoritative role within the hospital. Her ability to redirect Sean's focus highlighted her influence, even when another authority figure was involved. Her dismissal of Dr.

Plunkett's presence was a silent assertion of her power and a testament to her professionalism, as she didn't let personal issues interfere with her responsibilities.

The scene took an unexpected twist as Dr. Plunkett voiced his concerns to Dr. Gabehart. The accusations he levelled against Sean seemed to create a disjointed narrative, an incongruity between the allegations and Sean's character that was difficult for Dr. Gabehart to reconcile. The accusation of Sean recommending lethal treatment to a patient clashed with her understanding of him, adding an element of disbelief to the situation.

The dissonance in Dr. Plunkett's words created a cognitive dissonance for Dr. Gabehart. Sean's supposed lapse in professionalism seemed within the realm of possibility. Yet, the accusation of lethal recommendations felt jarring and out of character. The tension was palpable as Dr. Gabehart grappled with how to respond to this unexpected turn of events.

Dr. Gabehart's response was swift and matter-of-fact, reflecting her commitment to upholding the hospital's standards. Her decision to distance herself from Sean at this moment was pragmatic, reflecting her dedication to maintaining professionalism and safeguarding the hospital's reputation. Her abrupt departure left Sean standing in the wake of her departure, a stark realization of the potential consequences of his actions.

As the scene unfolded, it became evident that the hospital environment was more than just a backdrop. It was a microcosm of power dynamics, where authority figures clashed, allegiances shifted, and reputations hung in the balance. In this theatre of conflict, the characters grappled with their motives, professional responsibilities, and the delicate interplay between them.

As Sean simplified the matter that had caused this outrage

to Dr. Gabehart, her compassionate and patient-centred approach was revealed. Her immediate concern shifted from the internal power struggle to the patient's well-being, Mr. Gladstone. The gravity of the situation transcended personal disputes, showcasing her dedication to her role as a physician.

As Sean disclosed the details of Mr. Gladstone's condition, the scene pivoted from confrontation to shared concern for the patient's health. Dr. Gabehart's abrupt change in direction, halting her departure and returning to the conversation, underscored her commitment to her patients' welfare.

Dr. Plunkett's interruption echoed the undercurrents of authority and rivalry that persisted within the hospital's hierarchy. His assertion of his position as the head oncologist introduced a layer of complexity to the situation, as it challenged both Sean's involvement and Dr. Gabehart's decision-making.

The growing crowd highlighted the hospital's tightly knit environment, where news, conversations, and disputes could quickly escalate. Dr. Gabehart's instinct to move the conversation into her office underscored her desire to handle this matter privately, where the intricacies of the situation could be discussed without external scrutiny.

Dr. Gabehart's authoritative command demonstrated her control over the situation, reasserting her role as a leader and mediator amid professional discord. Her direct address to Dr. Plunkett and Sean emphasized the need for collaboration and communication, particularly regarding patient care.

Dr. Gabehart's explanation of her orders to Sean highlighted her authority in assigning responsibilities and her belief in Sean's capability to assist in patient care. This recontextualized

Sean's involvement, reframing it as part of a comprehensive plan overseen by Dr. Gabehart.

Amidst the charged office atmosphere, the clash of personalities between Dr. Plunkett and Dr. Gabehart was discernible. Dr. Plunkett's forceful entrance and immediate attempt to assert his authority were met with a firm response from Dr. Gabehart, who refused to be subjugated by his dominance. This tension unveiled itself as an ongoing power struggle between two strong-willed figures within the hospital's hierarchy.

Dr. Plunkett's outburst echoed his propensity for authoritarianism, "I'm still your boss, Gabrielle, and your student overstepped his boundaries!"

This trait seeped into his professional interactions and personal life. His determination to exert control was evident as he attempted to belittle Sean's standing and opinion, dismissing him as unworthy of being heard. However, Dr. Gabehart's refusal to bow down to his rank suggested a clash of equals, a testament to her strength and determination to maintain her autonomy within the hospital's framework.

Sean sat down and started telling his side of the story. "We used clubbing of Mr. Gladstone's fingers to make a presumptive diagnosis of lung cancer. However, during that time, I also noticed he was uncomfortable. I thought he needed one of his heart valves to be replaced. Initially, I didn't think the lung cancer and the back problems would've been related. I thought the same thing Dr. May had thought: that the need for valve replacement caused the back problem. The General removed the tumour and repaired the valve. Since we convinced him to go for a valve repair, I thought the problem would disappear. I saw his discomfort again after his surgery, and he told me he had had back problems for a couple of months, and it was still bothering him. It then occurred to me that the high calcium deposited on his valve was likely due to lung cancer, resulting in the need for a valve replacement, hence valve replacement or repair," he articulated.

Sean's narration unveiled the underlying complexities of Mr. Gladstone's case. His diagnostic journey, from the presumption of lung cancer through the clubbing of fingers to the unexpected connection to the heart's valve, showcased the intricate web of medical mysteries that physicians often grapple with. His meticulous recounting of the events highlighted his analytical thinking and dedication to pursuing a comprehensive understanding.

The duality of Sean's perspective emerged as he described his initial misconceptions and eventual realizations. The evolution of his diagnostic reasoning reflected the intricate, puzzle-solving nature of medicine. Sean's perception shifted, crystallizing around the realization that the seemingly disparate symptoms were, in fact, interconnected.

Dr. Plunkett's impatience was a clear manifestation of his domineering personality. His brash and aggressive demeanour underscored his lack of tolerance for what he perceived as unnecessary delays or obfuscations. The chasm between his authoritative approach and Sean's methodical narrative was palpable, with Dr. Plunkett's outburst serving as a stark reminder of his inclination to wield his power to achieve his ends.

In contrast, Dr. Gabehart's discerning nature allowed her to recognize the validity of Sean's explanation. She was the mediating force, bridging the gap between Dr. Plunkett's aggression and Sean's detailed discourse. Her intervention emphasized her role as a composed and pragmatic leader, seeking clarity and understanding even amid the turmoil.

Dr. Gabehart finished Sean's analysis, "And the high calcium was one of the things I picked up on that ECG. Lung cancer alone could have given him high calcium, but the addition of metastatic cancer to the bone meant the calcium was much higher. Unsurprisingly, most of this calcium started depositing around his heart valve. I talked to the General yesterday, and he told me the surgery had gone well, but I've not had a chance to talk to Mr. Gladstone. Good catch, Sean."

The puzzle pieces seemed to align, drawing an intricate connection between the patient's symptoms and the underlying medical complexities. The subtle nod to Sean's acumen from Dr. Gabehart was both a recognition of his diagnostic prowess and an endorsement of his rational approach to unravelling the intricate medical situation.

"I think we need to take things slow to make sure some people can understand the medicine involved in medical practice," Sean said as he looked at Dr. Plunkett.

Dr. Gabehart's suppressed laughter provided a moment of levity, easing the tension in the room. As soon as she caught sight of Dr. Plunkett's disapproving gaze, she abruptly ceased laughing.

Sean's deliberate focus on engaging with Dr. Gabehart while ignoring Dr. Plunkett's increasingly frustrated attempts at interjection painted a vivid portrait of the dynamics at play. Dr. Plunkett's isolation in the discourse symbolized the clash of egos and contrasting approaches to communication within the medical realm.

As Sean elaborated on Mr. Gladstone's shifting emotional state and the implications of his diagnosis, a sombre undertone settled over the room. The gravity of the situation was palpable, as Sean's words portrayed the intricate balance between medical diagnosis and the human emotions accompanying it.

Dr. Gabehart's thoughtful nod acknowledged this intersection, highlighting her deep understanding of the emotional nuances involved in patient care.

The mention of chemotherapy and symptomatic treatment as potential courses of action reflected the medical complexity faced by Mr. Gladstone. Sean's articulate explanation revealed his grasp of the intricacies of patient care as he seamlessly merged medical knowledge with a consideration of the patient's holistic well-being.

Dr. Plunkett's growing irritation was a reminder of his desire for recognition and control. His attempts to assert his authority became more evident as he voiced his frustration, attempting to steer the conversation back to himself. The sharp contrast between his forceful demeanour and Sean's composed responses heightened the tension, capturing the conflicting energies within the room.

Sean's quick-witted retort to Dr. Plunkett's outburst, "Don't worry, Dr. Plunkett. I'll write everything down for you to follow in your spare time," added a touch of humour and temporarily relieved the escalating tension.

Sean's playful exchange with Dr. Gabehart showcased their camaraderie and ability to navigate challenges with fun, even in the face of an infuriated superior.

Dr. Gabehart's restrained laughter hinted at her ability to find moments of humour amidst the chaos. Her ability to balance seriousness with lightheartedness underlined her leadership style, contrasting Dr. Plunkett's volatile demeanour.

In this charged scene, the intricacies of interpersonal relationships, medical expertise, and ego-driven conflicts converged, painting a vivid tableau of the multifaceted world of healthcare. The power dynamics, emotional depth, and communication nuances were all brought to the forefront, creating a narrative rich with tension and moments of relief.

The contrast between Dr. Gabehart's measured response and Dr. Plunkett's authoritative stance showcased the divergent approaches that often coexist within the medical field. Dr. Plunkett's insistence on his role as Mr. Gladstone's physician of record highlighted his need for validation and control. At the same time, Dr. Gabehart's willingness to navigate the situation diplomatically revealed her emphasis on patient-centred care.

Dr. Plunkett's demand that Sean should have sought his guidance before discussing treatment options with Mr. Gladstone echoed the hierarchical nature of medical practice. The assertion that a senior physician's opinion should precede a student's input underscored the traditional power dynamics ingrained within the profession.

Dr. Gabehart's conciliatory agreement with Dr. Plunkett reflected her adeptness at managing interpersonal conflicts while suggesting that she was aware of the need to maintain a harmonious work environment. Her acknowledgment of Sean's perceived breach of protocol was likely intended to appease Dr. Plunkett's concerns and maintain a semblance of professional decorum.

However, it was apparent that Dr. Gabehart recognized Sean's unique connection with Mr. Gladstone. Her understanding that Sean was a trusted source of information and comfort for the patient hinted at the compassionate side of medical practice. She subtly acknowledged that sometimes, the most effective treatment comes from medical expertise and establishing a meaningful rapport with patients.

The clash between tradition and patient-centred care was palpable in this complex interplay of personalities and perspectives. The narrative highlighted the multifaceted challenges healthcare professionals face in balancing their duty to their patients with the hierarchical structure of medical practice.

The dynamics in the room were a microcosm of the intricate ethical and professional dance that often characterized medical decision-making. Dr. Plunkett's failed attempt to assert his authority seemed to have temporarily quelled the immediate tension, but the underlying ethical questions remained unsettled.

Dr. Gabehart's stance on patient autonomy was a resolute reminder that medicine isn't just about prescribing treatments—it's about understanding and respecting patients' wishes and rights. Her commitment to maintaining a patient's agency was evident in her willingness to engage in an open discussion with Mr. Gladstone, enabling him to make an informed decision about his treatment.

Dr. Plunkett's assertion of authority based on seniority echoed the hierarchical structure that had long been a hallmark of the medical field. His demand for Sean to retract his advice demonstrated an approach rooted in traditional medical authority. However, Dr. Gabehart's counterproposal to jointly discuss treatment options with the patient revealed a more modern, patient-centred perspective.

The decision to visit Mr. Gladstone together underscored the ethical principle of shared decision-making. Involving the patient directly in the discussion about his treatment plan was a testament to respecting his autonomy and valuing his input. Dr.

Gabehart's suggestion to Dr. Plunkett that he present his case allowed for a balanced and comprehensive presentation of the available options, ensuring that Mr. Gladstone received the most accurate and unbiased information.

As they left the office to meet with Mr. Gladstone, it was clear that this situation embodied the complex interplay between medical expertise, patient autonomy, and ethical responsibility. The scene highlighted the delicate balance that healthcare professionals must navigate to ensure the best possible outcomes for their patients while upholding the principles of medical ethics.

The room held an unusual tension, with each person present having their own motivations and concerns. Mr. Gladstone, with his quick wit and astute perception, sensed that the atmosphere was charged with underlying issues that he had yet to comprehend fully. His sense of humour, showcased by his quip to Sean about his Rolex still up for grabs, was a defence mechanism and a way to gain insight into the situation.

Dr. Plunkett's frustration was palpable, fuelled by his perception of Sean's encroachment on his authority. His vocal insistence on Sean's lack of medical qualification revealed a deep-seated belief in the traditional hierarchy of medicine. However, Dr. Gabehart's deliberate choice to overlook this comment indicated her intention to focus on the patient's well-being rather than engaging in a professional power struggle.

As Dr. Gabehart explained the situation, Mr. Gladstone's initial skepticism gradually gave way to curiosity. His earlier interaction with Sean had planted the seeds of trust, making him more receptive to the information being presented. He seemed to be looking for reassurance that the conversation would be about his health and best interests rather than a confrontation of credentials.

As the conversation continued, it became clear that the clash of perspectives was emblematic of more significant issues within the medical field—namely, the evolving nature of medical authority and the growing emphasis on patient autonomy. With tensions simmering just below the surface, the room held the potential for either a collision of traditional and modern approaches or an opportunity for mutual understanding and collaboration.

The room's dynamics seemed to ebb and flow like a tense symphony, with each character's emotions and motives interplaying. Dr. Plunkett's attempt to assert his authority and discredit Sean was met with Mr. Gladstone's stubborn defence of the medical student's contributions. It was a classic clash between established hierarchy and the practical impact of experience.

Dr. Plunkett's approach was authoritative and blunt, reflecting his belief that medical decisions should be entrusted only to experienced professionals. His words, while calculated, failed to resonate with Mr. Gladstone, whose personal experience had been positively influenced by Sean's input. The reality of Sean's seemingly fortunate yet effective interventions challenged Dr. Plunkett's insistence on his competence.

Mr. Gladstone, displaying both his discernment and understanding of the situation, sought to maintain a diplomatic stance. His request to involve Dr. May in the conversation reflected his wish to include the physician who had been directly responsible for his care. His desire for fairness was evident, as he aimed to mitigate any potential division between members of his healthcare team.

Dr. Gabehart listened attentively as a mediator between Dr. Plunkett and Mr. Gladstone's strong personalities. Her diplomatic management of the situation was a testament to her experience in balancing patient needs, medical expertise, and interpersonal dynamics. Her silent role demonstrated her willingness to prioritize Mr. Gladstone's autonomy and comfort.

In this scenario, the dialogue was more than just a medical consultation—it was a microcosm of the broader debates within the medical community. Despite professional disagreements, the patient's empowerment to make informed decisions became a central theme. This exchange highlighted the evolving relationship between medical professionals and patients, emphasizing that medical authority should align with patient values and preferences.

Dr. May's entrance into the room introduced a new element to the complex tableau, her demeanour mirroring the situation's intensity. Mr. Gladstone's inquiry about Dr. Gabehart's stance indicated his desire for clarity and unity within the medical team. His trust in Dr. Gabehart and Sean was evident, and his apprehension about potential discrepancies was palpable.

Dr. Plunkett's attempt to sway Mr. Gladstone's opinion and gain an ally in the patient was driven by his conviction that only seasoned professionals should guide medical decisions. His strategic use of misinformation, claiming support from Dr. Gabehart, was a tactical move to bolster his argument. The tension between Dr. Plunkett and Sean was discernible, with each holding firm to their respective positions.

Perceptive and astute, Dr. May quickly detected the disarray in the room. She sensed a power struggle and ideological conflict threatening to undermine the patient's agency. Aware of Mr. Gladstone's relationship with Sean, she likely recognized the potential for a patient-physician alliance that could overshadow the conventional hierarchy. Yet, the exact nature of the issue remained a puzzle to her.

Amid this unfolding drama, Dr. Gabehart's role as a mediator and guardian of patient rights became more prominent. Her position, rooted in her dedication to patient autonomy, formed a buffer against the strong personalities at play. Her leadership was characterized by her ability to balance her roles as a physician and a patient advocate, ensuring that Mr. Gladstone's voice was heard and respected.

As the characters converged in this tense moment, the outcome hung in the balance, with each person's actions contributing to the resolution of the conflicting perspectives. The dialogue was a testament to the intricate web of relationships and values that underpin the world of medicine, where compassion and competence often intertwine in complex ways.

Dr. May's presence signalled a shift in the dynamics, introducing a fresh perspective that carried its own weight. Her deliberate approach to avoiding bias, combined with her genuine concern for Mr. Gladstone's wellbeing, positioned her as a neutral party seeking to understand the situation from the patient's point of view. This stance, coupled with her firsthand experience working with Sean, made her a valuable voice of reason.

She greeted everyone but avoided conversations to prevent appearing biased towards someone specific. She went to stand beside Dr. Gabehart to talk to Mr. Gladstone, "What's going on? Mr. Gladstone, are you okay?" she asked.

He replied, "This morning, you gave me a powerful drug, and I haven't felt so good in months. Why didn't you give me that medication when I first came into this hospital?"

Dr. May responded with a smile and a light tap on Mr.

Gladstone's shoulder. She navigated this intricate dialogue with professionalism and empathy, striving to ensure that Mr. Gladstone's questions were answered accurately and transparently.

Mr. Gladstone's method of using questions to assert his position, reflecting his somewhat arrogant nature, also underscored his desire for clarity and accountability. His approach turned the focus toward the facts, providing a counterpoint to the emotional tensions that had unfolded in the room.

In this charged atmosphere, Dr. Plunkett's anger and frustration had reached a boiling point. His dismissal of younger doctors as inexperienced was a testament to his seniority and arrogance, contrasting starkly with the evidence-driven approach that Dr. May and Dr. Gabehart had adopted. Dr. Plunkett's declaration that the back pain was unrelated to the cancer only fuelled the fire.

Dr. May's contribution to the scene with Mr. Gladstone's X-ray revealed her meticulous nature and commitment to providing airtight evidence to support her treatment decisions. Her careful preparation and thorough approach ensured that her interventions were grounded in medical certainty, particularly given her respect for Dr. Gabehart's authority. Her presentation of the X-ray, which corroborated Sean's initial diagnosis of metastatic cancer, was a pivotal moment that could not be easily dismissed.

The X-ray was a visual testament to the cancer's spread to Mr. Gladstone's backbone. Dr. May's action demonstrated her confidence in her diagnosis and her willingness to rely on solid medical evidence. In doing so, she challenged Dr. Plunkett's assertion that the back pain was unrelated to the cancer, compelling him to confront the reality of the situation.

Dr. Gabehart's endorsement of the X-ray findings underscored the doctors' unity and collaboration, cementing the credibility of their diagnosis and treatment plan. Her quick defence of Sean's presumptive diagnosis showcased their established support structure.

However, the situation took another turn as Dr. Plunkett sought to capitalize on the evidence presented. His abrupt shift to suggesting immediate chemotherapy due to the X-ray surprised everyone, signalling his desire to assert his authority and control over the patient's treatment. This move directly contradicted Dr. May's and Dr. Gabehart's cautious approach to allowing Mr. Gladstone autonomy in his treatment decisions.

As the conversation continued, Mr. Gladstone sought Dr. May's opinion, trusting her judgment. Dr. May's response, citing the X-ray evidence and suggesting the possibility of the cancer spreading to Mr. Gladstone's liver, further solidified her credibility and expertise. Her statement also demonstrated her awareness of the potential progression of the disease.

In this intricate exchange, a convergence of medical expertise, ego, patient autonomy, and communication styles became evident. The doctors' differing perspectives, grounded in their experiences and values, were juxtaposed against Mr. Gladstone's desire for transparency, respect, and a collaborative approach to his treatment.

Dr. May struggled to balance her commitment to ethical medical practice and the potential repercussions of disagreeing with Dr. Plunkett's authoritative stance. Her precarious position became even more evident as Mr. Gladstone encouraged her to continue sharing her thoughts, emphasizing his trust in her expertise.

Her hesitation to speak openly revealed the weight of her

decision. Going against Dr. Plunkett's opinion could have far-reaching consequences for her career and work environment. The delicate balance of power dynamics at AGH was a tightrope she had to navigate carefully.

Dr. Gabehart's response further complicated the situation. While her encouragement to speak her mind suggested an open-minded approach, Dr. May was aware of their complex dynamics. The undercurrent of Dr. Gabehart and Dr. Plunkett's marriage hinted at possible tensions that might arise from differing opinions.

Mr. Gladstone's plea for her honest opinion was a turning point in this charged atmosphere. His insistence on valuing her perspective elevated her role. It signalled that his trust in her judgment transcended the hierarchical structure of the hospital.

As Dr. May weighed her options, her decision would impact Mr. Gladstone's treatment and reflect her values as a healthcare professional. This moment tested her integrity, resilience, and commitment to patient-centred care, highlighting the intricate interplay of ethical considerations, personal relationships, and professional responsibility in medicine.

Dr. May explained, "I know Dr. Plunkett is inclined to put you on chemotherapy, but the cancer has spread too much for chemo to be effective at this point. You'll likely live longer with less stress on your body and mind off chemo than on chemo. Maybe it's time to make the most of the time you have remaining, however short or long it may be."

Dr. May's words hung in the air, a candid assessment and belief regarding Mr. Gladstone's condition. Her straightforwardness, while coming from a place of professional and ethical concern, had the potential to incite controversy, particularly considering Dr. Plunkett's well-known authoritative demeanour.

Dr. Plunkett's growing agitation was palpable as he struggled to assert dominance. The clash of medical perspectives and the assertion of who held the final word in a patient's treatment plan intensified the tension within the room. His demand for unquestioning adherence to his opinion underscored the power dynamics at play, where medical authority was at odds with the genuine interests and well-being of the patient.

Mr. Gladstone's situation now embodied the larger ethical question of medical autonomy versus medical paternalism. While Dr. Plunkett represented a traditional approach, where the superior physician's opinion was considered final, Dr. May's stance reflected the shift towards patient-centred care, allowing patients to participate actively in decisions about their treatment.

As the room hung in suspense, Mr. Gladstone's response would determine the course of his treatment and underline the fundamental principle of medicine – the sanctity of patient autonomy.

Mr. Gladstone's measured response struck a chord of understanding, illustrating his desire for a comprehensive understanding of his options before making a life-altering decision. His request for a second opinion was a respectful yet firm assertion of his autonomy as a patient, emphasizing his role as a partner in his own care.

Dr. Plunkett's decision to let the conversation proceed recognized the patient's right to explore various perspectives. The clash between the different doctors' views highlighted the complexity of medical decision-making, where expert opinions, patient wishes, and ethical considerations interweave in a delicate balance.

As the discussion moved forward, the room held an unspoken acknowledgment that medical practice wasn't merely about wielding authority but collaboration, patient education, and empowering patients to participate actively in their care. The unfolding interaction captured the essence of the evolving landscape of modern medicine, where patients' voices and choices were increasingly valued alongside medical expertise.

Dr. Gabehart made it easy for Dr. May to express her opinion, and Sean was going to express his opinion no matter what. This left Dr. Gabehart in a very tough position. Siding with Sean and Dr. May would have meant humiliation that would likely have led the dispute all the way to her bedroom.

It was a challenging position, but Dr. Gabehart couldn't let anything sway her. She didn't want to challenge her boss and husband like this, but she couldn't afford to lose the respect of Mr. Gladstone. She thought about it while trying to figure out the best way that wouldn't make things worse for anyone.

After a few minutes, she went for it, "I agree with Dr. May's assessment. Mr. Gladstone, if there's anything I can do to make you feel more comfortable, please let me know without hesitation."

It was two doctors against one, and just like that, it sealed defeat for Dr. Plunkett.

While stemming from his expertise and sense of authority, Dr. Plunkett's stance faced resistance in a medical environment that increasingly emphasized shared decision-making. A growing emphasis on the patient's right to participate actively in their treatment choices was challenging the power dynamics that often existed within medical hierarchies.

"Thank you very much, Dr. Gabehart. Sean, since you're not a doctor, it means you can't chime in on this, but as my friend, do you mind if I ask you for some advice about what these doctors have said to me about my treatment?" Mr. Gladstone enquired.

Sean quickly replied, "Certainly, O.G. I think we should go with what women say because women are always right. Who cares if they're wrong? They can always apologize in ways that a man like Dr. Plunkett can't."

Dr. May and Dr. Gabehart watched as Sean and Mr. Gladstone laughed.

Mr. Gladstone looked at Dr. Plunkett, "Dr. Plunkett, you really can't argue with that logic. No chemo, and I want Sean to sign off on everything you do on my case. I know you always want to get your way, Dr. Plunkett, but this is my life. I won't hesitate to bring my army of lawyers if I think for a bit that you're about to betray my trust in this hospital."

Dr. Plunkett replied as he stormed out, "I don't care. It's your life."

The lightheartedness of the situation underscored the complex dynamics within a hospital setting. Despite the tensions and disagreements, a sense of camaraderie and mutual respect prevailed among Sean, Mr. Gladstone, Dr. May, and Dr. Gabehart. This incident showcased the power of collaboration and the importance of fostering a supportive and respectful environment within the healthcare team.

All four laughed as they celebrated their victory over Dr. Plunkett and embraced the triumph of patient autonomy over medical malpractice.

Sean said to Mr. Gladstone, "You're such an ass. Why would you torment another man like that? You didn't care about Dr. May's and Dr. Gabehart's opinions."

Mr. Gladstone explained to Sean that he had heard a lot of nasty things about Dr. Plunkett, and he wanted to take this opportunity to embarrass him in front of his subordinates so he could learn some humility.

Dr. May seemed frustrated while walking towards the door, saying, "I think I'm going to start looking for another job now."

They all laughed. Each of them wished Mr. Gladstone a good day before heading out.

Turning Things Around

A palpable air of anticipation enveloped AGH as the sun painted the hospital corridors with warm hues on that awaited Friday. The dawn of the weekend seemed like a beckoning oasis after a week of professional rigour. Much like the previous day, the atmosphere was even more enthusiastic, akin to the exhilarating crescendo of a symphony's finale.

Amid this orchestration of activity, some patients, like migratory birds preparing to embark on a short hiatus, sought the final counsel of their physicians before departing for the respite of the weekend. The morning unfolded its busy canvas, with nurses and doctors weaving in and out of corridors, engaged in their compassionate hustle.

The caretakers, not mere observers but participants in the tapestry of healing, assisted patients in gathering their belongings, contributing to the kaleidoscope of humanity in motion. Meanwhile, a dedicated staff cadre orchestrated the evening's entertainment setting, an offering of joy and solace.

Sean's punctuality was unflagging, in his signature manner. He embraced the hours leading up to the weekend's collective exhalation as an opportunity to advance his work. Scribing notes and reviewing files, his diligence danced alongside the hospital's hum. His every action was part of a grand crescendo, leading him toward the harmonious symposium ahead.

Mother, the watchful guardian of this domain, assumed her role as the unseen hand that guided the gears of the hospital's intricate clockwork. Her presence was ubiquitous, a nurturing force tending to the many needs that arose. Yet even her boundless energy occasionally sought reinforcement, a testament to the cooperative nature of her orchestration. When the burdens became too weighty for her sole shoulders, the call to Dr. Gabehart emerged as an unsung harmony, demonstrating that even the conductor occasionally seeks a second baton.

The scene was akin to an old fable, where each character played a significant role, a cog in a greater wheel. The hospital buzzed with a kind of unity that resonated with the scheduled tasks and the unsung melodies of compassion and dedication. The spirit of collective purpose echoed an age-old saying: "Many hands make light work."

Yet within this well-tuned symphony, secrets lay hidden, and human dynamics existed as intricate layers. The corridors witnessed the flow of patients and the currents of interpersonal intricacies. The tale of the preceding day lingered, a story within a story, like a book concealed between the pages of another. Sean's rapport with the nurses had taken on a character beyond mere professionalism, embracing a camaraderie that was an art in itself, much like the varied hues in a painting.

Sean's demeanour became the calm before the storm, a stillness that masks the gathering tempest. It was a tale of voices, opinions, hierarchies, and humility entwined like the tendrils of ivy on an ancient stone wall. An amalgamation of power dynamics and ethical questions unfolded, painted against the backdrop of medical prowess. From the previous day, Dr. Plunkett's authoritative stride, imbued with the weight of seniority, collided with Sean's youthful fervour, creating ripples of tension that threatened the harmony.

Within the cadence of their discourse, echoes of respect and defiance reverberated, a dance of two wolves circling a prey. In the eye of this gathering storm stood Dr. Gabehart, torn between her loyalty to her husband and her commitment to medical ethics. The situation bore a stark resemblance to the timeless adage: "When two elephants fight, it is the grass that suffers."

As Friday unfolded at AGH, everyone enjoyed their extraordinary tradition, defying the conventions of medical institutions. Even Dr. Plunkett's formidable presence proved powerless against this unorthodox yet cherished ritual. This unique fusion of joy and healing phenomenon stood as a testament to the remarkable spirit that thrived within the hospital's walls.

Amid the structured corridors of medical routines, these Fridays emerged as a vibrant rebellion, a celebration of life that transcended the confines of illness. It was a paradox, a juxtaposition of disease and jubilation, a living parable that the human spirit can persist despite the most trying circumstances. The very essence of AGH seemed to harmonize with these days, nurturing a fusion of humanity, medicine, and unbridled joy.

The impact of this audacious concept extended far beyond its festive surface. Patient testimonials bore witness to its profound influence, a healing balm beyond medical prescriptions. They wrote of recoveries that were not just physical but emotional, a dynamic shift that propelled them towards wellness. In these weekend escapes, they found the solace of home, surrounded by the embrace of loved ones. The ward's symphony was not the sorrowful lament of departing neighbours but the hopeful rhythm of shared recovery.

In the embrace of these Fridays, hope flourished like an

ancient oak, its roots digging deep into the soil of possibility. Once bound by their ailments, patients found a reason to push their boundaries and strive for faster healing. These brief vacations into normalcy became their motivation, a beacon guiding them through the often demanding journey of recovery.

The symbiotic relationship between patient and caregiver underwent a metamorphosis. Once perceived as mere instructions, treatment plans transformed into collaborative journeys toward health. The once-dreaded therapies became stepping stones to the weekend reprieve, a bridge between medical necessity and personal reward. In this context, compliance wasn't just a medical term but a pact, a shared commitment to honour the healing process.

Dr. Gabehart's vision, a radiant star guiding the ship, garnered accolades that were more than just letters on paper. Her commitment to this radical paradigm shift resonated through every review and every heartfelt testimony of gratitude. Her approach wasn't just a departure from the norm but a beacon of compassionate leadership that transcended hierarchies.

Dr. Plunkett's attempts to thwart this movement were met with a chorus of support for the movement that echoed like a resounding ovation. The project's inception had ignited a fire of enthusiasm that refused to be extinguished. Like a mighty river, the collective will of patients, staff, and caregivers surged forward, overwhelming any resistance. The project had become a part of AGH and its heartbeat, a rhythm that resonated with the beating hearts of those who walked its halls.

As the sun painted its hues on the walls, music infused the air, a symphony that began with the first rays of dawn. The crescendo of volume grew with each passing hour like a morning bird chorus gaining momentum. It was an auditory manifestation of unity, a harmonious demonstration that echoed the sentiments of shared purpose.

The scene was almost poetic. The hospital, a realm often associated with sombreness, now resonated with the vivacity of life. The hallways, once avenues of sterile efficiency, transformed into lively thoroughfares akin to a high school during its most spirited moments. The music that embraced these corridors wasn't just a racket; it was an anthem of life, an audible affirmation that healing was more than just medical intervention.

As the Fridays of joy and healing persisted, they left an indelible mark. They became an embodiment of the saying "laughter is the best medicine," a testament that wellness wasn't merely the absence of disease but the presence of positivity. The hospital's reputation soared, and sterile statistics and stories of transformed lives elevated its ratings.

These Fridays were a chapter of AGH's legacy, etched into its narrative like an illuminated manuscript. They stood as a reminder that, amidst the realm of science and diagnostics, the human spirit is the most potent instrument of healing. In these moments of shared joy, the human spirit soared as resilient and magnificent as a phoenix rising from the ashes.

With the commencement of the morning shift, Sean found himself in the rare and enviable position of having accomplished the workload that might otherwise span the entire day within the span of a few hours. This efficient feat granted him a well-deserved break, an opportunity to extricate himself momentarily from the whirlwind of responsibilities.

His footsteps led him not to his workstation but to Mr. Gladstone's room. In the wake of delivering the sad news, Sean had forged an unspoken connection with the man. A bond that transcended the roles of doctor and patient had emerged, transforming their interactions into more than just medical consultations.

Sean's presence in Mr. Gladstone's room was not an obligation but a testament to the genuine camaraderie they had cultivated. Their interactions were less about medical prognoses and more about shared stories, laughter, and a lightness that momentarily lifted the weight of their circumstances. Their conversations echoed through the corridors like the lilting melodies of a duet, two souls finding solace in each other's company.

Laughter became the thread that wove their encounters together, a tapestry of joy and camaraderie that belied the stark reality of the hospital environment. Once a place of medical discourse, the room transformed into a haven of silliness, where the weight of illness was momentarily lifted. If one were to eavesdrop on their exchanges, they might be transported to a carefree world where two friends shared stories over late-night campfires.

The tempo of their laughter echoed teenage shenanigans as if they were naughty adolescents exploring the realms of humour with a sense of newfound liberation. These moments, laden with shared joy, represented an oasis of respite amidst the clinical corridors and the hushed conversations of the ill.

Their camaraderie transcended the sombre facade of medical discourse, infusing the room with an energy that was almost tangible. In these moments, Sean was not just a medical student; he was a fellow human, a friend providing a respite from the trials of illness. Mr. Gladstone, in his laughter, wasn't merely a patient; he was a companion embracing life's lighter side even in the face of adversity.

As the laughter spilled from the confines of Mr. Gladstone's room, it was as if a timeless bond had been forged, a connection that defied the boundaries of age and circumstance. Sean's visits were a testament that compassion and empathy were as much a part of healing as any medical prescription. The hospital walls seemed to dissolve in their shared moments, revealing the shared humanity that united them.

Sean brought a buoyant atmosphere, a ray of sunshine that illuminated even the gloomiest corners. In response, Mr. Gladstone's face was graced with a heartwarming smile and an anticipatory glimmer in his eyes. The air was infused with an unspoken agreement that each encounter would be laden with the promise of laughter, a welcome respite from the trials of their circumstances.

Warm greetings danced between them like familiar melodies exchanged between old friends who share an unspoken connection. Their conversations often began with light-hearted banter, an upbeat dance through topics encompassing the universal experiences of being a man—woman, work, dreams, and the complexities of life itself.

In this haven of camaraderie, age was both a common thread and a wellspring of jest. Mr. Gladstone's seasoned years were not exempt from Sean's quick wit, as he skillfully weaved lighthearted jibes around the concept of time's passage. Yet, even as Sean teased him about age, Mr. Gladstone reciprocated with a twinkle in his eye, ready to counteract with exaggerated tales of Sean's youthful exuberance akin to a teenage novice.

Their exchanges were a delicate dance, a tapestry woven with humour and companionship, each thread adding to the richness of their bond. Sean's jests about Mr. Gladstone's virility carried a note of endearing mischief, while Mr. Gladstone's playful retorts likening Sean to a pubescent youth elicited hearty laughter, proving that age was but a canvas for their shared laughs.

Amidst the jokes and laughter, their conversations gradually shifted to more profound matters. Life and love emerged as central themes, painted with strokes of wisdom and vulnerability. This seamless transition from jests to introspection was a testament to the depth of their connection.

As they settled into a more serious discussion, the atmosphere transformed, embracing a different kind of intimacy. Their shared laughter now lent an undercurrent of comfort, a cushion that allowed them to navigate conversations of greater weight. Their rapport transcended the roles of doctor and patient, forging a richer and more enduring connection.

Within the confines of that room, their conversations navigated the spectrum of human experience – from the whimsical to the profound, from the joys of jest to the depths of introspection. As the minutes turned into an hour, it was evident that their bond had transcended the boundaries of circumstance, illuminating the transformative power of companionship and shared laughter.

"So, how's the world treating you today, O.G.? Are you feeling like a million bucks?" Sean's voice was a comforting presence, and his question was wrapped in genuine concern as he inquired about Mr. Gladstone's well-being.

Mr. Gladstone's response carried a touch of lightness, a chuckle that seemed to ripple through the air. "I'm good, doc, just tallying up the days." His words held a mix of resignation and humour, a perspective that defied the weight of his circumstances.

In Sean's eyes, Mr. Gladstone's outlook remained enigmatic, a puzzle that intrigued him as much as it fascinated him. Despite challenges, the patient's approach to life was a study in resilience, a testament to the human spirit's capacity to find solace and humour amid adversity.

Sean marvelled at this unique bond they had formed, where Mr. Gladstone's candour had been the catalyst for a connection that transcended the traditional roles of doctor and patient. The older man's willingness to share his thoughts and emotions was a testament to his trust in Sean, a bond that was a privilege and a responsibility.

Their conversations sometimes took whimsical turns, Sean's concern manifesting in playful suggestions. He would raise the notion of seeking a psychiatrist's help, a feigned seriousness masking a wellspring of care. While the idea might have appeared grave in another context, their shared laughter reminded them that the bonds of camaraderie were strong enough to hold even the weightiest of subjects.

These moments of jest and laughter formed a tapestry of connection between them, woven with threads of empathy and understanding. This room became a sanctuary where walls could crumble and vulnerabilities could be laid bare, all under the watchful gaze of camaraderie.

In their space, Sean's genuine concern mingled with Mr. Gladstone's resilient spirit, crafting a bond that defied the norms and expectations of a medical setting. Their laughter became a balm for the trials of life, a reminder that even amidst uncertainty, human connection could serve as an anchor, a source of strength to weather the storm.

As Mr. Gladstone's words unfolded, Sean's attention became a finely tuned instrument, capturing each syllable with a mix of curiosity and respect. Seated before the older man, he felt like a willing disciple, ready to absorb the wisdom that flowed from Mr. Gladstone's story.

The backdrop of Mr. Gladstone's upbringing painted a picture of privilege and status, a life that danced in the circles of wealth and power. The remnants of those days still clung to his narrative, the echoes of arrogant laughter and the scent of luxury lingering in the air.

He spoke of parents who held a different creed, one in which the pursuit of money and influence stood above all else. While Mr. Gladstone might have easily harboured resentment toward such values, his demeanour hinted at something more profound, a layer of understanding that transcended judgment.

With the seasoned tone of a sage recounting lessons learned, Mr. Gladstone wove a tapestry of experience. The private school's corridors echoed with the footsteps of privileged children, a playground of arrogance and pride. Yet, he understood that it wasn't a world devoid of nuance. Within these circles, he learned the dance of appearances and expectations, where the world seemed to revolve around numbers and statistics.

As he spoke, the depth of his perspective became evident. He acknowledged the dissonance between one's ideal world and the reality that life often presented. This sentiment was tinged with the wisdom of someone who had navigated the waters of ambition and dreams. He recognized that conflating one's aspirations with the harshness of reality was a recipe for disillusionment, a path that often led to the shores of disappointment.

Mr. Gladstone added, "While that took the humanity out of me, I learned from these people that the world is mostly about numbers first and people second. Most people who fail in life focus on plausibility. However, if you focus on probability and maximize on it, you increase your chances of success."

The words hung in the air like pearls of wisdom, a testament to the clarity that comes with age and experience. Mr. Gladstone's philosophy was pragmatic, rooted in the principles of probability rather than the allure of possibility. It was a lesson in calculated risk, maximizing one's potential by understanding the odds and working within their confines.

Seated across from him, Sean absorbed every word with reverence. It was a privilege to glimpse into the mind of a man who had journeyed through the peaks and valleys of life, emerging not bitter but enlightened. In the resonance of Mr. Gladstone's story, Sean found the quiet wisdom that can only come from a life well-lived, a treasure trove of insights to be held close and cherished.

"And so, you made millions but couldn't have a family?" Sean asked.

Sean's inquiry pierced through the layers of Mr. Gladstone's story, revealing a chapter that held a tinge of sadness. The question hung in the air, delicate and poignant, a gateway to understanding the intricacies of a life lived within the realm of numbers.

Mr. Gladstone's response carried a weight that seemed to match the years of his experiences. He spoke of marriage, a union that should symbolize partnership and connection. But for him, it had been a transaction, a pact born from the exchange of status and material comfort. The woman he had chosen, or perhaps who had chosen him, was drawn not by love but by the allure of the lifestyle he could provide.

As he recounted this chapter of his life, he expressed a hint of bitterness rooted in his realization that his pursuit of numbers had left him isolated, a solitary figure amidst a family that mirrored his values. The echoes of his ambition had resonated in his wife and children, forging a bond built on materialism rather than the warmth of genuine affection.

Yet, Mr. Gladstone's journey was a paradox, a testament to the dualities that life often presents. While his family mirrored his fascination with numbers, they focused on expenditure rather than accumulation. They revelled in the fruits of his labour, viewing the world as a treasure trove to draw the spoils of his success.

In contrast, his perspective transcended the mere act of spending. He examined numbers with a discerning eye, seeking not just to consume but to position himself strategically within the framework of opportunity. The numbers weren't just units of currency; they were a language, a code that held the key to unlocking the doors of potential.

The nuances of Mr. Gladstone's story painted a portrait of a man who had navigated the landscape of ambition and desire, discovering the hollowness that often accompanied the pursuit of wealth. While his path was lined with success, it was marked by the absence of genuine connection, a solitude brought about by the numbers that had propelled him forward.

As Sean listened, he felt a mixture of empathy and reflection. Mr. Gladstone's narrative reminded him that the choices we make, even when driven by the pursuit of numbers, ultimately shape the contours of our lives. In the quiet tempo of their conversation, Sean recognized the fragility of relationships built upon inherently transactional foundations.

Within the confines of a hospital room, surrounded by the

rhythm of beeping monitors and the soft sighs of medical machinery, two individuals shared stories that bridged generations. It was a lesson in the intricacies of the human experience, a glimpse into the dance between numbers and emotion, ambition and connection, in a world where every interaction held the potential to shape the course of a life.

The revelation of Mr. Gladstone's family cut through the air like a sudden gust of wind, leaving Sean momentarily stunned. How had he missed such a significant detail? He prided himself on his observational skills, honed by countless hours spent in the hospital, where every glance and word held a world of information. Yet, this had eluded him entirely, wrapped in the enigma of Mr. Gladstone.

"O.G. Nothing at all about you screamed marriage to me. What happened to the wife and kids?" Sean inquired.

As Mr. Gladstone clarified the situation, Sean's internal landscape shifted, rearranging the puzzle pieces he thought he had already assembled. The word "married" resonated like a bell tolling in a quiet village, breaking the silence that had shrouded Mr. Gladstone's personal life. His calm exterior had masked a story of companionship forged not out of shared affection but out of calculated motives.

Sean's perspective's transformation was swift, like turning pages in a well-worn novel, revealing a previously concealed chapter. He had seen Mr. Gladstone through the lens of a friend, a patient, and even a mentor, but the presence of a wife and children added another layer, a layer painted with shades of complexity and contradiction.

Sean's question carried a weight of curiosity tinged with an undertone of sympathy. It was as if he had stumbled upon a hidden dimension, a truth obscured by the facades people so adeptly put forth. He had to know and understand what had led Mr. Gladstone down this path of seemingly calculated detachment from his own family.

The answer was blunt, delivered with a rawness that painted a portrait of familial bonds forged from convenience rather than emotion. Mr. Gladstone's words echoed with the bitterness of a man who had seen the reality of his relationships and recognized the shallow depths of his familial connections.

Mr. Gladstone corrected him, "Present tense, are married, and she's somewhere making plans for her life after I'm gone. The only way that woman and those kids are going to cry is if they realize I haven't left them every single penny I've made. I'm certainly going to make sure they cry when I'm gone."

Sean's empathetic response served as a bridge, a link between their two worlds that transcended the boundaries of generations and experiences. At that moment, as their conversation lingered on the underbelly of human relationships, Sean understood that the most intricate stories often lie hidden beneath the surface, woven into the fabric of existence, waiting to be unravelled.

Their room became a chamber of revelations, where words carried the weight of years and the complexities of emotions. It was a sanctuary of truths, where the vulnerability of a patient's confession met the genuine concern of a student seeking to comprehend the intricate tapestry of a life lived among numbers and aspirations.

As the conversation flowed, Sean realized that the lessons he learned within the confines of those hospital walls extended beyond medical textbooks and diagnoses. They delved into the depths of the human spirit, unravelling stories that painted the human experience in hues of sorrow and resilience, ambition and isolation, reminding him that every individual was a symphony of adventures waiting to be heard.

Mr. Gladstone continued, "My point is, when you understand the numbers you use to deal with the world and the numbers people will use to deal with you, you become more objective in how you do things in life. As much as you look for value in everything around your life, remember that everyone around you will also look for a similar value in you. In most cases, people are only interested in the value you can give them and not the value they can add to you. Know the truth and deal with it, and stop living a lie for its comfort. Remember, Sean, lies and myths are like an air mattress; there's nothing in it, but it's wonderfully comfortable. When someone pokes a hole in it, it'll cause discomfort and expose the reality of what was in it: nothing. Unchecked cracks in the foundation of your house will eventually lead to that house's collapse."

Mr. Gladstone's words fell like drops of rain on parched soil, each carrying a wisdom that seemed to seep into Sean's consciousness, nourishing his understanding. The analogy between numbers and life resonated deeply, like a symphony of truth playing in the chambers of his mind. It was as if Mr. Gladstone had handed him a key, unlocking a door to a broader perspective that extended beyond the confines of textbooks and medical knowledge.

The revelation that people often sought value in others for their gain rather than mutual enrichment was enlightening and sobering. It was a mirror held up to the intricacies of human interactions, revealing the complexities beneath the surface. As

Sean sat there, absorbed in Mr. Gladstone's narrative, he recognized the significance of this lesson not only in his interactions with patients but also in his broader relationships.

The metaphor of unchecked cracks in the foundation resonated as a cautionary tale, a reminder that neglecting the underlying truths in life could lead to the eventual crumbling of one's principles and aspirations. It was a message that spoke to the importance of facing reality, even when uncomfortable, and making choices that aligned with authenticity rather than convenience.

From Mr. Gladstone's perspective, Sean found a guide for navigating the unpredictable currents of life. The older patient, who had once seemed like a lighthearted jester, had transformed into a sage figure, offering insights that had been shaped by years of experience and contemplation. Sean admired how Mr. Gladstone had embraced life with an acute awareness of its complexities, finding solace not in denial but in acceptance.

As the conversation wound down, Sean felt a deep sense of gratitude for the privilege of connecting with Mr. Gladstone on such a profound level. Their discussions had moved beyond the realm of patient and student, transcending into a space of shared wisdom and mutual understanding. It was a testament to the unique bonds that could form within the walls of a hospital, where individuals from different walks of life intersected, leaving imprints on each other's journeys.

Mr. Gladstone added, "This isn't a predicament, doc. It's an opportunity for me. I've taught you about the Johari's window, and you're a smart kid. What am I hiding?"

The air seemed to hang still as Sean absorbed Mr. Gladstone's response. It was as if the curtains had been drawn back to reveal a hidden truth. Sean was grappling with the realization that he had only scratched the surface of this enigmatic patient's intentions. He marvelled at Mr. Gladstone's ability to navigate the intricate corridors of human psychology and weave his actions into a tapestry of motivations that extended far beyond the obvious.

The mention of Johari's window acted as a compass, guiding Sean's thoughts toward the realm of undiscovered truths. Mr. Gladstone's challenge was a puzzle that begged to be solved, an opportunity to peer beyond the obvious, to understand what lay beneath the surface. Sean's mind raced, sifting through memories, conversations, and actions he shared with Mr. Gladstone.

It was like piecing together a complex mosaic, with each interaction and revelation contributing a tile to the larger picture. Sean's voice carried a tinge of excitement as he responded, "So, that's something you know, but I don't. Let's see. You saved me from being expelled from this hospital because you liked that I was able to do something that your doctors had failed to do."

Mr. Gladstone quickly corrected him, "I thought you were smarter than that, Doc. That wasn't for my benefit. It was to humble those doctors, and I also thought this hospital needed at least one good brain before they kill people, if they haven't already."

As Sean listened to Mr. Gladstone's words, their interactions gained a new layer of complexity. What had seemed like lighthearted banter and moments of camaraderie had a deeper purpose.

The room seemed to buzz with intellectual energy, a meeting of minds transcending age, background, and position. Sean couldn't help but admire Mr. Gladstone's skill in navigating the hospital's social dynamics, effectively creating ripples of change through calculated actions and words.

After another moment of silence, Sean took another shot, "I think you're scared. Not scared of dying, but scared of not leaving a legacy. You didn't have much experience being part of a loving family and thought having your own would make up for that. That didn't turn out the way you hoped. You've made a lot of money in your life, but nothing will make you be remembered besides the size of your bank account. Some people would say you could give the money to charity, which you'd happily do, but that's still not a legacy because, to you, a legacy is something you achieve. You feel like your life is empty, and now you realize you no longer have time to fill that void, which scares the living daylights out of you."

A heavy moment settled in the room as if Sean's words had pierced through the layers of a carefully constructed facade. Mr. Gladstone's expression remained unchanged, but a flicker of something vulnerable danced in his eyes. It was as if Sean had laid bare the innermost corners of his thoughts, exposing the raw truth hidden beneath the surface.

The weight of Sean's analysis hung in the air, each word a brushstroke on a canvas that painted a poignant portrait of Mr. Gladstone's fears and desires. This interpretation transcended the superficial, delving into the depths of a man who had carefully guarded his emotions, motivations, and regrets.

For a moment, time seemed to hold its breath, caught between the reality of the present and the unspoken truths that had finally been voiced. Sean's words had peeled back the layers of Mr. Gladstone's stoicism, revealing the complex emotions that had been silently driving his actions.

Mr. Gladstone's gaze remained fixed on Sean, a mixture of surprise, acknowledgment, and perhaps a hint of resignation. It was as if Sean had articulated what had eluded him all this time, a summation of his deepest fears and the complex interplay between ambition, legacy, and the haunting spectre of time running out.

The room felt charged with a strange energy, a connection forged through vulnerability and understanding. Sean's empathy had broken through the barriers that Mr. Gladstone had erected, creating a bridge of shared experience between two individuals who had walked different paths but arrived at a common crossroad.

With a slow nod, Mr. Gladstone finally spoke, his voice carrying a weight that mirrored the gravity of the conversation. "You're perceptive, Sean. Legacy, or the lack thereof, can be a heavy burden to carry. The pursuit of success often blinds us to the richness of relationships. In the twilight of life, those missed connections become painfully evident. The fear you've spoken of—it's as real as the air we breathe, and facing it is a daunting endeavour."

The room was filled with camaraderie, a connection forged through vulnerability and the courage to confront uncomfortable truths. Their conversation would be etched into their memories, a reminder that beneath the exterior of strength and success lay a tapestry of hopes, fears, and unfulfilled desires.

Dr. May walked into the room holding a file, "Don't mind me; I'm just dropping off a few things and checking if Mr. Gladstone needs anything."

"Actually, if you don't mind, I need some more meds. The pain is coming back," Mr. Gladstone responded.

Dr. May explained to him that she was told not to increase

the medication by Dr. Plunkett. Apparently, Dr. Plunkett was concerned about Mr. Gladstone getting addicted to pain medication.

Mr. Gladstone's brows furrowed at Dr. May's response, a mix of frustration and incredulity colouring his expression. He let out a short, ironic laugh, a spark of sardonic humour in his eyes. "Addicted? At this point? I think I've got bigger things to worry about than becoming addicted to painkillers."

Sean could sense Mr. Gladstone's exasperation and disappointment. Mr. Gladstone looked at Sean, a wry smile tugging at the corners of his lips. "Well, they're not wrong. But my days of worrying about addiction are long gone, my friend."

He glanced back at Dr. May. "I've got the Grim Reaper knocking at my door, and he's not interested in painkiller counts."

Dr. May's expression softened, and her eyes were filled with understanding and empathy. She approached Mr. Gladstone's bed, holding the file against her chest. "I know it's frustrating, but we're trying to balance pain management with your overall health. We don't want to compromise your quality of life and must be cautious."

Mr. Gladstone sighed, his gaze fixed on the ceiling as if searching for answers among the patterns of the tiles. "I get it, Doc. But at this point, I think I've earned the right to make my own choices. If I want a bit more comfort in my final days, I should be able to have it."

Dr. May nodded sympathetically. "You're absolutely right, and I'll advocate for you. We'll work on finding a solution that provides you with the comfort you need without compromising your health."

After the previous day's events, Dr. May hadn't made much effort trying to argue with Dr. Plunkett's orders. Sean claimed Dr. Plunkett was never worried about anyone but himself. "He's worried about addiction for Mr. Gladstone for the next couple of months?" Sean asked.

Mr. Gladstone looked at Sean and said sarcastically, "Come on, Doc, I thought I had more time than that."

Sean proceeded to tell Mr. Gladstone that, of course, he had more time, but using numbers, Mr. Gladstone was likely going to have a heart attack while living his best life in his last months.

"Wouldn't it be crazy, though, when you die doing the horizontal dance, and instead of the cause of death being cancer, it becomes a heart attack during a moment of passion?" Sean said to Mr. Gladstone as both burst into laughter.

The laughter was a temporary reprieve from the weight of their conversation, another reminder that humour could offer a brief escape even in the most challenging circumstances. Mr. Gladstone's eyes sparkled with joy, and his laughter filled the room like a melody.

Mr. Gladstone nodded, his laughter subsiding into a warm smile. "Fair enough, kid. I'll try to keep my heart safe while having fun."

Their playful banter offered a moment of lightness, a counterbalance to the serious topics that often filled their conversations. It was a reminder that even in the face of uncertainty and adversity, human connection and shared laughter could provide solace.

Dr. May didn't find this exchange between Sean and Mr. Gladstone funny as she said disgustingly, "You, men, are sick. You need to grow up."

Mr. Gladstone took this as a soft pitch and decided to hit another home run, saying, "Nah, I prefer to stay this young."

Sean and Mr. Gladstone both laughed out loud again.

Dr. May found this even more annoying, so she packed and left the room. On her way out, she told Sean that Dr. Gabehart was looking for him and was waiting in her office. She also informed Sean that Dr. Gabehart didn't seem okay and thought it was a good idea for Sean to check on her immediately. Dr. May left the room and closed the door behind her.

The mention of Dr. Gabehart looking for Sean brought joy to Mr. Gladstone. His playful banter with Sean continued to provide a welcome distraction from the seriousness of his situation.

"You know I'm still giving away my Rolex? Don't let me die with it." Mr. Gladstone quipped.

Sean smiled as he examined the Rolex with fascination and mild desire, appreciating the craftsmanship that went into its creation. He responded, "Old man, don't make me risk my career for a watch. It's a good Rolex, though."

As Sean held Mr. Gladstone's hand, his fingers brushed against the timepiece's smooth surface. "You've got quite the taste, O.G. This is a beauty."

Mr. Gladstone chuckled, a mischievous glint in his eyes. "It's a symbol of time, isn't it? And boy, time has a way of catching up with all of us."

Sean grinned, his tone light-hearted. "I might let you die with it, but I can't guarantee I won't be tempted by its allure."

As Sean made to leave the room, he said, "You're going to hell for having these thoughts, O.G. I'm not a homewrecker."

Mr. Gladstone's response was swift and unapologetic, reflecting his straightforward nature. "Come on, you can wreck it for all I care. Help me crush Plunkett. He doesn't deserve Dr. Gorgeous!"

The bluntness of Mr. Gladstone's words made Sean laugh heartily, his steps echoing down the corridor. Seeing the older man's ability to find humour despite his health predicament was refreshing. Sean couldn't deny that Mr. Gladstone's candidness and lively spirit had a way of brightening even the most serious of moments.

As he walked away from Mr. Gladstone's room, Sean couldn't help but think about the various personalities and stories that filled the hospital's corridors. Each patient, each doctor, and each interaction was a tapestry woven with complexity, and Sean found himself increasingly grateful for the opportunity to be part of it all.

Sean entered Dr. Gabehart's office, the space bathed in warm sunlight that filtered through the partially drawn curtains. Dr. Gabehart sat at her desk, engrossed in what appeared to be a stack of patient files. Her welcoming smile and the comfortable atmosphere of her office set Sean at ease.

"Good morning, Sean," she greeted him with genuine warmth.

Sean returned her smile, his demeanour relaxed. "Good morning, Dr. Gabehart."

But as soon as Sean's reply left his lips, Dr. Gabehart playfully chided him, her tone feigning mock offence. "Oh? What happened to Dr. Gorgeous? I'm not gorgeous anymore? Wow, men really move quickly!"

A faint blush crept across Sean's cheeks as he realized her teasing caught him off-guard. He stammered a response, "I, uh, well, I didn't think you'd still remember that."

With a soft laugh, Dr. Gabehart leaned back in her chair, her eyes twinkling with amusement. "Thanks to you, Sean, I'm now Dr. Gorgeous to everyone around here."

Sean chuckled, slightly embarrassed yet enjoying the lighthearted exchange. "I guess I did start that, didn't I?"

Dr. Gabehart nodded, her smile radiant. "You did indeed. But don't worry, I don't mind. It's been a fun addition to my many titles."

Their conversation was infused with a camaraderie that had grown over the past few days. Sean appreciated Dr. Gabehart's ability to balance professionalism with moments of light-heartedness, especially in an environment that could sometimes be emotionally challenging.

Sean's cheeks grew warmer with every passing moment, and he fumbled for words as Dr. Gabehart teased him. Her playful demeanour made the situation both awkward and endearing at the same time. His initial apology had opened the door to a series of exchanges that seemed to have a life of their own.

Dr. Gabehart's laughter filled the room as she responded, her eyes dancing mischievously, "Thank you for the flowers. I appreciate an original way of sucking up to the boss. If you're asking to leave early using flowers, I wondered how you'd apologized when you screw up."

"Maybe a Rolex?" Sean said as he chuckled under his palm for the inside joke that only Mr. Gladstone would've appreciated.

Sean couldn't help but join in her laughter, his embarrassment giving way to a genuine sense of amusement.

Sean gratefully settled into the chair, feeling more at ease now that the initial awkwardness had passed. He looked at Dr. Gabehart with curiosity and readiness, waiting for her to explain why she had asked to see him.

Dr. Gabehart asked Sean what he thought of Dr. Plunkett. To answer the question, Sean wanted to know if he was giving an opinion about Dr. Plunkett, the oncologist and head of the hospital, or Dr. Plunkett, her abusive husband. Dr. Gabehart asked him if there was a difference.

After a brief pause, Sean agreed there was no difference because both the oncologist and the husband were overbearing, egotistic, and abusive with a grandiose complex. He expanded, "He'll do anything to get his way. He looks at people as possessions and tries to put everyone beneath him. He can ruin someone's life just for a laugh."

Dr. Gabehart listened attentively as Sean expressed his candid thoughts about Dr. Plunkett. His words resonated deeply, echoing sentiments she had experienced but had mostly kept concealed. She appreciated Sean's honesty, recognizing that it took courage to voice such opinions about someone in a position of authority.

As Sean continued, his description of Dr. Plunkett's behaviour struck a chord. It was as if he had tapped into the hidden chambers of Dr. Gabehart's mind, where she had carefully stored away her grievances against her husband. She nodded slowly, her expression a mix of understanding and quiet acknowledgment.

Dr. Gabehart's smirk reflected a hint of irony, reflecting the complex web of emotions surrounding their conversation. She acknowledged Sean's point, appreciating the distinction between his actions as a friend and his role within the hospital. Yet, she also understood that the lines between those roles could blur, and the repercussions could be far-reaching.

However, Dr. Gabehart found it confusing that Sean had seen all this in Dr. Plunkett but still decided to humiliate him and deny him the position he wanted: control.

Her appreciation for Sean's character deepened. "That's a noble sentiment, Sean. But you must also understand that your actions might have consequences for you and others."

The weight of their conversation seemed to rest heavily upon her shoulders, and she took a moment to gather her thoughts before speaking again.

Dr. Gabehart told Sean that Dr. Plunkett wanted him to get out of the hospital as soon as possible or for her to find a way to ruin Sean's path to graduation.

She told Sean she wanted him to tell her that he was worth it if she opposed her husband.

"Do you remember what you said you saw in me about my personal life?" she asked.

"The pain and loneliness?" Sean replied.

"Yes, Sean, pain and loneliness," she echoed softly, her gaze distant as if reliving the memories he had stirred. "I've built walls around myself for a long time; walls meant to protect me from... everything. Including my own vulnerability."

Sean's eyes were a mix of understanding and empathy, urging her to continue. "I married Dr. Plunkett for complicated reasons, but I also thought I could find a connection, a partner who understood the demands of this profession and the world we inhabit. But what I found was isolation, emotional detachment, and control."

She paused, her voice carrying a weight of unspoken emotions. "The hospital is my refuge in many ways, where I can exert control over my environment and my patients' outcomes. But it's also been a place where I've seen others like me, trapped by their circumstances."

Sean leaned forward slightly, his expression a mixture of concern and curiosity. "Dr. Gabehart, you don't have to—"

She held up a hand, signalling for him to let her continue. "No, Sean, I want to. You see, when I watched you stand up against my husband, against that oppressive control, I saw a reflection of the person I want to be—the person I need to be, not just for myself but for the patients who come through these doors."

Sean's brows furrowed slightly, his gaze intense. "Are you saying you want to stand up against him too?"

Dr. Gabehart's lips curved into a determined smile. "Yes. But it's not just about standing up against him. It's about standing up for what's right, justice, and compassion. It's about breaking down those walls and letting the world in, no matter how painful or vulnerable."

Sean's expression shifted to one of understanding. "You're taking a stand for the patients, staff, and this hospital's integrity."

Dr. Gabehart nodded, a spark of determination in her eyes.

"Exactly. And that includes you, Sean. I think you're worth it, worth every bit of effort it takes to challenge the status quo, even if it means going against my husband."

Sean's eyes held a mixture of gratitude and respect. "Thank you, Dr. Gabehart. But I don't want to put you in a difficult position."

She placed a reassuring hand on his arm. "It's a position I've chosen, Sean. And I believe that sometimes, change requires us to step into discomfort."

Sean listened attentively, his empathy for Dr. Gabehart growing as he learned more about her background. He could sense the weight of her past experiences, in her words, the complex web of family dynamics and societal pressures that had shaped her life.

"Yes. I got a raw deal in my life. My parents wanted to do business with Dr. Plunkett Sr., and they jumped when he told them his divorced son wanted to marry me. I didn't have much say in it since the money they would make would change their lives. I have two sisters, and I'm the middle child. The older sister is a single mother with two kids, both from different fathers, and the other sister calls herself an influencer despite never having enough money to pay her phone bill," she told Sean.

"I'm sorry you had to go through all that," Sean said sincerely. "It sounds like you were placed in a difficult situation without much control."

Dr. Gabehart nodded, her expression a mix of resignation and determination. "Yes, but I've also come to realize that the circumstances we're born into shouldn't define who we become. It's the choices we make, the actions we take, that truly shape our lives."

Sean's eyes sparkled with understanding. "That's true. And you've chosen to become a strong, compassionate, and dedicated doctor."

A faint smile tugged at the corners of Dr. Gabehart's lips. "Thank you, Sean. But I also want to ensure that the next generation of doctors don't have to face the same challenges and barriers I did."

Their conversation lingered in the air, and their unspoken understanding was palpable. At that moment, the bond between doctor and student went beyond the surface, transcending the hierarchy and the challenges ahead. They were united by a shared purpose, a determination to bring about positive change in a world that often resisted it.

Dr. Gabehart continued, "I love medicine. I knew that saying no to my parents' arrangement with Dr. Plunkett Sr. would destroy my family because they were all celebrating as if they had discovered a gold mine under the house. I knew I wouldn't like it, but the idea of a guaranteed, stable job appealed to me, so I went along with it. We got married in the first year of my cardiology fellowship, and all was okay for only a few months. He became controlling and physically abusive after only a couple of months."

Sean's heart sank as he listened to Dr. Gabehart's painful revelations. The weight of her words hung heavily in the room, a stark contrast to the cheerful atmosphere that usually surrounded them. He admired her courage in sharing such personal and painful details, knowing that opening up about such experiences was difficult.

"I'm so sorry you had to go through that," Sean said softly, his voice filled with empathy.

Sean was touched by Dr. Gabehart's honesty and the vulnerability she had shown him. He could sense the depth of her emotions and the weight of her past experiences that had shaped her life and decisions.

Sean asked her why she didn't report him to the police for the abuse, but she reminded him of the circumstances surrounding her marriage. A police report would've ruined Dr. Plunkitt's reputation and career, and the business relationship between the two families would've vanished into thin air and sent her family back to poverty by their standards.

She decided to put up with the abuse for the sake of everyone else. Had she lost this marriage, her parents and sisters would've never forgiven her.

"Fair enough. So, where do I fit in?" Sean asked.

"You came along and reignited my passion for medicine. It had become a chore, but I'm enjoying doing it again. You're amazing at what you do. I'd never want to take that away from you because I'd be depriving the world of a tremendous gift," Dr. Gabehart confessed.

"Thank you for sharing this with me," Sean said sincerely. "I'm honoured to be a part of your journey and to have helped rekindle your passion for medicine. It means a lot to me that I've made a positive impact."

Dr. Gabehart smiled warmly. "You've done more than that, Sean. You've reminded me of why I chose this path in the first place and how important it is to stand up for what's right."

Sean thanked her for the nice words, but he was still unsure if he was the right person to whom she should've been talking about this. In Sean's mind, she would either go along with it or ruin her marriage. He promised Dr. Gabehart that things would end on good terms between them, and he was sure he'd be able to figure something out for himself had he been let go from AGH.

Sean also assumed that Dr. Plunkett likely knew about Mr. Gladstone's threat of a malpractice lawsuit. Considering the kind of person he was, Dr. Plunkett would've been willing to fight that lawsuit than see Sean become a medical doctor.

Sean also reasoned that Dr. Plunkett likely had anticipated that the lawsuit would take years and that Mr. Gladstone was unlikely to see much of it.

Dr. Gabehart appreciated that Sean understood all the facts presented. All she asked was for him to think about it and help her figure it out. She also tried to explain to Sean that she didn't want to appear like the stereotype of wanting everything and making everyone happy, as that would have made her shallow.

Sean absorbed Dr. Gabehart's perspective and understood the complexity of her situation. He could see she was navigating a fine line between her happiness, professional ambitions, and family expectations. It was a tough spot, and Sean admired her for being open and honest about her struggles.

Dr. Gabehart never thought of herself as shallow, and she didn't want to give Sean that impression.

"Your perspective of this matter is quite reasonable. There is nothing shallow about looking for the best outcome by evaluating circumstances and determining the best course of action because it means you're living in the present. You understand the cause and effect and want to minimize risk and maximize positive outcomes. If you were looking for the best solution despite the circumstances, then you'd be shallow because you'd be talking about could've, would've and should've. I'll think about it and get back to you," Sean said.

Dr. Gabehart smiled warmly at Sean's thoughtful response. He clearly grasped her situation and concerns, reassuring her that he wasn't judging her but offering his support and understanding.

"Thank you, Sean. Your insights are truly valuable to me," she said, her voice carrying a touch of gratitude. "And you're right, living in the present and making informed decisions based on the circumstances is the best way to approach this."

Dr. Gabehart thanked Sean and told him she was really counting on him. But out of curiosity, Sean asked what made Dr. Gabehart think he could figure it out. She asked him if he had ever heard of something called the Johari's window.

Dr. Gabehart explained, "It's the idea that knowledge of our behaviour can be summarized as a combination of what we know and don't know about ourselves as well as what others know and don't know about us. We act and respond to situations like that. The best way to utilize this concept is by quantifying every aspect, looking at numbers and facts, and coming to a conclusion. You're already good at that, and that's how you naturally look at people and situations objectively while figuring out what you don't know in your thinking process. Let me guess, physics major?"

"That's very perceptive of you, and yeah, physics and math with a minor in psychology," Sean replied.

Dr. Gabehart smiled, her eyes reflecting a mixture of admiration and curiosity. "I thought so. Your way of thinking aligns quite well with that background. Physics and math, coupled with psychology, provide a unique lens through which to view the complexities of human behaviour and decision-making."

Sean nodded, impressed by Dr. Gabehart's observation. "You're absolutely right. I've always believed that approaching situations with a balance of objectivity and understanding can lead to the most effective solutions."

Dr. Gabehart's gaze shifted slightly as if lost in thought. "You know, Sean, the ability to look at people and situations through the lens of the Johari's window is a rare skill. It's about understanding the layers of human interaction, motivations, and vulnerabilities. That's why I trust you in this situation."

Sean's humility shone through in his reply, "I appreciate your confidence in me, Dr. Gabehart. I'll do my best to help you find a solution that aligns with your values and goals."

Dr. Gabehart asked Sean why he took psychology. Sean explained there weren't enough women in physics and math, and he needed a hobby, so psychology was the answer.

Dr. Gabehart called him terrible as she laughed at his response, but Sean felt the need to justify it. "Well, you like clothes and shoes, Dr. Plunkett likes beating you, and I like women. We all have our cravings, right?" Sean said, smiling.

Dr. Gabehart smiled back, telling Sean it was a hit below the belt. They laughed as Sean got up, turned around and started walking towards the door.

Dr. Gabehart's laughter followed Sean as he walked toward the door. "You're something else, Sean," she called out between chuckles.

He turned around, flashing a mischievous grin. "Isn't that what makes life interesting, Dr. Gabehart? Our quirks and eccentricities?"

She nodded, her smile warm and genuine. "You're absolutely right. It's those little quirks that add colour to the canvas of our lives."

Dr. Gabehart stopped him and asked why he hadn't asked her what she had studied in her undergraduate studies. "If I get it wrong, I'll be on any duty of your choice with anyone in this hospital, from changing bedsheets to mopping floors. If I get it right, I'll take you out for a nice dinner," Sean said to Dr. Gabehart.

She replied, "Not sure to call that audacity or arrogance, but sure, I'll bite. You can't get this one, so I'll make you change beds for a week.

"Electrical engineering and a minor in economics," Sean said with a huge smile.

Dr. Gabehart's eyes widened in surprise, and then she burst into laughter. "I can't believe you got that right! Electrical engineering and economics, you're absolutely right!"

Sean gave a triumphant grin, clearly pleased with himself. "Looks like I won't be changing beds anytime soon."

Dr. Gabehart playfully screamed at Sean, "GET OUT OF MY OFFICE. YOU SCUM!"

She threw something at Sean, but he ducked and closed the door. Sean opened the door again only to put his head into Dr. Gabehart's office. "Student council in high school, and likely started some sort of charity club in university." He said as Dr. Gabehart threw more things at him in playful banter, telling him to get out, leave her hospital, and never return to the hospital.

Sean closed the door again, but he also ran into Dr. May. She asked him what was happening, and Sean told her that he thought his days at AGH were numbered. Then, quickly, he changed the topic to discuss their date.

Dr. May raised an eyebrow, clearly intrigued by the sudden change of topic. Sean's ability to switch gears so quickly both impressed and amused her. She listened attentively as he spoke about their upcoming date, her annoyance seemingly fading away.

Dr. May was still annoyed by this upcoming date with Sean, but she was committed to meeting her end of the deal. To sweeten the deal even more, Sean promised to look at more files as a favour to Dr. May. However, Dr. May stipulated that the new terms of the agreement required Sean to bring these files with him, or else the date would be off. Sean was okay with this even though there was no additional benefit on his end.

Sean grinned back at her, glad to have lightened her mood. In his mind, Dr. May's demanding demeanour was all part of her way of showing her interest. As they parted ways, Sean couldn't help but feel a mix of excitement and anticipation for their upcoming date – and the challenge of the files only added to the thrill.

Sean then asked for the address, but she refused to give it to him. She told him that he gets by in life by giving everyone the impression that he was brilliant. If that was true, he shouldn't have any problem finding where she lived without her giving him the address. She also reminded him that she had asked everyone not to help him.

Sean didn't argue but smiled as he told Dr. May that he appreciated the challenge and wouldn't disappoint. He turned around and walked away.

As Sean walked away, he couldn't help but chuckle to himself. Dr. May's challenge only fuelled his determination. He knew he had a reputation for being resourceful, and this was a test to bring out his best.

Settling The Score

As the hospital's bustling Friday activity continued, Sean had his own arrangements quietly woven into the fabric of the day. The tempo of his responsibilities had begun to synchronize with the rhythm of AGH's routine. From the outside, it was just another day in the complex machinery of healthcare. However, for Sean, it was an opportunity to learn, contribute, and perhaps even outmaneuver challenges.

His pact with Dr. Gabehart had created a symbiotic relationship. He lifted the weight of some administrative tasks from her shoulders, allowing her to direct her energy toward broader organizational concerns. In return, Sean received a backstage pass to the intricate workings of the hospital machinery. This trade had a faint aroma of ancient bartering, a mutual exchange of value that drew from the pages of history.

Dr. Gabehart's guidance on discharging patients for the weekend had given Sean a glimpse into the transitional phase between medical care and home. He navigated this like a ship's captain, skillfully steering through tumultuous waters and preparing patients for their weekend reprieve. It was like choreographing a dance—ensuring that each step was coordinated and every detail accounted for lest someone stumble.

As the sun descended, the hospital corridors carried a sense of purpose, a culmination of the week's endeavours. But for Sean, it was also a prelude to something more personal – a date he had been challenged to secure. Dr. May's condition for this rendezvous had the flavour of a medieval quest, a test of wit and cunning. Her refusal to provide her address was akin to a locked gate, the key to which lay in the treasure trove of information he had amassed.

Among the ebb and flow of responsibilities, Sean was immersed in yet another intricate task: delving into case files, deciphering medical narratives, and seeking patterns that might elude the casual observer. This was akin to a scholarly monk poring over ancient manuscripts, translating the encoded wisdom.

As the evening sun cast a warm glow over the hospital, the atmosphere was electrified with anticipation. The impending weekly party was a celebration of camaraderie, a momentary release from the rigours of medical care. AGH's corridors had transformed into a sort of medieval feast, where laughter and camaraderie were the feast's offerings.

An invitation was also extended to Sean, a testament to his growing integration into the hospital's fold. But his steps took him only briefly into the festivity, his gaze wandering toward the gathering beyond. The atmosphere was festive, a fleeting pause amid life's hustle, and he was honoured by the invitation. However, the night held other plans for him.

The party's allure mingled with his resolve like the interplay of light and shadow in a painter's masterpiece. He had been handed an opportunity, a window into a realm where relationships and responsibilities converged. But he also knew that duty called, a responsibility to knowledge, preparation, and ultimately, a promise he had made.

The nurses' support added an extra layer of warmth to his efforts, and their kindness was a reminder that he was not alone in this journey. Their gestures mirrored the hospitality of ancient inns, where weary travellers found solace in the care offered by strangers-turned-friends. The hum of their conversations blended with the sounds of the hospital, thus creating a symphony of support that resonated within Sean.

For a moment, the party beckoned – a vivacious gathering, a crossroads of lives momentarily aligned. Yet, Sean's gaze was drawn to the task at hand, the case files for Dr. May, a condition for their date. The contrast between the festivity and his study was stark, a reminder that sometimes, the most valuable treasures lay hidden beneath the surface.

As the night advanced, Sean's steps led him back into the corridors he had traversed countless times. The echoes of laughter and the ambiance of companionship followed him like the distant whisper of a tale shared around a campfire. He had his own tale to unravel, an intricate puzzle of medical intricacies and diagnostic revelations.

In the tapestry of the night, as laughter mingled with conversation and music, Sean remained focused on his task. He was crafting his own narrative, piecing together the threads of information that would form the foundation of his interaction with Dr. May. The symphony of the party outside became a backdrop to his silent contemplation, a reminder that even amidst festivities, the pursuit of knowledge and duty held their allure.

As the clock ticked with the progression of the evening, Sean's efforts had borne fruit. The case files, analyzed and annotated, were a testament to his dedication. It was a journey not unlike an alchemist's pursuit, seeking to distill meaning and insight from the raw materials of medical data.

Sean felt a sense of accomplishment as he emerged from his task, the sun's last rays of the day painting the world with its gentle touch. The evening had been an exploration of different realms – one of camaraderie and festivity, and the other of study and preparation. In the tapestry of life, these threads wove together, creating a complex and harmonious composition.

As the shadows lengthened and the hospital corridors settled into a quiet rhythm, Sean's diligent efforts found their conclusion. Another load of case files, once a labyrinth of medical complexities, was now a testament to his meticulous analysis, neatly annotated and prepared for Dr. Gabehart's perusal. With this weight lifted, Sean embarked on a final round, a routine checkpoint to ensure that all was as it should be before the day drew to a close.

Like a ship readying for the night's journey, the hospital had its rituals. Patients were attended to, rooms were tidied, and last-minute arrangements were made for the night's watch. Ever the attentive steward of his responsibilities, Sean moved through these rituals with a sense of quiet satisfaction. Each interaction reminded him of the human aspect that underpinned the hospital's clinical machinery.

As the minutes ticked away, Sean's path converged on the doorway of Dr. Gabehart's office. A knock and a gentle push brought him into her domain. Yet, the atmosphere was palpably different, like the subtle shift in a room's temperature as a storm approached. He trod carefully, an observer of nuances and an interpreter of unspoken emotions.

Sean conveyed the tidings of his accomplished tasks with a casual ease. His careful penmanship now etched the discharge reports, documents of transition and healing. Dr. Gabehart's appreciation manifested in a subdued smile, a testament to the weight lifted from her shoulders.

Banter wove through their conversation, a fragile bridge of levity spanning the undercurrents of emotion. Sean, his tongue dipped in playful humour, prodded the realm of financial compensation for his endeavours. This dance of jesting, a time-honoured tradition, served as a reminder that even within the bounds of professionalism, humanity thrived.

Yet, within the confines of Dr. Gabehart's office, a particular air lingered – an unspoken invitation to share more than words. Sean's sensitivity picked up on it like a diviner's rod seeking truth beneath the surface. It was a space not just for business but for the resonance of feelings, a shared vulnerability amidst the clinical.

Their banter, however light-hearted, bore the weight of an evolving camaraderie. Dr. Gabehart's gentle smile was a testament to her acknowledgment of the connection that had gradually forged between them. While guided by an innate understanding, Sean skirted the boundaries of professionalism without crossing the line of propriety. He even joked that since he was her "shrink," she owed him much more than payment for his work on case files.

The exchange played out like a duet, a dance of words that swayed between the formal and the familiar. Dr. Gabehart's mock admonishments, reminiscent of a stern mentor, were met with Sean's jests, a counterpoint of playfulness. Within these seemingly inconsequential interactions lay the groundwork of trust, a bedrock upon which their understanding could flourish.

As the day's journey reached its twilight, Sean's interactions for the day drew to an end. His journey had been one of obligations and commitments, weaving responsibilities into the fabric of human interactions. In Dr. Gabehart's office, amid the dance of words and shared humour, a more profound connection had been nurtured – one that would serve as a guiding star in the uncharted seas ahead.

With a graceful, blushing smile, Dr. Gabehart said to him, "I'm going to teach you ECGs better than anyone you've ever met, so I think we're even on payment."

A symphony of understanding unfolded in the tranquil sanctuary of Dr. Gabehart's office. Her smile, a beacon of encouragement, spoke volumes about her intentions. The promise to unveil the intricate world of ECGs was not just an academic offer but an extension of trust and mentorship. With this offer, she positioned herself as a superior and a guide who would illuminate the path with expertise and patience.

The exchange transitioned seamlessly to the topic that lingered beneath the surface, much like the hidden currents of a river. Dr. Gabehart's query about their earlier discussion regarding Dr. Plunkett and his threat, laced with a blend of curiosity and cautious hope, hung in the air. Ever the thoughtful strategist, Sean spoke of his ongoing efforts, assuring her that the gears of his plan were turning smoothly.

His words were laced with an undercurrent of assurance, a testament to his calm and meticulous approach. In his terms, one could perceive the diligence of a chess player surveying the board, evaluating each move with precision.

The tension in Dr. Gabehart's eyes hung heavy like a storm-laden sky, threatening to unleash torrents of uncertainty. Her distress was palpable as her smile faded, each word laden with an urgency that refused to be ignored. The stakes were high, and the patience that was once a virtue now teetered on the edge of a precipice.

Desperation coloured Dr. Gabehart's plea as she implored Sean to share his progress. It was the plea of someone caught in the currents of uncertainty, reaching for a lifeline to steady themselves. Though laced with his signature playful charm, Sean's response carried an undercurrent of reassurance. He likened the situation to a baker offering dough that had yet to rise fully, promising her a richer reward if only she could wait a bit longer.

However, the whimsical comparison couldn't entirely quell Dr. Gabehart's anxiety. The need for a solution, even a partial one, was undeniable. She cut through Sean's jests with a stark reminder of her emotional state. Anxiety had a way of transforming even the most composed individuals, and she made it clear that Sean would be the first to bear the brunt if her anxiety escalated.

But Sean wasn't one to be deterred by this veiled threat. His retort danced on the edge of audacity and jest, a proposal as unconventional as it was unexpected. He suggested the solution to her dilemma lay in divorcing her husband and eloping with him. His words were playful, a whimsical attempt to lighten the mood, yet they might have held a kernel of truth beneath the surface.

Dr. Gabehart's satirical smile in response was a testament to their camaraderie, their ability to share even the most audacious thoughts without offending. However, she was quick to pivot to the gravity of the situation. This wasn't mere banter but a crossroads that could reshape her life.

The exchange encapsulated the duality of their connection. It seamlessly transitioned from lighthearted flirtation to a poignant acknowledgment of the importance of the moment. The unspoken understanding that underscored their words was a testament to the depth of their rapport.

With the weight of the situation bearing down upon them,

Dr. Gabehart's approach to Sean had shifted from mere professional interaction to something more personal. Her earlier revelation paved the way for a newfound camaraderie, a connection forged through shared vulnerability.

Her proposal hung like a question mark, a plea for a lifeline in a sea of uncertainty. The offer was steeped in desperation and underscored by a genuine sense of urgency. The stakes were not just professional or practical; they reached deep into her very essence, the life she had known.

Sean, however, wasn't one to be easily swayed by the allure of money. He was keenly aware of the gravity of the situation, and his response was a testament to his unflinching integrity. Dr. Gabehart's financial enticement was met with a counterproposal that displayed his unwavering commitment to his principles. Five thousand dollars wasn't just a number; it was a declaration of the value he placed on his ethical stance.

Their dynamic danced between professional detachment and a deeper understanding during this negotiation. Dr. Gabehart's readiness to write the cheque was a tangible expression of her desperation, a manifestation of her willingness to do whatever it took to secure actionable advice. Like a key unlocking the door to her inner turmoil, the chequebook spoke volumes about the magnitude of the issue at hand.

Sean's surprise and humility in the face of this gesture revealed his character. He wasn't just a student or a temporary fixture within the hospital but an individual of integrity and conviction. Dr. Gabehart's willingness to part with a substantial sum of money before receiving any concrete information was both an acknowledgment of his credibility and a testament to her vulnerability.

The exchange wasn't just about a business transaction; it was a negotiation rooted in the complexities of human relationships. The power dynamic shifted as Dr. Gabehart wielded her influence not just as a superior but as someone who recognized Sean's value beyond the confines of his medical skills.

"You're giving me the cheque before I tell you anything?" Sean asked.

"I know where you work, and your career is in my hands right now. So, out with it." Dr. Gabehart replied.

In this charged atmosphere, their unspoken trust took centre stage. Their interaction was not just about transferring money or information but the interplay of individual motives, mutual understanding, and the complex tapestry of their evolving connection.

Sean sat down and got comfortable as Dr. Gabehart looked at him keenly. "The entire issue is about learning to deal with your husband. Considering the circumstances, you married him out of obligation, and divorce is likely not an option. You need to use a few psychology tricks on him. It would be best to have believable tricks to keep his mind busy without getting angry at you. Most abusers crave control, and abusing their victims sometimes is the only way for them to exercise that control. You can't give him control anymore, but you can certainly give him the illusion of control. This illusion will feed his appetite for power while occasionally stroking his ego if done right. He craves that because he has been primed for that for most of his life, so it will be an easy trap for him." Sean explained as Dr. Gabehart listened pensively.

Sean's words hung like a carefully woven tapestry of insight and strategy. Dr. Gabehart's eyes remained fixed on him, absorbing every word as if each syllable contained the key to unlocking a new reality. At this moment, the room held a tangible aura of tension, as if the air was charged with the weight of their discussion.

Sean's voice carried a sense of measured confidence, an assurance that he had dissected the situation and was now offering a prescription for its resolution. His words were not just a string of sentences; they were a roadmap, a pathway to navigate the intricate landscape of Dr. Gabehart's challenges.

Dr. Gabehart's gaze remained unwavering, her expression an intricate mosaic of hope, skepticism, and yearning. Sean's analysis wasn't just advice; it was a lifeline, a potential lifeline that could offer her the semblance of control she desperately craved in a tumultuous situation.

Keeping his gaze on her, he cleared his throat and continued, "You live with him, and he uses you to build his public image. Manipulating him should be easy because you were never emotionally connected to him. Living with him is the only problem you can't solve right now. The way I see it is that you're not married to him, but you're married to your work. As long as he's happy with his illusion of control, he'll leave you alone, and you get to focus on doing what you love. Always remember that people like him are prone to make big mistakes that they will never want to become public because they're too proud. His ego and pride will lead him to screw up so bad you'll be able to get something big you want."

The depth of Sean's understanding of human psychology came to the forefront as he delved into the intricacies of manipulation and control. His insights were like a collection of ancient scrolls, revealing secrets hidden within the human psyche. He spoke not just as a medical student but as a student of human behaviour, a discipline that transcended the confines of hospital walls.

The concept of the illusion of control was presented like a magic trick, a sleight of hand to distract the mind from its true intent. It was a psychological dance, a careful choreography to appease the hunger for dominance that fuelled Dr. Gabehart's husband. Sean's strategy was pragmatic and intricate, a delicate interplay of ego and perception.

The room seemed to hold its breath as Sean painted a picture of a life lived in parallel, where the illusion of marriage was a shield against the storm of abuse. His words resonated as a theoretical discourse and a possible salvation, a lifeline thrown to Dr. Gabehart amidst the tempest of her existence.

In Sean's analysis, the threads of manipulation were interwoven with the strands of inevitability. His conclusion, a poignant crescendo, echoed the inevitability of a man's pride leading to his downfall. It was a classic narrative, a tale as old as time, where hubris blinded the protagonist to the snares laid before him.

As Sean's voice faded, the room seemed to reverberate with the gravity of his words. Though still locked onto his, Dr. Gabehart's eyes seemed to reflect an array of emotions—relief, uncertainty, determination. The seeds of a plan had been sown, a strategy that could reshape the trajectory of her life.

Their exchange was a dialogue and a pact forged in the crucible of adversity. Sean's advice was not merely a strategy but a lifeline extended to a woman seeking respite from the storm. The room bore witness to a moment of profound connection, where the boundaries of hierarchy dissolved, and two individuals stood united in the face of adversity.

The weight of Sean's words still hung in the air as Dr. Gabehart gazed at him with a mixture of contemplation and concern. His strategy was sound, a calculated dance that could lead her to calmer waters.

Still, there was a massive piece of the puzzle missing. "What about you? How do I handle that?" she asked.

His response to her question was unexpected, casting a new shade on the canvas of their conversation. His assessment of himself was candid and unsparing, painted in strokes of self-deprecation and sobering honesty. The room, which had absorbed their earlier exchange, now absorbed this new layer of vulnerability that Sean laid bare.

"I'm an arrogant kid with a brain on fire. I only look out for myself, and you could be a victim of my actions one day. I'm not worth saving. Tell your husband he was right about me, but you don't think getting rid of me right now is a good way to handle this. Instead, tell him to wait until I'm done with my clerkship, and then he can write me the worst review to ensure no one hires me. He wouldn't want the backlash from the staff that already like me if he gets rid of me now. If he does it in a letter, he can deny that to anyone that confronts him. Don't forget to convince him that the letter will carry much weight for a letter written by an oncologist who runs a hospital where I interfered with life-saving treatment for a cancer patient. To make it more believable, make something up I did today that made you so angry that you changed your mind about me, that made you agree with his assessment of me. You really must sell it, though," Sean explained.

Dr. Gabehart began to tear up because although the strategy may have been effective, she didn't want to use it on someone she had just started to see as a true friend.

This response to her question was unexpected, casting a new shade on the canvas of their conversation. The room, which had absorbed their earlier exchange, now absorbed this new layer of vulnerability that Sean had laid bare.

In his words, there was a hint of resignation, a conviction that his personality could bring harm, not just to himself but potentially to others. The juxtaposition of his earlier wisdom with this stark self-assessment created a complex portrait of a young man grappling with his identity and place in the world.

Dr. Gabehart's question was a turn in the conversation, a reminder that this wasn't just about her challenges; it was also about the entwined fate of two individuals navigating a convoluted journey. Sean's response was a testament to his analytical mind, offering a practical solution to a problem that lay ahead.

The scenario he painted was a masterpiece of manipulation, a choreographed dance of influence and perception. He was willing to play a sacrificial pawn in this elaborate game, presenting himself as the antagonist in a narrative that would serve Dr. Gabehart's purpose. This gambit required careful orchestration, a symphony of emotions and motives.

Dr. Gabehart's eyes glistened as Sean's words penetrated her defences. This was more than just a strategy; it was a poignant revelation of the depths of Sean's character. His willingness to sacrifice his reputation for her exposed a noble and tragic facet of himself.

Their roles had shifted again, from doctor and student to confidants bound by a shared secret. At this moment, Dr. Gabehart felt a surge of conflicting emotions: gratitude, guilt, and a profound sense of responsibility for the young man before her.

The room felt intimate as if they were wrapped in a world of their own making. In this sanctuary, vulnerabilities were laid bare, and walls crumbled. Sean's words had ignited a transformation, an evolution of their relationship from professional to personal, detached to interconnected.

As their gazes lingered, the unspoken words reverberated— a silent promise of trust, a shared commitment to navigate the uncertain waters ahead. Theirs was a story woven from the threads of adversity, and it would forever mark this chapter in the tapestry of their lives.

Given all the options and her knowledge of her husband, this may have been the only way to handle things at the moment, but she was not yet ready to do so.

In that quiet, tension-filled moment, Dr. Gabehart grappled with the weight of the decision she was contemplating. The choices before her were like a crossroads, each path leading to a different outcome, and none of them were without their own set of sacrifices.

"Do you really want that? You know I don't have the heart to do that," she said to Sean.

He reassured her he would be fine and suggested she take this as a temporary solution. At the same time, she buys herself more time for a better solution.

The exchange was a delicate dance, a harmonious duet of hearts and minds. Sean's assurance was a balm to her inner turmoil, a reminder that there were alternatives, even if they weren't as immediate or apparent. His words held a thread of optimism, suggesting that there was always a way forward, even when the present road seemed impassable.

The future he painted was a canvas filled with possibilities. Research and teaching—two avenues that diverged from the clinical path—offered him new horizons to explore and fresh challenges to conquer. In his casual tone and humour, he revealed a resilience that had become characteristic of him.

Dr. Gabehart's eyes remained fixed on Sean, her expression a blend of gratitude and concern. The choice that loomed before her concerned not only her predicament but also the young man who had become an unexpected anchor in her tumultuous world.

As they lingered in their conversation, the space between them seemed to narrow, a bridge connecting their separate existences. Sean's willingness to embrace uncertainty and chart a new course unwittingly taught her the art of resilience and adaptability.

The clock ticked on, and yet time seemed to stand still at that moment. Their unspoken understanding, forged through vulnerability and honesty, created a connection that transcended their assumed professional roles. It was a bond forged in the crucible of adversity, one that had the potential to leave an indelible mark on both their lives.

Dr. Gabehart's heart swayed between the dilemma at hand and the unexpected alliance she had found in Sean. Her choices carried the weight of her destiny and the ripple effect they might have on another's life.

Her heart ached as she listened to Sean's words, and she felt the weight of the situation bearing down on them. Although she had come to admire his resilience and intelligence, she recognized the vulnerability he sometimes concealed beneath his wit and humour.

Dr. Gabehart was heartbroken. She knew the severity of the situation and how it could harm Sean's career. His easy laughter, even while discussing such serious matters, was reassuring and disconcerting. It was a facade she had seen in people who masked their pain with smiles and jokes. Dr. Gabehart wondered if this was Sean's way of reaching out, hinting that he needed someone to understand the turmoil he might be experiencing.

As Sean spoke of the potential consequences of her actions, her heart sank. She had never intended for her decisions to have such a significant impact on him. This realization of the interconnectedness of their lives, even within the confines of their professional roles, was sobering.

His advice about dealing with her husband's abusive behaviour was a mix of practicality and dark humour. Despite the gravity of the situation, a small chuckle escaped her lips. The image he painted of her husband's reputation crumbling in the face of public exposure was tempting, even if only in theory.

But then Sean's tone shifted, and his words carried a weight that hit her like a blow. His insistence that he wasn't worth sacrificing her family for cut deep. It was a perspective Dr. Gabehart hadn't fully considered, a reminder that her choices had far-reaching implications beyond her own life.

As Sean got up and walked up to Dr. Gabehart, the room seemed to contract around them, leaving them in an intimate cocoon of shared vulnerability. Dr. Gabehart met his gaze, and in that moment, she saw not just a talented young man with a bright future but someone who had become an unexpected anchor in her turbulent journey.

"Sean," she began, her voice laced with emotion, "You're worth more than you think. Your future is important, and our choices now have consequences that stretch beyond us. This is certainly a tough situation, but I hope we can find a solution that doesn't sacrifice either of us."

She held his gaze, her eyes reflecting determination and gratitude. Amid their shared uncertainty, they stood as two individuals united by circumstance, confronting the challenges with an unspoken understanding.

Sean's gesture of offering tissues to Dr. Gabehart was a simple act of kindness that carried a more profound message of empathy and support. It was a moment of vulnerability shared between two people who, despite their professional roles, were now navigating the complexities of their personal struggles together.

He acknowledged the significance of her advice, recognizing that her medical insights were valuable far beyond his initial assumptions. The hug that followed was a silent acknowledgment of their shared understanding, a reassurance that they were in this together, facing professional and personal challenges.

As they held each other, it was a fleeting but decisive moment of connection, a bond forged in the crucible of difficult decisions and uncertain paths. When they eventually parted, Sean's resolve was palpable as he expressed his appreciation and reassured Dr. Gabehart that he was ready to face whatever came next.

However, the conversation turned unexpectedly as Dr. Gabehart asked Sean about his affinity for poetry. His playful response showed he was still the same person, a young man who often masked his emotions with humour and a touch of bravado. Yet, her question piqued his curiosity, and he couldn't help but inquire further.

Her revelation about receiving flowers and poems over the last few days introduced a touch of mystery to their conversation. It was as if a subplot had emerged, intertwining with the larger narrative of their lives. Sean's interest was piqued, and he couldn't help but ask, "So, what did the poems say?"

As Sean listened to Dr. Gabehart's account of the mysterious flowers and poems, he felt a mix of intrigue and concern. Her story painted a picture of someone reaching out to her, someone who remained shrouded in anonymity. His immediate reaction was to reassure her that he only sent her flowers once. His intent was clear: to provide her with a sense of comfort and security.

When she called the florist to ask who was sending her flowers, they had no information as the person was paying in cash. It was a puzzle that seemed to have no clear solution, leaving Dr. Gabehart to wonder who could be behind this thoughtful yet enigmatic gesture.

Sean's logical thinking kicked in, and he suggested a practical course of action: visiting the flower shop to inquire further. This suggestion was rooted in his affinity for numbers, facts, and evidence. The idea that someone was paying in cash for the flowers didn't fit his usual modus operandi, and he was keen to help her uncover the truth.

As he left her office, the weight of the situation was apparent. Dr. Gabehart's whispered words conveyed a yearning, a wish for a particular outcome that had yet to materialize.

Her vulnerability was laid bare as she lowered her head onto her desk, overcome with emotions she had likely been suppressing. "I wish it was you."

At this moment, the narrative took on a deeper emotional layer. The flowers and poems were more than a simple gesture — they were a lifeline, a connection to something potentially beautiful and significant. As the door closed, it was as if a veil had fallen, revealing the depth of her feelings and the complexity of her heart.

The story had woven together themes of friendship, adversity, and hidden desires, painting a tapestry of human experiences that resonated with Sean and Dr. Gabehart. With each turn of the narrative, their lives became more intertwined, their struggles and shared moments shaping their paths in unexpected ways.

The cold air nipped at Sean's skin as he navigated the transition from fall to winter. He had utilized his hospital connections to unearth the location of Dr. May's place of residence, and now he found himself on a determined journey. Braving the chilly winds, he alighted from the bus and embarked on the final leg of his trip, walking along the frost-kissed streets.

The winds, carrying the promise of the impending winter, seemed to gnaw at him with every step. Yet, his resolve was unwavering. He had a mission to fulfill, a promise to keep. As he approached the building, he couldn't help but reflect on the journey that had brought him here, literally and metaphorically.

Upon reaching the building's entrance, a new challenge presented itself. Sean realized that gaining entry was contingent on Dr. May herself opening the door for him. This realization threw a wrench into his plans. He knew that even a phone call would likely not suffice — Dr. May's characteristic curiosity and skepticism would undoubtedly lead to a barrage of questions about how he had tracked down her residence.

As he stood outside, he grappled with his options. His

mind raced through scenarios, trying to predict Dr. May's reactions and devise a strategy to counter them. The clock ticked, and the brisk air only intensified his anticipation. Yet, despite the mounting obstacles, Sean remained resolute, determined to overcome whatever hurdles stood in his path.

In the lobby's stillness, time seemed to stretch, and the biting cold air only enhanced the suspense. Just when the uncertainty began to feel overwhelming, a figure emerged on the horizon. Burdened with her grocery bags, an older woman slowly approached the building's entrance. Sean's instinct kicked in, and he rushed out to assist her without hesitation.

The wind seemed even more unforgiving now, whipping around him as he moved to help the woman. He eased the weight of her groceries from her grasp, shouldering the burden himself. With a warm smile, the woman thanked him, her gratitude painting a momentary canvas of human connection in the cold air.

As they entered the building together, Sean's kind gesture didn't go unnoticed. The woman unlocked the door, allowing him to carry the groceries all the way to her apartment. Gratefulness filled the air as they climbed the stairs together, their footsteps echoing in the corridor. The woman's genuine appreciation radiated, and she insisted on repaying him. However, Sean politely declined, explaining that he was simply embracing the chance to do something good for someone else.

As he left the woman's apartment, Sean's heart was whole. But he still had his mission ahead – a ten-flight ascent up the stairs to Dr. May's floor awaited him. The rapid climb left him breathless, starkly contrasting the warmth he had just shared with the grateful woman. Finally reaching his destination, he paused to catch his breath before approaching Dr. May's door, his heart pounding with excitement and apprehension.

The echoes of Sean's knocks seemed to linger in the hallway as he waited, hope mingling with uncertainty. When no response came after his first knock, he didn't falter, trying once more. Still met with silence, he considered the possibility that perhaps Dr. May had changed her mind or some unforeseen circumstances had arisen. But dismissing such a notion, he remembered the kind, understanding woman he had come to know.

A wry smile tugged at his lips as he mused about the unlikelihood of her intentionally being that cold-hearted. No, Dr. May's personality was anything but that. Her compassion and kindness had shone through in their interactions. So, with a renewed determination, he rapped on the door a third time, a rhythmic beat that carried the weight of his anticipation.

Finally, as if his persistence had summoned her, she screamed from her apartment, "Who's it?"

Sean's voice was light as he replied, "Aren't you expecting someone?" His playful tone was bracing for the intriguing evening ahead.

Dr. May unleashed a torrent of pent-up emotions as the door creaked open. Her voice carried the weight of her frustration as she bombarded Sean with questions, her words flowing in an exasperated torrent. Her initial reaction wasn't what he had hoped for, but he understood her concerns. She had every right to be cautious, and he took it in stride.

He listened patiently as she expressed her vexation about his presence in the building, her anger directed at him, and the circumstances that had allowed him to reach her apartment. Even though he was the target, he couldn't help but find a hint of amusement in her fiery tirade. It was a testament to how deeply she valued her privacy and control over her personal space.

Yet Sean was skilled in navigating such situations, a mixture of genuine concern and well-timed sarcasm, his secret recipe. As her words swelled around him, he injected humour into the dialogue, turning her anger into something funny. He knew the key to disarming her frustration was to help her see the situation differently.

His compliment, delivered with a sincere smile, appeared to break through the last of her defences. A subtle shift occurred as the storm of emotions ebbed, replaced by a more relaxed atmosphere. With time, the exchange morphed into a dance of comfort and familiarity, each moment contributing to the foundation of their growing connection.

Eventually, the door that had initially opened with skepticism seemed to swing wider, ushering in a shared space that was inviting and filled with potential. Sean stepped into her home, an unspoken understanding between them – that this evening would be unique and memorable, marked by their candid conversations and perhaps a touch of unexpected magic.

Sean complied with Dr. May's request, slipping off his shoes and finding a seat. Her instruction to not get too comfortable struck a chord of playful banter between them. It was as though their conversations were woven with a delicate balance of tension and ease, a symphony of verbal exchanges that reflected their unique dynamic.

The mention of the elderly ladies brought a chuckle to Dr. May's lips, a knowing smile that hinted at the identities of those who had assisted Sean in reaching her apartment. Sean's playful admission had unmasked the truth, yet it only amused her further. Their connection was marked by an understanding that required little explanation – a quiet acknowledgment of their roles in each other's lives.

"Is this how you welcome guests into your home?" he asked.

"As someone doing this under protest, trust me, I'm being very nice to you right now," she replied.

Dr. May was clearly relishing the opportunity to exercise a little teasing authority over him. As they engaged in this verbal dance, it became evident that despite her initial resistance, Sean's presence was not entirely unwelcome. A peculiar blend of hospitality and mock reluctance encapsulated their interaction.

At that moment, the air in the room seemed to shimmer with an unspoken understanding, as if the words exchanged were just a surface layer of the connection that was forming between them. Each comment and response was a step in a carefully choreographed dance of emotions and vulnerability, building a bridge between their lives that neither could have anticipated.

Sean's wit and charm made Dr. May smile, and the atmosphere lightened between them. He playfully nudged her to loosen up, highlighting that they still had professional matters to attend to. His humour gently reminded her that their interactions weren't solely based on personal dynamics but also involved their work relationship.

Sean's threat to involve Dr. Plunkett in their case exchange brought Dr. May another bout of laughter. Clearly, he effectively used his ability to turn a potentially tense situation into a lighthearted exchange. In response, she feigned concern that Dr.

Plunkett harboured resentment because she had not supported him in his encounter with Mr. Gladstone.

Then, in a vulnerable twist, Dr. May opened up about her own struggles. The mention of her grandmother's Alzheimer's diagnosis added a layer of depth to her character. The weight of her confession hinted at the emotional toll the situation was taking on her. Despite being at home, the lines between work and personal life seemed blurred as she struggled to find answers for her grandmother's condition.

Sean's demeanour shifted subtly, his eyes reflecting a more profound empathy. He understood the gravity of her situation, and his earlier teasing tone gave way to a more compassionate demeanour. He could sense that this was an area where his unique talents as a "psychiatrist" could be of help beyond the walls of the hospital.

At that moment, their connection deepened, and he assured her, "Well, if you ever need a fresh perspective or someone to talk to about it, I'm here."

Sean asked to see her grandmother's file, but Dr. May refused, telling him he didn't have to.

She told him she had to learn to accept it and find a way to live with it. Sean didn't fight it, which offended Dr. May.

"Really? Why are you giving up on Grandmother so quickly? You're helping a smoker, and you can't lift a finger to help an elderly woman who has lived her whole life to make others happy?" she asked in frustration.

Sean asked if she had forgotten that he wasn't a doctor. Dr. May handed Sean the file with all her grandmother's medical records.

As Sean flipped through the file in silence, the weight of Dr. May's frustration and sorrow hung in the air. Her plea for help for her grandmother had clearly touched a nerve.

Dr. May's inner conflict was palpable. Her actions in preparing the table were almost mechanical as if her thoughts were far away. Her grandmother's condition was a heavy burden on her heart, and she had reached a point of desperation, seeking any possible avenue for hope.

As Sean read through the medical records, his brow furrowed in concentration. He wasn't a doctor, but his analytical mind was hard at work. His unique perspective, honed by his psychology skills and natural inclination for problem-solving, allowed him to see patterns and connections that might not have been immediately apparent to others.

Finally, Sean looked up from the file, his expression a mix of seriousness and contemplation. He saw the pain in Dr. May's eyes, the emotional turmoil she was grappling with. He cleared his throat before speaking, his voice gentle but resolute. "I'm not a medical expert and can't offer you a miracle. But I can offer a different way of looking at things."

In that intimate setting, their roles had shifted. Sean, the aspiring medical professional, was now the compassionate listener and problem-solver. Dr. May, the accomplished doctor, was the one seeking solace and guidance. This exchange was a testament to the power of understanding, empathy, and how people can come together to support and uplift one another, even in the face of the most challenging circumstances.

As Sean shared his insights and suggestions, he was acutely aware of the delicate nature of the situation. Dr. May's hope was fragile, hanging by a thread, and he didn't want to extinguish it inadvertently. He chose his words carefully, aiming to balance realism and empathy.

"You're right," Sean said, his tone soft but earnest. "It's tough to reverse a confirmed diagnosis. Medical science has its limits, and sometimes the best we can do is to enhance the quality of life and provide comfort."

Dr. May's eyes glistened with unshed tears, her emotions raw and exposed. Sean's honesty, delivered with empathy, had created a bridge of understanding between them. They were two individuals grappling with the weight of uncertainty, seeking solace and support from each other in a moment of vulnerability.

"I can see that your love and concern for your grandmother are boundless," Sean continued. "And even though we can't change the diagnosis, we can explore ways to make her days more comfortable, filled with moments that bring joy and connection."

As they talked, Sean shared his thoughts on creating a supportive environment for her grandmother, where sensory experiences, familiar routines, and emotional connections could be nurtured. He suggested involving other family members, sharing stories and memories, and finding activities that might still resonate with her grandmother's personality and preferences.

Dr. May listened intently, her expression a mix of gratitude and aching sadness. Sean's willingness to engage in this discussion and lend his insights even when he wasn't a medical professional was a testament to the depth of his compassion. It was a reminder that sometimes, the most meaningful support comes from a genuine heart willing to walk alongside another in their pain.

The dining table was a tapestry of colours and flavours, a feast for the eyes and the palate. Sean marvelled at the spread before him, the array of dishes a testament to Dr. May's culinary skills and her genuine desire to create a memorable evening. The lamb chops glistened under the soft lighting, the mashed potatoes were creamy and inviting, and the shrimp in the fried rice looked tantalizingly succulent.

Sean's skepticism about Dr. May's involvement in preparing such a lavish meal was met with her good-natured response. Her smile, a mixture of playfulness and warmth, reassured him that this was indeed her handiwork. As they sat down to eat, Sean couldn't help but admire the effort she had put into every detail, from the arrangement of the dishes to the careful pairing of flavours.

"Apologies if I doubted your cooking prowess," Sean chuckled, his tone light. "You've truly outdone yourself."

Dr. May raised an eyebrow, a mock expression of indignation on her face. "Well, I do have some skills beyond diagnosing patients, you know."

As they savoured each bite, their conversation flowed effortlessly. They discussed everything from hospital anecdotes to favourite travel destinations, creating a sense of comfort and camaraderie that belied their initial meeting's tense circumstances. The meal had become a bridge connecting their worlds, allowing them to share a moment of respite from the challenges that awaited them outside the walls of Dr. May's apartment.

Amid the laughter and anecdotes, a sense of gratitude lingered. Sean felt grateful for the opportunity to step into Dr. May's world, to offer his insights and share a meal that transcended mere sustenance. Dr. May, in turn, was grateful for the unexpected company and the chance to let her guard down and find solace in Sean's presence.

In a world marked by high-stakes medical decisions and complex relationships, breaking bread together allowed them to connect on a profoundly human level.

As the dinner conversation flowed and the meal was savoured, Sean was genuinely surprised by Dr. May's culinary expertise. The variety of flavours and meticulous attention to detail she had put into each dish spoke volumes about her dedication to creating a memorable dining experience. It was a far cry from what he had initially expected—a simple, casual meal.

"Dr. May, you've truly managed to exceed all expectations," Sean exclaimed with a hearty chuckle. "I've had my fair share of homecooked meals, but I must say, this might just take the cake as the best one yet."

Dr. May's eyes sparkled with amusement and pride at his words. "Well, I'm glad you're enjoying it. I rarely get to play chef, so I figured I'd make it a special occasion."

Sean's playful skepticism about her culinary abilities had been put to rest, replaced by genuine admiration. He couldn't help but tease her about her hidden talents, joking about becoming a regular visitor to her kitchen.

A smile played on Dr. May's lips as she responded, "Oh, you're more than welcome to visit anytime, though I can't promise a gourmet meal every time. Tonight is a bit of an exception."

As they finished the main course, the promise of dessert—a homemade cheesecake—hung in the air, adding an extra layer of excitement to the evening. Dr. May's thoughtful gesture of suggesting wine to complement the dessert only enhanced the overall experience.

With a nod of appreciation, Sean responded, "Dr. May, you

have outdone yourself. I'll gladly get that bottle of wine for us."

As he left the dining area to retrieve the wine, Sean felt a deep sense of gratitude for the unexpected turn the evening had taken. It was a stark reminder that people hold hidden depths and surprises and that sometimes, the most memorable moments can arise from the simplest gestures.

Sean returned to the dining area with a bottle of wine, ready to uncork and enjoy the dessert. As he settled back into his seat, he noticed Dr. May's thoughtful expression. He could sense that her mind was still grappling with her grandmother's health despite attempting to shift the conversation away from herself.

With a gentle smile, Sean decided to engage in some light banter. "You know, I've been thinking about it. I'd give that meal a solid 9.5 out of 10. The only way it could've been a 10 is if you somehow managed to make the cheesecake from scratch, too."

Dr. May rolled her eyes, though her lips curled into a playful smile. "You're impossible. I hope you realize that."

Sean chuckled. "Oh, I definitely realize it. And I'd say that's a key part of my charm."

They both laughed, the tension from earlier in the conversation slowly dissipating.

Dr. May asked Sean what he thought of her grandmother's file. Sean dodged the question by begging her not to talk and let him savour the moment.

"Typical, insensitive," Dr. May mumbled.

Sean asked her why she was always tense. He told her that she was too rigid, which showed in how she handled her cases. He advised her to relax and enjoy life's simple things.

"Could we not discuss me, please?" she asked, and Sean obliged.

Sean then leaned back, his expression turning thoughtful. "On a serious note, though, I can tell that your grandmother's situation is weighing on you. But hey, let's not make this evening about that. Let's just enjoy the good food, the wine, and the company."

Dr. May nodded, appreciating the attempt to lighten the mood. "You're right. Thank you for reminding me to take a break from my own thoughts."

The atmosphere eased as they indulged in the delicious homemade cheesecake. The weight of their responsibilities was momentarily set aside, replaced by the simple pleasure of good food and the camaraderie that had developed between them.

Sean's playful demeanour faded as he realized the depth of Dr. May's emotions. He put down the wine bottle and looked at her with concern. "Hey, you don't have to do that. We're here to enjoy the evening, not drown our sorrows."

Dr. May's expression softened, and she offered a small smile. "I know. But sometimes, it's tempting to just forget about everything for a moment."

Sean nodded, understanding the sentiment behind her words. "I get it. Life can get overwhelming, and we all need an escape sometimes. But you have a strong spirit and are not alone in facing challenges."

Dr. May's gaze met his, and for a moment, they shared a connection that went beyond the surface. "You're right. I guess it's just a tough time. Thanks for being here, Sean."

"Always," he replied, his tone genuine. "And you know, you can lean on your friends. We're here to help you through the tough times."

Dr. May smiled appreciatively, and they continued their conversation, discussing lighter topics and sharing laughter. As the evening unfolded, they found solace in each other's company, offering support and understanding amidst life's complexities.

Sean got up and stood beside Dr. May. He poured her a glass of wine and guided her hand to get up. Then, he started playing music and dancing slowly with her.

"You are like a shining star in the sky - radiant, brilliant, and captivating. Your intelligence is like a sharp sword, cutting through problems with ease. Your compassion is like a sturdy oak tree rooted firmly in the ground. And your sense of humour is like a refreshing breeze, bringing joy and laughter wherever you go. Interacting with patients is like a warm embrace, making them feel cherished and important, even during a busy day. Your unique disposition is like a rare gem, treasured and admired by all who have the privilege of knowing you," Sean articulated.

Dr. May blushed as she began to enjoy the moment while they danced to multiple songs.

Soft music filled the room, creating an intimate atmosphere as Sean and Dr. May swayed to the rhythm. Dr. May's initial awkwardness melted away, and she smiled at Sean's words, feeling a warmth spreading within her. She had always prided herself on her professionalism and dedication, but hearing Sean's perspective made her realize that her efforts were indeed making a difference.

"Thank you, Sean," she replied, her voice soft and genuine. "It's not often I hear such kind words about myself."

Sean's eyes met hers, his gaze sincere. "Well, it's important to recognize when someone's doing something great. And you definitely are."

The room seemed to fade away as they danced, leaving just the two of them lost in the music and the moment. Dr. May was usually so focused on her work, her responsibilities, and her worries that she rarely allowed herself such moments of relaxation. But in Sean's presence, she found herself letting go, embracing the simple joy of dancing and connecting with someone on a deeper level.

"Sean," she began, her voice a mixture of vulnerability and gratitude, "you've brought a different perspective into my life. I appreciate that you're not like anyone else I've met."

Sean smiled warmly. "And you've brought something special into mine too. You're not just a good doctor but a person with a big heart and a unique spirit."

As the music played, their steps became more synchronized, and their movements flowed naturally. At that moment, it felt as if their challenges had been temporarily forgotten and replaced by a sense of shared understanding.

Dr. May looked up at Sean, a soft glow in her eyes. "Thank you for this, Sean. It's been a while since I've felt so carefree."

Sean grinned. "Well, I'm glad I could help you find some relaxation in the chaos. And remember, whenever you need a break from the storm, I'm here."

Dr. May nodded, her gaze a mixture of emotions. They stood there for a moment, appreciating the bond that was growing between them. Amid life's challenges, they had found solace in each other's company, which was exceptional.

Dr. May asked Sean if he meant all those nice things he said earlier, and Sean responded, "You're like a solid eight."

Dr. May pulled away from Sean in frustration. "An eight?!" she exclaimed.

Sean couldn't help but chuckle at Dr. May's reaction. Her frustration was mixed with a hint of incredulity, and he could see that his comment had struck a nerve. He tried to suppress his amusement as he met her gaze, still wearing that mischievous grin.

"Hey, I'm just being honest," he said with a playful shrug. "You're a solid eight."

Dr. May crossed her arms, her expression a mixture of annoyance and amusement. "And what exactly makes me an eight? Care to explain your rating system?"

Sean pretended to ponder for a moment, his finger on his chin. "Well, let's see. You're smart, beautiful, compassionate, funny if you're in the mood, and you've got that whole doctor thing going for you. But," he added with a wink, "no one's perfect, right?"

Dr. May rolled her eyes. "And what would make me a ten, in your esteemed opinion?"

Sean raised an eyebrow. "A ten? Well, that's reserved for the truly exceptional, the absolutely mind-blowing. Think about it like this: a ten is a once-in-a-lifetime, out-of-this-world kind of person. For you, I think confidence will do it. Learn to take charge in your work, and your subordinates, including the nurses, will respect you."

Dr. May's irritation softened, and she playfully nudged Sean's shoulder. "You're lucky you're funny, Mr. Charming Six."

"Ah, so I'm Mr. Charming now?" Sean teased.

Dr. May's lips curved into a smile. "Well, maybe a solid five, only a soft six if you get rid of your arrogance. You were like a hard two the first time I worked with you."

They both laughed, the tension dissipating into lighthearted banter. Moments like these made Sean appreciate the connections he was forming and how they brought unexpected laughter into his life.

As their playful conversation continued, the evening became more relaxed and comfortable. The walls they had built were slowly crumbling, replaced by a genuine camaraderie that grew stronger with each passing moment. Amid their laughter and friendly jabs, a more profound connection was blossoming, one that neither of them had expected, but both were beginning to cherish.

Dr. May's laughter mixed with a hint of self-awareness. Sean's words were both accurate and revealing. He had managed to grasp one of the aspects of her personality that she had often struggled with.

Sean explained, "Dr. Gabehart is a beautiful, intelligent professional with great humour. She is confident in her abilities and believes in herself, which allows her to succeed in this field. In contrast, while you are also intelligent, you struggle with self-doubt and question your every move. However, I think you are determined to improve your confidence and strive to succeed like Dr. Gabehart in your career. She gets those two points for confidence, and you're going to work for those two points."

Dr. May laughed as they resumed dancing.

Sean continued, "You knew about the lady with the schizophrenic daughter and the law student with arrhythmias.

However, you second-guessed yourself and asked me for a second look. Don't be afraid to be wrong, but always learn from your mistakes."

"You've got a point," she admitted, her eyes meeting his as they continued to dance. "I do tend to overthink things, even when I know the answers. It's like I need that extra validation."

Sean smiled warmly at her. "Validation isn't bad, as long as it doesn't hinder your confidence. You're more capable than you give yourself credit for."

She sighed, her fingers tightening slightly on his hand. "I know, it's just... harder than it sounds."

Sean's voice softened. "I get it. It's not easy to change how we see ourselves, especially when we've gotten used to certain patterns of thinking. But hey, you've got a great skill set, compassionate and willing to learn. Those are all qualities that make you an exceptional doctor."

Dr. May's gaze dropped, and she seemed momentarily lost in thought. When she looked up again, her eyes had a mixture of vulnerability and determination. "You know, you're not just a charming six. You're also surprisingly perceptive."

Sean chuckled, guiding her in a gentle twirl before bringing her back into their dance. "Well, what can I say? I've got my moments."

As the music continued to play and they swayed together, the atmosphere between them had shifted into something more intimate. A unique connection was forming, built on honesty, vulnerability, and a shared understanding of each other's complexities.

As the evening wore on, the laughter and conversations flowed freely. They exchanged stories, shared dreams, and discovered more about each other's lives. It was a simple evening, yet it held a special kind of magic that comes from genuine connection.

As they continued to dance and talk, Sean couldn't help but feel grateful for the unexpected turns life had taken, which had led him to this moment, this place, and the beginning of something meaningful and authentic.

Dr. May was getting more comfortable as she danced with Sean, and he went into his second gear as he moved in for a kiss. She was receptive at first, but she soon pulled away. She apologized as she tried to explain that she had no idea why she did that.

Sean asked if she was okay, and she said she would be fine. She pulled away from Sean, poured more wine, and took a huge sip. "As soon as this kicks in, I'll be ready," she quipped.

"Hey, it's okay," he said softly, a reassuring smile on his face. "There's no rush. We're just here enjoying each other's company, right?"

Dr. May nodded, taking another sip of her wine, her eyes momentarily avoiding his. Sean could tell that something was bothering her beyond just the kiss.

She tried returning to Sean's arms to keep dancing, but Sean pulled away. He finally realized she wasn't joking when she insisted that he repelled her.

Dr. May tried to apologize and kept promising she could do this; she just needed a little more time and maybe help from him. Sean started walking away, packing up his things to get ready to leave. Dr. May was standing in despair as she started crying.

Sean turned around and apologized, "I'm sorry for making you feel this way about me and for making you do this. I thought that maybe with some charm over dinner and music, this would all be a huge joke, and we could have some adult fun. I meant everything I said about you. You are an exceptional woman, and I hope your patients know how lucky they are to have you as their guardian angel. I hope everyone will see and appreciate the value you bring into this world one day."

Dr. May's tears continued to flow as Sean's words sank in. She felt a mix of emotions, from frustration and embarrassment to a deep sadness at the turn of events. She had genuinely wanted to enjoy the evening and connect with Sean, but her emotional struggles had gotten in the way.

Sean's sincerity was evident in his voice and his eyes. He wasn't trying to hurt her or make her uncomfortable. He had intended to create a relaxed and enjoyable atmosphere, but sometimes things don't go as planned.

Dr. May wiped away her tears and took a shaky breath. "Sean, it's not your fault," she said, her voice quivering. "I appreciate your efforts and your kind words. It's just... I have my own battles to fight, and I thought I was ready to step out of my comfort zone tonight, but clearly, I'm not."

Sean nodded, understanding the depth of her feelings. "It's okay, really. We all have our struggles, and respecting our boundaries is important. You don't owe anyone an explanation for how you feel."

Dr. May looked at him, her gratitude mixed with sadness. "Thank you for understanding."

Sean gave her a reassuring smile. "Of course. And don't

think for a second that this changes how I see you. You're an incredible person, and I'm here to support you, whatever you're going through."

Dr. May managed a small smile. "You're too kind."

Despite Dr. May's apologies and pleas for him to stay, Sean reassured her there was no need to apologize as he was at fault. He acknowledged and appreciated all the help she had provided him and expressed admiration for her willingness to sacrifice her well-being for the sake of her patients. He reassured her that her consideration of the offer of a date, even with the possibility of unwanted intimacy, was a testament to her dedication as a great doctor who would do anything to help her patients.

Dr. May kept crying, apologizing to Sean, and begging him not to leave, but Sean was already walking towards the door.

When he reached the door, he stopped, turned around, and pulled some files from his backpack. He handed them over to Dr. May and said, "Here're the files I promised I'd work on, and I've written notes on all of them. You were on the right track on most of them, but you need to be more confident and assertive with your opinions because your patients are counting on you."

Dr. May took the files from Sean's hands, her tears still flowing, but her expression now a mix of gratitude and determination. She nodded as she wiped her tears with the back of her hand.

Sean offered a reassuring smile. "You're an excellent doctor, Dr. May. Just believe in yourself as much as your patients believe in you."

Despite Dr. May's insistence, Sean was determined to leave, especially given her current condition. However, she asked if there was any other way she could make things right with him. Sean requested she bring him a cup of coffee and a muffin on her next workday to even the score.

Dr. May asked Sean if he was okay, and he replied, "Never felt better. And, by the way, I don't think your grandmother has Alzheimer's. Look over the tests again, and your solution is found over the counter in any drug store. She should be feeling better in a month or two."

"Can you just tell me what it is?" she asked.

"You asked for a perspective, and it'd mean more to you if you figured it out yourself. Thank you for one of the greatest meals of my life. Good night, Dr. May," Sean replied as he walked out.

Dr. May watched as Sean walked away, his confident stride a stark contrast to the emotional turmoil in her apartment. She felt a mix of emotions: gratitude, confusion, and a renewed sense of purpose. She stood there for a moment, processing everything that had transpired.

With Sean's words echoing in her mind, she found herself drawn to the files he had left behind. She retrieved them from the couch and began to sift through his notes. As she read his insights and suggestions, she realized that his perspective was incredibly valuable. It wasn't just about the medical cases but also about her journey as a doctor.

As she looked over the medical records of her grandmother once again, her eyes widened as she spotted something she had missed before. She couldn't believe it—it was a potential explanation for her grandmother's symptoms that had been overlooked.

Filled with hope and anticipation, Dr. May decided to investigate further. She made a mental note to conduct additional tests and research the over-the-counter solution Sean had mentioned. It was as if a new door had opened, shedding light on a different path she hadn't considered before.

No Smoking

The hospital corridors were like the silent passages of time, winding and echoing with the distant whispers of footsteps. While others were still wrapped in the embrace of slumber, Sean was already orchestrating his day with the precision of a seasoned conductor. Dawn's soft light filtered through the windows, illuminating the hospital's hushed halls.

In the heart of this early morning tranquillity, Sean was a steadfast sentinel, tending to the needs of patients like a guardian of the night. In these pre-dawn hours, Sean found solace, his fingers dancing across the keyboard as he diligently tackled paperwork and organized patient files. His dedication was as unyielding as a sentinel guarding the gates of time.

After the nourishing embrace of his breakfast that Mother had prepared, Sean embarked on his daily pilgrimage to Mr. Gladstone's room. This ritual was a testament to his dedication, like the tides that never failed to kiss the shore. Mr. Gladstone's room became a haven where conversations flowed freely, a symphony of voices sharing stories across generations.

Sean's compassion was a guiding star in this dynamic dance of life. His interactions with Mr. Gladstone were more than just routine check-ins; they were moments of connection painted with the hues of empathy. Sean's presence was a soothing balm, easing the weariness of illness with the simple yet profound act of listening.

As the sun gradually ascended the sky, casting gentle rays through windows adorned with hope, Sean moved through the hospital corridors like a guardian angel in human form. The clock's hands continued their relentless journey, and the hospital buzzed to life with the promise of a new day.

Yet, amid the bustling current of medical duties and patient care, Sean's resolute commitment remained unwavering. He embodied the notion that the most significant rewards often emerge from the quiet moments, the ones shared between heartbeats, between breaths, where human connection forged bonds more potent than the mightiest fortresses.

The hospital's early hours bore witness to Sean's dedication, which mirrored the passage of time itself—an eternal cycle of giving, receiving, compassion, and connection. The morning symphony of footsteps, whispers, and the occasional beep of medical equipment created a canvas upon which Sean painted his legacy of care.

In the ever-turning wheel of existence, Sean's actions illuminated the truth that the most impactful gestures often take place when the world is still waking, when the soul's whispers are loudest. He was a testament to the sentiment that the smallest acts of kindness, like ripples in a serene pond, could reverberate far beyond the present moment.

Their conversations wove through the hospital's hushed corridors like a pair of elusive spirits. The exchange of words between Sean and Mr. Gladstone was a dance of eccentricity, a duet of minds as diverse as the tapestry of life itself. It was a symphony of laughter and contemplation, a canvas painted with hues of silliness and profoundness.

The mundane and the cosmic intertwined in their conversations, creating a peculiar yet endearing bond. From the ordinary humdrum of daily occurrences to the far-reaching depths of human existence, they navigated it all as though each topic was a star in their shared galaxy.

The conversations often took a whimsical detour, reeling off the beaten path and into the realm of the absurd. They were like jesters in the court of life, their discussions traversing the spectrum from crazy to outright insane. In these moments, the hospital walls seemed to lean in, eager to catch every word that echoed through the air.

However, there were occasions when the waters ran deep, when their discussions transformed into a voyage through the labyrinth of life's intricacies. The two minds would cast aside the veil of levity and venture into the territory of introspection. They'd explore the landscapes of relationships, traverse the mountains of philosophy, and dance through the valleys of existence.

Yet, even within these profound discussions, the essence of their camaraderie remained unchanged. Their exchanges were tinged with an unspoken understanding—a recognition that their connection would always be a beacon of light. At the same time, the world outside might be gloomy.

Then, there were times when they engaged in debates that could rival any intellectual duel. The pinnacle of their friendly sparring was the epic debate over the hypothetical fate of Dr. Gabehart's beauty in the literal absence of her nose. Facts and theories were exchanged like knights on a grand chessboard; each move steeped in the intrigue of medical knowledge and human physiology.

As Sean and Mr. Gladstone sparred in good humour, their laughter was a melody that reverberated through the hospital's walls. Their conversations were like bubbles of joy, rising from the depths of their hearts and bursting into the open, scattering laughter like sunlight.

In their conversations, there was no hierarchy, no distinction between doctor and patient. Instead, there was only a shared journey of exploration that carried them from the whimsical to the profound, from the ordinary to the extraordinary, and from laughter to contemplation. Theirs was a connection woven from the threads of conversation. This bond transcended the ordinary and embraced the extraordinary in every breath of dialogue.

The peculiar rapport between Sean and Mr. Gladstone wasn't confined to the face-to-face moments. It was like a river, meandering through time, occasionally taking unexpected turns and merging with new tributaries of conversation. Even after one discussion ended, its ripples continued to influence their interactions hours or days later.

Both were skilled debaters with a vast arsenal of arguments and witty retorts. Yet, their shared ability to carry snippets of these debates into other aspects of their conversations truly set them apart. The lines between their jovial sparring and reality often blurred as their arguments became the playful backdrop against which their lives unfolded.

For instance, the debate over the finest timepiece proved to be a catalyst for countless jests. Mr. Gladstone's steadfast conviction that a Rolex was the epitome of horology became a wellspring of humour. The assertion that a mere wristwatch could claim the title of "best" became an ongoing joke between them.

So, when scheduling a meeting or a walk, Sean would slyly toss the punchline, "Why don't you ask your Rolex?" It was a banter-filled reminder of the timepiece dispute that had captured their energies not too long ago.

On another occasion, Sean's resourcefulness in using a nurse to bolster his argument became a legendary tale in their shared history. The mere mention of a nurse's opinion was enough to turn the tide of a debate in Sean's favour. It was an inside joke that demonstrated the lengths to which their discussions could traverse.

The exchanges might have seemed like the mad ramblings of two individuals with an irreverent sense of humour to outsiders. Yet, their interactions were not just playful banter but a manifestation of their deep connection. Their shared eccentricity created a universe of its own, where seemingly nonsensical debates and quirky arguments were treasured jewels in the tapestry of their camaraderie.

Listening to them might have prompted raised eyebrows and bemused chuckles. Still, the congruence of their eccentricities made their dynamic so endearing. Their shared wavelength, a symphony of jests and laughter, was their secret language— understood only by them. This language transcended the ordinary and bound them together in a web of shared experiences and endless amusement.

Dr. May's entrance into Mr. Gladstone's room brought an unfamiliar twist to the atmosphere Sean had cultivated there. The mirthful banter was momentarily interrupted, replaced by an unspoken tension that hovered in the air. Her presence was a reminder of their awkward rendezvous, an unexpected detour on the path of their budding relationship.

Sensing her unease, Sean extended a symbolic bridge to her, the lines on his face softening as he tried to salvage a sense of normalcy from the situation. The room seemed to widen as he reassured her that his conversation with Mr. Gladstone was nothing more than a lighthearted exchange devoid of urgency or gravity. It was an attempt to paint over the awkwardness, to blur the edges of the unfinished business they had left behind.

Yet, for Dr. May, the embarrassment she had carried since their failed date was like a persistent shadow, refusing to be cast aside. The space between them was a bridge not yet crossed, and her longing for a return to their previous rapport mingled with her apprehension of what lay ahead.

To break free from the uncomfortable confines of the room, Dr. May suggested a change of scenery, a respite outside the patient's quarters, where the walls wouldn't echo their shared misstep. Sean exchanged a knowing look with Mr. Gladstone, their laughter a silent agreement that life's imperfections were best faced with humour.

As they stepped out into the corridor, Sean's stride was measured, his voice a blend of warmth and casualness. He tried to steer the conversation toward familiar waters, to remind Dr. May of the professional rapport they had managed to preserve despite the abrupt halt of their personal connection. But Dr. May's eyes held a mix of emotions, hinting at the commotion beneath her composed exterior.

The exchange of emails and their continued collaboration on cases had been a lifeline—keeping their interactions grounded in their shared purpose, minimizing the uncomfortable void left by their faltering date. Yet, despite their professional partnership, the unresolved tension lingered, an unspoken question waiting to be addressed.

The corridor felt like armour, providing a momentary sanctuary where the outside world could be held at bay. Dr. May's gaze finally met Sean's, her eyes an open window to the vulnerability she had tried to mask. They both stood on the precipice, grappling with the aftermath of a failed attempt at something more.

At that moment, the hospital's bustle seemed to recede, allowing their voices to float between them, a fragile bridge over the emerging gap. Their journey of connection, once paved with laughter and shared moments, had hit an unexpected detour. The path ahead was uncertain, but with every word spoken and every glance exchanged, they inched closer to the possibility of reclaiming the comfort they had once known.

They stood in the corridor, a candid moment in life's usual whirlwind. Dr. May's words were like a gust of fresh air, direct and earnest, slicing through the undercurrent of uncertainty that had settled between them. Her voice held a mix of relief and apprehension as if she had finally mustered the courage to confront the situation head-on.

"Can you stop acting nice and tell me what's happening with you? I'm very sorry about that night, but you seem to be ignoring me. I haven't seen you around for the last couple of days," she told Sean.

Sean's response, though simple, carried a tone of reassurance. The words he chose were like a calming balm, promising that the awkwardness of their previous encounter hadn't left any lasting marks on their camaraderie. He deftly downplayed the significance of that night, subtly sweeping its memory under the rug as if to say, "No harm done."

Dr. May's gaze reflected her mixed emotions. Her curiosity and concern simmered beneath her composed exterior, evident in how her eyes searched his face for hidden meanings. She was determined to address the elephant in the room, to mend the unravelling thread of their connection.

Sean offered a logical explanation for his absence, a tangible reason for his reduced presence in her world. The ECG lectures from Dr. Gabehart, a mentor he had often alluded to, lent credence to his explanation. It was as if he was saying, "Life has been busy, but not because of what you might be thinking."

Dr. May's decision to accept Sean's response without further probing was a mix of her longing to maintain their professional camaraderie and her reluctance to unearth deeper layers of emotion. Sometimes, the unspoken is easier to bear than the raw truth, and in that moment, she chose the path of least resistance.

As they stood in the corridor, their words and silences formed an unspoken pact—an agreement to set aside their personal complexities and revert to the easy familiarity that had marked their professional rapport. It was a silent understanding that the road they had travelled together was winding, and sometimes, it would lead them into the shadowed corners of their uncertainties.

With that quiet reconciliation, they seemed to reclaim a semblance of equilibrium. The hospital's rhythm continued around them, reminding them that life surged forward with its challenges and unanticipated moments.

"By the way, you were right about my grandmother. She didn't have Alzheimer's. She had a B12 deficiency, but I also took the liberty to check her hormones and got her psychiatric help to evaluate and treat any underlying depression. I wonder what I owe you now." she mused.

Amid their conversation, a sudden interruption shattered the casual atmosphere. The nurse's voice was laden with urgency, like a siren piercing through the calm. Her desperate plea was a stark reminder that in medicine, tranquillity could be shattered in an instant, replaced by the urgent call to heal.

The words, "Doctors! Please help. I gave a patient their medication as it said on his chart, and he developed a strange reaction. Please, come and look at this!" reverberated through the corridor, summoning Sean and Dr. May to a new crisis that demanded their attention, skill, and quick thinking.

It was as if fate had taken a detour, steering them away from their personal discourse and plunging them into the immediacy of a life-or-death situation.

The patient's room loomed before them, a microcosm of chaos within the controlled environment of a hospital. The air was charged with tension, heavy with a sense of urgency. Dr. May's mind raced as she assessed the patient's condition—a man trapped in a vortex of suffering, hives and redness painting his skin like a grotesque canvas. His laboured breathing was a haunting melody that underscored the gravity of the situation.

As a doctor, Dr. May was well-versed in the theoretical aspect of emergency medicine. However, faced with the raw reality of a patient's critical state, her training was put to the test. In her eyes, one could glimpse the gears turning as she analyzed the symptoms, trying to match them with her knowledge.

Beside her, Sean absorbed the situation with a practiced calmness. His analytical mind kicked into gear, his instincts honed by years of exposure to the unpredictable nature of medical emergencies.

The nurse's panicked explanation was like a puzzle piece, "I gave the patient his medication as scheduled, and a couple of seconds later, this started. I've never seen anything like this, and it's freaking me out."

As Dr. May grappled with the situation, the nurse's explanation flowed like a river of information into Sean's receptive ears. Her words vividly depicted a routine action gone awry, injecting a sense of urgency into the otherwise sterile room. The nurse's uncertainty and fear fuelled Sean's resolve, his calmness starkly contrasting her distress.

Dr. May and Sean formed a seamless partnership—two minds that operated in tandem in this critical moment. Their collective experience and knowledge became a potent force channelled into diagnosing the underlying cause and determining the appropriate course of action. Time was of the essence, and their synchronized movements mirrored the rhythm of a symphony, each note building towards a crescendo of hope and healing.

Their minds raced in tandem as they stood before the patient, and their actions danced with precision and expertise. The patient's suffering was another poignant reminder of the fragility of life, an echo that reverberated through the hospital's corridors. As they worked together to unravel the mystery behind this unexpected reaction, they held the power to steer the course of fate—one decision, one action, one heartbeat at a time.

Dr. May's hands moved with practiced precision, her focus unwavering as she assessed the patient's condition. Each movement was deliberate, a carefully choreographed sequence in the delicate ballet of medicine. The tension in the room was palpable, a living entity that pulsed with the gravity of the situation.

As she prepared to intubate the patient, her determination was a force of nature—a reflection of her commitment to healing.

Beside her, Sean's eyes were fixed on the patient's chart. His mind sifted through the information like a detective searching for clues. His gaze dashed from the chart to the patient and back again, his analytical mind racing to make connections. The chart was a treasure trove of insights, a map that might lead them to the heart of the problem.

Amid this critical juncture, a new figure entered the scene—Dr. Gabehart, a pillar of authority in the chaos. Her swift movements and decisive actions were a testament to her experience, a reminder that split-second decisions could spell the difference between life and death in medicine.

Dr. Gabehart briefly examined the patient, retrieved an injection from a drawer, and administered it immediately, instructing Dr. May to forego intubation.

"Not this again! I really need to start firing some people here. Who changed the patient's medication without looking at his chart?" Dr. Gabehart asked as she administered the injection.

The injection was like a magical elixir. Its effects were swift and transformative, breathing life back into the patient's struggling body.

Dr. Gabehart's voice cut through the tension like a surgeon's scalpel, slicing through the confusion and revealing the root of the issue. Her frustration was palpable, a testament to the recurrent challenges that could arise within a complex medical institution. The patient's medication had been changed without proper consideration, a mistake that carried dire consequences. Her words were a stark reminder that human error could have profound and far-reaching effects in medicine.

As the medication took effect, a gradual transformation overtook the patient's features. The once-distressed breathing eased, the hives receded like a retreating tide, and the room sighed with relief. Dr. May's shock was mirrored by Sean's bewildered expression—two individuals grappling with the unexpected twists and turns that their profession could bring. In the aftermath of the storm, the nurse's relief was palpable, a tangible exhale after a held breath.

Time seemed to stand still in that room, frozen within the frame of an averted medical crisis. The delicate balance between life and death had teetered on a precipice, but the effort of skilled hands had pushed it back from the edge. The patient's struggle was a reminder of the fragility of existence, a lesson etched into the memories of those who had fought to restore his breath.

Dr. Gabehart explained, "It's called experience. Once you see a sulphur allergy, you'll never forget it. This is a classic type one hypersensitivity reaction. The patient has been here for a couple of weeks, and this is the first time this has happened."

The air in the room seemed to settle as Dr. Gabehart's words lingered, carrying the weight of years of experience and wisdom. Her explanation flowed like a river, carrying knowledge carved into the banks of time. Sean and Dr. May listened intently, their eyes fixed on her as though she held the keys to a secret realm. In her words, the diagnosis became a tapestry woven from threads of medical history and clinical expertise.

With the diagnosis established, Dr. May's mind raced, each synapse firing like stars bursting into life. She pieced together the puzzle before her—medications, allergies, and reactions interconnecting like constellations in the night sky. It was a detective's work, a delicate unravelling of the patient's medical narrative. As the pieces fell into place, a portrait emerged—one of a patient in need, a life held precariously in the balance.

Sean's voice added another layer to the conversation, his words woven from the fabric of meticulous chart examination. He painted a picture with his words, each line and detail contributing to the collective understanding. The revelation that the patient was allergic to penicillin added another twist, a reminder that medical histories held secrets that could unlock the doors to understanding.

Dr. May's mind was a symphony of connections, each note resonating with the next. Her memory was an archive of medical knowledge. In her recollections, she unearthed the fact that sulphur allergies often extended beyond a single drug. The implications rippled through the room—a medication switch gone awry, an allergy overlooked, and a patient thrust into the throes of a hypersensitivity reaction.

But amid the complexity, a sense of awe lingered—the way Dr. Gabehart had navigated the situation with calm authority. Her demeanour was a lighthouse guiding them through the storm, a beacon of reassurance that in the face of the unknown, experience was their North Star. Sean and Dr. May were captivated by her poise as if witnessing a master at work, a conductor orchestrating the chaos into a harmonious whole.

The incident was a microcosm of medicine's relentless demands and unforgiving nature. It was a reminder that each decision and action carried profound consequences. The patient's struggle became a canvas upon which their collective efforts painted a portrait of healing—a portrait coloured with knowledge, experience, and a shared commitment to the well-being of those in their care.

As the room settled, a newfound sense of purpose lingered. The threads that wove their professional tapestry were the unity of minds, the exchange of ideas, and the swift response to crisis. In the midst of it all, they were reminded that medicine was not just a science but also an art—a dance of skill and compassion, where every movement held the potential to shape lives.

The nurse received some quick instructions from Dr. Gabehart, who appeared to be in a hurry. She also exchanged a few words with the patient before leaving the room. Then, she led Sean and Dr. May to her office, briskly walking ahead of them. Together, the three of them headed toward Dr. Gabehart's office.

As they walked, Dr. Gabehart spoke. "I think it's high time we revisit our protocols and communication systems," She began, her voice firm and commanding. "Today's episode was a stark reminder that even the smallest oversight can have severe consequences. It's not enough to simply diagnose and treat. We must ensure that our practices are watertight, that every link in the chain is fortified."

Her words were a rallying cry, a call to arms that resonated deeply with Sean and Dr. May. The incident exposed vulnerabilities and cracks in the façade of their well-oiled machine. It was a humbling reminder that in medicine, every detail matters—a mantra that Dr. Gabehart had always championed.

"We need to reassess our medication administration procedures," she continued. "This incident should never have occurred, and it's our responsibility to prevent such mishaps in the future. Each patient's chart should be meticulously reviewed before any changes are made to their treatment plan. I want a system in place that leaves no room for error."

Sean and Dr. May were drawn into her orbit as she outlined

her vision. Her determination was infectious, a contagion of purpose that permeated the corridors. They concurred, their commitment to the cause cemented by the gravity of the situation.

"But beyond protocols," Dr. Gabehart emphasized, "communication is paramount. We need to foster an environment where every team member feels empowered to voice concerns, ask questions, and challenge assumptions. Our collective knowledge is our greatest asset, and it's imperative that we leverage it fully."

Her words were a call to unity, a reminder that they were all integral pieces of a puzzle that relied on each other to form a complete picture. Sean and Dr. May exchanged a meaningful glance, recognizing that their roles weren't just defined by their titles but by their shared mission to heal and safeguard lives.

As the trio entered Dr. Gabehart's office, it felt like a courtroom. Her stern gaze served as the judge's gavel. The two men seated before her desk were caught in the crosshairs of accountability, their expressions a blend of apprehension and defensiveness. The weight of their anxiety weighed heavily on the room, and a palpable silence spoke volumes.

Sean and Dr. May stood as witnesses, their presence a reminder that their patients' well-being extended beyond the confines of the hospital walls. They listened to Dr. Gabehart's words with a mixture of understanding and empathy, the gravity of their roles as physicians intersecting with their responsibility towards their patients' families.

Telling Sean and Dr. May while referring to the two men, "Doctors, these two men are the sons of the patient who was admitted for uncontrolled hypertension and received psychiatric treatment upon your recommendation. It has been over a month since their mother has been here, and neither of the sons has visited her. As the patient's caretaker, I suggest that at least one of these men visit their mother daily to ensure her well-being. I kindly request that you notify me immediately if there are any days when no one visits her."

She turned to the two men and continued, "Gentlemen, I hope you understand that your mother and sister are going through a difficult time and need your support. I know you have your personal responsibilities, but your mother has been here for almost six weeks, and neither of you has visited her. I strongly urge you to consider visiting her more frequently. However, if you choose not to, I may have to take an even more unorthodox route, like offering a free seminar at your workplaces on caring for loved ones, using your situation as an example of what not to do. Please think about your choices carefully."

Dr. Gabehart's reprimand was a mix of disappointment and stern resolve. Her words were laced with an urgency that transcended professional boundaries, carrying the weight of compassion for the family they had under their care. The two men, sons who had fallen short in their obligations, listened to her words with a sense of humility, perhaps even shame.

The threat of a seminar on responsibilities hung in the air like a sword of Damocles, a reminder that their actions—or lack thereof—had consequences far beyond their personal lives. The seminar, offered as a cautionary tale, symbolized the power of their role in their mother's life and the potential for growth in the face of their shortcomings.

As Dr. Gabehart concluded her address, the room seemed to exhale a collective breath, the moment's tension easing slightly. The two men, chastened and perhaps even inspired, nodded their agreement, their eyes a mix of remorse and determination. The air felt charged with the potential for change, the realization that their actions had the power to mend the fractures in their family.

Dr. Gabehart's words lingered like an echo, a reminder that their roles as healers extended beyond medical treatments. Sean and Dr. May exchanged a knowing glance, recognizing that their duty encompassed medical expertise and the power to inspire change, compassion, and understanding in those they encountered.

Dr. Gabehart's intervention was more than just a directive—it was a catalyst for growth, a reminder that compassion and responsibility were threads in the complex tapestry of healthcare, weaving together to create a brighter, more caring world.

The exit from Dr. Gabehart's office felt like a collective retreat from the battlefield. The men, their shoulders slumped and pride wounded, left the office with a clear understanding of their responsibilities. It was as if the weight of Dr. Gabehart's words had etched the weight of their obligations into their very beings.

Dr. Gabehart requested the attention of the two men before they crossed the threshold out of her office.

"Gentlemen, are we clear?!" she yelled as she looked for a verbal or physical response.

"She's not joking. Just say yes and head out," Sean said as he tried to cover his laugh.

"Sean, shut up and get out too!" Dr. Gabehart exclaimed.

As they walked out, Sean's suppressed chuckle offered a moment of levity, a temporary respite from the intensity of the situation. Sometimes, admitting defeat was the first step towards growth, a lesson the two men seemed to be learning the hard way.

Following behind them, Dr. May wore a pensive expression, her thoughts likely occupied by the power dynamics within the realm of healthcare. She understood that their roles went beyond treating ailments; they were entrusted with caring for families, the guardians of physical health and emotional well-being.

The encounter was a stark reminder that compassion, responsibility, and accountability were integral to their roles as healthcare providers. Though seemingly harsh, Dr. Gabehart's unrelenting stance reflected the seriousness with which she regarded their shared mission.

As the hallway swallowed them up, the tension that had filled Dr. Gabehart's office began to dissipate, leaving behind a sense of hope. It was a hope that these two men, touched by the moment's urgency, would find a way to honour their responsibilities and mend the fractures within their family.

In the grand tapestry of healthcare, the threads of duty and empathy intertwined, weaving a story of healing that extended beyond medical treatments and charted the course toward understanding, growth, and change.

Sean decided to take a break from his work and revisit Mr. Gladstone's room. As he entered, he detected an unusual scent. Initially, he suspected that his sense of smell was deceiving him, but his doubts were dispelled when he observed Mr. Gladstone emerging from the washroom with a cigarette in his mouth.

Sean lost it. "You must be kidding me! What the hell is wrong with you?!" he started lambasting Mr. Gladstone.

His fury was evident in his tensed muscles and glare.

"You, ungrateful, sorry excuse of a life. You have stage four cancer likely caused by smoking, and now you're back to smoking again? Is this a joke to you?! I'm here trying to help you day in and day out, and sometimes I find it hard to fall asleep worrying about you." Sean had lost it, and Mr. Gladstone couldn't say anything back as he was caught with guilt and shame.

Sean continued, "I'm trying to ensure you're as comfortable as possible considering your fate. Now, you go behind everyone's back to make things worse for yourself by smoking again? I know you're the reason I came back, but for what? Are you this egotistic to try controlling everything without accountability? I'm trying to build a house with you, and you're removing two bricks for each brick I lay. How the hell do you expect me to help you?"

Sean began to run out of breath from yelling, but he continued, "I'm not going to be here for long. With the little time we have, you decide to make things worse for yourself. You were depressed, in pain, lonely, and without a proper diagnosis before I came here. And guess what? You had gone for over ten years without smoking. Now, you're not depressed, pain-free, somewhat lively as you find the world entertaining, and in control of your health again, but back to the one thing that caused your problems."

Sean dropped the magazine he had brought for Mr. Gladstone and threw his arms in the air as he said in exasperation, "I really don't need this. You can smoke your life away as you please for all I care, but I'm done with your nonsense. I know in my heart that I tried and did what I could to make your life better in this hospital. I'm okay with giving up here. This is the end of the line for me; I'm done. You know what? Dr. Gabehart said she saw smoking on your ECG, and I should've known then because there's no way nicotine would've been in your body ten years after you quit smoking. This means you've been smoking for weeks, at least!"

The air in Mr. Gladstone's room hung heavy with guilt and tension. Sean's outburst was an eruption of frustration built upon the foundation of countless hours spent trying to improve Mr. Gladstone's quality of life. The room felt confined and suffocating as the weight of Sean's words settled around them.

The scent of cigarette smoke lingered, a bitter reminder of Mr. Gladstone's defiance of his own well-being. Sean's anger was palpable, a storm of emotions swirling and clashing within the room's confines. The intensity of his fury was etched in every word he hurled, each accusation landing like a blow to Mr. Gladstone's conscience.

Silence enveloped the room momentarily as the shock of Sean's tirade reverberated. Mr. Gladstone stood there, a portrait of guilt and shame, his cigarette reduced to a mere stub in his trembling hand. His eyes dropped to the floor, unable to meet Sean's gaze, his shoulders heavy with the weight of his actions.

Sean's words had cut deep, slicing through the layers of Mr. Gladstone's defences. The truth in Sean's accusations had struck home, and the reality of his recklessness weighed heavily on Mr. Gladstone's heart. It was as if he had been stripped bare, exposed for all his weaknesses to see.

As Sean stormed out of the room, the echo of his footsteps seemed to hang in the air, a stark reminder of the finality of his decision. The sound faded, leaving behind an emptiness that matched the void in Mr. Gladstone's chest. He stood there, his eyes staring at the closed door, grappling with the consequences of his choices.

The room became a sanctuary of introspection, a space for Mr. Gladstone to confront the reality of his actions. The cigarette butt dropped from his fingers, its embers fading like his resolve. It was a bitter pill to swallow, the realization that he had pushed away the one person who had cared enough to fight for him.

Outside the room, the hospital bustled with its own rhythms, unaware of the storm that had just transpired. The hallway stretched into the distance, a corridor of uncertainties and decisions. As the dust settled within Mr. Gladstone's room, the unspoken question lingered: Would this encounter be the catalyst for change or the marker of a fractured bond?

Someone had heard the yelling and informed Dr. Gabehart. Just a few minutes after Sean had left, she came into Mr. Gladstone's room to see him sitting on his bed, drenched in tears.

"Mr. Gladstone, are you okay?" she asked.

Mr. Gladstone kept sobbing, now seated on his bed staring at the wall.

"I think I just ruined things for myself. The only friend I've had for as long as I can remember just walked out of my life because I betrayed him," he said as he tried to keep himself together.

Dr. Gabehart's presence in the room was a calming force, a steady anchor amidst the emotional turmoil. Her concern was genuine, and her voice rang with empathy and understanding as she addressed Mr. Gladstone's shattered composure.

She pulled up a chair and sat beside him, allowing the weight of his words to settle between them like a shared burden. The room's atmosphere was heavy, charged with the residual tension from Sean's departure. The echoes of their conversation seemed to linger like a poignant melody in the air.

Dr. Gabehart's voice was soft and reassuring as she spoke.

"Mr. Gladstone, relationships can be complex, especially in times of distress. People get frustrated, and sometimes emotions run high. But that doesn't mean everything is irreparably broken."

Mr. Gladstone wiped his tears with the back of his hand, his gaze still fixed on the wall. He let out a shaky breath, his voice catching as he continued, "I've been so foolish. He tried to help me, and I only pushed him away. I don't know why I did it, Doc."

Dr. Gabehart's gaze was steady, her eyes reflecting her compassion. "Sometimes, we sabotage the things that can improve our lives out of fear or self-doubt. It's not uncommon to react this way, especially when faced with change or the possibility of healing. But you have to remember, Mr. Gladstone, that it's never too late to make amends."

Mr. Gladstone sighed, the weight of his actions heavy on his shoulders. "I just want him to know how sorry I am, Doc. I want to make things right, but I don't know if he'll listen."

Dr. Gabehart placed a reassuring hand on his arm. "He's a caring person, Mr. Gladstone. I have a feeling he'll eventually come around. You just need to give him some time. And in the meantime, focus on taking care of yourself."

As the room seemed to hold its collective breath, neither of them could ignore the significance of this moment. Mr. Gladstone's journey toward self-forgiveness and reconciliation had just begun, and the road ahead was uncertain. But within that uncertainty lay the potential for growth, redemption, and the rekindling of a friendship that had weathered the storm.

In the quiet aftermath of Sean's departure, Mr. Gladstone and Dr. Gabehart sat together, the echoes of their emotions mingling in the space around them. It was a moment of vulnerability, confronting mistakes, and desiring to make things right. As the seconds ticked away, it became a reminder that even amid turmoil, there was always room for healing and renewal.

Dr. Gabehart's expression remained compassionate and understanding as she listened to Mr. Gladstone's heartfelt confession. She could see the depth of his remorse and the genuine desire to make things right, which moved her. She gave him a reassuring smile and placed her hand on his shoulder, a gesture of support and comfort.

"Well, all I can say is I never cared for people staying in my life. They can stay if they want or leave as they please, but I've felt how it is to hurt someone else for the first time in my life. I don't care much about him leaving; that's his prerogative. I betrayed him; I broke his heart. That's killing me because that would've been the last thing I'd have wanted to do. I've never voluntarily apologized to anyone, but Dr. Gabehart, can you please help me apologize and try to win my friend back? I never meant to betray him like that. Please help me. Please tell me anything I can do, and I'll do it without questioning you. How can I make amends with my friend?" tears streamed down his face as he gazed at Dr. Gabehart.

"Mr. Gladstone, it takes a lot of courage to confront our mistakes and admit when we've hurt someone, especially someone we care about," she began gently. "The fact that you're willing to take responsibility for your actions is a significant step towards healing."

She paused momentarily, letting her words sink in, before continuing. "Apologizing is important, but it's also about understanding the impact of your actions and showing through your behaviour that you're committed to change. Sean needs to see that you're sincere and willing to work on rebuilding the damaged trust."

Dr. Gabehart leaned in slightly, her eyes locking onto Mr. Gladstone's as she emphasized her words. "Start by reaching out to him. Be honest about your feelings and your journey towards realizing your mistake. Sometimes, putting our feelings into words can be incredibly powerful."

She sighed softly and continued, "But don't stop there. Show him through your actions that you're committed to change. Be patient and give him the time he needs to process everything. And when he's ready, be open to talking things through and listening to his perspective."

Dr. Gabehart patted his shoulder gently and offered him an encouraging smile. "Sometimes, mistakes are the stepping stones to growth and stronger relationships. Just remember that true friendships can weather storms and come out even stronger on the other side."

Dr. Gabehart sighed gently, taking a moment to choose her words carefully. "I'm not sure if I should be telling you this, but Mr. Gladstone, Sean has been dealing with personal and professional challenges. He might not have been in the best place emotionally when this incident happened. Sometimes, when dealing with our own difficulties, even small things can feel overwhelming, and our reactions might be stronger than they would be under different circumstances."

She paused, watching Mr. Gladstone absorb her words. "I'm not making excuses for him, but rather trying to give you some perspective. It's possible that his frustration and anger were amplified by other things going on in his life. It doesn't change what happened, but it might help you understand his reaction better."

"What do you mean? What's going on?" Mr. Gladstone inquired.

Mr. Gladstone listened to Dr. Gabehart's words, the gravity of the situation sinking in, "I believe he is deeply concerned about his future after finishing his clerkship in this hospital because Dr. Plunkett is set on ruining his career because you chose Sean's medical advice over his, which is likely why he has reacted so strongly."

Mr. Gladstone was surprised by the extent of Sean's challenges and potential consequences. Sean's actions clearly reflected the immense pressure he was experiencing, and this realization deepened his understanding of his friend's reaction.

"I had no idea," Mr. Gladstone admitted, his voice heavy with concern. "He's been carrying all that and still managed to remain cheerful throughout the hospital."

Dr. Gabehart nodded sympathetically. "Sean is the type of person who puts others first. He's a dedicated and compassionate individual; sometimes, that dedication to others can take a toll on his well-being. He's been trying to balance a lot, and it's caught up to him."

Mr. Gladstone sighed, feeling a mix of gratitude and guilt. "I owe him an apology and an explanation. I need to let him know I'm here for him just as he was for me."

As Mr. Gladstone contemplated his next move, he felt a renewed determination. He was ready to reach out to Sean, not just to apologize for his actions, but to let him know that he was there as a friend, willing to help and support him in any way he could. He realized their bond was worth fighting for, and he was willing to try to mend it.

Mr. Gladstone's heart felt heavy with the weight of his actions and the realization that his actions had inadvertently caused pain to someone who had been a steadfast friend and advocate during his time in the hospital. He wished he could turn back time and handle things differently, but he knew that wasn't possible. All he could do now was try to make amends and show Sean that he valued their friendship.

Dr. Gabehart's words about Mr. Gladstone's significance in Sean's medical journey resonated deeply. The bond between a doctor and their first patient was unique and profound. The circumstances under which Mr. Gladstone had come into Sean's care had shaped their lives in unexpected ways. Mr. Gladstone realized how significant his actions were beyond the surface and felt a sense of responsibility to address the situation.

He knew he had to find Sean and have an open conversation, acknowledging his mistake and reassuring Sean that their friendship was important to him. But he also understood that rebuilding the trust they once shared would take time and effort. He wanted to make it right for the sake of their friendship and alleviate some of Sean's burdens.

Mr. Gladstone sighed in frustration, feeling the weight of the complexities and limitations of the situation. He had hoped that there might be some way to help Sean, to prevent the vengeful actions of Dr. Plunkett from derailing Sean's career. But it seemed the cards were stacked against them, and there was little room for maneuvering.

Dr. Gabehart's analysis of the legal and ethical constraints resonated with Mr. Gladstone. He understood the potential repercussions of involving himself in a legal battle that could inadvertently harm Dr. May's career, especially considering the positive rapport they had developed recently. It was a difficult choice, and Mr. Gladstone found himself grappling with the situation's complexity.

"Now, I feel worse than before you came in here. That's tough. He truly loves what he does, and your husband will take it away from him?" Mr. Gladstone said as he got up from his bed and started walking around.

He stopped pacing and turned to Dr. Gabehart with a mix of frustration and determination. "So, we're stuck? There's nothing we can do to stand up against this injustice?" he asked, his voice tinged with a hint of desperation.

Dr. Gabehart sighed, empathizing with Mr. Gladstone's frustration. She knew how much he cared about Sean and how helpless he must feel in this situation.

"You really have thought about this from every angle. You certainly care about this kid. You're smart, and I admire that about you. With your brains and feminine instincts, I'm sure you'll figure something out for him before time runs out," he told Dr. Gabehart as he took a sigh of relief and sat back down on his bed.

After pondering for a while, he requested Dr. Gabehart to give him a dose of his pain medicine so he could try catching up with Sean and have a conversation with him. He was eager to reconcile with Sean without any delay.

"These are the matters of the heart, and we must act accordingly," he remarked as Dr. Gabehart administered an injection.

Mr. Gladstone sat for a few minutes, waiting for the medication to kick in before getting up.

Dr. Gabehart smiled as she asked Mr. Gladstone, "What do you mean by my feminine instincts?"

She blushed as she told Mr. Gladstone that she didn't have a crush on Sean. She explained that she was his teacher and a married woman.

Mr. Gladstone was determined to explain and did not let the matter go, "I didn't have to twist your arm too hard to get you to get him back here; you sided with him in front of your husband when you know how your husband doesn't like to lose face in front of those beneath him; you value his opinion, and I see the way you pay attention when he speaks than when other doctors speak; you've been a happier person since he started working here; and you twirl your hair when you laugh with him. He has an effect on you that no one else does. He may not end up in bed with you, but he already has your heart. Like I said, these are matters of the heart, and we must act accordingly."

Dr. Gabehart couldn't help but laugh, her face turning even redder as Mr. Gladstone pointed out all the observations he had made. She playfully rolled her eyes at his teasing, realizing that perhaps her feelings towards Sean were more apparent than she had thought.

As Mr. Gladstone left the room, Dr. Gabehart trailed behind him.

"I don't twirl my hair!" she exclaimed.

"Interesting how you only objected to that, don't you think?" Mr. Gladstone responded.

Mr. Gladstone's mischievous banter had certainly left Dr.

Gabehart flustered. As she sat on the bed, her fingers lightly touching her cheeks, she couldn't help but replay their conversation in her mind. She realized there might have been more truth in Mr. Gladstone's observations than she had initially wanted to acknowledge.

"Twirling my hair... Really?" she muttered to herself with amusement and disbelief.

It wasn't a gesture she had consciously noticed herself doing, but now that it had been brought to her attention, she couldn't deny its occasional occurrence.

Dr. Gabehart had always prided herself on her professionalism and level-headed approach to her work and interactions. She was known for her poise and confidence, traits that had helped her earn respect in her field. But perhaps, in her efforts to maintain that composure, she had unintentionally revealed more than she had intended.

She sighed softly, her fingers still resting on her cheeks. It was true that Sean's presence in the hospital had brought a new dynamic to her daily routine. She admired his enthusiasm, dedication, and genuine concern for patients. If she was honest with herself, she also enjoyed his presence.

However, she also knew that the complexities of her personal life and the responsibilities of her position had led her to compartmentalize her emotions. The idea of allowing her heart to lead in matters beyond medicine intrigued and terrified her.

With a determined exhale, Dr. Gabehart stood up from the bed. As she straightened her lab coat and composed herself, she reminded herself that her focus should remain on her patients and her role as a mentor to the upcoming generation of doctors.

Mr. Gladstone inquired with multiple people about Sean's whereabouts, searching familiar locations without success.

He searched many rooms and spoke with numerous people before discovering Sean conversing with nurses in a lounge. Sean had his backpack and appeared prepared to depart. The entire room fell silent upon noticing Mr. Gladstone's arrival, and the nurses turned their attention to Sean.

Mr. Gladstone broke the silence, "Hello, angels. Is there any chance I can steal your husband for a few minutes? I promise he'll be back in a moment."

The nurses laughed as Sean excused himself and left the lounge with Mr. Gladstone.

Outside the lounge, the corridor was bustling with the usual hospital activity. Mr. Gladstone led Sean to a quieter area, away from the prying ears and curious glances of others. He leaned against the wall, looking at Sean with a mix of earnestness and regret.

Sean and Mr. Gladstone had a very informal relationship for nearly two weeks. However, at this moment, Sean addressed him formally, "Hey, Mr. Gladstone, what can I do for you?"

"Come on, can we talk properly? Look, I've always levelled with you, and I won't stop now. You've given me in two weeks more than everyone I've met in my adult life. You gave me hope; you gave me a shoulder on which to lean; you gave me answers to life through your friendship; and you gave me the biggest gift of all, what it feels like to be alive and enjoy the small things in life," Mr. Gladstone responded as he started getting emotional again.

Sean nodded, his expression a mixture of empathy and appreciation for Mr. Gladstone's heartfelt words. He leaned against the wall, giving Mr. Gladstone his full attention.

Mr. Gladstone continued, "Right now, I feel terrible because I betrayed you, and with everything you've given me, this isn't the repayment you or I had in mind. Dr. Gabehart has told me about your situation, and I believe she'll figure something out for you. I don't know what it is, and I've no clue what's in her power to help you, but I saw in her eyes that she cares a lot about you. She'll figure something out. What I did was selfish and ignorant, and I deeply apologize for that. Sean, I'm sorry for letting you down like that. I promise this won't happen again." Mr. Gladstone struggled to contain his emotions.

Mr. Gladstone wiped a few tears from his eyes, his emotions still very much on the surface. "You've been like a guiding light in this place, Sean. And even though I've stumbled and caused some bumps in the road, I want you to know that I truly value our friendship."

Mr. Gladstone took a deep breath, visibly trying to compose himself. "I really want you to be a part of my life, even if it's just for a short time. I want to make the most of the time we have left together."

Mr. Gladstone chuckled through his lingering emotions. "I suppose we'll have our share of craziness and debates along the way, won't we?"

"You know, Sean, you're like that rare gemstone that brightens up everything it touches," Mr. Gladstone said with a twinkle in his eye.

Sean listened attentively to Mr. Gladstone's words, his expression a mix of understanding and forgiveness. He could sense the sincerity in his voice, which touched him deeply. He knew that

Mr. Gladstone's regret was genuine and that he truly valued their friendship.

Mr. Gladstone continued, "You've been carrying so much weight on your shoulders already, and I just added to it. I can't bear the thought of burdening you further, especially after everything you've done for me."

Their connection felt stronger as they stood in a hospital hallway filled with bustling activity. It was a reminder that true friendships were forged through shared laughter and mutual understanding, forgiveness, and the willingness to support each other, no matter the circumstances.

"I only have a few months to live, and I'll spend every day making it up to you. I'm going to start now. I know you take a bus here every day, which takes you about two hours each way. Here are the keys to my apartment, and it's a small walking distance from here on a sunny day. It's been my sanctuary since I got married. No one uses it right now, and I'm just paying the bills for nothing. You can live there for as long as you need. These are the keys to my car; it comes with the apartment. This's the least I can do for now, and I hope it's a good start," Mr. Gladstone said as he gave Sean the keys to his apartment and car.

Sean was taken aback by Mr. Gladstone's offer. The keys in his hand felt heavier than their physical weight, carrying a sense of responsibility and gratitude that was hard to put into words.

"O.G., I don't know what to say..." Sean began, his voice filled with a mix of astonishment and gratitude.

Mr. Gladstone held up a hand to stop Sean. "No need to

say anything, my friend. Just promise me that you'll take care of yourself and use them to make your life a bit easier during these tough times."

Sean nodded, his eyes slightly misty. "Thanks, O.G. This means more to me than I can express."

"Consider it a small gesture to repay your kindness," Mr. Gladstone replied, a faint smile tugging at the corners of his lips.

The keys in Sean's hand were more than just keys; they were symbols of trust, friendship, and the remarkable way people could impact each other's lives in the most unexpected ways.

Sean was overwhelmed with emotion as the apology humbled him to the core. Despite their best efforts, both parties failed to conceal their feelings.

Sean told Mr. Gladstone that he was having a rough day, but he'd bounce back soon. He even made light of the situation, saying that the nurses were already working on his recovery. Sean then invited Mr. Gladstone to the lounge for a brief chat before he left for the day. Although Mr. Gladstone kept apologizing for the earlier incident, Sean reassured him that these things happen in life. Sean quickly changed the subject to discuss his plan to ask some nurses out on a double date, which made them both chuckle. They shook hands and walked into the lounge.

As they sat in the lounge, the tension built up earlier was replaced by a sense of camaraderie and mutual understanding. Mr. Gladstone's sincere apology had mended a rift that had unintentionally formed between them, reminding them of the value of their friendship.

They talked about lighter topics, sharing anecdotes and jokes that brought smiles to their faces. Sean appreciated Mr. Gladstone's ability to lighten the mood, even in the face of emotional moments. It was as if they had come full circle, from a serious conversation to shared laughter.

As their conversation continued, the other nurses in the lounge gradually joined in, creating a warm and friendly atmosphere. Sean's ability to connect with people was evident as he engaged in light banter and exchanged stories. It was clear that he had formed meaningful relationships with his colleagues, a testament to his character and the positive impact he had on those around him.

As the day came to an end and Sean prepared to leave, Mr. Gladstone walked him to the hospital exit.

"Remember, my friend, take care of yourself and use those keys to your heart's contention," Mr. Gladstone said, his eyes reflecting a genuine admiration.

"I will, O.G. And thank you again," Sean replied, his voice filled with gratitude.

With a final handshake and a heartfelt goodbye, Sean walked out into the evening. The weight of the keys in his pocket served as a constant reminder of the unexpected twists that life could take and the enduring bonds that could be formed along the way.

Second Time is a Charm

The third week of Sean's cardiology clerkship dawned like a challenge waiting to be embraced. This stretch of time saw his relationship with Dr. Gabehart take on a more intense hue. The hours stretched long, with lectures lasting up to two hours each day and an ECG analysis and interpretation load that could give anyone a cold sweat. It was a true test of Sean's mettle, a crucible through which he would have to prove his worth.

The week unfurled like a grand tapestry woven with threads of knowledge and pressure. Dr. Gabehart was a stern instructor, demanding his utmost attention and dedication. In the realm of cardiology, there was no room for errors and no tolerance for hesitation. Sean was thrown into the thick of it, the pressure mounting as he navigated through a torrent of information, ECGs, and lectures.

Despite the stress that hung over his days like a heavy fog, Sean's spirit remained unwavering. Like a sailor navigating a stormy sea, he steered through the dense material, determined to make the most of this opportunity. The clock's ticking hands did little to daunt him; they seemed to fuel his determination.

From dawn until dusk, Sean dedicated himself to his work. He embraced the hours not merely as a grind but as a test of his limits. He arrived at the hospital when the sky still held the night's remnants and departed when the stars had fully emerged. The hospital walls had become his fortress, and his resolve was the foundation upon which he built his experiences.

This timetable might have seemed insurmountable for another medical student, a burden too heavy to bear. But Sean was cut from a different cloth. He thrived in adversity, finding solace in the very challenge that might have deterred others. His energy surged like a river fed by melting glaciers, unyielding and determined.

Amidst the bustling corridors and hushed examination rooms, Sean laboured with a purpose. He absorbed knowledge like parched earth soaking up rain, embracing the intricacies of cardiology with an enthusiasm that illuminated his passion. Each ECG he scrutinized and lecture he attended were pieces of a puzzle he was determined to solve.

As the week drew to a close, a sense of accomplishment, a quiet satisfaction, resonated through the hospital's walls. Sean had faced the tempest head-on, emerging unscathed and strengthened by the challenges he had encountered.

Mr. Gladstone's generous gesture had turned Sean's daily transit ordeal into a breeze, transforming a marathon of four hours into a mere sprint of twenty minutes. Those early mornings were now like a quick dash, leaving him invigorated rather than drained. The shortcut to the hospital was a gift that felt like finding a secret passage through the labyrinth of city streets.

In the labyrinth of life, Mr. Gladstone had handed Sean a compass that pointed directly to convenience. The exhausting treks were now a distant memory, replaced by a smooth journey that allowed Sean to channel his energy into his work. It was like trading a rugged and arduous path for a paved highway, a transformation that mirrored the shift in Sean's professional trajectory.

With his belongings shifted from his old abode to Mr. Gladstone's offered apartment, Sean felt like a traveller who had finally found his haven. Moving was not just about transporting physical possessions; it was about transitioning into a new phase of life. The boxes unpacked like chapters of a story unfolding, and as Sean set up his new space, it was as if he were scribing the opening lines of his next chapter.

The apartment, once Mr. Gladstone's sanctuary, now bore Sean's imprint. It was a cozy cocoon where Sean could retreat after the intense days at the hospital. The walls seemed to hold whispers of stories from the past, blending with Sean's aspirations for the future. By the time the third Friday of his clerkship arrived, Sean had woven himself into the fabric of this new space, finding a refuge amidst the hustle and bustle.

As the Christmas weekend beckoned, Sean longingly sought a respite, a chance to step away momentarily from the demanding rhythm of hospital life. Christmas Eve falling on a Friday felt like the universe's way of gifting him a well-deserved breather. It was as if the stars had aligned to offer a reprieve, a moment to embrace the joy of the season.

He approached Dr. Gabehart, seeking the blessing to step out of the whirlwind momentarily. The request was not just about taking time off but acknowledging the importance of rest in a journey that demanded his all. With her understanding nod, Sean felt a weight lift, an assurance that there was room to pause and rejuvenate even amidst the intensity of his clerkship.

The anticipation of the Christmas weekend bloomed like a peaceful melody, soothing the strains of exertion. Sean looked forward to those days when the hospital corridors would echo with a different tempo, when the warmth of celebration would replace the rush of medical urgency. Sean found himself at the crossroads of dedication and self-care at this juncture, embracing both with the same passion that had fuelled his journey thus far.

Amid his demanding schedule, Sean decided it was time to embrace the spirit of celebration. He had embarked on a journey to conquer his medical clerkship and discover the art of balancing work and life. This new apartment had become the canvas on which he would paint his relaxation, inviting a touch of social warmth to complement the rigorous medical environment.

With the afternoon sun gently casting its glow through the windows, Sean moved with purpose, orchestrating his new space into an atmosphere of friendliness. The living room exuded an inviting aura as if each piece of furniture held a whisper of anticipation for the evening's company. He had poured his attention into the details, ensuring that the arrangement echoed his pleasant personality.

His choice of guests reflected the vibrant diversity of his newfound professional life. Bella and Bonita, the two nurses he had affectionately dubbed, were more than just colleagues; they were the threads of camaraderie woven into his hospital routine. Tonight, they would transition from the clinical corridors to the comfort of his living room, bridging the gap between professional and personal.

As the clock ticked closer to their arrival, Sean's heart danced in rhythm with the anticipation. He surveyed his efforts with a sense of satisfaction, acknowledging that he had transformed this space into a haven of togetherness. The rooms felt like characters in a story, ready to play their part in an evening that would intertwine laughter, stories, and shared experiences.

With its spacious dimensions, this duplex apartment felt

like an expansive canvas upon which the strokes of connection and camaraderie would be painted. The grandeur of the dining room and living room symbolized the expanse of possibilities this gathering promised. It was a tribute to the human capacity to carve out sanctuaries of joy amidst the hustle and bustle of life.

Sean's choice of words, "a good touch on the bachelor pad," spoke volumes about his attitude towards this space. It was not just a place to lay his head; it was a canvas where he could express his individuality and hospitality. The upper level, with its cozy bedrooms, seemed like a sanctuary for his moments of solitude, a reminder that solitude and connection have their rightful place in the symphony of life.

Sean's excitement grew as the sun dipped lower in the sky, casting warm hues across the apartment. The doorbell's chime would soon usher in an evening of joy and camaraderie, a temporary respite from the rigours of medical practice. The condo had transformed into a tableau of fellowship, a reminder that even amidst the hustle of life, there are moments to cherish, friendships to nurture, and corners to call home.

Sean's christening of the apartment was not merely a celebration of physical space but a poignant testament to the interweaving of lives, aspirations, and the essence of human connection. Before orchestrating this evening of laughter and camaraderie, Sean had sought the blessing of an unlikely benefactor—Mr. Gladstone.

This gesture stood out as a symbol of trust and respect in a world where permissions and approvals often dictate our actions. Mr. Gladstone's simple yet profound words echoed like a benevolent decree, granting Sean the freedom to shape his surroundings as he saw fit. This was not a transaction; it was a legacy of trust that spoke of their friendship's depth.

As Sean reflected on this unique permission, he marvelled at the layers of meaning beneath it. Mr. Gladstone's implicit understanding of the unspoken had touched Sean deeply. The old man's reluctance to delve into the inevitabilities of life and death only added to the aura of mystery that surrounded him. The notion of inheritance was reframed in their bond, for it wasn't material possessions that were transferred but rather a sense of autonomy and kinship.

This act of extending permission transcended the realm of mere ownership. It spoke to a shared understanding, an unspoken pact formed between two disparate souls. Mr. Gladstone's wealth, which others might view as a measure of success, seemed inconsequential compared to the richness of this friendship. For him, wealth wasn't just about amassing possessions; it was about having the freedom to live on his own terms, bestow kindness without expectations, and foster friendships beyond the confines of social norms.

The apartment itself became a microcosm of this philosophy. As Sean prepared for the evening, he recognized that this space was not just bricks and mortar—it was a canvas upon which memories would be painted and relationships would be nurtured. The christening wasn't just about "breaking-in" the apartment; it was about blessing it with shared laughter and stories with friends.

As the evening drew near and the apartment began to buzz with the hum of anticipation, Sean's heart swelled with gratitude. The walls seemed to hold a certain warmth as if they were embracing the joy that was about to unfold. The gathering wasn't just a celebration of a new living space; it was a celebration of friendship, trust, and the beauty of two lives intertwining in unexpected harmony.

Sean's journey from medical student to friend, from apprehension to belonging, was mirrored in the walls of this apartment. The layers of paint and the furniture arrangement seemed to echo the layers of their relationship—complex, textured, and rich with meaning.

In the presence of friendship, the apartment was more than just an abode; it was a sanctuary of connection. It was a reminder that the most beautiful spaces are the ones where laughter reverberates, stories are shared, and bonds are forged. The christening had gone beyond its literal meaning, transforming the apartment into a haven of human connection, a testament to the profound impact of trust and friendship.

Mr. Gladstone's journey through life had been a tale of twists and turns, aspirations and disappointments. He had amassed a fortune through diligent work and ambition, envisioning a life where his wealth would be a cornerstone for a flourishing family. Yet, life's capricious hand had dealt him a different set of cards.

The dream of familial bliss, built on shared dreams and mutual love, had eluded him. The woman he had chosen to be his partner on this journey didn't prove to be the companion he had envisioned. The cold currents of circumstance had prevented them from nurturing the warmth of love.

In a world where divorce might seem the logical conclusion, he had remained tethered to a marriage of convenience. His reasons, steeped in a pearl of practical wisdom, illuminated a path that was neither ideal nor affectionate but served a purpose.

Instead of allowing himself to be trapped by a relationship

that lacked the harmony he sought, Mr. Gladstone crafted his own existence. He found solace and independence, choosing a divergent path away from the spotlight of matrimony. His world, then, became a private universe where he could wield his wealth on his terms and cultivate a life that was uniquely his.

However, a void lingered amidst this life he had carefully cultivated. The absence of genuine companionship, the lack of a true friend who saw him for who he was, gnawed at the edges of his contentment. Money had granted him luxury but couldn't fill the emotional chasm that craved human connection. The irony was stark—a man with riches at his disposal yearned for something money couldn't buy.

Then, Sean walked into his life, an unexpected guest in this symphony of solitude. In the brief span of a few weeks, Sean etched himself into Mr. Gladstone's world with the grace of understanding, the artistry of empathy, and the authenticity of his friendship. Sean's appreciation of Mr. Gladstone, beyond his financial worth, was a breath of fresh air in a world often clouded by ulterior motives.

Their camaraderie was a bridge that spanned generations, linking their souls through a bond that transcended their differences. Sean's ability to peer into the intricate layers of Mr. Gladstone's mind, to grasp the essence of his philosophy and emotions, was a treasure. It was as though he had been handed a key to unlock the vault of Mr. Gladstone's heart, revealing the hidden treasures within.

The significance of their friendship was not lost on Mr. Gladstone. He recognized the rarity of finding a confidant who cherished him for who he was without being swayed by the allure of his wealth. Sean's presence was a salve for the emotional wounds he had accumulated over time. The hope he brought, the genuine camaraderie they shared—it was as though Sean had breathed life into the dormant chambers of Mr. Gladstone's heart.

Through their interactions, the walls of Mr. Gladstone's private world crumbled, replaced by an exchange of ideas, laughter, and experiences. Sean's friendship was a testament to the fact that wealth, while a source of comfort, was eclipsed by the true treasures of life—connection, understanding, and kinship. Their friendship was a beacon that illuminated the dark corners of Mr. Gladstone's existence, revealing the joys that had long eluded him.

In Sean, he had found not just a friend but a guardian of wisdom, a repository of experiences, and a bridge between two distinct eras. Sean's gift of companionship surpassed any material offering. It was a priceless exchange of souls, a symphony of shared moments that enriched their lives. The lessons they learned from each other, the perspectives they gained—it was a mutual enrichment that money could never replicate.

For Mr. Gladstone, Sean wasn't just a friend; he was a revelation. In turn, Sean found a mentor, a confidant, and a genuine bond that defied the conventional boundaries of time and age. The tapestry of their lives had been woven together in a way that defied explanation, leaving an indelible mark on both of their hearts.

Amidst the tapestry of their intertwining lives, one thread remained unspoken yet profoundly woven into the fabric of their bond—intelligence. In all his brilliance, Sean had often taken the gift of his intelligence for granted, using it as a mere tool to outshine his peers. But in the company of Mr. Gladstone, he discovered the true depth and worth of his intellectual prowess.

Mr. Gladstone's insight and wisdom, carved through years

of experience, offered a mirror to Sean's potential. He was more than a guide; he was a catalyst that ignited the flames of Sean's potential. Their conversations weren't just exchanges of ideas; they were lessons that resonated beyond the spoken words. Through these exchanges, Sean unearthed the value of his intellect, not merely as a tool for self-validation, but as a beacon that could illuminate the world in unique ways.

As for Mr. Gladstone, he found in Sean a mind that wasn't just intelligent but receptive and curious. Their camaraderie was a testament to the adage that true friendship was not about finding someone similar but someone with complementary qualities. Theirs was an unconscious synergy, where Sean's youthful exuberance kindled Mr. Gladstone's spirits, and Mr. Gladstone's wisdom guided Sean's endeavours.

The lament echoed silently—why hadn't they met earlier? The beauty of their friendship was tempered with the regret that life's clock had ticked away before bringing them together. The brevity of time had sharpened the significance of their connection, making each shared moment a treasure beyond measure. Though blossoming in a later season, their friendship was rich with depth, authenticity, and the profound realization that true friendship transcends time.

One truth remained unshaken for all the uncertainties that the future held—they had found immeasurable value in each other. It was a connection that surpassed material wealth, a bond that resonated in the chambers of their hearts. Though their paths might soon diverge, the echoes of their shared laughter, deep conversations, and mutual respect would linger, etching an indelible memory.

Mr. Gladstone's time was a finite resource, yet even in the

shadow of this truth, he vowed to carry Sean in the annals of his memory. His wisdom whispered that temporal boundaries never limited true friendships; they persisted in the corridors of recollection, immortalized by their impact on one's soul. He knew that even as life's current carried them apart, the imprint of their connection would remain steadfast.

Sean, too, felt this eternal resonance within him. Though relatively brief, their time together had woven a narrative of kinship and camaraderie that would forever remain a cherished chapter in his life. Mr. Gladstone had enriched Sean's world with his friendship, forever shaping his perspective and kindling a fire of gratitude and admiration.

Different beginnings had culminated in shared richness. They had embarked on distinct journeys, often diverging their perspectives and experiences. Yet, they had converged at a juncture where their hearts recognized each other's inherent worth. Their friendship was a testament to the extraordinary connections that could be forged when hearts recognized kindred souls.

In this convergence, they discovered a wealth that transcended material possessions. Richness wasn't confined to bank accounts or possessions; it resided in the intangible realm of connection, understanding, and shared moments. Through their union, they unlocked a treasure trove of mutual growth, kindness, and the profound beauty of companionship.

As the sands of time continued their relentless march, Sean and Mr. Gladstone stood on the threshold of a parting, enriched by the lessons they had taught each other, the memories they had created, and the value they had found in the unlikeliest of friendships. Though the future held uncertainties, the tapestry of their shared experiences remained a constant, an enduring testament to the extraordinary richness of their bond.

The anticipation in the air was palpable as Sean meticulously prepared his apartment for the evening's festivities. He didn't just tidy the place; he orchestrated a symphony of arrangements, ensuring every corner exuded an inviting charm. The gentle hum of music set the ambiance like a beckoning melody inviting the night to dance.

Sean's dedication to the occasion was reflected in the abundance of drinks and snacks that he had thoughtfully laid out. His preparations spoke of enthusiasm and anticipation as if he was crafting a canvas of memories that would linger long after the evening was over.

As the clock's hands inched closer to eight, Sean poured himself a drink, his concoction of relaxation and readiness. His reflection in the glass mirrored the eagerness in his eyes. He stood on the threshold of an evening that promised camaraderie and laughter, hoping his efforts would yield a night to remember.

The door swung open like a movie scene, revealing Bella and Bonita's entrance. Their presence brightened the room, and their elegance radiated an aura of sophistication laced with an intriguing hint of adventure. Sean was momentarily stunned by their beauty, his heart echoing with an incredulous "Wow."

Dressed for the occasion, Bella and Bonita embodied a perfect blend of class and a touch of the unpredictable. Their attires were like a secret promise of a night filled with laughter, shared stories, and perhaps a sprinkle of mischief. Sean's pulse raced as he took in their appearances, a silent tribute to the transformation that unfolded when scrubs were swapped for something more enchanting.

As the evening unfolded, Sean marvelled at its surreal quality. The girls' presence was like a magic touch, casting a spell that transformed the ordinary into the extraordinary.

At this moment, Sean stood at the nexus of past and present, realizing that life had taken an unexpected turn. The medical student, who had immersed himself in studies and responsibilities, had become the host of an evening about to brim with joy and vibrancy. It was a moment of realization that life was as much about seizing opportunities as it was about pursuing knowledge.

Sean was about to find himself caught in the middle of a beautiful mosaic painted by friendship, festivity, and the exhilaration of new experiences. Bella and Bonita were bringing a touch of enchantment to his world, reminding him that there was more to life than stethoscopes and textbooks. As his eyes beamed with excitement, Sean marvelled at the fate that had brought them all together on this Christmas Eve—a night destined to be etched in memory as the beginning of a new and exhilarating chapter.

Sean stood there with a welcoming smile, inviting Bella and Bonita into his transformed abode. He had meticulously prepared the space, but now it was time for them to infuse it with their energy, to make it their sanctuary of laughter and shared moments.

With a lighthearted chuckle, Sean reassured the girls that they were in a no-rules zone tonight. They were here to let loose, savour every second, and etch this night into their memories as a testament to their friendship. His words carried a touch of promise, a pledge to make this evening unforgettable.

The ambiance perfectly blended music, laughter, and the soft glow of lights. As they settled in, their fingers instinctively reached for the snacks, delighting in the little culinary treasures that

Sean had prepared. The crunch of chips and the clinking of glasses composed a rhythm that echoed through the room, orchestrating the soundtrack of the night.

It wasn't long before the irresistible lure of the music tugged at their hearts. Spontaneously, they began to sway, to move to the rhythm that seemed to breathe life into the room. The space was transformed into a dance floor, a canvas where their movements painted their emotions, joy, and shared bond.

As the tempo quickened, laughter intertwined with the melodies, creating a symphony of ecstasy that seemed to reach beyond the walls. They danced as if time was their ally, as if the night was a canvas they were determined to fill with their vivacity. With each step, each twirl, they painted memories that would colour their souls long after the music ceased.

Yet, as the night progressed, the physical exertion began to take its toll. The swaying and dancing, once effortless, now left a glistening sheen on their skin. The music carried them on its wings, weaving a tapestry of sweat and shared joy. Realizing they were becoming too "shiny," as Bella playfully put it, they decided to pause their dance. It was time to momentarily shift gears, to allow their hearts to slow down before they embarked on the next phase of their evening.

With a laugh, they found themselves seeking refuge on the comfortable seating, a contrast to the energetic dance floor they had commandeered earlier. The change was refreshing, and the quiet moments between their conversations allowed them to catch their breaths and exchange stories. It was as if the night was guiding them through its rhythm, seamlessly transitioning from one beat to another.

As the clock's hands moved forward, the night still held

many unwritten chapters. The evening had begun with the promise of festivity. Gathering in the cozy corners of Sean's apartment, they were crafting the tale of their shared experience. Laughter, dance, and heartfelt conversations were threads woven into the tapestry of this remarkable night. On this night, three souls connected, laughed, and revelled in the magic of camaraderie.

Amid the comfortable cocoon of friendship, their conversation meandered through various topics, each revelation drawing them closer together. The clinking of glasses and the shuffling of cards seemed to harmonize with their laughter as if the room was enchanted by the warmth they exuded.

Bonita's words struck a chord, her genuine curiosity wrapping around Sean's decision to leave the hospital. Her question echoed the whispers that had danced around the hospital corridors, whispers of an impending departure that left many puzzled.

Sean made a conscious effort to avoid ruining the pleasant atmosphere of the evening by tactfully avoiding the question at hand. He diverted the attention to the enjoyable pastimes of drinking and playing cards, thus ensuring that the mood remained light and pleasant.

"Yes, why can't you stay? The hospital has been more fun since you joined, and I don't want that to end," said Bella.

Amid the warm camaraderie and the gentle coaxing of his friends, Sean found himself torn between the desire to share the whole story and the determination to protect the positive atmosphere they had managed to create.

As the girls comforted Sean by rubbing his arms, they exchanged concerned looks. Bonita proposed starting a petition to keep Sean around, confident she could gather over a hundred signatures in just a few hours. She believed that if Sean saw how much people wanted him to stay, he would change his mind. However, Bonita was unaware of the whole story, and her assumption was based on a faulty premise.

As Bella's words mingled with Bonita's suggestion, he couldn't help but smile at their genuine concern, a testament to the genuine connections he had formed in such a short time.

He sipped his drink, the rich flavour momentarily distracting him from the weight of his worries. Their hands on his arms, their genuine concern evident in their eyes, brought a touch of comfort he hadn't realized he needed. The night was still young, and the laughter and shared moments were an antidote to the challenges he was battling.

Setting his drink down and pushing the cards aside, Sean met their gaze with a small, appreciative smile. "You guys have no idea how much your support means to me. It's like a ray of sunlight breaking through the clouds. But honestly, the situation is a bit more complicated than a petition can fix."

Bonita's brows furrowed slightly, her concern deepening as she listened to his words. Bella's fingers tightened gently on his arm, a silent gesture of solidarity. Sean leaned in a little closer, his voice lowering as he continued to share his thoughts.

"Believe me, if it were up to me, I'd love to stay here. The hospital, people, and experiences have become an important part of my journey. But a lot going on behind the scenes is making it difficult for me. It's not just about a job; it's about a future, a career. And I don't want to put myself in a position where I'm fighting an uphill battle that could compromise my entire career."

He paused, his gaze shifting between the two friends who were now leaning in, hanging onto his words. The room seemed to fade away, leaving just the three of them in their bubble of understanding.

"I'm humbled and truly grateful for your support. But sometimes, you have to make tough decisions that are best for you in the long run, even if they're not the easiest or most popular. And right now, that's what I'm trying to do. I appreciate your friendship and your concern more than I can express. But I need to figure out my path in a way that ensures my future isn't compromised."

The room settled into a thoughtful silence, their words and emotions hanging in the air like delicate threads woven into a tapestry of understanding. Bella and Bonita exchanged glances, their expressions a mix of empathy and respect for Sean's journey. The gravity of the situation had deepened their bond, transforming a simple evening into a profound connection.

Bonita reached over and gently squeezed Sean's hand. "We understand, Sean. Your future is important, and you have to make the right choices for yourself. Just know that whatever you decide, we're here for you."

Bella nodded in agreement, her eyes reflecting their genuine support. "You've got a whole team of cheerleaders, even if we don't fully understand the game you're playing."

The tension seemed to ease from Sean's shoulders as he offered them a grateful smile. Amid their shared understanding, he realized that sometimes, the support and friendship of a few can illuminate even the darkest paths, making the journey a little less daunting.

Bella and Bonita listened attentively as Sean spoke, their

expressions a mix of understanding and a touch of disappointment. The room seemed to hold its breath, each word he uttered carrying a weight that extended beyond the immediate conversation. As he shared his desire to explore new horizons, their thoughtful expressions showed their grasp of the intricacies he was navigating.

"I hear you, Sean," Bella said softly, her gaze steady on his. "It's important to chase your dreams and broaden your horizons. We all know you're incredibly talented and driven. Whatever path you choose, you'll excel, and we'll be rooting for you every step of the way."

Bonita nodded, her smile carrying an undertone of bittersweetness. "Hospitals will come and go, but your growth and success are what truly matter. It's just that... well, you've become a sort of beacon of positivity around AGH. You brought a new energy, and it's going to be tough not having that."

Sean's heart swelled with a mixture of emotions. These were his friends and colleagues, and their understanding touched him deeply. He knew his impact during his short time at the hospital, and it was heartening to realize that his presence had created ripples of positivity.

"I'll miss all of you too," he admitted, a genuine smile touching his lips. "You've made this experience unforgettable for me. And you never know; life has its way of bringing people back together. Who's to say we won't cross paths again in the future?"

Bella and Bonita glanced at each other and then looked back at Sean with smiles that expressed hope and a touch of mischief.

"Oh, we'll definitely hold you to that," Bella said with a chuckle.

As the conversation continued, the atmosphere shifted from discussing the complexities of career decisions to sharing lighthearted anecdotes and dreams for the future. The night pressed on, each passing moment a testament to the bonds they had formed in such a short time.

They raised their glasses in a silent toast, a shared understanding passing between them. It was a night of friendship, genuine connection, and accepting that sometimes life takes people on different paths. But as they laughed and talked, they also knew that true friendships could withstand time and distance, even as they embarked on new chapters of their lives.

The music swelled, enveloping the room in a vibrant rhythm that seemed to echo the trio's heartbeats. Sean couldn't help but chuckle as Bonita pulled him into the middle of the room, her energy infectious. He let himself be swept up in the moment, dancing with a freedom that mirrored the conversations of the night.

As the music flowed through them, Sean's gaze shifted between the two nurses, their expressions a mix of playfulness and earnestness. Bonita's eyes sparkled with determination as she twirled him around. At the same time, Bella's smile held a touch of wistfulness as she watched them.

"You see, Sean, we're not going to let you go without a fight," Bonita declared, her voice lighthearted but her message clear.

Bella stepped closer, gracefully joining the dance. "We know you have your plans, and we respect that. But we also want you to know how much you mean to all of us. The hospital won't be the same without you."

Sean laughed as he spun around, the camaraderie of the moment warming his heart. "Well, you two are making it really hard for me to leave."

Bonita grinned mischievously. "That's the point!"

They danced, lost in the music, and shared laughter. Their steps were a silent promise of the connections they had formed during these few weeks. The night continued with a blend of heartfelt conversations, spontaneous dances, and camaraderie that made the imminent farewell seem bittersweet yet inevitable.

Sean looked at his friends, his voice carrying a note of gratitude. "Thank you, both of you, for this incredible night. You've made this christening truly unforgettable."

Bella leaned back, her smile warm. "It's the least we could do for someone who's brought so much joy to our lives."

Bonita nodded in agreement. "We might not be able to change your plans, but we can at least send you off with great memories."

With the night growing deeper and the music still echoing in the apartment, the trio's inhibitions faded further into the embrace of alcohol. The apartment pulsed with vibrant energy, reflecting the joy and harmony that had filled the space throughout the evening.

Sean looked at the two women by his side, their smiles illuminated by the soft glow of the room. "You know," he said with a playful grin, "This is quite the unforgettable evening."

Bonita leaned back against the couch, her gaze fixed on the ceiling. "It really is. I don't think any of us will forget this night."

Bella chuckled, her head resting on Sean's shoulder. "That's for sure. A night of dancing, laughter, and friendship."

"Ladies, take me to heaven!" he said as he removed his shirt.

"Let's make this a night to remember," Bonita affirmed as Bella added, "I'll drink to that!"

As Sean's shirt came off, laughter and cheers filled the room. Bonita and Bella joined in the spirit of the moment, their inhibitions melting away as they matched his carefree attitude. The alcohol had worked its magic, loosening the strings of reserve that often held them back.

Dancing took on a new form, more playful and daring, each movement a testament to the freedom of the night. The music continued to weave its spell, wrapping around them like a warm embrace. Laughter filled the air as they twirled, swayed, and moved to the rhythm, creating their little haven of glee.

The hours passed in a blur, and the boundaries between the trio faded as they shared stories, dreams, and secrets. The alcohol lent a sense of vulnerability, allowing them to open up in ways they might not have otherwise. The room felt like a sanctuary, where time held no sway and worries were set aside.

The apartment seemed to sigh with contentment as if it, too, had felt the weight of the evening's memories. The trio's hearts beat in rhythm with the music that still played softly in the background, a reminder of their shared magic.

Sean suggested they go upstairs to the bedroom if they were going to continue drinking. They all laughed and agreed because they acknowledged they might not make it up the stairs if they drank too much. They gathered the essentials - liquor, snacks, and a deck of playing cards - and headed upstairs.

Mr. Gladstone had installed speakers throughout the house, so the music was just as loud in the lounge as in each bedroom. He had also added a touch of sophistication and intimacy to the apartment, ensuring that every aspect of it was welcoming to anyone who entered.

The stairs seemed like a playful challenge as they navigated their way upstairs. The laughter and tipsy companionship made the ascent a delightful adventure. Each step promised more fun and drew them closer to the bedroom, where they could continue the night's festivities.

As they reached the upper level, the atmosphere shifted from the open space of the living area to the cozy confines of the bedrooms. Soft lighting cast a warm glow, creating an intimate ambiance that invited relaxation and enjoyment. The girls couldn't help but compliment the tasteful decor, each room reflecting Mr. Gladstone's attention to detail.

With the music still accompanying them, they settled into one of the bedrooms, the soft melodies weaving a sense of comfort around them. The night was still young, and the possibilities felt endless. They spread out their chosen refreshments on a small table, the colourful bottles and snacks adding a festive touch.

As they played cards and enjoyed their drinks, the conversation flowed effortlessly. The barriers of formality had long been abandoned, leaving only the genuine connections they had formed. They shared stories of their lives, their dreams, and even their embarrassments, the night's intoxication fostering an atmosphere of trust and harmony.

The cards and the drinks created a rhythmic pattern, like the heartbeat of the night. The conversation shifted from one topic to another, and laughter punctuated every tale and joke. Time ticked by unnoticed.

The music, carefully chosen to match the mood, swirled around them, wrapping them in its comforting embrace. Mr. Gladstone's thoughtful installation of speakers throughout the apartment ensured that the melodies were a constant companion, weaving a seamless connection between the lounge and the bedrooms.

As the night progressed, the laughter grew softer, the anecdotes becoming more intimate. The room seemed to hold its breath, the shared experiences creating an unbreakable bond. The alcohol had not only dulled their senses but also ignited a sense of unity, an unspoken understanding that this night was meant to be cherished.

As the music played and the conversation became hushed, they settled into a comfortable silence. The cards were forgotten, and the drinks rested untouched as they enjoyed each other's presence. Their connection was a treasure, a testament to the magic of unexpected friendships and unforgettable nights.

A knock interrupted the moment as the bedroom atmosphere became more lively with giggles and relaxed attitudes. Sean was new to the apartment, and nobody knew his address. It was probable that the person at the door was searching for Mr. Gladstone, so Sean chose to disregard it.

The knocking grew louder, escalating from knuckles to a pounding. The girls asked Sean to deal with the interruption so they could enjoy their time undisturbed. Sean obliged and went to answer the door.

"Who's there?" he inquired.

"It's me. Please open the door," Dr. May replied, her speech slurred.

The door swung open to reveal Dr. May in a somewhat inebriated state, her usually composed demeanour utterly dissolved by the alcohol she had consumed. Sean's concern was evident as he tried to comprehend what had led her to this state.

"May, are you drunk? What happened to you?" Sean asked.

"I only had one beer, officer. I promise I don't drink and drive. " Her words slurred, and her balance compromised. She attempted a feeble joke that garnered a small smile from Sean despite the situation.

"May, come on in," he said, his tone a mix of sympathy and exasperation. Helping her steady herself, he guided her into the apartment and towards the living room. The room seemed to have its own glow, a contrast to the muted lighting of the bedroom she had just interrupted.

Bella and Bonita exchanged curious glances, their expressions a mixture of surprise and amusement at the unexpected visitor. Sean couldn't help but chuckle under his breath at the sight of Dr. May's attempt at levity, even in her intoxicated state.

"May, what happened?" he asked, his voice laced with concern and amusement. He couldn't help but be taken aback by the sight of his usually poised colleague in such a vulnerable state.

Dr. May flopped onto one of the couches with an exaggerated sigh, her posture exuding a sense of dramatic exhaustion. "It's been... one of those days, Sean," she mumbled, her words blending into each other as if they were part of some hazy dream.

Sean fetched a glass of water from the kitchen and handed

it to Dr. May, encouraging her to drink it to mitigate the effects of the alcohol.

"You're lucky Mr. Gladstone isn't here to witness this," he teased gently, a smile tugging at the corners of his lips.

Dr. May's laughter, though slightly slurred, echoed through the room as she took a sip of water.

"Oh, you just wish I get humiliated, don't you?" she responded, her tone a mix of embarrassment and amusement.

As the evening took an unexpected turn, the apartment seemed to absorb the unusual energy with an open embrace. The combination of alcohol, unexpected guests, and the already festive atmosphere created a tableau of spontaneity and camaraderie that none of them would soon forget. The night had turned into the realm of the unexpected, transforming what was meant to be a simple gathering into a memory that would be retold with laughter for years to come.

The room's dynamics shifted as Bella and Bonita, who had been part of the festive scene upstairs, made their way downstairs. The unexpected sight of Dr. May in her intoxicated state triggered their instinct to offer help and support. With a sense of fellowship, they joined Sean in ensuring that Dr. May was comfortably settled on the couch.

Bella and Bonita offered her friendly smiles, their curiosity piqued by this unexpected turn of events. In this unconventional scenario, the camaraderie they had built with Sean throughout the evening extended to Dr. May.

"Dr. May, are you okay?" Bella asked, her voice laced with genuine concern as she positioned a cushion behind Dr. May's head.

Dr. May responded with a passive smile. Her eyes were half-closed as if the effort to keep them open was monumental. Bonita fetched a blanket and covered her with care as if she were tending to an ailing friend.

Sean appreciated the girls' kindness and willingness to help, but he couldn't ignore the reality of the situation. The festive atmosphere that had filled the apartment earlier had been replaced with a sense of responsibility for their colleague's well-being.

With the music's volume lowered, Sean spoke, addressing the girls and Dr. May. "I think it's best if we call it a night. Dr. May needs some rest, and it wouldn't be right to continue the party while she's like this."

Bonita and Bella exchanged understanding glances with Sean, nodding in agreement.

"Of course, Sean. We completely understand," Bella assured him, her voice soft and empathic.

Dr. May seemed to drift in and out of awareness, occasionally mumbling something unintelligible. Her state was a poignant reminder of the evening's unpredictability.

As Sean exchanged a look with the girls, he couldn't help but feel a twinge of disappointment. The night had taken an unforeseen turn, veering away from the excitement and company they had shared earlier. Yet, as he looked at his colleagues and friends, a sense of unity prevailed – a shared understanding that some situations called for a shift in plans, even if it meant putting aside their desires for the sake of someone in need.

With a sense of responsibility, Sean fetched another glass of water. He placed it within Dr. May's reach, ensuring she was comfortable. As Bella and Bonita helped tidy up, their laughter replaced by a quiet camaraderie, the apartment seemed to emanate a different kind of warmth – the kind born from empathy and shared experiences.

Ultimately, the night may not have unfolded as they had initially planned. Still, their bond grew stronger through their collective care and understanding. Sometimes, the most memorable moments emerge from unexpected situations, a reminder of the importance of compassion and the ability to adapt to the circumstances life presents.

As the girls departed, their infectious smiles promised better times to come. Although the atmosphere within the apartment had shifted, their spirits remained resilient, buoyed by the understanding that friendship and celebration could still be in the cards for the following night. Sean watched them walk down the hall, their laughter echoing faintly as they disappeared from view.

Turning back to the living room, he found Dr. May still sprawled on the couch, her sense of reality dancing on the edges of her consciousness. The situation was far from ideal, but Sean's compassionate nature kicked in, urging him to ensure she was as comfortable as possible.

"May, how about we get you more water and another blanket? You can rest here tonight," he suggested gently, approaching her with an empathetic smile.

Dr. May's response was a contented sigh, accompanied by a nod that seemed to require more effort than it should. Sean fetched a glass of water, placed it within her reach, and gently covered her with a blanket. Despite the unexpected turn of events, he couldn't help but admire the resilience of his colleagues – the girls' willingness to come back another time and Dr. May's desire to create a memorable night despite her current state.

A sense of serenity filled the room as Sean settled into the space. The music had subsided, and the apartment felt wrapped in a tranquil embrace. Though the raucous festivities had transformed into a quiet night of care and solace, the sense of camaraderie that had been present throughout remained unwavering.

Sean sat nearby, his watchful gaze occasionally resting on Dr. May. In this unexpected moment, he realized that true friendships were forged not only amid laughter and excitement but also in moments of vulnerability and compassion. The night had taken an unforeseen turn, yet its lessons were profound – the importance of adaptability, the power of empathy, and the ability to find joy even amidst unexpected challenges.

As minutes ticked by and the room fell into a gentle hush, Sean's thoughts turned to the promise of laughter and celebration that lay ahead the following night. As he looked at Dr. May, who had drifted into a more peaceful slumber, he couldn't help but feel grateful for the connections they had formed and the unbreakable bond that had been woven through the tapestry of their shared experiences.

Sean's concern deepened as he observed Dr. May's condition and tried to assess the possible causes of her behaviour. Despite the unexpected situation, his medical instincts kicked in, guiding him through a methodical examination to ascertain if there were any signs of substance use or abuse.

He gently checked her hands for signs of needle marks, his movements deliberate yet delicate, mindful of the situation. His brows furrowed in concentration as he meticulously scanned her skin, hoping to uncover clues that might shed light on her unusual state. The room seemed to hush around them, the only sound being the soft rustle of fabric as Sean worked methodically.

But the search yielded no telltale signs of injection. There were no needle marks and no signs of recent punctures. It appeared that whatever had caused Dr. May's intoxicated state wasn't linked to intravenous drug use. Sean's mind raced, considering other possibilities. Had she consumed something without realizing its potency? Could there be a medical condition that was causing her symptoms?

Dr. May's drowsy eyes met Sean's concerned gaze, and she seemed to muster a faint smile. "My head's all fuzzy."

Sean's worry shifted from potential illicit substances to the realm of medication. "May, did you accidentally take the wrong medication? Do you have any allergies or underlying medical conditions I should know?"

Dr. May reassured Sean that she hadn't taken anything dangerous and reminded him she was too smart to do anything stupid.

Sean's eyes widened in astonishment as he processed Dr. May's revelation. The situation had taken a sudden turn, veering into territory that was not only unexpected but also worrisome. He was torn between disbelief and concern, struggling to reconcile the confident and composed Dr. May he knew with the person in front of him who seemed to be revealing a hidden side.

"This is atypical of you. What happened?" Sean asked.

Dr. May was intoxicated, although she attempted to conceal it. Despite her condition, she tried to engage in conversation and behave normally. She sat on the couch and informed Sean that she had consumed only a few drinks at home and had taken a "happy" pill.

"Don't worry, I knew exactly what to take. I just wanted to get high without ending my life. I walked out, and right outside my building was a taxi, and here I am!" she said to Sean in her semi-comprehensible voice as she leaned into Sean to kiss him on his cheek.

Sean instinctively pulled back slightly, the mixture of alcohol on her breath and the weight of her confession creating a whirlwind of emotions within him. He tried to hide his shock, his face a mask of composed concern even as his mind raced to find the best way to handle the situation.

"May, I understand that you're trying to cope, but mixing alcohol with any kind of medication can be dangerous," Sean said, his voice a careful balance of firmness and empathy. "I appreciate your honesty, but I can't condone this behaviour. We need to ensure your safety."

Dr. May's eyes flickered with a mix of defiance and vulnerability as she tried to maintain her bravado. "I told you, Sean, I knew exactly what I was doing. I've taken these before, and it's never been a problem."

Sean's concern deepened as he recognized the signs of someone trying to rationalize their actions, even when they were aware of the risks involved. "May, I get that you're intelligent and capable, but there's always a risk when mixing substances. You might think you're in control, but unexpected reactions can happen."

The room seemed to hold its breath as their conversation hung in the air, tension palpable between them. Sean's priority was Dr. May's safety, but he also wanted to approach the situation with sensitivity and understanding. He knew there was more beneath the surface and hoped to uncover the root causes of her actions.

"May, if you're struggling, I'm here for you," Sean said gently, his voice carrying the weight of his genuine concern. "You don't have to go through this alone. Whether it's stress, pressure, or anything else, there are healthier ways to deal with it. And I'll support you through that."

Dr. May's slurred words and erratic behaviour portrayed someone in distress, trying to navigate her emotions and find solace through means that were clearly uncharacteristic of her usual self. Sean's concern deepened as he listened to her explanations, piecing together the series of events that had led her to his doorstep.

"And how did you know to find me here?" Sean asked.

Dr. May continued mumbling, but Sean deciphered that Mr. Gladstone was still feeling bad about the fight he had with him, and he thought maybe she could spend some time with Sean to cheer him up. She went home, got ready, had a few drinks, and took a taxi to Sean's apartment.

"You're not happy to see me? I thought you'd be happy to see me," Dr. May muttered.

"Of course, I'm happy to see you, but I'm trying to understand why you are like this because this is out of character for you," Sean responded.

Dr. May shifted on the couch, her gaze avoiding his as she fidgeted with her fingers. "I just wanted to forget, even for a little while. I didn't want to think about everything that's been going on."

Sean's heart went out to her as he recognized the desire to escape from the weight of one's thoughts and emotions. He knew that life in a hospital could be incredibly demanding and emotionally draining.

"I get it, May," Sean said softly, his voice carrying empathy. "But numbing your feelings with substances isn't the answer. It might provide temporary relief but won't solve the underlying issues. It's okay to feel overwhelmed, and it's okay to ask for help."

She continued speaking in her disoriented voice, explaining to Sean that she wanted to make up for the date she had ruined. She also argued that it was likely that she would never see him again after the following week, and this was her last shot to do so.

"So, what do you say? I'm all yours tonight," she said to Sean as she moved in to kiss him.

Sean's voice was gentle but firm, his words a lifeline of sobriety amid Dr. May's intoxicated advances. He held her gently by the shoulders, his expression a mix of concern and compassion.

"May, I appreciate your honesty and willingness to make amends," Sean said, his voice steady. "But this isn't the right way, especially given your current state."

Dr. May's eyes were a cocktail of emotions — embarrassment, frustration, and a hint of clarity from his words. She nodded, her face flushing with a mix of alcohol-induced warmth and her own realization.

"You're right," she admitted, her voice subdued. "I shouldn't have let things get this far. I'm sorry, Sean."

"There's no need to apologize, May," Sean reassured her, his grip on her shoulders remaining gentle. "We all have our moments, and what's important is learning from them."

She nodded again, her gaze dropping as she tried to process the situation and the emotions that had driven her actions. Sean guided her back to the couch and made sure she was comfortable.

Sean went to the kitchen and came back with a glass of juice for Dr. May to rehydrate. He gave her the drink and told her it was a special mix he had prepared for her to prevent a hangover.

"I'll finish this, and we'll start having some fun, okay?" Dr. May said as she winked at him and blew a kiss.

She tried to drink the juice but choked immediately. Sean helped her hold the glass and told her to drink it slowly and try not to puke. She did as asked and slowly drank it, with hiccups in between, while still trying to convince Sean that she was ready to have the night of her life with him.

Sean watched with concern and amusement as Dr. May navigated her way through the glass of juice. Considering her intoxicated state, her determination to salvage the night was endearing and slightly comical. He chuckled softly and shook his head.

"May, I appreciate your enthusiasm, but I think it's best for you to rest and sober up," Sean advised with a caring tone.

Dr. May pouted playfully, her attempts at seduction giving way to a more childlike demeanour in her drunkenness. "You're no fun, Sean. I promise I'm feeling much better now."

Sean raised an eyebrow, clearly unconvinced by her declaration. "You might feel better, but I still think it's a good idea to take it easy for the rest of the night."

Dr. May sighed dramatically, then grinned. "Fine, Doctor's orders. But only if you keep me company."

Sean smiled, his expression softening. "Of course, May. I'm here."

With a contented sigh, Dr. May settled back against the couch. Her eyes were half-lidded as the effects of the juice started to kick in. Sean grabbed a cozy blanket and draped it over her, ensuring she was comfortable. He sat nearby, ready to keep her company.

Despite the unexpected turn of events, the night had taken on a different kind of intimacy, one borne out of vulnerability and authenticity.

The evening that had started with chaos and impulsiveness had transformed into a testament to the unpredictability of life, the beauty of vulnerability, and the bonds that could be forged in the most unexpected circumstances.

Finishing the drink was one thing, but making it stay down was another. Sean told Dr. May not to move too much and to relax to let her body process the drink.

"Sean, you're a great guy, and you will make an amazing doctor. You saved my job, saved my grandmother's life, and you're just a really cool guy," she mumbled as she slowly got drowsy.

"I just want you to know that I really want to spend the night with you. I'm sorry I'm drunk, but I really mean that; you are a great guy. You're not taking advantage of me at all," she paused before adding, "You're a really good guy, Sean."

Sean sat there, listening to Dr. May's slurred words, touched by her genuine sentiments and concerned for her well-being. Her vulnerability was apparent in her words and her struggle to keep her eyes open.

He leaned back in his seat, his gaze resting on her, and replied softly, "Thank you, May. I appreciate your kind words."

Sean recognized the sincerity in her speech, but he also knew that her judgment was impaired due to the alcohol. He wanted to make sure she was safe and comfortable. "I think you're a great person, too, but your health is more important right now. Let's focus on getting you back to feeling better."

Dr. May's eyelids grew heavier, and she nodded sleepily. "Okay, Sean. You're right. Thanks for taking care of me."

With a small smile, Sean kept watching her, ensuring she was okay as she drifted into a peaceful slumber. He thought about the evening's unpredictability—how plans had shifted, emotions had surfaced, and unexpected connections had formed. The night had taken on a life of its own, revealing different layers of himself and Dr. May.

As the apartment fell into a quiet calm, Sean reflected on the complexities of human interactions, the fragile balance between professionalism and personal connection, and the unpredictable twists that life often presented. At this moment, with a drowsy and vulnerable Dr. May resting nearby, he found a renewed appreciation for the depth and richness that relationships could bring to his journey.

Dr. May passed out into Sean's arms, and he lifted her to one of the bedrooms. He made her bed and tucked her fully dressed. He ensured she had nothing on her that could hurt her while she slept. Before leaving the room, he also left a bowl, water, and a few towels for Dr. May in case she started throwing up in the middle of the night.

With Dr. May settled and comfortable, Sean quietly left the bedroom, gently closing the door behind him. He sighed, a mix of relief and concern for her. It had been an unexpected turn of events, a night that had taken an unusual course. He looked around the apartment, the remnants of the earlier festivities scattered about. The music that had filled the space with energy now hung in the air as a distant hum.

As he stood there, he pondered the complexities of the connections he had made during his time at the hospital. From Mr. Gladstone to Dr. Gabehart and now to Dr. May, each person had brought their own story, struggles, and unique qualities into his life. In return, he offered his care, expertise, and friendship.

With a sense of gratitude and humility, Sean appreciated the intricate web of human interactions that had woven around him. The highs and lows, the challenges and triumphs, all played a role in shaping his path to becoming a medical doctor. He knew that while he couldn't predict the twists that life would throw his way, he could always choose how to respond—with kindness, empathy, and a willingness to learn.

A promising evening of an unforgettable night had ended differently than he had imagined. After tucking Dr. May in, he wasn't ready to sleep and still had a lot of energy. He went to the living room, cleaned up the place from top to bottom before pouring himself a drink, and started watching a movie. Bella and Bonita would likely have been home by now, and there was no chance he'd get them to come back. Besides, he had to look after the intoxicated Dr. May.

In the silence of the night, as the movie played softly in the background, Sean lay in bed, his thoughts drifting. The events of the evening had been a whirlwind, an unexpected mix of emotions, interactions, and revelations. He reflected on the bonds he had formed, the challenges he had faced, and the choices he had made.

As the movie played on, casting gentle shadows across the room, Sean felt a sense of fulfillment. He had come a long way since the start of his clerkship, both professionally and personally. He had forged connections that had enriched his life and broadened his understanding of human nature.

With the movie's end, Sean turned off the television and settled further into the stillness of the night. Tomorrow was a new day, a fresh opportunity to continue his journey of growth, build his career, and nurture the bonds that had come to mean so much to him.

As he closed his eyes and drifted off to sleep, he carried with him the memories of the day—the laughter, the conversations, the challenges—and the realization that every experience, whether anticipated or unexpected, was a thread woven into the intricate tapestry of his life's story.

Upon awakening, Dr. May found herself in a state of confusion. She was unsure of her whereabouts and how she had ended up there. Although alone in her bed, she was fully clothed and lacked any signs of injury, ruling out several possibilities. Despite this, the fact that she was in a stranger's bedroom left her feeling embarrassed. Attempting to recall the previous night's events, she found herself at a loss for several key details. After a few minutes of fruitless effort, she gave up and headed to the washroom.

Dr. May splashed some water on her face, hoping it would help clear her head. She stared at her reflection in the mirror, trying to remember the events of the previous evening. Fragments of memories started to come back to her like pieces of a puzzle slowly falling into place.

She remembered the decision to take a "happy" pill, her determination to make amends with Sean after the previous date's fiasco, and the hazy taxi ride that somehow brought her to Sean's apartment. The events following her arrival were fuzzy. Still, she vaguely remembered drinking a special concoction Sean had prepared for her to prevent a hangover.

As the memories slowly returned, embarrassment, regret, and gratitude washed over her. She was grateful that Sean had cared for her, ensuring she was safe and comfortable despite her intoxicated state. Her embarrassment stemmed from her behaviour and the realization of being completely out of character.

In her usual state of mind, she had always tried to prove to Sean she deserved his respect. Things had been awkward since she "humiliated" him in her apartment. Waking up like this in Sean's apartment was not how she wanted to be remembered.

Dr. May moved carefully, trying not to make any noise as she gathered her belongings. Her head was still fuzzy from the previous night's events, but she was determined to leave before Sean woke up. She felt a mix of embarrassment and regret for her actions. She hoped that slipping away unnoticed would spare her from facing Sean again.

As she made her way to the door, she hesitated. A part of her felt the need to apologize and explain her behaviour, but another part wanted to avoid any potential awkwardness. She had always prided herself in her professionalism and composure, and this situation was far from that.

Taking a deep breath, Dr. May opened the door slowly to leave the bedroom where she had spent the night. Just as she stepped out of the bedroom, she heard a voice behind her.

"May, leaving so soon?"

She turned to see Sean standing in the hallway with a gentle smile. Her heart skipped a beat, and she felt a mixture of relief and trepidation. Her attempt to sneak away had been in vain.

"Sean, I... I didn't want to disturb you," she stammered, her cheeks flushing with embarrassment.

"No worries. Good morning, cheap drunk. How was your night?" Sean greeted Dr. May while handing her a cup of tea.

"How am I a cheap drunk?" she asked in embarrassment while also trying to be furious at Sean.

"What do you call a few drinks and a happy pill to make a fool out of yourself?" Sean asked.

Dr. May's cheeks turned a shade of red that matched her embarrassment as she realized the previous night might've been worse than she thought. She took the cup of tea from Sean, feeling grateful for the gesture even as he teased her.

"I don't usually drink that much," she mumbled.

Sean chuckled, his playful demeanour putting her at ease. "Well, we all have our moments, May. And trust me, I've seen worse."

She managed a weak smile, grateful Sean wasn't making her feel worse about the situation.

"Listen," Sean said, his tone more serious now. "Last night might've been a bit unexpected, but I want you to know that I don't judge you for it. We've all had our moments of vulnerability."

Again, she tried to put together a complete picture of the previous night's event in relation to Sean's comment. Sean tried to brush it off as he told her not to worry about it and started walking to his bedroom.

Dr. May followed him to his bedroom because his earlier

comments piqued her curiosity. She was concerned that she may have done something that could harm her professional reputation. She wanted to know every detail of what occurred the night before.

As they entered Sean's bedroom, Dr. May's curiosity got the best of her. She couldn't shake off the feeling that there might have been more to her drunken escapade than she could remember. She cleared her throat, feeling a bit awkward but determined to understand the whole story.

"Sean, I know you said not to worry about it, but I need to know if I did anything embarrassing or inappropriate last night."

Sean turned to face her, his expression serious yet reassuring. He could sense her concern and wanted to put her mind at ease. "May, don't worry. You were a bit drunk, but you didn't do anything that could harm your career or image. You were just... in a really good mood, let's put it that way."

She let out a sigh of relief, her shoulders relaxing. "Thank goodness. I was really worried."

Sean chuckled, his smile kind. "Trust me, May, you're not the first person to have a wild night."

As she stood by the bedroom door, Dr. May's memory started to piece together more fragments from the previous night. Sean's comment triggered a sequence of events in her mind. She remembered the girls, Bella and Bonita, and the disappointment on their faces when they left.

"Wait a minute," Dr. May began, her brows furrowing as she recalled, "I remember seeing those two girls... Bella and Bonita, right?"

Sean nodded, looking slightly amused. "Yeah, that's right.

They came over for a little get-together."

Dr. May's memory was becoming more apparent. She remembered arriving at Sean's apartment, and there were the two nurses she had seen at the hospital before. Her embarrassment deepened, realizing that her drunken state had disrupted their evening.

"Oh gosh, I must've ruined your party," she exclaimed, covering her face with her hand. "I'm so sorry!"

Sean chuckled, trying to alleviate her embarrassment. "Don't worry about it. They understood what was going on. They're actually coming back tonight after work. We planned to continue our little hangout."

Relief washed over Dr. May. At least she hadn't completely ruined Sean's night with his friends.

She smiled sheepishly. "That's good to know. And I'm glad it's not as bad as I thought."

Sean grinned. "See, no harm done."

When Sean accused her of coming over to sleep with him, she immediately denied it, insisting that she would never do such a thing. However, after reflecting on the events leading up to that moment, she began to think that Sean might be telling the truth.

Dr. May gradually connected the previous night's events and was still trying to piece together a clear picture. She felt disappointed in herself for ruining Sean's night when he visited her. Two weeks later, she again spoiled his night, this time at his house. She couldn't help but cry, yet she found some humour in how ridiculous everything seemed.

As Dr. May's emotions oscillated between embarrassment,

realization, and a strange mixture of laughter and tears, Sean watched her with a compassionate smile. He could see the internal struggle she was going through, and he understood the complexity of her emotions.

"Hey," he said gently, moving closer to her on the bed. "It's okay. We all have our moments, and sometimes things don't go as planned. But you know what? These moments make life interesting."

Dr. May looked up at him, her eyes still glistening with tears. "I know, Sean. It's just... I've always been so careful about my image and how I present myself. And now, here I am, making a complete fool out of myself in front of you."

Sean placed a comforting hand on her shoulder, then turned around to get back into bed. "You're human, May. We all have our vulnerabilities, and it's okay to show them sometimes. Besides, you've achieved so much, and one silly night isn't going to define you."

As the conversation between Dr. May and Sean unfolded, Dr. May couldn't help but feel remorseful for ruining Sean's night once again. She knew she wasn't a terrible person and didn't intend to cause him harm, but she also knew that her recent behaviour had been questionable.

Sean reassured her that he had no negative feelings toward her. Nevertheless, he asked her to be truthful about what was happening with her, which was a valid request given the circumstances.

Dr. May took a deep breath and struggled to articulate her thoughts and actions. She knew she needed to be honest with Sean, but expressing her struggles proved difficult. In an effort to change the subject, she asked Sean if he had any plans for the day. Sean replied that he was going to have a simple Christmas at home, watch a few movies, and maybe visit Mr. Gladstone at the hospital later. It was a simple plan, but it sounded like just what he needed.

When asked why she wanted to know about his plans for the day, she replied, "I'm not very good with words, especially under these circumstances, so I'd rather show you," as she moved in to be close to Sean.

As Dr. May's actions became more apparent, Sean's expression changed from puzzled to a mixture of surprise and realization. He looked flustered and unsure of how to react.

"Dr. May, what are you doing?" he asked, his voice a mix of shock and concern.

Dr. May looked at him, her expression a blend of determination and vulnerability. "I told you, I'm not good with words. But actions speak louder, right?" She reached out to gently touch his arm, her gaze earnest.

Sean's mind was racing as he tried to process the situation. Before Sean could piece everything together, Dr. May's tongue was doing a tango with his. It looked like Sean was about to christen his new apartment, finally.

When Duty Calls

Christmas had ushered in a scenario entirely unforeseen. If one had told Sean just a day before that Dr. May would awaken in his bed on this particular day, he might have dismissed it as the stuff of dreams. Yet here they were, wrapped in a tranquil embrace, a tableau of unexpected intimacy that coloured the day's canvas with hues he had never predicted.

Light streamed through the windows, glowing gently upon their intertwined forms. Her head nestled against his chest, and she stirred slightly as consciousness tiptoed back into her world. The rise and fall of their breaths formed a rhythmic flow, an intimate duet between two souls navigating uncharted waters.

In this fragile, fleeting moment, they found solace, an escape from the complexities that often engulfed their lives. The world outside, with its expectations and norms, seemed distant and inconsequential. It was as if time had suspended its relentless march, allowing them to savour this reverie.

As the minutes unfolded like delicate petals, they remained nestled in their haven of stillness. It was a rare instance of vulnerability, where their professional facades had crumbled, revealing the raw authenticity beneath. The world may have judged them, but judgment held no dominion in this sanctum of dawn.

The customary exchange of presents seemed almost redundant in the wake of the unanticipated intimacy they had shared. Yet, they exchanged smiles and subtle nods, recognizing that sometimes, the most meaningful gifts were the intangible ones—trust, understanding, and the courage to traverse uncharted territories.

Sean contemplated the enigma of human connections. It was as if life had orchestrated this unique interlude, a respite from the trials and tribulations that accompanied their respective roles. The ancient adage, "Fortune favours the bold," echoed in his mind as he acknowledged the audacity it took to forge unexpected bonds.

The day's magic was not confined to its fleeting hours; it had left an indelible mark on Sean and Dr. May. They had ventured into the realm of vulnerability, embraced it, and emerged stronger for it.

Sean found himself pondering the unpredictability of existence. Life's narrative was an intricate tapestry woven with threads of chance encounters, unforeseen twists, and the resilience to navigate unanticipated terrain. The tale of this Christmas day would forever remain etched in his memory, a reminder that even amidst the ordinary, the extraordinary could unfold.

Ultimately, it wasn't the presents exchanged or the celebrated festivities that defined this Christmas. The human connection, fragile and genuine, had coloured the day with shades of authenticity. Sean couldn't help but muse that the most meaningful gifts often came wrapped in the cloak of the unexpected.

Within the cocoon of the luxurious apartment, Sean found himself awash in a surreal sense of contentment. The extravagant dwelling, a realm of opulence he had often glimpsed in glossy magazines but had never dared hope to experience, was now his reality. Nestled within its lavish embrace was Dr. May, a figure whose motives he pondered little, for the present moment held his entire focus.

As he lay there, minutes trickled by, and the world outside seemed to blur into insignificance. The enchantment of the morning had woven a tapestry of comfort, an embrace so profound that Sean found himself suspended in a tranquil trance. Dr. May's presence, her head resting gently on his chest, radiated a sense of calm that enveloped him like a protective cocoon.

The outside world may have bustled with activity, its noise a distant echo, but time had yielded its tyranny in this cocoon of warmth. Sean's consciousness danced on the precipice between dreams and reality, fully ensnared in the embrace of a moment he had never dared put on his Christmas wish list. As if under a spell, he allowed himself to be carried by the current of serenity, cherishing each heartbeat that connected him to the world he had discovered.

When consciousness stirred within him, as it invariably must, Sean's eyes fluttered open. Yet, he made no move to disturb the stillness of the moment. Dr. May's form remained serenely nestled against him, her breathing a melodic rhythm that mirrored the peaceful cadence of his own heart. It was a tableau frozen in time, a momentary pause from life's relentless march.

Gazing at the ceiling, Sean felt a profound connection to the world around him. The luxury apartment, the embodiment of comfort and opulence, seemed to cradle them in its embrace. The air held a whisper of magic, a reminder that life could occasionally paint masterpieces that transcended ordinary existence.

While a part of him recognized the practicalities of time, the other part yearned to remain in this sanctum of tranquillity. He knew that reality's obligations would soon knock at the door, urging them to embrace the day beyond these walls. But for now, he relished the calm that enveloped them, savouring the stillness that few could claim in a world defined by chaos.

Sean's thoughts meandered into introspection. The sensation of Nirvana, the profound peace he had glimpsed, reminded him that life was a tapestry woven with diverse threads. Moments like these, woven with simplicity yet laden with significance, were the fabric of existence that truly mattered.

He savoured the connection, tranquillity, and intangible sense of unity that bound him to the world he had discovered. The outside world might have beckoned, but for now, he remained in this oasis of stillness, basking in the exquisite symphony of peace.

Dr. May's tranquillity was disrupted by the persistent intrusion of her phone's ringing. It was a disruption akin to a calm pond disturbed by ripples as if fate conspired to break the moment's enchantment. She silenced the device twice, hoping to reclaim the tranquillity she had briefly tasted, but destiny was unrelenting.

The third ring roused her from her slumber once again, and she finally answered the call in a mix of frustration and resignation. Bella's urgency was unmistakable, and it shattered the serene bubble that had enveloped Sean and Dr. May. The world beyond their cocoon had woven its tendrils into their sanctuary, demanding their attention.

As Bella detailed the gravity of the situation, the words painted a vivid picture of chaos and urgency. A major car pileup had unleashed a torrent of injured patients, and the hospital's resources were stretched thin. The holiday season had claimed many of the staff, leaving an insurmountable void in the face of this emergency.

"That's terrible. Have you reached Dr. Gabehart?" Dr. May inquired.

Bella informed her that she attempted to contact Dr. Gabehart but reached her voicemail, stating that she was away with her husband and would return on Monday morning.

Dr. May's thoughts raced as she considered the severity of the situation. Her concern for the patients was genuine, as was her awareness of the shortage of medical personnel. But equally pressing was the reality that her presence in this unique sanctuary, this cocoon of tranquillity, was now under threat.

Amidst the chaos and clamour of Bella's voice, Dr. May's mind was a whirlwind of decisions and possibilities. She knew she couldn't ignore the plea for help, for her dedication to her profession was steadfast. But simultaneously, she found herself reluctant to relinquish the sense of peace she had stumbled upon. She yearned to remain cocooned in this haven, to bask in the rare serenity that had embraced her.

Turning to Sean, whose attentive presence had not wavered throughout the call, she found empathy and understanding in his gaze. Their shared moment of bliss had created a bond that transcended the mundane. Their connection spoke volumes without the need for words.

"I have to go," Dr. May informed Bella, her voice a mixture of responsibility and reluctance. "I'll do my best to rally the remaining staff and coordinate the response. Stay safe and keep me updated," she added before ending the call.

As the weight of the situation settled upon her, Dr. May met Sean's gaze again. There was an unspoken understanding between them, an acknowledgment of the ebb and flow of life's currents. It reminded them that even in the face of disruption, the cocoon they had shared was not lost; instead, it had given them the strength to navigate the challenges ahead.

Sean's inquiry about the emergency's seriousness and extent delved beyond the immediate staff shortage, seeking insight into the scale of the unfolding catastrophe. Dr. May's response carried a mixture of realism and exasperation, reflecting the systemic challenges that often plagued medical institutions during critical times.

As they navigated the conversation, the tone of Dr. May's words was imbued with a deep sense of resignation as if she had reluctantly accepted the unfortunate truth. Her assessment cut through the rosy facade that one might hold about the medical profession, particularly during the holiday season. She painted a picture of doctors and nurses who might be more concerned with their paycheques than with the well-being of the patients in their care.

The candidness in her words revealed a sobering reality that many would prefer to overlook. In this reality, personal grievances and discontent could sometimes overshadow the oath to serve and heal. While candid, Dr. May's characterization of the situation was not without a tinge of disappointment, hinting at her unwavering dedication in contrast to others' lack of commitment.

Sean absorbed her words, recognizing the gravity of the situation. Her frank admission of not being the first choice for assistance in a crisis highlighted the moment's urgency. In the face of this emergent crisis, it seemed that all notions of hierarchy and pride had been cast aside, leaving only the dire need for medical expertise.

Their conversation testified to the complexities of the healthcare system and the human factors that often dictated its operation. Dr. May's revelation painted a sombre yet illuminating picture of the challenges faced by those genuinely dedicated to their vocation and the disheartening reality of those who sought refuge in complacency.

Sean's admiration for her dedication only deepened. Their shared cocoon of tranquillity had been temporarily disrupted, yet in its place emerged a profound understanding of the world they both inhabited. Their connection, forged in the quiet moments of an interrupted afternoon, would remain a poignant reminder of the intricacies of life, the healthcare system, and the individuals who navigated its turbulent waters.

Sean's words of encouragement and guidance flowed like a gentle stream of wisdom, each sentence carrying the weight of his experience and insight. As he spoke, his voice resonated with the calm authority of someone who understood the nuances of medicine and human behaviour.

Dr. May was drawn to his words like a thirsty traveller to an oasis in the desert.

His advice struck at the heart of the matter – it was not just medical expertise needed in times of crisis, but the confidence to wield that expertise effectively. His perspective illuminated the dual nature of competence and confidence, how knowledge could only truly shine when paired with an unwavering belief in one's abilities.

The symbolic torch he passed to her was one of empowerment, a reminder that even amidst chaos, the strength to act lay within. He didn't simply offer platitudes; his words carried a genuine concern for her growth as a physician, driven by a desire to see her overcome her self-imposed limitations.

Dr. May's response was a testament to her willingness to evolve and stretch beyond her comfort zone. Her vulnerability reminded her that even accomplished professionals had moments of uncertainty. Her decision to seek Sean's assistance acknowledged his unique insights, even though he was still a medical student. In her eyes, his perspective was valuable due to his medical knowledge and ability to see situations from a different angle.

Sean's playful retort, highlighting his status as a medical student, added a touch of levity to the conversation. The exchange was a nod to the dynamics of their relationship, which had evolved from teacher-student to something more profound – a camaraderie built on shared experiences and mutual respect.

Their agreement to work together was a testament to the strength of their bond, a partnership forged in unexpected circumstances. As they prepared to face the challenges awaiting them at the hospital, their shared determination became a testament to the resilience of the human spirit and the power of genuine connection to overcome even the most daunting of obstacles.

As Dr. May got ready, her demeanour emanated renewed determination. It was as if Sean's words had breathed life into her confidence, turning mere words into a tangible force propelling her forward. The transformation was akin to rekindling a once dormant flame, casting a warm and unwavering light around her.

Her plan of action showcased her newly embraced authority, a testament to the evolution of her mindset. Her instructions to Sean weren't just about delegation; they were about recognizing and harnessing the strengths of each team member. By assigning him the role of the brain behind their strategy, she acknowledged his unique analytical prowess and emphasized the collaborative spirit that would guide their approach.

A quiet understanding flowed between them – a shared commitment to navigate this storm together. The symbiotic partnership they'd built over time was no longer just about medical knowledge but a mutual trust that transcended hierarchies. Sean's role was not diminished by his status as a medical student; instead, it was amplified by his distinct perspective and insightful observations.

Sean initially had doubts, but she reassured him by highlighting their successful collaboration on numerous cases during the past three weeks. She expressed certainty that they could handle this emergency together.

"Fine, if you want me to take charge, I'll start right now. Go to the hospital, try to calm everyone, and give the nurses and doctors some leadership. Focus on stabilizing everyone and moving on to the next patient," Sean instructed Dr. May.

Dr. May smiled, knowing this was going to be an adventure. She was finally being honest about trusting Sean and felt confident in her decision.

"I know you will figure this out. I'll keep you posted. Let me know if there's anything you'd need when you get to the hospital so I can get it ready for you," she said to him as she leaned in to kiss him passionately before heading out.

As Sean pondered his next steps, he felt that the severity of the crisis had been downplayed. He turned to the Internet to gather information about the alleged incident. His instincts told him the accident would have been reported in the news if it had been as significant as he suspected.

Sean's analytical mind was like a detective's, piecing together the puzzle with fragments of information. The blizzard outside added a layer of complexity to the situation. It was as if nature had conspired to test their courage on this challenging Christmas late afternoon.

As he delved deeper into the online articles, his hunch proved correct. The accident was a catastrophic pileup involving numerous vehicles, including buses. The limited details painted a grim picture of the scene – twisted metal, shattered glass, and the potential for a high number of casualties. Sean's heart sank at the thought of the lives affected by this tragedy.

He picked up his phone and made a call. In the blink of an eye, Sean had seamlessly transitioned from the medical realm to a battlefield analogy that only those well-versed in military jargon could comprehend. His words were laden with urgency and purpose, reflecting the gravity of their situation.

"Hey, General, I'm sorry to call you like this, but we've been caught behind enemy lines, and we're outnumbered. We were caught off-guard, and some of our men have gone AWOL and deserted the squad. One of our soldiers is landing on the battlefield as we speak, and the reserves are likely exhausted," Sean explained.

Sean and the General had a distinctive way of communicating during their discussions on serious matters. With over twenty years of experience as a surgeon in the Air Force, the General continued to uphold the principles of the armed services even after returning to civilian life.

Sean had never experienced war firsthand, only watching TV shows about it. However, spending ample time with the General during and outside surgeries allowed him to learn and use military terminology to connect with him.

"Hey, Sean, good day, and a Merry Christmas to you too. Get your artillery and get to the battlefield on the double. I'll meet you there. We need to act fast before we get slaughtered behind enemy lines. Over and out," the General replied.

Equally imbued with the same language, the General's response conveyed a sense of camaraderie and shared mission.

As Sean hung up the phone and stood before a mirror, his heart felt heavy with emotion. Although he had always been sure of his skills as a prospective medical doctor, he had never envisioned a scenario where he would have to provide care in such a setting so soon. The gravity of the situation weighed heavily on him as he took in the moment and the challenge ahead of him.

Dr. May had placed her complete trust in him. He had to gather his courage and move forward with determination and confidence. With Dr. May entrusting him with this responsibility, he was now responsible for over a hundred individuals who required agent care. This realization was quite daunting.

Sean attempted to make a phone call but only reached voicemail, prompting him to leave a voice message before gathering his belongings and departing. He opted for a brief jog in the snowstorm as he made his way to the hospital, which was only minutes away.

A quiet introspection settled over him as his footsteps crunched in the fresh layer of snow. The events of the day were going to be a testament to his resilience and adaptability as he navigated the uncharted territory of a medical crisis with the guidance of Dr. May and the General. The weight of responsibility bore down on him, reminding him of the delicate balance between his medical training and the gravity of real-life situations.

The winter landscape mirrored his internal landscape—serene yet challenging, calm yet potentially turbulent. Each step he took manifested his commitment to the patients waiting for him. This commitment transcended the comfort of theory and embraced the urgency of action.

The gentle yet persistent snowfall seemed to mirror patients' relentless flow into the hospital. As he jogged through the blizzard, Sean's mind churned with a mixture of emotions – from the overwhelming weight of responsibility to the gratitude for his education and the chance to make a difference.

As Sean reached the hospital, his breath misting in the frigid air, he was ready to face whatever challenges lay ahead. The blizzard and the chaos within the emergency room were a reminder that life's storms could be unpredictable and demanding. Yet, armed with his knowledge, his mentorship from the General, and the trust of Dr. May, Sean was prepared to weather this storm and emerge stronger on the other side.

The journey from his apartment to the hospital wasn't just physical; it was a journey of growth, resilience, and self-discovery. It was a journey that transformed Sean from a medical student to a capable and confident medical professional, ready to face the ever-changing healthcare landscape with courage and compassion.

Amidst the chaotic backdrop of the emergency room, tension simmered as egos clashed and emotions ran high. The scene was reminiscent of a battlefield where competing forces vied for dominance, and the true test of leadership was about to unfold.

As Sean entered the emergency room, he was met with screams and yelling from the patients. Despite the challenging situation, the staff were doing their best to handle it. Some doctors and nurses were present, and Dr. May led the team. Upon seeing

Sean, she called for everyone to gather for a brief meeting.

She told the group, "Great job, everyone, for your hard work. As the most experienced physician present, I would like to designate Sean to take over. Let's all work together to support him and continue with our efforts. Thank you."

Dr. May's pronouncement marked a defining moment. This decision carried the weight of authority and the echoes of years of training. Her words placed Sean at the forefront and underscored the power struggle that often accompanies high-stress situations. The gathered medical staff, weary yet resolute, found themselves on the cusp of an unanticipated shift in command.

With his dissenting voice, Dr. Bates represented the voice of tradition and hierarchy, a reminder of the established norms within the medical profession. His challenge was more than a mere objection; it was an assertion of the established order, the tried-and-true path that had guided medical practice for generations.

"With all due respect, Dr. May, Sean's only a student, and your arrangement with Dr. Gabehart regarding this student doesn't extend here." Dr. Bates pointed at Sean, telling him to get out.

Dr. May replied, "Dr. Bates, with all due respect, I'm in charge here, and I say this is how we go about it. I'm still responsible for everything that anyone does here. Is that understood?"

The tension between Dr. May and Dr. Bates symbolized the clash between the old and the new, the traditional and the innovative. Dr. May's decision to trust Sean was not merely a display of hierarchy but a reflection of her newfound confidence and belief in the potential of unorthodox solutions.

As Dr. May stood her ground, her response was a testament

to her courage and demonstrated her commitment to the greater good. Her assertion of authority was a declaration that leadership was not bound by titles but driven by necessity and capability.

During this confrontation, Sean's role as an unexpected catalyst became evident. The uneasy silence that followed Dr. May's response was a pause pregnant with the possibilities of change. Sean's presence, once questioned by Dr. Bates, now represented a beacon of fresh perspective and potential innovation.

The battlefield of opinions and egos had transformed into a battlefield of ideals—the traditional versus the unconventional, the hierarchy versus the meritocratic. The unfolding drama in the hospital mirrored the complexities of the medical field itself—a dynamic interplay of experience, expertise, and the urgency to save lives.

The chaos of the emergency room was a constant reminder that lives hung in the balance, vulnerable to the decisions made in that moment. As Sean stood amid the storm, he embodied hope, a symbol of a new generation of medical professionals ready to navigate uncharted waters, challenge conventions, and forge a path toward a better future in healthcare.

Amid the tumultuous clash of opinions, the general's entrance was a turning point. He cast an aura of authority that quelled the rising tension. His presence demanded respect like a seasoned commander stepping onto a battlefield to restore order and discipline.

As the General positioned himself beside Dr. May, his mere presence silenced the uproar like a gust of wind extinguishing a raging fire. The weight of his experience and the unspoken promise of swift action hung in the air like a poised sword, ready to strike down any dissenting voices.

The General's resonant and commanding voice cut through the air like a trumpet call, rallying the troops for an impending battle. His words carried the weight of authority, a reminder that hierarchy was not just a formality but a crucial structure for efficient operation. It was akin to a seasoned captain stepping onto the deck of a ship to steer it through a storm.

Dr. May's role as a bridge between the medical staff and the General highlighted her significance as a leader in her own right. Her unwavering stance and willingness to assert her authority spoke of a newfound strength as if she had metamorphosed from a hesitant observer into a decisive leader.

"Thank you, Dr. May, for handling this, and I'll take over from here. Sean, this's your show. Get it going, and we'll all follow your lead. If any of you are tired, rest or go home because I only want people with the energy to work here. Dr. Bates, get in line, or I'll throw you out into this blizzard with your pants over your head," the General declared.

The General's decree, delivered with unwavering confidence, affirmed the power dynamic and marked a leadership transition. Standing at the forefront, Sean was akin to a young commander entrusted with a battalion, ready to lead with fresh insights and innovative strategies.

The General's dismissal of Dr. Bates' objections was a display of uncompromising authority, a clear message that unity and collaboration were paramount in times of crisis, like the stern command of a seasoned marshal putting an unruly soldier in their place.

With the General's passing of the torch to Sean, the room transformed into a symphony of purposeful movement, each medical professional finding their role in the unfolding narrative, resembling a choreographed battle formation, where individual skills melded into a collective force.

As the General retreated to his "office," his departure symbolized a change in personnel and a transition of power. Sean's journey from a medical student to a pivotal decision-maker was a testament to the evolving nature of leadership, where innovation and adaptability trumped convention.

Once a battleground of conflicting opinions, the emergency room was now a theatre of collaboration. It was guided by the vision of a new generation of medical professionals ready to face adversity head-on, determined to ensure the well-being of those in their care.

Amid the unfolding drama, Sean stepped forward, his voice cutting through the tension like a clarion call. It resonated with a blend of assertiveness and calm determination like a seasoned commander addressing his troops on the eve of a crucial battle.

"Okay, guys, I'm sorry that some of you don't like how things are, but it is what it is. Dr. May, do quick assessments on each patient and make a note on their chart."

His words carried the weight of authority, echoing through the room like a rallying cry demanding attention and respect. Sean's demeanour had shifted from a medical student to a leader in the face of adversity. It was akin to a young captain taking command of a ship navigating treacherous waters.

Although intended to be discreet, Dr. Bates' muttered objection was like a discordant note in a symphony, disrupting the harmony that Sean was trying to instill. But Sean's response was swift and decisive, reminiscent of a general dismissing a subordinate whose actions threatened the cohesion of the unit. The sternness in Sean's voice as he dismissed Dr. Bates for the night reflected his newfound authority and commitment to maintaining order and discipline.

The conversation between Sean and Bella epitomized a moment of strategic decision-making, where the weight of staffing shortages clashed with the need for a functional team. Sean's reply was imbued with confidence, reflecting his unwavering belief in the power of a motivated and cohesive group, reminiscent of a commander who knew that quality was more valuable than quantity on the battlefield.

As Sean urged those who had been working for an extended period to take a break, his voice carried the compassionate assurance of a leader who recognized the importance of rest amid chaos. It was like a general offering his troops a moment of respite before the next battle. Bella's plea to reconsider dismissing Dr. Bates for the night mirrored the concerns of a tactical advisor, reminding Sean of the dire circumstances they were facing.

Sean's response promised unwavering conviction like a commander-in-chief assuring his forces that the situation was under control. His words were a testament to his confidence in his strategy, echoing the sentiment that sometimes quality was more important than sheer numbers.

In that moment, Sean's leadership had transcended his role as a medical student. He had become a unifying force, rallying the troops with the promise of a well-thought-out plan and the assurance that, despite the challenges, they would emerge triumphant. Once a chaotic battleground, the emergency room had transformed into a symphony of purpose and coordination, guided by Sean's steady hand and unyielding determination.

In this whirlwind of organized chaos, Sean's strategic mind

was at its prime. He orchestrated a dance of medical efficiency more akin to a military operation than a hospital emergency room. He had taken the helm with a commander's precision, his instructions cutting through the frantic atmosphere like a seasoned general issuing battle orders.

His request for some nurses to accompany the General was akin to assigning elite scouts to gather vital intelligence on the battlefield. Just as skilled surveillance can mean the difference between victory and defeat, the role of these nurses was crucial in ensuring that the medical teams were informed and ready to address each patient's specific needs.

Sean's new triage system was a stroke of tactical brilliance, a testament to his ability to think beyond the confines of convention. In the heart of the storm, he had engineered a symphony of medical evaluations, assigning each doctor a distinct role, much like a skilled conductor assigning different instruments their unique melodies in a grand orchestral performance.

The patients, brought in by paramedics like wounded soldiers returning from the frontlines, were met with a rapid succession of medical assessments. It was as if a battalion of doctors had descended upon them, each specialist conducting their examination with focused efficiency. The assembly line of care they had created was reminiscent of a war production line, ensuring that no time was wasted in the battle to save lives.

The synchronized movement of the doctors from one patient to the next mirrored the coordinated maneuvers of a military unit, advancing together with precision and purpose. Sean's systematic approach allowed the medical team to address a multitude of issues on each patient, ensuring a thorough evaluation that left no stone unturned.

As observations were meticulously jotted down on each patient's chart, it was as if the battle strategy was being mapped out with meticulous care. The scribbles and notes symbolized the tactical decisions made by a commander on the field, shaping the course of action to ensure the best possible outcome.

Sean's leadership was the beacon that guided the medical team through the storm. His ability to harness their collective skills and channel them towards a common goal was reminiscent of a military leader rallying his troops, ensuring that every member understood their role and executed it flawlessly.

In this dire situation, Sean's innovative thinking and unshakable confidence transformed the emergency room into a theatre of precision and efficiency. His leadership and strategic approach were the driving force that turned a potentially overwhelming crisis into a well-coordinated operation that showcased the prowess of the medical team under his command.

In this fast-paced medical symphony, Sean's role as the final checkpoint was as crucial as the watchtower overlooking a battlefield. His meticulous eye for detail and unwavering commitment to quality ensured no potential oversight went unnoticed. Just as vigilant generals survey the progress of their troops, Sean's discerning gaze scanned each patient's chart, confirming that all observations were accurately recorded and all necessary assessments had been performed.

The operation's rhythm was relentless, like the rhythmic pounding of drums on a battlefield. Every ten minutes or so, a new set of patients arrived on stretchers, and the specialized doctors swiftly assessed their condition and needs. Like a well-oiled war machine, they moved with synchronized precision, addressing each patient's condition with practiced expertise.

Sean's final assessment was like a commander reviewing the battle plans before giving the final order to advance. It demanded clarity of thought and an unwavering commitment to excellence.

His decisions – whether to admit, treat, or provide respite – held the weight of a commander choosing the optimal course of action on the battlefield. His judgment was informed not only by his medical knowledge but also by his ability to identify patterns and discrepancies that might have been missed in the heat of the moment.

By positioning himself as the ultimate arbiter of patient care, Sean created a system in which his oversight enhanced the operation's overall effectiveness. His ability to spot potential pitfalls and recommend course corrections ensured that the medical team operated as a well-coordinated unit, maximizing their collective impact on patients' outcomes.

In this role, Sean's actions transcended the realm of medical practice and symbolized leadership in its purest form. Just as a battlefield commander's decisions can determine the outcome of a conflict, Sean's decisions had the potential to shape the trajectory of each patient's journey toward recovery. His presence was a reassuring constant, a beacon of stability amid chaos, guiding the medical team toward victory over adversity.

In those intense hours, as the clock seemed to race against their efforts, Sean's presence and leadership were a testament to the power of effective collaboration, strategic thinking, and unyielding dedication to the well-being of those in their care. As he continued to navigate this intricate dance of medicine and leadership, he was writing a chapter of his own in the annals of medical history – a chapter marked by resilience, innovation, and the unwavering commitment to uphold the sanctity of life, even in the face of the fiercest challenges.

Dr. Gabehart's unexpected entrance was like a sudden gust of wind disrupting the medical team's carefully choreographed dance. As the snow-covered figure stumbled in, breathless and dishevelled, the intensity of the situation momentarily shifted to accommodate this new arrival. Dr. May's swift response, like a field medic rushing to aid a fallen comrade, was a testament to the camaraderie that had formed among the medical professionals.

The following scene echoed the ethos of unity and care established within the hospital walls. The swift removal of wet clothes and the offering of blankets to warm her up were gestures of compassion, mirroring the unwavering support soldiers extend to one another in times of crisis. Dr. May's assessment of Dr. Gabehart's condition was a clear example of medical expertise and teamwork in action – a reminder that even in the chaos, the well-being of each individual was paramount.

The bruises that adorned Dr. Gabehart's form were like battle scars, a visual testament to her challenges on her journey to the hospital. Dr. May's attentive assessment and immediate action showcased the essence of their profession – to heal and care for one another, just as they did for their patients.

As Dr. Gabehart recounted her harrowing journey, her words held an air of vulnerability that transcended professional titles. The unpredictability of life's circumstances was a reminder that even those who stood as pillars of medical knowledge were not immune to the unpredictability of the world around them.

Dr. Gabehart's experience was a microcosm of the larger struggle they all faced – navigating the treacherous terrain of the snowstorm-ravaged city. Everything was good until she got to the hospital when her car slipped and crashed into a wall. Despite the dangerous conditions, her determination to respond to Sean's voicemail mirrored the dedication of soldiers answering the call to defend their homeland.

In this tableau of events, the hospital corridors became a sanctuary of warmth and compassion amidst the wintry chaos outside. The bonds forged through shared experiences and a common purpose shone bright, much like the camaraderie that unites soldiers on the battlefield.

Dr. Gabehart's entrance into the intricate tableau added another layer of complexity to the unfolding story. Her swift and efficient assessment resembled a seasoned general gauging the battlefield conditions before formulating a strategy. Dr. May's preliminary evaluation revealed no internal injuries or trauma, offering a glimmer of relief amidst the prevailing chaos.

Dr. Gabehart's determination to continue her duties despite her personal ordeal was like a bold commander rallying her troops on the front lines. Her insistence on resting for just a few moments echoed the resilience of a leader who understood the importance of tending to her well-being in order to guide her team effectively.

The exchange between Dr. Gabehart and Dr. May resonated with a shared purpose and mutual respect. The passing of the torch – or rather, the stethoscope – from one capable leader to another was a testament to the camaraderie and trust fostered among the medical professionals. Dr. May's act of providing fresh scrubs and running shoes was reminiscent of a fellow soldier ensuring her comrade was equipped for the challenges ahead.

"Sean, you need to change your approach in whatever you plan to do. More people are making their way into this emergency room within an hour. I told them I was sending someone from here to help stabilize patients on the scene. So, Sean, go help them, and I'll take over from here," she instructed.

As Dr. Gabehart departed to change into her fresh attire, the scene became a brief interlude, a pause in the ongoing turmoil. The hospital's corridors had transformed into a sanctuary of physical and emotional support, where the night's struggles were met with a sense of unity and compassion. The staff, each facing their own battles, were bound by a common goal – to provide care and healing to those in need.

With Dr. Gabehart's directive to Sean to change his approach, a new chapter of the night's events was set to unfold. The situation's urgency was heightened, much like a commander receiving critical intelligence that demanded swift and decisive action. Sean's impending mission was not just about medical expertise; it was about channelling his dedication and resolve to stabilize patients on the scene amidst the tumultuous backdrop of the snowstorm.

As the narrative continued to weave together these moments of action, reflection, and interaction, the larger tapestry of unity, compassion, and unwavering commitment to the well-being of others became increasingly evident. The story stood as a testament to the indomitable spirit of those who face adversity with resilience, empathy, and the shared purpose of serving and healing.

Amidst the flurry of intense activity, a surprising figure stepped into the emergency room – Mr. Gladstone, a character whose previous role in life had been more aligned with the administrative and financial aspects of life. At this moment, however, he transitioned seamlessly into a new position, one of an organizer and coordinator, akin to a field marshal orchestrating the movement of troops on a complex battlefield.

Sean took his bag and was ready to leave when he saw Mr. Gladstone entering the emergency room. He told him they could use his help, "O.G, you know how to run factories. I was hoping you could keep this place organized and keep things moving. Make sure you keep this place in order for Dr. Gorgeous. I have to run to a car pileup and try to manage things from there."

Sean's direct and unconventional approach to involving Mr. Gladstone in the emergency efforts was reminiscent of a strategic commander delegating specific responsibilities to an able lieutenant.

Sean's choice of words – "keep things moving," "keep this place in order," and "organize for Dr. Gorgeous" – evoked a sense of mission and purpose. It underscored the idea that each individual's contribution, regardless of their background or primary role, was crucial in ensuring the smooth operation of the emergency room during this critical time.

In a situation where verbal communication might have been secondary to the urgency of the moment, Mr. Gladstone's unspoken compliance was a vivid testament to his commitment. His physical presence and gestures carried weight, embodying the concept that actions can often speak louder than words. This shift in his role highlighted the adaptability and resilience that can emerge when unexpected challenges arise.

The passing of the torch of organization from medical professionals to Mr. Gladstone alleviated the pressure on nursing staff, allowing them to focus more on direct patient care. This act showcased Sean's ability to see beyond traditional roles and utilize available resources to their fullest potential, much like a strategist who maximizes the strengths of each division on the battlefield.

As Sean geared up to venture into the heart of the storm, his departure was marked by a moment of levity—a contrast to the gravity of the situation. His rendition of "Jingle Bells" echoed through the corridors, serving as a reminder that even amid the chaos, there could be moments of shared humanity and a touch of light-heartedness.

At this moment, the narrative encapsulated the diverse range of roles and talents that converged within the confines of the emergency room. The characters, each contributing uniquely, symbolized the collective effort to weather the storm, both literal and metaphorical.

Amid this orchestrated chaos, Dr. May's small act of preparing a cup of coffee for Dr. Gabehart carried a profound significance. It was a gesture that transcended the frantic pace of the emergency room – a symbol of care and camaraderie amidst the whirlwind of urgency. Dr. Gabehart settled into her new role like a seasoned commander taking charge of a well-organized battalion, building upon the foundation Sean had established.

The torch of responsibility was passed seamlessly, a testament to Sean's transparent approach. The process he had initiated had become a well-oiled machine, moving with precision and purpose, guided by the expertise of medical professionals who understood the importance of their roles. Dr. Gabehart's transition into this rhythm reflected her experience and confidence, her presence seamlessly interwoven into the symphony of activity.

The smaller number of patients in the emergency room was a brief respite, a moment of calm before the storm. With the combined efforts of the staff and Mr. Gladstone's capable organization, the situation was tenuously manageable. It was akin to a ship navigating through turbulent waters, with the crew working harmoniously to steer it towards calmer seas.

The patients who entered the emergency room were a diverse cross-section of humanity, each with their own story and needs. Some required only minor interventions, a mere stitching of the wounds they had sustained. Others, however, needed more comprehensive care, and they were directed toward the General, a figure who symbolized the commanding presence, ready to tackle the intricate and complex surgical challenges.

Dr. Gabehart's parting words to Sean – "Be careful out there and get back soon" – held a sentiment that resonated deeply. It reflected the unspoken bond shared among those who worked on the front lines of emergencies, a reminder of the vulnerability that existed even within the realm of medical professionals. Sean's response carried a sense of determination and purpose, encapsulating the spirit of his commitment to the task at hand.

"Don't worry, this's how I like my Christmas," Sean replied.

Amidst the urgency and intensity, this interlude in the narrative highlighted the multifaceted aspects of human connection and resilience. It showcased the interplay of individual roles, the harmony of collective effort, and the pursuit of purpose, all set against the backdrop of an eventful Christmas day.

A moment of clinical acumen and collaboration stood out in the ongoing medical ballet. Dr. May's approach showcased her ability to analyze complex situations and make critical decisions swiftly. Her proactive step of involving Dr. Gabehart in a patient's case demonstrated her commitment to thoroughness and seeking input from her colleagues.

Dr. May approached Dr. Gabehart and informed her of the need to send a patient for dialysis. Dr. Gabehart inquired about the reason for dialysis and how the patient ended up in that state. Dr. May explained that the patient's blood sugar levels were excessively high.

"The patient has just been in an accident. Of course, the blood sugar will be high!" Dr. Gabehart exclaimed.

Dr. May calmly showed Dr. Gabehart the blood sugar level that alarmed her.

"Blood sugar doesn't get this high even with the worst physical trauma," she said to Dr. Gabehart as she handed her a clipboard.

Dr. Gabehart responded in shock, "Oh my god, admit the patient and get a nurse to set up the machine. Good call, Dr. May, good observation."

The interplay of emotions within her mirrored the rollercoaster of the emergency room itself, where every diagnosis and decision could alter the course of a patient's life.

The dialogue was a testament to the power of medical knowledge and experience. Dr. May's calm presentation of evidence, in the form of the alarmingly high blood sugar levels, illustrated the art of rational clinical deduction.

The realization that the patient's blood sugar levels were beyond what physical trauma alone could explain was a turning point — a shift from focusing solely on the trauma to recognizing an underlying medical issue that needed immediate attention.

Dr. May's keen observation influenced the patient's care. It showcased the collaborative essence of a well-functioning medical team, where individual insights collectively lead to comprehensive patient management.

This short exchange underscored the complexity of medical decision-making, the depth of knowledge, and the significance of teamwork. As the emergency room continued to bustle with activity, this moment stood as a reminder of the precision, intuition, and expertise that defined the medical profession.

For over two hours, Dr. Gabehart attended to patients one at a time and quickly evaluated them before sending them to rooms to rest and recover. She met a few that needed thorough evaluation and set those aside.

Amidst the organized chaos of the emergency room, a particular case had ensnared Dr. Gabehart's attention, presenting a medical puzzle that defied easy diagnosis. This instance illuminated the complexity inherent in medical practice, where symptoms and signs could often challenge even the most experienced professionals.

She had to call Sean. "I have a senior with low blood pressure and high pulse but no sign of a bacterial infection. I've looked everywhere and can't find any sign of bleeding. I asked the patient nearly every question, but I can't figure this one out," she said on the phone.

Sean told her to ask the patient about the colour of his stool the last time he checked.

"How do you know I haven't asked him that already?" Dr. Gabehart asked.

"You're too much of a lady to directly ask a male patient about their bowel habits, especially under these circumstances. If you think the patient's blood pressure and pulse are likely due to blood loss, look everywhere until you find it. You're dealing with a senior patient, so go to the most obvious source before you try to rule out anything else," Sean told Dr. Gabehart.

Dr. Gabehart's response, a mixture of embarrassment and amusement, unveiled the intricate dynamics of a medical team's camaraderie. The chuckle that followed Sean's guidance showcased the genuine connection between professionals who shared the same commitment to unravelling medical mysteries.

"Alright, doctor," she responded with a blush and a chuckle.

"By the way, did you know there are six places into which a person can bleed to death without a drop of blood leaving their body?" Sean asked.

"Come on, Sean. I'm not in the mood for a lecture," Dr. Gabehart interrupted. She hung up on him, laughing at herself and shaking her head.

In this exchange, diagnosing a patient became a tapestry woven with knowledge, empathy, and collaboration. The spotlight on this case was a reminder that medicine was not just a science but also an art that required equal parts intuition and expertise to navigate the intricate landscape of the human body's complexities.

In the ongoing medical battlefield, Sean continued to work diligently, stabilizing patients and meticulously documenting their conditions. Each note he left was a snapshot of his critical thinking and medical assessment, capturing the essence of patients' conditions.

Yet, one patient still eluded the grasp of diagnosis, a riddle that intrigued Sean's analytical mind. This case was akin to a locked chest, its contents hidden beneath layers of signs and symptoms that defied an easy solution. Sean's commitment to his profession compelled him to unravel this enigma.

Sean contacted Dr. Gabehart to inform her that additional patients were being referred to her. Although he had successfully stabilized most patients, he was still working on one case that required further investigation. Sean planned to accompany this patient during transport back to the hospital.

Dr. Gabehart asked what the problem was with the patient.

"Well, let's see. A young woman looks healthy and has no signs of any current treatment. Signs and symptoms of a disseminated bacterial infection. No significant medical history. She has otherwise been healthy and happy," Sean told Dr. Gabehart before she asked if the patient was a teenager.

"Yeah, fifteen. How did you know?" Sean replied.

"Because you're right, she is likely in septic shock, but only a young girl who recently became a woman doesn't know the importance of proper feminine hygiene. You're too much of a gentleman to think about that. Remove the tampon that has probably been there for several hours and treat her for septic shock," she explained.

The conclusion to this medical mystery, delivered by Dr. Gabehart's words, was a reminder that medicine was about understanding the intricate interplay of the human body and its various facets. In this moment of revelation, the connection between medicine and life's intricacies shone brightly, a testament to the holistic nature of healing.

The impending conclusion of the crisis was a beacon of hope, promising a return to normalcy for both patients and exhausted medical staff. Sean's suggestion to check on Mr. Gladstone revealed his compassionate nature. He extended his concern beyond the medical sphere to the well-being of those who supported the operation from the sidelines.

"Thanks, Doc, very impressive. I guess I'll see you guys shortly. Check on O.G. in case he needs another dose for his pain. The poor guy has been standing for hours while he's supposed to be in bed. We should be able to round up everything in a few hours so you can all return to enjoy what's left of your Christmas. Which reminds me, why did you leave your vacation for this?" Sean said to Dr. Gabehart.

"So, you wanted to have all this fun without me? Besides, I'd rather spend the night here than return to that sorry excuse of a husband. Want to join me and work on these reports for these patients all night?" she replied.

The camaraderie among the medical team shone through Sean's interaction with Dr. Gabehart. Her decision to leave her vacation and join the medical frontlines revealed a shared dedication to the profession. Their banter, a playful exchange of words, showcased the bonds forged through the shared trials and triumphs of medical practice. Her invitation for Sean to join her in this healing marathon echoed the unspoken unity of purpose that had guided them through the crisis.

Sean's delight in accepting the invitation was a testament to his commitment to his duties and the shared journey of healing. As the phone call concluded, a sense of impending closure hung in the air. The General's departure and Dr. May's announcement of completion marked a turning point in the narrative. Yet, amid the chaos and exhaustion, a sense of camaraderie and shared purpose lingered that transcended the moment's challenges.

Amid this medical odyssey, Sean's steps were a testament to the profound impact of his dedication and resolve. As he embarked on the journey back to the hospital, the warmth of the camaraderie and the promise of a job well done filled his heart. The night's events had been a crucible, forging connections, testing resilience, and reminding everyone involved of the profound meaning of their chosen path.

Second Chance

As the dawn of New Year's Eve illuminated the hospital corridors, Sean embarked on a reflective journey, each step laden with the weight of his experiences yet buoyed by an air of contentment. This day marked the end of his clerkship and the culmination of his medical school journey. The path that lay ahead was cloaked in uncertainty. Yet, his heart resonated with a sense of fulfillment, much like a traveller who has reached a scenic summit and stands there, pausing to absorb the grandeur before him.

In the spirit of this bittersweet occasion, Sean's demeanour radiated warmth and goodwill. Like a benevolent spirit weaving through the hospital's tapestry, he engaged with patients whose lives he had touched during his tenure. It was a reminder that medicine wasn't just about treatments and diagnoses; it was about human connection, about being a beacon of empathy in moments of vulnerability.

With small tokens of appreciation in hand, Sean gracefully moved through the hospital's corridors, his steps a rhythmic dance that mirrored the melody of gratitude he carried within. His familiar presence was like a comforting tune, and this melody resonated in the hearts of those he had encountered. As they met his gaze, their faces lit up with the warmth of recognition, a silent acknowledgment of shared moments and mutual growth.

The act of embracing, a universal gesture that transcends words, became a poignant ritual. It was as if these embraces held within them the essence of the countless lives he had touched, a tapestry of shared experiences woven together by the threads of compassion. It was a scene reminiscent of a harvest festival, where the bounty of human connection was celebrated and shared.

Amidst these interactions, Sean's movements seemed choreographed by an inner harmony, a symphony of gratitude that played softly within his heart. As he traversed the hospital's landscape, his dancing steps mirrored the joyous rhythm of the moment, a reminder that even amidst the rigours of medical training, a symphony of shared humanity existed.

Sean's presence left an indelible mark on the hospital and its inhabitants. His gestures of appreciation were not just tokens; they reflected the profound impact of his journey. With each smile exchanged, each embrace shared, the hospital resonated with an unspoken truth—that medicine, at its core, is a symphony of empathy, compassion, and human connection.

While the world outside celebrated the impending arrival of a new year on this New Year's Eve, the hospital's inhabitants knew that time adhered to a different rhythm within its walls. For them, it was not just the eve of a new year; it was another Friday, a day that held its own significance in the tapestry of their lives.

The hospital's pulse followed a rhythm that was independent of the calendar, and Fridays were etched into its heartbeat as days of importance. With each Friday came a sense of anticipation, a spark of energy that infused the air. It was a day when routines shifted, and the familiar corridors seemed to hold secrets waiting to be unveiled.

Since the early hours of the morning, Sean had been a steady presence in this bustling microcosm. His footsteps echoed in harmony with the hospital's heartbeat as he traversed its halls, engaging in conversations and sharing moments with the various souls who called this place their second home. Yet, his role seemed to transcend the conventional tasks one might associate with a medical student.

Amidst the flurry of activity, Sean's hands remained unburdened by the weight of medical instruments or documents. Instead, they were open to receiving and giving, to grasping the hands of colleagues and patients, to embracing and sharing tokens of appreciation. His conversations flowed like a river, carrying with them a sense of connection, of unity in a shared experience.

Although the world beyond those walls was abuzz with celebratory preparations, the hospital's inhabitants knew that their Fridays were special enough to warrant their own anticipation. As Sean moved from one interaction to another, he was enacting a ritual that had become woven into the fabric of this unique environment. He embodied the spirit of camaraderie, reminding everyone that even amid their demanding routines, there was space for shared moments of humanity.

Sean illuminated the hospital like a sunbeam breaking through a cloudy sky. He moved among the night shift staff, his energy seemingly endless even after spending hours engaged in heartfelt conversations and shared laughter. His enthusiasm mirrored the mood of someone deeply in love. This infectious joy spread like wildfire among those fortunate to cross his path.

As morning's light heralded the arrival of the new shift, Sean's spirit remained unwavering, a reflection of the uncontainable joy of a contented baby, the unbridled excitement of a teenager exploring the world anew, the profound love of a father cradling his precious newborn, and the quiet pride of a grandparent watching generations unfold.

In this moment, Sean's aura encapsulated the essence of celebration, a reverie in honour of completing his medical school journey. The title of "Doctor" was only days away, but for now, he basked in the joy of his present accomplishment. His heart overflowed with gratitude for those who had walked alongside him, who had shaped his experiences and made his path richer and brighter.

With each interaction, Sean was weaving the final stitches of this chapter, a tapestry of shared moments and meaningful connections. As he rejoiced with his colleagues, his spirit resonated with theirs, harmonizing in a chorus of celebration that echoed through the hospital's corridors.

This day was more than just a milestone; it was a testament to the power of community, the strength of human bonds, and the beauty of shared dreams. As Sean continued to infuse his energy and love into the hospital's heartbeat, he celebrated his achievement and honoured the journey that had brought him to this point.

Among the many faces that lit up at Sean's presence, only Dr. Gabehart and Mr. Gladstone held the intimate understanding of the crossroads at which Sean now stood. They alone comprehended the complex blend of emotions, hopes, and uncertainties that swirled within him.

Sean had spun a tale for the others, a narrative carefully woven to cloak his true intentions. A story that painted his immediate future with the hues of research, teaching, and reflection. This skillfully crafted tale had served as a shield against probing inquiries. It had garnered little more than nods of agreement in its reasonable simplicity, freeing Sean from the need to divulge the intricacies of his heart's journey.

Among the flurry of farewells and well wishes, a particular

individual stood out – someone with the uncanny ability to infuse every occasion with heartfelt sincerity. This unassuming figure was known for her thoughtful gestures, knack for making others feel cherished, and extraordinary ability to create an atmosphere of genuine connection.

As the hospital staff bid Sean adieu, some extended small tokens of farewell while others grappled with the profound emotions that such partings tend to stir. Yet, amid this array of reactions, her presence radiated warmth, enveloping the occasion in an aura of camaraderie and empathy.

She never allowed moments like these to go unnoticed, nor did she let them pass without leaving their mark. For her, celebrating someone's journey was not just a courteous formality but an authentic expression of compassion and appreciation. Her actions were not guided by a sense of obligation but rather by an innate understanding of the human connection that underpins every shared experience.

The anticipation had been palpable among the hospital staff, each person eager to witness her signature brand of heartfelt celebration. Sean, perhaps immersed in the emotional whirlwind of his departure, had never envisioned this as a possibility.

In the heart of this bittersweet farewell, a beacon of sweetness transcended the confines of spoken words. Mother, a master of culinary artistry, had conjured a masterpiece in the form of a cake—a true testament to her boundless love and a feast for both the eyes and the palate. This confectionery creation was a tangible embodiment of her unwavering support and pride in Sean's contributions and achievements.

The cake, a veritable work of art, bore the indelible mark of her artistic ingenuity, reflecting her painstaking efforts and meticulous attention to detail. Each stroke of frosting was a testament to the love that had guided her hands, transforming baking into a profound expression of maternal devotion. It stood as a token of celebration, honouring Sean's accomplishments and the profound journey that had brought him to this pivotal moment.

The tantalizing aroma that enveloped the cake drew the attention of the hospital staff, who were no strangers to the delectable treats that Mother lovingly crafted. Yet, this particular creation was more than just a culinary delight; it symbolized unity, a shared memory that spoke of community and connection. Mother had poured her skill and heart into this masterpiece, ensuring that each slice would hold the promise of culinary delight and the warmth of her love.

The staff, many of whom had witnessed Sean's growth and dedication, eagerly awaited their turn to indulge in this scrumptious creation. The cake held within its layers the spirit of celebration. This gesture extended its embrace to include the entire hospital community. It was a silent reminder that in moments of transition, joy, and even parting, the shared experience of a delectable treat can forge bonds that endure, reminding us all that love and connection transcend the passage of time.

Amid the gathering of hospital staff, a peaceful and respectful silence fell as Mother stepped forward, bearing not just a cake but the weight of emotions that flowed within her. Her speech was a testament to the gratitude and admiration that had grown within the hearts of those who had the privilege of working alongside Sean during his brief yet impactful tenure.

Her words, soft but resonant, acknowledged Sean's quiet dedication, which had left an indelible mark on the hospital's corridors. As her voice carried through the room, it was evident that her sentiment echoed the unspoken thoughts of those present. Her speech was a tribute to his unwavering commitment to patients, relentless pursuit of excellence, and innate ability to uplift spirits even in the midst of challenging circumstances.

The applause that followed her words was an expression of approval and a collective recognition of Sean's transformational effect on the hospital's environment. It was a spontaneous outpouring of respect, a manifestation of the appreciation that had grown within the hearts of colleagues and beneficiaries of his care. The applause held within it a sense of unity, a shared acknowledgment of the positive change he had brought to AGH.

Mother's heartfelt wish for Sean's future endeavours contained pride and a hint of sadness, affirming her unconditional love and support. Her expression of disappointment, albeit selfish, reminded her of the void his departure would create. In her words, her promise that he would always be a part of the AGH family resonated deeply, solidifying the sense of connection that transcended the walls of the hospital.

As the applause subsided and the cake stood as a symbol of this shared sentiment, it was clear that Sean's impact went beyond his medical knowledge – he had become an integral thread woven into the tapestry of the hospital's community. While his journey was about to take him elsewhere, his legacy would remain etched in the hearts and memories of those he had touched.

The atmosphere brimmed with celebration as the harmonious notes of "For He's a Jolly Good Fellow" filled the air. The uplifting melody was a fitting tribute to Sean's positive influence, creating a shared cadence of joy that resonated through the room. At this moment, Sean was more than just a medical student completing his clerkship – he was a cherished member of a united community honoured for his contributions and embraced by those he had touched.

The dance began with Sean lifted on the shoulders of two staff members, a symbolic gesture of support and camaraderie. The corridor became a whirlwind of movement, each step a testament to the unity that had grown among those who had shared this journey with Sean. The dance embodied the rhythm of the music and the pulse of the connections forged during his time at the hospital.

Amid the joyful melody, Mother stood at the centre, her smile radiant as she took in the moment – a tangible representation of the collective gratitude that flowed within every heart present. Her invitation for others to share their wishes was a gesture that showcased the inclusivity of the occasion. As the space echoed with brief but heartfelt well-wishes, each word was like a drop of sincerity in a sea of emotion.

Though the words were concise, they carried the weight of all the interactions, smiles, and moments shared with Sean. Each speaker spoke not just for themselves but for everyone who had come into contact with him. The space, filled with a chorus of diverse voices, united in the desire to convey their appreciation, best wishes, and hopes for his future.

These brief yet powerful speeches revealed the depth of the bond forged over weeks of shared moments. The emotion in the air was palpable, a fusion of gratitude, fondness, and the bittersweet recognition that this was a farewell. Amidst the whirlwind of celebration, Sean was enveloped in a profound sense of belonging that extended far beyond the hospital walls, touching hearts and lives in ways that words could only attempt to express.

With the room's emotions hanging in the air, Sean's gratitude flowed like a soothing melody. His words wove a tapestry of appreciation, compassion, and a tinge of wistfulness. He spoke with a sincerity that touched hearts, acknowledging the privilege of his brief yet meaningful tenure at AGH. His words were a gentle reminder that even the shortest connections can leave an indelible mark on the human spirit.

In his words, Sean mirrored the collective sentiment of heartbreak, echoing the unspoken emotions that lingered in the room. The poignant admission that he wished he could have started his journey as a medical doctor at AGH resonated deeply, reflecting the inevitability of life's unpredictable turns. His yearning for the chance to have begun his medical career at AGH revealed a bond that transcended time, echoing the sentiment that sometimes circumstances challenge even the most heartfelt desires.

Amidst the shared emotions, Sean's sincerity became a unifying thread, weaving the moments they had shared into a tapestry of appreciation. His acknowledgment of the staff's welcome resonated with the sentiment that their embrace had created a sense of belonging he would carry with him. His gratitude was a bridge that connected his heart with theirs, reminding them that even though he was leaving physically, his spirit remained intertwined with theirs.

The cake-cutting ceremony symbolized unity, as Sean held the knife to divide the cake, representing their shared experiences. The invitation for Mr. Gladstone to share in this moment spoke volumes, reflecting the familial camaraderie that had been established between them. The feeding of the cake became a playful manifestation of the bond they had formed—a bond that extended beyond formalities to moments of carefree laughter and genuine camaraderie.

As laughter filled the space, Sean's face adorned with cake cream became a testament to the joy that transcended the bittersweet undertones of the occasion. The cream symbolized the shared memories and the undeniable connections that had been built. At that moment, as the room reverberated with laughter and warmth, Sean's presence became a living embodiment of the hospital's spirit – a spirit that would persist long after he had left, a spirit that was, in essence, the heart and soul of AGH.

Amidst the chorus of gratitude and warm goodbyes, Bonita stood like a guiding presence, leading Sean towards an individual who sought him out. As she pointed out the man, the moment took on an air of anticipation, a thread connecting the past to the present.

In that instant, as their gazes met, Sean and Mr. Carroll's familiarity transformed into a reunion that defied the passing of time. Sean's exuberance echoed through the corridor like a musical note of genuine joy. Their embrace was like an old friendship rediscovered, a testament to the impact of even the briefest connections in healthcare.

Mr. Carroll's presence exuded a sense of gratitude that words could hardly capture. His demeanour reflected resilience and recovery, and one could see his journey in the lines of his face. This journey had brought him from illness to healing. As Sean greeted him with familiarity, Mr. Carroll's quiet gratitude spoke volumes. His appreciation manifested in the simplicity of his words and the genuine warmth of his smile.

The exchange between them was a poignant moment in the tapestry of medical care. Sean's modesty, his humble assertion that he had done nothing, emphasized the compassion that often goes unnoticed. These small gestures create an enduring impact.

The hug that followed symbolized the bond formed between a doctor and a patient. This bond transcended medical treatments and became a connection grounded in empathy and shared humanity.

As Sean's voice echoed through the room and the two men embraced, their interaction encapsulated the heart of healthcare—the art of healing and the art of forming connections. At that moment, they were not just a doctor and a patient; they were two individuals united by a shared experience, a memory that would linger in their hearts long after they parted ways.

Amidst the backdrop of a farewell celebration, Sean's exchange with Mr. Carroll became a reminder that the impact of a physician's care goes beyond medical treatments – it touches lives, leaves imprints of compassion, and bridges the gap between vulnerability and healing. It was a moment that resonated with the essence of the journey Sean was about to embark on – a journey where the power of human connection would complement his medical skills.

The corridor stretched before them, a quiet space of connection away from the celebratory crowd. The camaraderie between Sean and Mr. Carroll was palpable, an unspoken understanding that transcended the boundaries of medical interactions. The hallway seemed like a timeless conduit, allowing them to traverse through moments of shared laughter and heartfelt conversation.

Amidst Sean's light-hearted compliment, the room resonated with genuine solidarity. Their shared laughter painted the hallway with the hues of harmony, each chuckle a testament to their bond. This bond had transformed into a real friendship, a testament to the authenticity that often emerged amidst the corridors of healing.

Yet, as the laughter subsided, the tone shifted into a more reflective register. Mr. Carroll's words weaved an intricate narrative, a tale of transformation spurred by Sean's care. The vulnerability in his voice carried the weight of his journey, and his recounting embodied profound introspection.

In Mr. Carroll's words, a story of redemption, of coming to terms with personal weaknesses and striving to amend them, unfolded. The contours of his journey unfolded—the chaotic and heartrending episodes that had led him to that hospital bed. Sean's words and insights ignited a spark of self-awareness, leading Mr. Carroll on a path to mend his health and marriage.

The impact of Sean's care went beyond physical healing; it had kindled a resolve to prioritize what truly mattered in life. The admission of gratitude, the acknowledgment of Sean's role in his metamorphosis, reverberated through the hallway like a profound affirmation of the doctor-patient bond.

Sean, in his characteristic humility, downplayed his role. He viewed his actions as natural extensions of his commitment to patient well-being. He assured Mr. Carroll that the important thing was that everything turned out well. In his response, Sean embodied the essence of a dedicated healer—one who did not seek grand accolades but whose fulfillment came from the happiness of those he served.

As they walked, their exchange encapsulated the profound influence that medical professionals can have on their patients. Beyond science and medicine, moments of genuine connection, sincere words, and empathetic understanding leave lasting imprints. Sean's care had catalyzed Mr. Carroll's transformation, a testament to the incredible power of compassion in healthcare.

Mr. Carroll's revelation about his profession cast a new light on their encounter, unveiling yet another layer of the complex tapestry of human connections. The hallway seemed to hold within its walls the stories of countless lives, each with its own narrative arc, merging and diverging with those of the hospital staff like Sean. The revelation that Mr. Carroll was a sports agent underscored the variety of people who crossed paths in the sphere of healthcare and how the threads of destiny wove their tales in unexpected patterns.

As Mr. Carroll extended four tickets, a symbol of gratitude and a gesture of appreciation, the atmosphere seemed to shimmer with an ethical dilemma. Sean's internal conflict between protocol and genuine gratitude played out in real-time. At that moment, the hallway, usually a conduit for movement, became a stage for a moral introspection that demanded an answer.

Sean's initial hesitation and acknowledgment of the rules and guidelines governing doctor-patient relationships showcased his commitment to professionalism and ethical integrity. Yet, as his eyes scanned the details of the tickets, a subtle shift occurred – an electrifying realization that transcended the boundaries of protocol. The tickets held the promise of an experience, a moment of joy, and a rare chance to enjoy something beyond the confines of the hospital walls.

The transformation from reserved consideration to unbridled enthusiasm was written across Sean's face. The tickets represented more than mere passes; they offered an opportunity to partake in an experience that held personal significance for him. As he gleefully accepted the tickets, the crescendo of Sean's excitement painted the hallway with a vibrant hue of joy and gratitude, an emotion shared between doctor and patient in this unique interchange.

Their exchange encapsulated the nuanced dynamics of human interaction. Sean's decision to accept the tickets was twofold: a sincere acknowledgment of gratitude and a recognition of the profound impact medical professionals can have on their patients' lives. The tickets were tokens of appreciation but embodied the notion that sometimes, in the delicate balance between rules and compassion, an exception can yield something extraordinary.

As they shook hands, their interaction echoed a moment of harmonious understanding. Mr. Carroll's reflection on his journey and how the entire episode had catalyzed a paradigm shift in his perspective resonated deeply. Sean's role in this transformative process was humbling yet affirming. The hallway became a realm of mutual respect, a testament to the potential for meaningful connections to emerge from the intersection of healthcare and life experiences.

Mr. Carroll then turned around and started walking away. The echoes of their conversation lingered in the corridor, a reminder of the profound interactions within the walls of a hospital. Sean's parting wish, a lighthearted yet earnest expression of hope for Mr. Carroll's continued well-being, carried the essence of their connection – one rooted in care, gratitude, and an enduring bond forged in the crucible of healing.

Amid the quiet confines of Mr. Gladstone's room, Sean's exuberance burst forth like a ray of sunshine, casting aside the shadows of illness and infirmity. The energy that radiated from him was palpable, akin to the infectious enthusiasm of a child stepping into a candy store for the first time. It was a stark contrast to the otherwise serene ambiance as if a wellspring of joy had surged forth, momentarily dispelling the solemnity of the hospital environment.

The magazine in Mr. Gladstone's hands was forgotten as Sean engaged him with the tale of his unexpected gift. The words tumbled out, laced with genuine excitement, as if Sean was reliving the moment again. Mr. Gladstone watched this jubilation with amusement, feeling a sense of camaraderie with the young man who had become a friend and confidant during his time in the hospital.

Amidst Sean's fiery enthusiasm, a question that raised ethical concerns arose—medical professionals' acceptance of gifts from patients. This topic has long been discussed and debated, representing a delicate balance between gratitude and the ethical boundaries that define doctor-patient relationships. Mr. Gladstone posed this question to Sean in his astute way, fully aware of its complexities.

Sean quickly replied, "Well, thanks to Dr. Plunkett's never-ending lecture, I'm not a doctor!"

Sean's words were light, as if he were aware of the paradox of his statement yet unapologetically embraced it. His distinction between being a medical student and a doctor seemed almost like an ingenious twist, turning the tables on a seemingly stringent rule. The quirkiness of Sean's logic carried an undeniable charm, and Mr. Gladstone found himself laughing heartily.

At that moment, Sean's unique perspective, his ability to find a silver lining even in the face of ethical dilemmas, resonated with Mr. Gladstone. The notion that a seemingly negative situation could be transformed into a positive one through a shift in perspective struck a chord. It was a testament to the resilience of the human spirit and the capacity to navigate challenges by reframing them in ways that empower rather than constrain.

Their laughter filled the room with a sense of communion,

understanding, and shared appreciation for the quirks that make each person unique. Sean's lighthearted approach to life and ability to extract joy from even the most unexpected corners lit up the lives of those around him. As Mr. Gladstone looked at the young man before him, he realized that the most profound lessons are sometimes hidden within the simplest, most unassuming moments of connection.

Mr. Gladstone's room became a sanctuary of sorts. This cocoon safeguarded him from the external world, surrounded by the watchful eyes of the medical staff. His condition, delicate and demanding, made him a unique case, necessitating a level of caution that extended beyond the hospital's walls. His pain medication, a potent elixir capable of alleviating his suffering yet perilous in even slightly higher doses, underscored the fragility of his situation. Every step in his treatment had to be meticulously orchestrated, and his temporary escape from the hospital seemed like a logistical puzzle with no clear solution.

Amid this carefully constructed reality, the news of Sean's plans for a night out brought a glimmer of excitement and a wave of concern to Mr. Gladstone's eyes. He was glad to be included in Sean's celebration, to share in a moment of joy and camaraderie that transcended the confines of illness and hospital walls. Yet, the inherent risks posed by his condition cast a shadow on the festivities that lay ahead.

In his typical fashion, Sean responded with an air of reassurance and determination. His words resonated with a quiet confidence that seemed to say, "Trust me, I've got this."

There was a subtle shift in the atmosphere, a sense that in Sean's capable hands, the seemingly impossible was not only possible but probable. Mr. Gladstone's unease began to yield to a burgeoning excitement as he surrendered his doubts to the hands of the person who had become more than just a medical student – a friend, a confidant, a beacon of light amid adversity.

As they conversed, their shared laughter echoed through the room, punctuating their conversations with a touch of warmth and familiarity. Amid the beeps of monitors and the rustling of hospital sheets, they shared stories, exchanged plans, and forged a connection that was as much about genuine friendship as it was about medical care.

In this unique bond between patient and companion, a celebration of life's triumphs and challenges unfolded. Sean's impending achievement—the culmination of years of hard work and dedication—was a personal milestone and a testament to the resilience of the human spirit. Mr. Gladstone's unwavering confidence and ability to find humour and grace in the face of adversity inspired Sean in a way that transcended medical textbooks and hospital routines.

As the anticipation of the night ahead built, a shared understanding settled between them. Theirs was a journey marked by grit, friendship, and the unwavering belief in the power of connection to transform even the most difficult circumstances into moments of shared joy.

As they prepared to venture into the night, a sense of friendship and anticipation hung in the air – a tribute to the strength of the human spirit and the bonds that can be forged in the unlikeliest of places.

Dr. May walked into Mr. Gladstone's room and saw Sean and Mr. Gladstone celebrating something. The room momentarily held its breath in response to Dr. May's inquiry about the reason behind the celebrations. This palpable silence encapsulated unspoken emotions.

"I have tickets to the big basketball game tonight, and I want you to join us!" Sean replied.

Dr. May regretfully declined the offer as she had a hectic schedule ahead of her at the hospital.

Dr. May's comment lingered in the air, casting a shadow of longing and perhaps a touch of melancholy. It was as if the bustling hospital activity outside the room was momentarily suspended, allowing the weight of unspoken desires and unfulfilled plans to settle.

In this silence, Mr. Gladstone's gaze shifted from Sean to Dr. May, his eyes carrying a depth of understanding that transcended mere words. He recognized the unsaid sentiments, the yearning for a break from the relentless demands of their roles. He knew, perhaps better than anyone, the toll that dedicating oneself to the care of others could take, the moments of solitude and self-care that often became elusive in the whirlwind of medical practice.

Sean's gaze shifted from Dr. May to Mr. Gladstone, and a silent connection formed in that exchange. It was a connection forged from shared experiences from understanding the weight of responsibility that came with their chosen paths. It was a connection that recognized the unspoken sacrifices and yearnings that often remained hidden beneath the surface of professionalism.

As the room slowly exhaled its held breath, the atmosphere shifted, and a soft chuckle from Mr. Gladstone broke the silence. With a glint of mischief in his eyes, he offered a piece of wisdom, "You know, they say the best way to get what you want is to ask for it. And sometimes, we need to permit ourselves to take a break, even when the world around us keeps spinning."

The words hung in the air, a gentle reminder of the importance of seizing moments of respite amid life's chaos. The room came alive again, infused with a renewed sense of purpose and possibility.

Sean's face lit up, and his eyes flickered with determination. He glanced at Dr. May with a hopeful smile, his words a blend of sincerity and gentle persuasion: "Dr. May, I know you have a busy schedule, but maybe just this once, you can take a break and join us for the game. It's not just about celebrating the end of medical school—it's about celebrating life, friendships, and the moments that make the journey worthwhile."

Dr. May's gaze held Sean's for a moment, a complex interplay of emotions dancing in her eyes. She considered the invitation, the allure of a temporary escape from the rigors of her responsibilities. The room held the promise of a decision, a choice that could bridge the gap between duty and personal fulfillment.

The moment lingered, pregnant with possibility, as the echo of unspoken sentiments resonated. In the backdrop of hospital corridors and the hum of machinery, a small group of individuals stood at the intersection of shared experiences, contemplating the power of camaraderie and the potential for a simple night out to be the balm that soothes weary souls.

The idea of inviting Dr. Gabehart to join them had taken root, and the possibility of expanding their small celebration to include her was tantalizing.

"Maybe you can ask Dr. Gabehart in the O.R. after her surgery. She might use a night out if she can recover quick enough," she added as she invited total silence in the room.

Sean's face mirrored a blend of surprise and despair, his features reflecting the delicate dance of hope and resignation.

Sean and Mr. Gladstone grew anxious, wondering if something had happened to Dr. Gabehart since she had looked well the last time they had seen her.

"Oh? What happened to her? She seemed fine to me," Mr. Gladstone inquired.

Sean didn't even give her a chance to reply as he asked, "Is she sick? Do you know more about the surgery?"

According to Dr. May, Dr. Gabehart was likely diagnosed with breast cancer and was undergoing a mastectomy. However, Dr. May also considered that Dr. Gabehart might have opted for the surgery as a precautionary measure. Sean was not provided with much information, but Dr. May suggested he could visit the operating room to check on Dr. Gabehart.

Following Dr. May's advice, Sean promptly left Mr. Gladstone's room and proceeded to the surgery department.

Sean's hurried footsteps echoed down the corridor, his mind spinning with concerns for Dr. Gabehart. The revelation of a possible diagnosis felt like a sudden gust of cold wind, a jarring reminder of the fragility of life that could strike even the most resilient individuals. The atmosphere had shifted from a celebratory to an unhappy state as the weight of uncertainty settled upon Sean's shoulders.

He arrived at the entrance to the operating room, his heart thudding in his chest, his mind grappling with the gravity of the situation. As he walked through the sterile surroundings, the scent of antiseptic hanging in the air, he felt a surge of admiration for the medical professionals who worked tirelessly to heal others. Yet, at this moment, the realization struck that even healers themselves were not exempt from the vulnerabilities of their own bodies.

With a determined stride, Sean navigated the familiar hallways of the surgery department, each step carrying him closer to the room where Dr. Gabehart was preparing for her surgery. The memories of his time spent here during his clerkship under the General provided a sense of familiarity, a comforting backdrop to the uncertainty ahead.

As he approached the door, he paused momentarily, taking a deep breath to steady his thoughts and emotions. He knew this encounter required sensitivity and respect, a delicate balance between offering support and respecting Dr. Gabehart's privacy. With a gentle knock, he announced his presence and stepped into the room.

The door swung open to reveal Sean, his face etched with concern and care. Dr. Gabehart's heart skipped a beat as she welcomed him into the room. His unexpected presence brought a surprising surge of relief, a balm to the nerves that surgery always seemed to evoke.

"Come in," she invited, her voice blending surprise and gratitude. She watched as he stepped into the room, radiating comfort in the sterile environment.

Without hesitation, Dr. Gabehart rushed forward, her arms enveloping Sean in an embrace that held an intensity born from a mix of emotions. The warmth of the hug, the human connection, offered a brief respite from the weight of the situation at hand. She held on as if to anchor herself in this moment of connection and reassurance.

The hug lingered for a while, an unspoken exchange of support and understanding passing between them. Sean's presence was like a soothing balm, easing the tension that often accompanied the anticipation of surgery. In his embrace, Dr. Gabehart found a moment of solace, a reminder that even in the face of uncertainty, there were those who cared.

As the hug finally began to loosen, Dr. Gabehart's emotions swirled beneath the surface. She had been a pillar of strength for so long, but in this moment, vulnerability revealed itself in the misty shimmer of her eyes. She composed herself, taking a step back, her gratitude evident in her soft smile.

"Thank you for being here," she said, her voice carrying a depth of emotion that words alone couldn't convey.

Sean met her gaze, understanding the significance of this encounter. "I wanted to check on you. How are you feeling?"

Dr. Gabehart took a deep breath, allowing herself a moment to reflect. "Nervous, I suppose. It's always a bit daunting, no matter how many times you've been on the other side of the scalpel."

Sean nodded, a gesture of empathy and understanding. "You've dedicated your life to caring for others. It's okay to let others care for you now."

The words hung in the air, reminding Dr. Gabehart that vulnerability was not a sign of weakness but a testament to the depth of one's humanity. Her eyes held a mixture of gratitude and acceptance. In Sean's presence, she found the strength to embrace her vulnerability, knowing that she was not alone in this journey.

Sean's visit was a beacon of light, a reminder that even amid uncertainty, a sense of community and support could uplift the spirit.

Sean understood her emotional state from the hug and tried to say something that wouldn't make her uncomfortable, as she was emotionally and physically vulnerable.

Sean was in a tricky situation as he contemplated telling a joke. The potential for the joke to be received positively or negatively left him unsure of what to do. After careful consideration, he decided to opt for something neutral that would likely evoke positive feelings. He harkened back to the same conversation starter that had served him well when he first met Dr. Gabehart.

Sean expressed himself, "Your smile is truly breathtaking, capable of stopping anyone in their tracks. It's a daily reminder of the beauty in the world. Your voice is equally enchanting, like a melody that soothes my soul. Your voice and smile are my go-to for a pick-me-up when I'm feeling down. As my time here comes to an end, I couldn't possibly say goodbye without hearing your angelic voice one last time."

Sean's words floated in the room, carrying a blend of admiration and sincerity that painted a soft smile on Dr. Gabehart's lips. His choice of words was unexpected yet charmingly familiar, a throwback to their initial meeting. As his voice wove, a tapestry of compliments and kind words, a subtle blush tinted her cheeks, a testament to the genuine warmth of his sentiments.

Like a melodic note, her laughter escaped her lips, punctuating the air with a touch of lightness. "Well, Mr. Charming, you certainly have a way with words."

Sean chuckled softly, a warm sparkle in his eyes. "I just speak from the heart."

Dr. Gabehart's smile deepened, and she shook her head playfully. "You always know how to catch me off guard."

"It's a skill I've been working on," Sean replied with a wink, breaking the moment's intensity with a hint of humour.

Their exchange was lighthearted, a brief interlude amid the weightier matters that often occupied their days. In each other's company, they found a balance. Their roles as physicians could momentarily blur in this space, replaced by the genuine connection that had developed over time.

"I'm glad you came to see me," Dr. Gabehart admitted, her tone softer now, touched by a warmth that only human connection could bring.

"I wouldn't have missed this moment for the world," Sean replied, his gaze meeting hers with unwavering sincerity.

Dr. Gabehart was filled with gratitude and momentarily forgot about her upcoming surgery. She expressed her appreciation to Sean for his kind words and conveyed how much they meant to her. Despite this, she tried to lighten the mood and joked, "My secret admirer didn't send me flowers today, and it broke my heart, so I'm here for treatment."

As they exchanged smiles and embraced, Sean took hold of her hand and spoke with heartfelt sincerity, "You truly are the most remarkable woman I have ever had the pleasure of meeting. The moments we have shared, whether laughing, discussing complex cases, or simply conversing about life, will forever be etched in my heart. Your beauty speaks to my heart, and your intellect speaks to my soul. When I am in your presence, I find myself wanting to make the world a better place for you so that you never have to experience pain or shed a tear. In the short time we have known each other, I have become more self-assured, content with my life, eager to embark on a lifelong journey in medicine, grateful for everything the world has bestowed upon me thus far, and hopeful for what the future holds. You have helped me become a better man, student, and friend, and for that, I am eternally grateful. Wherever the winds of life may take me, you will always remain the woman who changed my life, made me a better person, and opened my eyes to the beauty of the world. You are the exceptional woman I had always dreamed of meeting, with whom I could share a cup of coffee. I feel incredibly privileged to have been your student over the past four weeks. Although I wish our paths did not have to diverge, you will forever hold a special place in my heart. I only hope that I was able to have at least a fraction of the same positive impact on you as you have had on me. As today marks my last day here at AGH, I feel that there could be no better time to express these sentiments."

Despite the overwhelming surge of emotions he was experiencing then, he managed to compose himself and carry on. "My upbringing was quite challenging," he continued, his voice steady and firm. "I had to fend for myself from a very young age. All I ever wanted was a stable job to afford my own place and a modest vehicle. I had nothing but my intellect, and people often ridiculed me for being a freak of nature. I navigated my way through life using my wits and the skills I acquired along the way. Scholarships funded my education, but I still had to work multiple jobs to make ends meet. When I started medical school, one of my professors recognized my potential as a capable physician."

Dr. Gabehart stood there, deeply moved by Sean's heartfelt words. As he spoke, she could feel the sincerity radiating from him, each word carrying a weight of significance that touched her heart. His confession was like a melody, resonating in the room, weaving through the air and wrapping around her like a warm embrace. She had been a pillar of strength for many, but Sean's vulnerability and honesty reminded her that even those who appear strong are allowed moments of genuine emotion.

Listening to him share his feelings was like witnessing a cascade of emotions that had been building up within him. He bared his soul, revealing his journey, his aspirations, and the transformative impact their interactions had on him. It was a testament to the profound connection that had grown between them in a relatively short period.

Dr. Gabehart's eyes shimmered with unshed tears as Sean's words echoed in the room. It was a rarity for her to find herself speechless, her usual eloquence momentarily evading her. Yet, in that silence, her heart swelled with gratitude and admiration for the young man before her.

Dr. Gabehart struggled to hold back her tears as Sean continued expressing his gratitude. He spoke of his past struggles with discipline as a student and how his professor had arranged for him to work with her husband for twelve weeks, which had helped straighten him out. However, it wasn't until he met Dr. Gabehart that he truly understood the significance of medicine beyond just solving cases. He had learned that patients were seeking not only a cure but also a sense of hope, and Dr. Gabehart had recognized his potential to become the kind of doctor who could provide both.

Through her mentorship, Sean was shown that he mattered in this world and developed a newfound passion for wisdom and life. He had always been driven by a thirst for knowledge, but Dr. Gabehart inspired him to seek more from life and believe that he had more to offer. By welcoming him into her life, she gave him a fresh perspective on the world, and he would always be grateful for everything she had taught and shared with him.

Dr. Gabehart had been searching for someone who would truly see her for who she was, and finally, she had found that person. His words of understanding and acceptance had a profound impact on her, and she couldn't help but feel overwhelmed by the emotions that were stirred within her.

They forged a deep and meaningful connection through their shared experiences and the knowledge they gained from one another. They both recognized the emptiness within them, and it was only through each other's presence that they could fill that void. As they stood there, lost in their thoughts and feelings, Dr. Gabehart couldn't help but wonder what might have been if they had met in a different time and place.

Dr. Gabehart's eyes shimmered with mixed emotions as she listened to Sean's words. It was as if he had reached into the depths of her heart and uncovered feelings and desires she had long kept hidden. She had always been a strong and capable woman, but Sean had managed to touch the chords of her vulnerability and bring forth a side of her she hadn't shared with anyone before.

His words resonated deeply within her, touching upon the essence of what it meant to be a healer, a mentor, and a friend. It wasn't just about solving medical puzzles or delivering treatments; it was about understanding the human experience and providing physical and emotional healing. Sean's insights into the nature of medicine and patient care mirrored her beliefs, reaffirming that he wasn't just a student but a kindred spirit on a journey of growth and understanding.

Tears welled up in Dr. Gabehart's eyes as she found herself at a loss for words. The vulnerability and raw emotion in Sean's confession mirrored her feelings. For a moment, they were two souls laid bare, connected by their shared experiences and mutual respect. She reached out to gently touch his hand, a silent acknowledgment of the profound impact he had on her life.

She finally found her voice, her tone carrying a mixture of tenderness and sincerity. "Sean, your words have touched me deeply. You have a gift, not only for medicine but also for understanding and empathy. Your journey is a testament to your resilience and determination. Your transformation is a testament to your open heart and willingness to learn and teach. You have a bright future ahead of you, and I'm honoured to have played a small part in your journey."

Dr. Gabehart's gaze held Sean's with unwavering warmth. She felt a connection, a mutual respect that defied the conventional boundaries of teacher and student. "Remember, the best physicians aren't just the ones who possess vast medical knowledge, but those who approach their patients with compassion and understanding. You have that gift, and I don't doubt that you'll make a difference in the lives of many."

Emotion welled up in her chest as she offered a reassuring smile. "And as for your influence on me, well, let's just say that even the experienced can learn a thing or two from the students." Her voice was accompanied by a playful glint in her eyes, a glimpse of the humour that had become a part of their interactions.

Their embrace felt like a shared moment of solace, a culmination of their shared emotions. It was a farewell that wasn't defined by distance but rather by their lasting impact on each other's lives.

"Sean," she continued, her voice a whisper that carried a weight of emotion, "You've touched my heart in ways I can't adequately express. Your presence has been a gift, a reminder of the beauty and potential that lies within each individual. You've shown me that the learning process is a two-way street, and that every interaction, every exchange, has the power to change us for the better."

A small smile graced her lips as she continued, "While our paths may diverge, and life may take us on separate journeys, I want you to know that you'll always carry a special place in my heart, too. The world needs more people like you—compassionate, driven, and willing to learn from books and life itself."

Their gazes met with a shared understanding that transcended words. It was a moment of profound connection, a silent promise that the impact of their interactions would remain etched in their hearts, guiding them on their respective paths.

"As you embark on the next chapter of your journey, know that you're not alone. You carry the wisdom you've gained, the friendships you've formed, and the memories that have shaped you. And remember, the lessons we learn from one another often ripple through time, creating a chain of positive influence that extends beyond what we can see."

Dr. Gabehart's voice was gentle, and her words soothed the stirred emotions. She offered Sean a warm smile, a gesture conveying gratitude and a sense of shared understanding. Amid their heartfelt conversation, she realized that sometimes, the most profound connections remain unspoken, held within the heart's sacred chambers.

Dr. Gabehart grasped Sean's hand with a firm yet tender grip, searching her mind for the most fitting words to express her gratitude and admiration. In the comfortable silence, she realized now was the perfect moment to convey how much Sean meant to her. She held his hand with a renewed passion, cherishing this moment of intimacy and connection between them.

Her words were heartfelt and genuine as she spoke, expressing her gratitude for the thoughtful gesture. "I must say, flowers would have been more than enough, but your kindness has left me at a loss for words. Sean, you have inspired me since the day you walked into this hospital with your infectious energy and charm. For most of my life, I have been treated as nothing more than a pretty face, which caused me to doubt my intellect and worth. However, your presence in my life has allowed me to reflect on all the things I am grateful for rather than dwell on my regrets. As a doctor, I have always cherished my work and education, but how the world has treated me has often made me question my path. For a long time, I have battled depression alone, feeling like a lonely and bitter woman. But you have changed all that and given me a gift I never expected from anyone, not even my family - hope. You have touched my soul in a way I never thought possible. If there were anything I could do to help you stay here, I would do it without hesitation. Though my husband has given me an ultimatum, know that I haven't stopped thinking about how I can help you. I am sorry for any inconvenience I may have caused. Still, I wish you all the best in everything you do because you have an extraordinary talent for making everything you interact with better, including me. Thank you for being the wonderful person that you are."

As their hands remained entwined, the weight of their emotions hung in the air, creating a cocoon of vulnerability and understanding. Dr. Gabehart's words flowed with a sincerity that resonated deeply within Sean's heart. He listened intently, hanging onto every word she spoke and feeling a profound sense of gratitude that he had significantly impacted her life.

Tears glistened in Sean's eyes as he absorbed the depth of Dr. Gabehart's confession. He had never anticipated the extent of his presence's impact on her, and her words filled him with a mixture of humility and awe. Her vulnerability in sharing her struggles and doubts touched him profoundly, reminding him of the power that simple acts of kindness and genuine connections could have on a person's life.

Once again, they embraced, savouring their final precious moments as colleagues in this hospital. Their gazes met, and they took in each other's presence, uncertain if this was the last time they would be in this setting. Just then, a nurse entered the room and inquired if Dr. Gabehart was ready. She responded with a request for additional time.

"Dr. Gorgeous," Sean began, his voice laced with genuine sincerity, "I am truly honoured to have been a part of your life in this way. Your strength, dedication, and brilliance have always shone through, and it's an absolute privilege to know that I've been able to play even a small role in bringing that light back into your life. You are far more than just a pretty face; you are an incredible physician, a remarkable woman, and a source of inspiration for all who have the privilege to know you."

He gently wiped away tears from her cheeks, his own eyes reflecting a deep well of emotion. "Your words mean the world to me, and I want you to know that you've given me a gift as well— the gift of hope, of perspective, and of knowing that even in the darkest of times, connections can be formed that transcend our circumstances. You've touched my life in ways that words can't fully express, and I am eternally grateful for the moments we've shared."

They held each other in a tender embrace, their hearts communicating a depth of emotion of which words could only scratch the surface. It was a bittersweet moment, knowing that their time together in this capacity was coming to an end, yet also cherishing the profound bond they had formed.

Although their paths diverged, the lessons learned, the connections made, and the memories forged would forever remain a testament to the power of human connection and the potential for growth and change, even in the midst of life's challenges.

Once Sean overcame the initial awkwardness, he sat beside Dr. Gabehart on the bed, determined to address the elephant in the room.

"Now that we've managed to get that out of the way," he began, "I'm curious to know what's going on with you. I truly hope you aren't considering any measures to alter your beauty, as you are absolutely stunning just the way you are," he added, causing her to blush with a mixture of surprise and pleasure.

She playfully punched Sean and said, "You're spoiling me with compliments and then leaving? That's mean," before telling her story.

"Well, approximately six months ago, during a routine self-breast exam, I discovered a lump in my left breast. I made a conscious effort not to panic. Still, I couldn't help but assess some of the significant risk factors: I'm over thirty, childless, not particularly slender, had early development, and have relatively large breasts. Given these factors, I knew it was crucial to have it checked out. After undergoing a biopsy, it was evident that I needed to take action. My husband urged me to start chemotherapy right away, which was five months ago, but at that point, I hesitated. There was so much to process, and I needed time to come to terms with everything. Then, out of the blue, a young man entered my life and imparted a valuable lesson about embracing every moment. That revelation prompted me to take action, and I decided to schedule a mastectomy."

As she spoke, her demeanour exuded acceptance as though she had made peace with her fate.

As Dr. Gabehart shared her journey, Sean's attention was entirely on her. His eyes reflected the depth of his empathy and concern. He listened with an open heart, nodding in understanding as she spoke about the various emotions and decisions she had faced.

"Thank you for opening up to me about this, Dr. Gabehart. Your strength and resilience are truly admirable," Sean said, his voice soft and reassuring. "It's not easy to navigate such challenging times, especially when you have so much on your plate. Taking the time to process everything and make decisions that align with your feelings is a testament to your courage."

He gently squeezed her hand, a gesture of support and understanding. "You know, from the moment I met you, I could sense your determination and dedication. Whether it's in the hospital or your personal life, you approach everything with a level of strength that is truly inspiring. And I have no doubt that you will face this situation with the same grace and resilience."

Sean's eyes locked with hers, his gaze filled with admiration. "No matter what path you choose, whether it involves changes or not, your inner beauty and strength shine through. You've taught me much about being a compassionate and dedicated physician and embracing our vulnerabilities. You've impacted my life in ways you might not even realize."

He leaned in slightly, his voice softening even more. "Remember, you're not alone in this journey. I'm here to support you however I can, even if it's just offering a listening ear or a shoulder to lean on. You've made a lasting impression on me, and I want you to know that you have someone who cares deeply about you."

As they sat together, the room seemed to hold an unspoken understanding. Their connection had evolved into a bond forged through shared experiences, vulnerability, and a mutual appreciation for their impact on each other's lives.

Sean nodded, reflecting his genuine concern for Dr. Gabehart's well-being. He leaned forward slightly, offering her a reassuring smile. "Life has a way of throwing unexpected challenges our way. It's in those moments that we truly discover our strength and resilience. And I do not doubt that you have both in abundance."

He paused for a moment, carefully choosing his words. "It's okay to feel a mix of emotions about all of this. Sadness, frustration, and even anger are all part of the process. But it's also important to remember that this challenge does not define you. You're defined by the incredible person you are, the lives you've touched, and the dedication you've shown to your patients and your work."

Sean's gaze remained steady, and his sincerity was evident in his words: "I know you have the strength to get through this. And while it may not be how you envisioned your thirties, I believe you'll emerge from this experience even stronger and more resilient. You have an army of people who care about and support you, myself included."

He reached out and gently placed his hand on hers, a gesture of comfort and solidarity. "If there's anything I can do to help, please don't hesitate to let me know. You've been my mentor, friend, and inspiration, and I want you to know that I'm also here for you."

Dr. Gabehart looked at Sean, her eyes reflecting gratitude and emotion. In that moment, as they sat together, they shared a connection that transcended the boundaries of their roles in the hospital. They were two souls supporting each other through life's unexpected twists and turns, finding strength in their shared vulnerability.

"Just so you know, it's breast density and not breast size that is a risk factor for breast cancer," Sean said as he looked at Dr. Gabehart putting a finger in her mouth and pretending to induce vomiting before he continued, "How're you feeling about it, though?"

She explained to him that it was sad. She had been depressed about it for a couple of months, but she was just happy that it'd be all behind her after the surgery. She insisted she would be fine as this was just a tiny part of her life.

"This isn't exactly how anyone thinks about their thirties and the rest of their lives, but here we are," she said as she covered her face in exhaustion.

There was a moment of silence as they both processed what was happening. Dr. Gabehart looked at Sean; he had a look that would typically be peculiar for most, but she had become accustomed to it. Sean looked like he was trying to figure something out, which was confirmed when he asked, "Did you get a second opinion?"

He looked at her with a confused look as he added, "This has your husband written all over it, and I wouldn't trust him to watch a hamster in its cage. Trust me, I've met the guy and no offence, but I think he needs oversight in everything he touches."

Dr. Gabehart laughed and admitted to Sean that she agreed, but she told him, "He's an oncologist after all, so, like I said, here we are."

Sean's nose flared as he became increasingly concerned about the lack of a second opinion on such a serious case.

Sean's concern was palpable as he leaned forward, his voice laced with a sense of urgency. "Dr. Gabehart, I know you're going through a lot right now, and I can't imagine the weight of the decisions you're facing. But this is your health, your life, we're talking about. Getting a second opinion isn't a sign of doubt; it's a responsible step to ensure you're making the best decision for your well-being."

He continued, "Even the best doctors can have biases, and sometimes, they can be clouded by their familiarity with a situation. Having a fresh set of eyes and a different perspective can provide valuable insights. I've seen patients live with a misdiagnosis because they didn't seek a second opinion, and it's heartbreaking. To make matters worse, we're talking about a diagnosis made by your husband here."

Sean's expression softened as he looked at her, his concern evident in his eyes. "You deserve to have unimpeachable information before making such a significant decision. And if you're worried about your husband's reaction, he should understand that this is about your health and peace of mind. If he truly cares about you, he'll support your decision to seek a second opinion."

Sean was visibly in denial that Dr. Plunkett had correctly

diagnosed Dr. Gabehart. He asked her if she'd care for a second opinion right then.

"Look who's in denial now. It's okay, Sean. The biopsy confirmed that he was right. You can let it go. Thanks for the offer, though," she said.

Dr. Gabehart considered Sean's words, her brow furrowing. She appreciated his concern and honesty, even if it meant confronting a difficult situation. Deep down, she knew he was right—a second opinion was a sensible step.

As their conversation continued, it became apparent that their bond extended beyond the medical setting. They were confidantes, allies, and friends, navigating both the challenges of medicine and the complexities of life itself. They found strength in each other's presence—a testament to the profound impact that genuine connections can have on our lives.

With a sigh, she nodded. "Maybe you're right. I've always preached the importance of seeking different medical perspectives, and it's only fair that I follow my advice. I don't think it'll make any difference, though."

"Come on, humour me," he tried to convince her.

After thinking about it for a while, Dr. Gabehart gave in to Sean's offer. "Okay, fine. Someone might as well touch them one more time before I get rid of them," she said as she laughed at her joke while taking off her gown.

Sean wasn't looking at her as she undressed. He got up from the bed, took a few steps away, turned around to look at Dr. Gabehart, and exclaimed, "Holy Jesus! Those things are amazing!"

Dr. Gabehart burst into laughter, her amusement evident

as she covered her mouth with her hand. Sean's reaction had caught her off guard, and his words had broken the tension that had been lingering in the room. Amidst the uncertainty and heaviness of the situation, his unabashed compliment was like a breath of fresh air.

"You're ridiculous, Sean!" she exclaimed, her laughter infectious. She shook her head, still laughing, as she put her gown back on. "You are definitely one of a kind."

As their laughter subsided, a comfortable silence settled in the room. It was a moment of connection, shared laughter, and genuine friendship. In that instant, they weren't teacher and student but two individuals who had formed a unique bond. Dr. Gabehart's impending surgery and Sean's imminent departure seemed temporarily forgotten as they enjoyed the simple pleasure of laughter and companionship.

Dr. Gabehart was still embarrassed after putting her gown back on, but she laughed at Sean's reaction. His reaction was hilarious, and the fact that he had the guts to do it right before her made everything even more comical.

"I knew this was a bad idea," she said to Sean as she told him to get out.

"I'm sorry. Come on, I'll do better this time. They took me by surprise, that's all. Do you blame me?" he responded as he tried to convince her to allow him to try the clinical breast exam again.

Dr. Gabehart agreed, but under the condition that if he reacted like that again, she would expel him from the hospital herself and write him the worst review of his life.

Sean raised his hands in mock surrender, grinning mischievously. "Deal! I promise, no more unexpected reactions from me."

With Dr. Gabehart's consent, Sean promised to approach the examination with a more composed demeanour.

Dr. Gabehart repositioned herself and took off her gown again. Sean was looking down when she took off her gown, and when he looked up and directly at Dr. Gabehart, he once again exclaimed, "God damn! Those things are making me hungry!"

Dr. Gabehart burst into a huge laughter as she covered herself. This time, the reaction was even more hilarious. She couldn't stop laughing, shaking her head in disbelief and signalling Sean to leave.

As they shared a final laugh, the tension that had been lingering earlier had completely dissipated. Their interaction had turned from a serious discussion into a comedic episode, reminding them that, despite challenging circumstances, finding moments of lightness was essential.

Sean covered his eyes with both hands, embarrassed beyond belief. "Oh my gosh, I'm so sorry! I promise I didn't mean to... I don't know what's wrong with me today!" he stammered, his words a mixture of mortification and apology.

Dr. Gabehart laughed so hard that she had to lean against the wall for support. Tears of laughter streamed down her face as she regained her composure. "Sean, I can't believe you said that... twice!"

Dr. Gabehart's infectious laughter slowly overtook Sean's embarrassment. Despite his shock, he couldn't help but join in, his laughter mixing with hers.

"I swear, I'm usually much more composed than this,"

Sean managed to say between chuckles. "I think I've just officially lost my ability to maintain professionalism."

Dr. Gabehart finally caught her breath, wiping away the tears from her eyes. "Well, you've certainly made my day quite memorable. I don't think I'll ever forget this consultation."

Sean grinned sheepishly. "Well, if I can bring some laughter to your day, I guess I've accomplished something, even if it's at the expense of your dignity and my reputation."

With all the jokes Sean told her and all the comments Sean was always blurting out, she didn't expect Sean to have the audacity to say such things about her right in her face. Considering her state of mind and the circumstances that had brought them to this point, Sean provided Dr. Gabehart with laughter and distraction from her predicament.

"You're terrible. I take back every good thing I ever said about you!" she exclaimed as she continued laughing hard.

Sean was now laughing even harder.

"Wow, I even surprised myself with that one," Sean confessed as he kept laughing while trying to catch his breath.

Dr. Gabehart's laughter was a beautiful melody to Sean's ears, a temporary reprieve from the seriousness of the situation. He wiped a tear from his eye as he managed to control his laughter. "I apologize, Dr. Gabehart. I promise I'll try to keep my comments professional from now on."

She shook her head, still grinning. "How dare you? I should've let Dr. Plunkett kick you out of this hospital long ago."

Sean chuckled, "Well, if my future medical career fails, maybe I can become a stand-up comedian instead."

After several minutes of rib-cracking laughter, Dr. Gabehart screamed at Sean, "Dr. Sodeman! Can we be professionals for a moment?!"

Sean stopped laughing and turned professional in seconds. "My apologies, Dr. Gabehart. I'm going to assess your breasts in your current sitting position visually," he said as he started a clinical breast exam.

He asked her to lift one arm and put it over her head to touch the ear on the opposite side and hold the position for a couple of seconds. After a couple of seconds of observation from that position, he asked her to do the same with the other arm.

Dr. Gabehart relaxed for a few seconds before Sean asked her to put both arms on her side and push on her hips while sitting in that position. Sean was looking for irregularities using these positions, from skin discolorations to visible lumps.

"Now, I'm going to examine your breasts manually and start with your lymph nodes. If you feel uncomfortable at any moment during the procedure, please let me know. Meanwhile, tell me about how you ended up a department head so young," he said as he started doing the manual breast exam on Dr. Gabehart.

Dr. Gabehart didn't object to talking about herself while Sean did the exam.

Dr. Gabehart sighed in relief as Sean shifted his focus to the professional aspect of their interaction. She knew it was essential to balance humour and seriousness, especially given the nature of their discussion. She answered Sean's question as he continued the clinical breast exam, his movements methodical and respectful.

Dr. Gabehart started, "I come from a middle-class family

with three daughters, and I am the middle child. My older sister claims to have street smarts, but she has never held a job as an adult and is a single mother of two children from different fathers. My younger sister considers herself an influencer, though she struggles to pay her own phone bill. She is content with her current lifestyle and has no plans of settling down. My parents work in sales, which can be stressful, as they can go months without a good sale. I never had the best relationship with my sisters, as I consider myself more intellectually inclined, and, well, they are not. Understanding my family dynamics gives you an idea of how I grew up. Though I was always a good student, I didn't stand out until high school, where I became involved in many activities."

"It sounds like you come from a diverse family with a range of personalities," Sean remarked, a faint smile on his lips. "Middle child syndrome is a real thing, isn't it? It seems like you found your own path amidst the variety."

"Absolutely. Being in the middle, I often felt like I needed to carve out my own identity. I immersed myself in academics and extracurricular activities, trying to stand out in a positive way." Dr. Gabehart responded.

Sean's eyes showed a hint of understanding. "It's interesting how our family dynamics can shape us, sometimes pushing us to become the person we aspire to be."

Dr. Gabehart chuckled. "Yeah, you could say that. I was the studious one, the responsible one. I wanted to prove to myself and others that I could achieve something meaningful."

"I'm sure your determination and hard work were noticed," Sean said. "And you've come quite a long way from those high school days."

Dr. Gabehart shrugged. "Definitely. Medicine has been quite the journey. It's been a mix of challenges, growth, and learning. But even in the midst of it, there are moments when I feel a bit disconnected from my family. We're all so different, and our priorities and values don't always align."

Sean nodded in understanding. "Family dynamics can be complex. Sometimes, we find our support systems beyond our immediate family. Have you found that in your friends or mentors?"

Dr. Gabehart's eyes brightened. "Absolutely. I've been fortunate to have some amazing mentors throughout my journey, including you, ironically. You've been a source of inspiration and emotional guidance, and I've learned so much from you."

A warm smile graced Sean's lips. "I'm honoured to hear that, Dr. Gabehart. Mentorship is a two-way street, and it's been a privilege to witness your rejuvenation and enthusiasm."

Dr. Gabehart's expression turned thoughtful. "I've always believed that true success goes beyond academic achievements. It's about our impact on others, the lives we touch and the positive change we bring. That's why moments like this, where we can connect on a personal level, mean a lot to me."

Sean nodded in agreement. "You're right. Meaningful connections are what make work for medical professionals so rewarding. It's about more than just the science and the diagnoses—it's about empathy, understanding, and making a difference in people's lives."

They shared a brief moment of quiet reflection, the weight of their words hanging in the air. The bond they had developed over the weeks felt more potent than ever, fortified by their shared experiences and candid conversations.

Sean paused the exam briefly as he asked Dr. Gabehart to lay on the bed facing the ceiling so he could examine her breasts in that position.

She obliged before continuing her story: " Anyway, my high school culminated with me running the student council and winning several science accolades, neither of which impressed my family. I left home for university at seventeen to study electrical engineering. One day, I was watching the movie A Beautiful Mind, in which a mathematical genius who suffered from schizophrenia struggled to find a thesis on patterns in life for his dissertation."

Sean interrupted, "Oh yeah, I've watched that movie. Great movie. Was it John Nash's schizophrenia that motivated you to study medicine?"

Although Sean had assumed otherwise, Dr. Gabehart quickly denied his assumption. However, she acknowledged that the movie was fascinating to watch and that the producers had done an excellent job of portraying mental health in a realistic and empathetic manner.

Dr. Gabehart resumed her story as she lay on the bed, her gaze fixed on the ceiling as she reminisced. "It wasn't John Nash's schizophrenia that influenced my decision to pursue medicine. But that movie triggered something in me—a curiosity about the human mind, its complexities, and how we decipher the patterns of life."

Sean leaned against a nearby table, listening intently. "So, you started in electrical engineering. How did you transition from that to medicine?"

Dr. Gabehart replied, "I'm getting there. Don't be impatient. You asked, so now you have to hear the whole story."

She continued, "Anyway, there's one scene where he's at a bar with friends, and they were trying to talk to a group of girls. John Nash mentioned Adam Smith's theory that "individual ambition is good for any group," but he added that "individual ambition with the group's interest" is paramount. He applied that to his solution of how they could all get to take the girls out. He argued that if they strictly followed Adam Smith's theory without considering the group's interest, there was a chance none of them would get a girl. This was an interesting way to approach women, igniting my interest in economics."

Sean was intrigued, piqued by the connection she made between a movie scene and her fascination with economics.

"At the end of my freshman year, I looked for a copy of Adam Smith's "A Wealth of Nations," and I read that cover to cover. I fell in love with economics. It opened up a whole new world of understanding for me. I realized that economic principles can apply to various aspects of life, not just finances. It's about how choices are made, resources are allocated, and individuals and groups interact. I also read most publications by the Nobel Prize-winning economist Dr. Milton Friedman, leading me to Dr. Thomas Sowell's work. The following school year, I started taking courses towards a minor in economics."

Dr. Gabehart chuckled, the memory vivid in her mind. "I started studying economics alongside engineering, and it opened up a whole new world of understanding for me."

Sean nodded, engrossed in her story. "That's quite the leap—from electrical engineering to economics."

She grinned playfully. "I guess you could say I have a penchant for making unexpected leaps. But in all seriousness, economics taught me to analyze situations from different perspectives and consider the broader implications of our actions."

"I can see how that analytical mindset would be invaluable in medicine and life," Sean remarked.

Dr. Gabehart's expression grew contemplative. "Absolutely. It's about recognizing that our decisions and actions ripple through a network, affecting us and those around us."

Sean looked pensive and engaged in the conversation. "And that ties into what you said earlier about individual ambition with the group's interest."

"Exactly," she affirmed. "That concept has guided many of my personal and professional decisions. It's about finding that delicate balance between pursuing our ambitions and contributing to the greater good."

"It's fascinating how a single moment, like that movie scene, can set someone on such a transformative path," he commented.

Dr. Gabehart nodded, a thoughtful smile on her face. "Absolutely. Sometimes, all it takes is a spark to ignite a passion that reshapes the course of our lives."

Sean interjected again, "And how did you get into medicine? First, engineering, then economics, and you seem to love both."

Dr. Gabehart explained, "In the winter semester of my sophomore year, when I was driving home from school for Christmas after midnight, I saw a small car pile up. The accident had just happened, so I rushed over to help. It was a mess; two people died as I scrambled to help and manage the situation alone, and six were seriously injured. I thought that maybe if I had known more about medicine, those people wouldn't have died. I was home crying for days, blaming myself for those deaths."

She paused as she fought back tears before she continued, "This is the first time I'm opening up about that incident."

She was quiet for a moment before continuing, "My junior and senior years were primarily spent in different social clubs and applying to medical school.

Sean listened attentively, his expression a mixture of empathy and understanding. "I can't even begin to imagine how that experience affected you," he said softly. "But it's clear that it ignited a desire within you to make a difference, to learn how to save lives and help people in those critical moments."

Dr. Gabehart nodded, her gaze distant momentarily as she recalled those difficult memories. "Exactly. I realized that my passion for understanding systems and making them work efficiently could also be applied to medicine. It was like connecting the dots—my love for problem-solving and my yearning to help people merged into a single path."

Sean smiled warmly. "It's incredible how life has its way of guiding us, isn't it? Sometimes, the most unexpected moments lead us to where we're meant to be."

Dr. Gabehart returned the smile, her eyes reflecting a sense of resolve. "Absolutely. And in a way, those moments of uncertainty and doubt can pave the way for growth and transformation. Just like my journey from electrical engineering and economics to medicine."

Their conversation lingered in the air, blending shared stories and unspoken understanding. At that moment, they had forged a bond through vulnerability and the shared pursuit of purpose.

Dr. Gabehart continued, "I got into medical school at twenty-one, and it wasn't a breeze. I had a lot of sleepless nights, but I found the work relatively easier than I had been led to believe. I got into residency at twenty-five at a different hospital without issues as I had great grades, and that's where I met my mentor, who was my boss in internal medicine residency. He was like the cardiology guru. I learnt most of the things I now understand about cardiology from him."

She looked at Sean dead in his eyes for emphasis, " The man could look into a patient's eyes and make a diagnosis of a heart murmur that needed surgery."

She returned her gaze to the ceiling and continued, "I found it very impressive, so I became a loyal disciple. After finishing my residency, he retired, so I came here to do my fellowship in cardiology. That's when I met Dr. Plunkett."

Sean looked scared momentarily as the character set out to ruin his career entered the scene.

"His wife had just left him, but that's another story altogether. He started pursuing me relentlessly, but I kept turning him down. He talked to his dad, and they did some digging about my parents. They made an offer to my parents that they couldn't refuse. All my parents had to do was instill enough guilt in me to give in, and my parents are very manipulative." Dr. Gabehart said as she rolled her eyes in disgust.

"Dr. Plunkett Sr. sweetened the deal by handing me over the cardiology department after finishing my cardiology fellowship. I was never much of a romantic, thinking about love, happiness, and such. Men had been trying to get into my pants since puberty hit me. Even when men showed real interest, it was still a huge turn-off for me because, in my mind, they were all after just one thing."

She stopped talking like she had just awakened from a dream and asked Sean, "Hey, it's been a while. You're not done yet?"

Sean told her he was done but asked her to finish her story first.

Dr. Gabehart's story continued, her tone reflecting a mix of bitterness and resignation. "So, there I was, with everything I ever wanted professionally handed to me on a "silver platter." I was successful, respected, and the head of a department before I even turned thirty. But then, it hit me. I realized I had never really lived for myself. I had followed a path that was laid out by others—my parents, my mentors, and even society's expectations."

She sighed and looked at Sean, her eyes filled with regret and contemplation. "I married Dr. Plunkett because it was expected of me. I thought maybe being married would bring me some semblance of happiness, but it was just another way to prove myself to everyone else. And now, here I am facing this battle with breast cancer, and I can't help but wonder if I've lived my life for me or if I've been living it for others."

Sean listened intently, his gaze unwavering. "It sounds like you've been carrying a heavy burden for a long time. But remember, it's never too late to take control of your life and start living for yourself."

Dr. Gabehart nodded slowly, her expression a mixture of contemplation and determination. "You're right. As difficult as it is, this diagnosis has also been a wake-up call. It's made me realize that I can't keep living for others and must prioritize my happiness and well-being."

Sean offered a reassuring smile. "You have the strength within you to overcome this, and not just the cancer. You have the power to redefine your life, to live it on your terms. And I don't doubt you'll make the most of this second chance."

Dr. Gabehart's gaze met Sean's; in that moment, she felt a sense of connection and hope she hadn't experienced in a long time. "Thank you, Sean. Your presence here today, your words, they mean more to me than you know."

They sat silently for a moment, the weight of their shared stories hanging in the air. In that room, amidst the challenges and uncertainties, they found a moment of genuine connection and understanding that had the power to shape their futures in unexpected ways.

Sean's expression became more serious as he listened to Dr. Gabehart's explanation. "I'm really sorry to hear that you've been going through such a difficult time, both personally and professionally," he said sincerely. "No one deserves to be in an abusive situation, and regrettably, you've had to endure it."

Dr. Gabehart nodded, her gaze thoughtful. "Thank you, Sean. I've managed to keep it hidden for a long time, but with this diagnosis, I'm reevaluating everything in my life. I don't want to continue living like this, feeling trapped and powerless."

"You don't have to," Sean replied firmly. "You have the strength to make changes, to take control of your life. And you're not alone in this. There are people who care about you and want to support you."

Dr. Gabehart's eyes welled up with tears, and she looked at Sean with gratitude and vulnerability. "It's been a long time since someone showed genuine concern for me. Thank you for listening, Sean."

"If Dr. Plunkett went through all that to get you, why does he hit you?" Sean inquired.

Dr. Gabehart didn't hesitate to explain, "He was a gentleman at first, but I later found out he was very jealous and a borderline psycho. He saw me talking to one doctor at a conference. There was an exchange of nasty words when we got home, and that's when he lost it. It became a bit of a habit after that. To my family, I have a great life, and complaining about "minor" things like physical abuse was a nuisance to them, so I kept everything to myself since there was no recourse."

"How about talking to his dad, friend, counsellor, or anyone?" Sean asked.

Dr. Gabehart explained that Dr. Plunkett Sr. never took the issue seriously and always told her that his son was a good man deep inside, and this was his way of showing his affection. Taking matters outside of that would've ruined everyone, including her family. If she had reported it to the police, her husband would've been arrested, and her father-in-law would've been angry. That would've likely led him to take everything away from her parents, something he had promised he'd do in an instant if she ever got his only son into trouble.

Sean listened carefully, his expression filled with concern. "I'm sorry you've had to go through all of this, Dr. Gabehart. It's never easy to be trapped in such a difficult situation, especially when there's so much at stake. But I want you to know that you deserve to live a life free from fear and abuse. No one should have to tolerate that."

Dr. Gabehart nodded, her eyes heavy with the weight of her experiences. "I know deep down that you're right, Sean. I've always told myself that I'll endure it for the sake of my career, for my family's reputation, for so many reasons. But with the cancer diagnosis, I can't ignore my well-being any longer."

"That's a courageous realization to come to," Sean said, his voice steady and supportive. "You have the right to prioritize your happiness and safety. It won't be easy, but I think it can be done."

Dr. Gabehart managed a faint smile. "It's scary, though. The thought of standing up for myself, making such a huge change..."

"I can only imagine how daunting it must feel," Sean admitted. "But sometimes the scariest decisions are the ones that lead to the most positive transformations. And you're not alone in this. You have people who care about you, who want to see you thrive."

Dr. Gabehart looked at Sean with a mixture of gratitude and determination. "Thank you, Sean. It's strange how conversing with you has given me more clarity and strength than I've had in a long time."

Sean smiled warmly. "I'm glad I could be here for you. Just remember, you have a choice in how your life unfolds."

The weight of her burdens felt a little lighter with each word spoken, and a sense of empowerment began to replace the sense of helplessness she had carried for so long.

"Wow, that was huge, but at least there's a bright side for you," Sean said, surprising Dr. Gabehart.

"Have you been listening to anything? What's the bright side?!" she angrily asked.

Sean replied with four words she never thought she'd ever hear, "You don't have cancer."

She was overwhelmed with emotions but sincerely asked him to be serious because she couldn't buy it.

Sean looked at Dr. Gabehart with a sincere expression, his voice calm yet filled with conviction. "I'm serious, Dr. Gabehart. I believe Dr. Plunkett might have misled you about your diagnosis. Based on the information you've shared and what I've observed, I strongly doubt his accuracy."

Dr. Gabehart stared at Sean in disbelief, a mixture of hope and skepticism crossing her face. "Are you saying there's a chance I don't have cancer?"

Sean nodded. "Yes, that's exactly what I'm saying."

Tears welled up in Dr. Gabehart's eyes as the weight of Sean's words sank in. "But how can I be sure?"

Sean understood she was unlikely to believe him because she thought he was in denial. He offered to get her a third opinion immediately.

"The General is not only an amazing surgeon, but he's also a great pathologist. He hates putting effort into something he doesn't have to do, so he checks every patient file before starting any surgical procedure." Sean laughed as he continued, "One time, a patient was scheduled for the removal of a brain tumour, and it turned out it was a cyst that would've been treated with antibiotics. I've never seen a man so angry."

While Sean was laughing, Dr. Gabehart saw the humour in

the joke, but this was not the time.

"Sean! What does it have to do with me?!" she exclaimed.

He told her to call the General, who'd likely confirm that she didn't have cancer. He also reminded her that the General doesn't mince his words.

Dr. Gabehart's emotions were running high, torn between disbelief, hope, and a flicker of trust in Sean's words. She thought about it momentarily, skeptical about the General picking up the call. She even wondered how Sean got him to come and help on Christmas Day.

"We're buddies, and if you don't believe me about this and I turn out to be right in both getting the General here and you being cancer-free, I get to take you out tonight. In this city, we have one of the best French restaurants in the world in a hotel downtown. I know someone that can get us a reservation there tonight. We'll have dinner around six, be at the game by eight and come back to the hotel for drinks if you still have the energy," Sean proposed.

Dr. Gabehart looked at Sean with a mix of surprise and amusement. "You have this all planned out, don't you?"

Sean shrugged, his grin mischievous. "Well, if I'm going to make a bet, I might as well make it memorable, right?"

She chuckled, shaking her head. "Alright, you're on. If the General confirms what you're saying, and I'm not dealing with cancer, then I'll take you up on your offer. But just so you know, I don't have the energy for a wild night out."

Sean raised an eyebrow playfully. "Oh, come on, a fancy dinner and a basketball game? What could be wild about that?"

Dr. Gabehart smirked. "You underestimate the excitement of fine dining and intense sports, my friend."

Dr. Gabehart was lost in the thought of going to the French restaurant. It's a place she had heard about for years, but it was nearly impossible to get a reservation there. It was her dream to have dinner at that restaurant.

"I just sent the General a message, and we should hear from him in less than ten minutes. As for your earlier question, while I was examining your left breast, I saw you flinching, and that told me the mass was likely painful," Sean said.

Dr. Gabehart remembered that cancer was generally not painful unless it had grown enough to compress a nerve. She also remembered that dead breast tissue due to physical trauma and cancer can strikingly look similar on a biopsy.

Dr. Gabehart felt a mix of emotions as she considered the possibility that Sean might be onto something. She appreciated his persistence and concern, but she couldn't help but feel guarded. The idea of not having cancer was a relief, but she had to remind herself not to get her hopes up too high until they had more concrete information.

Sean continued, "That was in the first few minutes. The most common reason for a painful breast mass is the death of breast tissue, commonly caused by blunt trauma to the breast. This could be one powerful blow like one from an abusive spouse or repeated mild blunt trauma like playing intense dodgeball. You don't play dodgeball, as far as I know. If there is one mass due to physical trauma by an abusive spouse, there will likely be others, so I started looking for them. You have two smaller masses in your right breast. I'm guessing you stopped doing self-breast exams after the initial scare. I thought maybe all three masses could be cancerous, but that would be statistically unlikely, considering that your husband likes to use you as his punching bag."

He paused and looked straight into Dr. Gabehart's eyes with deep concern. "Dr. Gabrielle Gorgeous Gabehart, I'd be doing humanity a disservice if I don't encourage you to make your husband stop hitting you before he kills you. I understand you can't get out of the marriage, but at least find a way to make him stop hitting you."

Dr. Gabehart was taken aback by Sean's straightforwardness and deep concern for her well-being. She had never had anyone speak to her about her situation in such a direct and honest manner. His words struck a chord within her, stirring up emotions she had buried for so long.

"Maybe you're right," she admitted, her voice tinged with vulnerability and determination. "I've been trying to handle this alone, thinking that it's something I just have to endure. But hearing you say it like that... it's like a wake-up call."

Sean nodded, his expression serious. "Dr. Gabehart, you deserve so much better than this. No one should have to endure abuse, and you especially don't deserve it."

Tears welled up in Dr. Gabehart's eyes as she looked at Sean. "Thank you, Sean. Thank you for caring enough to say something. I know I have to do something about it. It's just... complicated."

As they shared this heartfelt moment, Dr. Gabehart felt a renewed sense of determination. Sean's words had given her the courage to confront her difficult situation. With the news that she might not have cancer, it felt like a new chapter was beginning— one in which she could reclaim her life and make the changes she needed.

"Thank you, Sean," she said, her voice filled with gratitude. "You've been an unexpected source of support and strength for me, and I'll never forget that."

Dr. Gabehart wiped away her tears and took a deep breath. She was ready to face the challenges ahead, armed with newfound hope and the support of a friend who had shown her the way.

The General walked in as Sean finished evaluating Dr. Gabehart's case. The General was also the one doing the surgery, so he came in with a grave concern, thinking there was something wrong. He looked at Dr. Gabehart, who seemed anxious, but nothing unusual for someone about to have surgery. He then looked at Sean and asked, "Lieutenant, what's going on?"

Sean briefed the General on the matter at hand. Dr. Gabehart thanked the General for the impromptu consultation. The General opened the file and examined it for a few minutes. Then, in anger, he looked at Sean and said, "You couldn't figure this out?"

Sean tried to explain, but the General interrupted and told him to leave the room.

Embarrassed by the General's reaction, he nodded to Dr. Gabehart and the General and quietly left the room.

The General continued to review the file and briefly examined Dr. Gabehart. After a few minutes of silence, he finally spoke, his tone more composed. "Dr. Gabehart, based on my evaluation and the previous test results, I can confirm that you do not have breast cancer."

Dr. Gabehart's face lit up with relief. She had been carrying the weight of fear and uncertainty for so long that this news was a tremendous weight off her shoulders. "Thank you, General. Thank you so much," she said with genuine gratitude.

The General nodded and offered a small smile. "You're welcome, Dr. Gabehart. I'm glad I could clarify things for you."

The General sat on a chair and made sure Dr. Gabehart was comfortable before he started talking, "As you know, my wife works at the university. She was so impressed with Sean that she asked me to take Sean for his surgery clerkship as a personal favour. That was a big deal to me, and I asked her for compensation for the work because I don't like doing favours for anyone. Yes, that includes my wife. On his first day, Sean was nervous."

Dr. Gabehart interrupted, "Everyone is nervous when they meet you for the first time, General."

He looked at her with a grin and ignored her as he continued, "Very funny. That day, we had a morbidly obese patient. The anesthesiologist was struggling to find the right dose to prevent the patient from waking up in the middle of a sixteen-hour surgery or from dying on the table. Sean was watching everything very analytically without saying a word. He quietly raised his hand and asked if the patient drank alcohol so we could use that as a baseline to titrate the anesthesia. You'd think every doctor in the room would've thought about that first, but nope, that came from a third-year medical student. The anesthesiology team was annoyed but used his idea to put the patient to sleep. They ignored him after that, and he was quiet. I had told him that if he wanted to learn from me, he had to stay for the entirety of every surgery I was going to do during his entire time with me, and he was surprisingly okay with it. Sixteen hours later, the anesthesiologist couldn't wake the patient up. They tried everything, and nothing was working. Sean raised his hand again, and they dismissed him right away. He asked me if I trusted my wife, which was an odd question that annoyed me. I wanted to see where he was going with it. Quite frankly, I was too tired for this, but I played along. The patient was off the ventilator, and everything seemed fine except for the absence of breathing. Every doctor was stressing and rumbling about what to do, and I was looking at Sean, trying to figure out what was going through his brain. He went around and inspected everything from the monitors to the patient's physical state. Suddenly, I heard a thunderous slap. Yup, Sean had just smacked the devil out of the patient."

Dr. Gabehart couldn't help but laugh at the unexpected turn of events in the General's story. The mental image of Sean smacking a patient to wake them up was both humorous and absurd.

"He what?!" she managed to say between bouts of laughter.

The General chuckled with her before continuing, "Yes, you heard me right. He slapped the patient hard enough to shock the patient's system into waking up. The whole room went silent for a moment. And you know what? It worked! The patient woke up groggy and confused, but alive."

Dr. Gabehart wiped tears of laughter from her eyes as she gasped, "Oh my goodness, I can't believe he did that!"

The General continued, "All doctors suddenly turned to him and wanted to lynch him for what he had done, but they were also distracted by the patient's breathing as she woke up, finally. Of course, the patient wasn't happy being woken up like that."

Still, Sean said to the patient, "I'm sorry for waking you up like this, but we were having a hard time bringing you back as you were told this would be a possibility before we started this surgery."

He turned to the anesthesiologist and explained the neuroscience behind his actions. I was genuinely impressed that he could think that fast on his first day of his surgery clerkship. I dismissed him for the day and called my wife right away."

"To tell her she made a great recommendation to you?" Dr. Gabehart inquired with a huge smile.

The General replied, "Don't be ridiculous. I told her she didn't owe me anything, and instead, I wanted to do something she had been asking me to do for over twenty years: spend an afternoon in a museum. I've been buddies with Sean ever since, and I know he knows what he's talking about when he gives you his medical opinion."

Dr. Gabehart listened intently to the General's story, her smile growing as she realized the depth of Sean's connection with the highly respected surgeon. The General held Sean in high regard and their bond went beyond just a professional relationship. As the General finished speaking, Dr. Gabehart felt a renewed sense of confidence in Sean's assessment of her situation.

"I have to admit," she said, still smiling, "your stories about Sean are both enlightening and entertaining. It's clear that he's a remarkable individual."

The General nodded in agreement. "Remarkable is one way to put it. He has a unique way of approaching things and is not afraid to challenge the status quo if he believes it's for the better. That's a trait that's becoming rarer these days."

Dr. Gabehart's expression grew thoughtful. "You know, I never expected to form such a bond with him during his time here. He's brought a lot of laughter and positivity into a situation that's been difficult for me."

The General smiled warmly. "Well, that's Sean for you. He has a way of brightening up even the darkest of situations. And I have no doubt that he genuinely cares about your well-being."

Dr. Gabehart nodded, her appreciation for Sean growing even more substantial. She thanked the General for the consultation and an insight into Sean. It was sad that her husband was determined to stop him from practicing medicine.

The General told Dr. Gabehart not to worry about Sean and that he would be fine. He explained, "I know he cares about you, and you care a great deal about him too. There's nothing that says you guys can't stay friends, and he can be the guy to give you free consultation on some of your most challenging cases. Unfortunately, things had to be this way, but you might as well make the best of the circumstances."

Dr. Gabehart nodded in agreement with the General's words. "You're right. Unfortunately, things have turned out this way, but I am grateful for Sean's friendship and support. I've learned a lot from him, not just about medicine but also about approaching life with positivity and determination."

The General offered a reassuring smile. "Sean has a way of leaving a lasting impact on those he crosses paths with. And as for your situation, remember that you have the strength to face whatever comes your way. Surround yourself with people who genuinely care about and uplift you."

Dr. Gabehart's gaze shifted to the window, lost in thought. "I will. And I appreciate your perspective on this. It's given me some clarity."

Dr. Gabehart again thanked the General. As he was about

to leave, she couldn't resist asking him why he hadn't talked Sean into doing his residency in surgery with him.

The General turned around and replied, "He said, and I quote, 'Surgery is not intellectually stimulating for me. I need something more interesting.' Can you believe that nitwit?!"

The General was so frustrated that he spoke with his fist clenched as Dr. Gabehart burst into laughter. She kept laughing for a while before calming down as she looked at the disappointed General. She told him not to feel bad as he had said the same thing to her about cardiology.

The General's stern expression softened into a grin. "Well, it seems like we both have one opinionated mind in our lives, don't we?"

Dr. Gabehart chuckled. "Indeed. But I guess that's what keeps medicine and our fields evolving. We all bring our unique perspectives and passions to the table."

The General nodded in agreement. "You're right. The diversity of thought often leads to breakthroughs and progress."

The General walked over to Dr. Gabehart and took her hand as he told her, "Look, Gigi, my wife and I weren't blessed with children. I admire and envy your courage and hard work in everything you do around here, and it's always an honour working with you. Maybe one day I'll have the privilege of working for you if you run this hospital before I die. Each time I see you, I see the daughter I never had. So, tell your husband that if he keeps hitting you, I won't think twice about dropping a truck engine on his back, and that's not a metaphor."

Dr. Gabehart was deeply touched by the General's words and protective stance. She held his hand tightly, feeling emotions swirling within her. "Thank you, General," she said with genuine gratitude. "Your support means more to me than you can imagine."

The General gave her hand a reassuring squeeze. "Remember, Gigi, you're never alone in this. We're a team, and we look out for each other. If you ever need anything, don't hesitate to reach out."

"I will," she replied, her voice steady with determination. "And I'll make sure to pass along your message to Dr. Plunkett." She chuckled.

She started sobbing as the General left the room. She collected her belongings and got ready to get out to start preparing for the day to celebrate dodging a bullet.

The Mother of All Nights

As the afternoon sun bathed the hospital corridors in a warm and golden glow, Dr. Gabehart and Sean found themselves immersed in a conversation that felt like a gentle refuge from the storm that had been raging in her life. The cloud of a potential breast cancer diagnosis had hovered over her like a persistent shadow, casting doubts and fears into her thoughts.

Contemplating the possibility of cancer was akin to treading through a dense forest shrouded in mist; the path ahead seemed obscured and treacherous. The mere notion of her susceptibility to this affliction was akin to a sad refrain echoing in the chambers of her heart.

In those quiet moments, when the whispers of doubt were most insistent, Dr. Gabehart had often found solace in the words of an old English saying: "Forewarned is forearmed." Her understanding of the risk factors associated with breast cancer had been a double-edged sword, equipping her with knowledge but also burdening her with apprehension.

The intricate interplay of risk factors, like the complex patterns of delicate lacework, had woven a tapestry of concern in her mind. Her age without kids, medical history, and body composition—all these threads of destiny had converged to create a fabric of uncertainty.

Yet, as Sean's words reached her ears, a glimmer of hope

pierced through the clouds of worry. The revelation that she had been spared from the clutches of cancer felt like sunlight breaking through after a long and stormy night. It was a reprieve that resonated deep within her soul, like the sweet sound of birdsong heralding the dawn.

Dr. Gabehart's acceptance of her situation was reminiscent of a proverb often spoken by her grandmother: "Acceptance is the first step to peace." She had embraced the news with a stoic grace, ready to confront whatever lay ahead. Her commitment to facing her challenges head-on was a testament to her strength of character, like a ship navigating stormy seas with an unwavering helm.

Amid the storm, she had found an unexpected anchor in Sean. Their connection had evolved into a lifeline of support and understanding. It was as if two travellers had met on a winding path, sharing stories by the fireside as they rested their weary souls.

As they conversed, Dr. Gabehart's heart felt like a chamber of secrets being gently unlocked. She shared fragments of her life, revealing the contours of her journey—from the shadows of her family dynamics to the heights of her professional aspirations. Each word spoken was like a brushstroke on a canvas, painting a portrait of a woman whose resilience was as remarkable as a phoenix rising from the ashes.

In the tender moments of vulnerability, Sean unveiled his own truths. His recounting of their early interactions, laced with humour and candour, was like a master storyteller weaving a narrative of unexpected friendships in the most unlikely circumstances.

Their conversation was a dance of emotions, as laughter intermingled with tears, and stories flowed like tributaries merging into a mighty river. Their comfort in each other's presence was akin to seeking shelter beneath a grand oak tree during a sudden downpour. In this haven, they could be themselves, stripped of pretence.

As the day waned, they stood at the threshold of a new chapter. The prospect of an elegant dinner at a prestigious French restaurant seemed like a fitting celebration, a jubilant symphony to mark the triumph over adversity.

Their laughter echoed through the air like the tinkling of wind chimes on a gentle breeze. It was a moment suspended in time, a snapshot of friendship and joy that they would cherish as a rare gem in the treasury of their memories.

The resonance of their laughter and shared stories created a harmonious melody, soothing their souls like a lullaby sung by the universe.

Their hearts were heavy with gratitude and hope. Dr. Gabehart had navigated the storm, finding the truth about her health and a friend who illuminated her path with compassion and empathy. With every step forward, she carried with her the wisdom of her journey and the enduring bond she had formed with Sean — a bond forged in the crucible of vulnerability and fortified by the fires of friendship.

As the final week of Sean's extraordinary clerkship concluded, a bittersweet nostalgia settled in the air. The bonds he had formed with Dr. Gabehart, Dr. May, Mr. Gladstone, and most of the staff had become an indelible mark on his journey. This period had transformed his perspective, kindling the flames of camaraderie and knowledge in equal measure.

In the corridors of the hospital, Sean had not only gained

medical insights but also friends for life. The relationships he had forged were like the intricate patterns of a tapestry, woven with threads of shared experiences, laughter, and moments of profound learning. Every encounter, every diagnosis, and every patient interaction had left an imprint on his heart, shaping his path in ways he had never imagined.

While the shadow of Dr. Plunkett's opposition loomed over Sean's future in medicine, he had come to realize that his journey was not confined to a single road. The winding paths of opportunity beckoned him, and he had begun to explore alternative routes to fulfill his passion for healing. The wisdom of an old English saying echoed in his mind: "When one door closes, another opens."

Sean's heart was a mix of emotions – gratitude for the lessons learned, hope for the future, and a touch of wistfulness for the bonds he would leave behind. His relationship with Dr. Gabehart, marked by humour, compassion, and shared experiences, had become a beacon of light in the darkness. Their connection was like a flame that had ignited his passion for medicine and human connection.

Then, there was Mr. Gladstone, the unexpected mentor who had embraced Sean's presence with open arms. Their friendship had blossomed like a rare flower in a garden of challenges. From the serendipitous encounter that had brought them together to the moments of guidance and shared laughter, their bond was a testament to the power of human connection that transcends age and circumstances.

Sean carried with him a treasure trove of memories – the camaraderie, the laughter, the challenges, and the triumphs. It was the end of something special, a chapter that would forever hold a special place in his heart. They had journeyed together, navigating the intricate landscape of medicine with courage and determination.

The air was charged with excitement, for it was New Year's Eve – a night of celebration and reflection. The city's skyline would soon be painted with fireworks, a dazzling display of light and colour that mirrored the fireworks of emotions within Sean's heart.

Sean found himself looking back at his remarkable journey. The people he had met, the stories he had shared, and the lives he had touched had transformed him profoundly. The night was a tapestry of memories woven with the threads of joy, growth, and the promise of a new beginning.

Sean's heart was filled with gratitude. He knew that the connections, lessons, and bonds he had made were gifts that would stay with him and guide him on his path. Just as the fireworks were going to illuminate the night sky, these experiences had illuminated his soul, making this New Year's Eve a celebration of both the past and the future.

Dr. Gabehart and Sean's companionship had bloomed into a deep connection, a shared understanding that transcended the confines of the hospital. Their bond was unique, blending camaraderie, empathy, and genuine care for each other's well-being.

As she stepped out of the hospital, a renewed sense of gratitude filled her heart. The weight of an unnecessary mastectomy had been lifted from her shoulders, and she was determined to embrace life with newfound zeal. Her first order of business was to shed the sterile hospital attire and slip into something that resonated with her true self. With a change of clothes and a hint of a smile playing on her lips, she embarked on the journey of celebration.

The hours that followed were like a canvas painted with the hues of joy and friendship. Sean and Dr. Gabehart's interactions were a testament to the beauty of companionship, marked by laughter, heartfelt conversations, and moments of shared vulnerability. The day felt reminiscent of youthful escapades as they navigated the city with the enthusiasm of teenagers in love.

Yet, their dynamic was layered with respect and mutual understanding, mirroring the bond of siblings. Their shared experiences had forged an unbreakable connection, and the trials they had faced together had solidified their trust in one another. In each other's presence, they found solace, support, and the freedom to be themselves without judgment.

Their celebratory activities for the day were carefully chosen to avoid raising eyebrows. They revelled in each other's company while being mindful of the complexities that surrounded Dr. Gabehart's situation. They didn't want to inadvertently create misunderstandings or complications that could jeopardize her well-being with her husband. Instead, their day was a delicate dance of shared moments, a celebration of life, and a reaffirmation of the importance of human connections.

Their shared journey was like an exquisite secret they held close to their hearts. Their laughter echoed through the city streets, a testament to the beauty of finding joy amid challenges.

In their carefully planned day of celebration, Dr. Gabehart and Sean each chose activities that resonated with their tastes and interests. It was a thoughtful gesture, a way of sharing their passions while enjoying life's simple pleasures.

Dr. Gabehart's choices reflected her love for culture, beauty, and the pursuit of inspiration. She led Sean through the doors of a museum, where they wandered among timeless artifacts and immersed themselves in the stories of the past. The art gallery was a symphony of colours and emotions where they could appreciate the creativity of the human spirit. As they strolled hand in hand, Dr. Gabehart's eyes sparkled with the joy of sharing these treasures with a kindred spirit.

Shopping, with its promise of finding something special, became an adventure. Dr. Gabehart's promise to buy Sean something nice added a touch of excitement to the experience. As they browsed through stores, Sean couldn't help but be charmed by her infectious enthusiasm. The day was a testament to their budding connection, filled with laughter, shared anecdotes, and an understanding beyond words.

On Sean's part, he treated Dr. Gabehart to a different kind of entertainment – bowling. Sean's choice to take her bowling was a playful invitation to embrace lighthearted competition, where they could enjoy each other's company in a relaxed setting.

Their conversations flowed seamlessly throughout the day, delving into their dreams, aspirations, and challenges. The passing of the year became a symbol of new beginnings, a chance to look beyond the present difficulties and envision a future illuminated by friendship and shared experiences.

As the evening sun began its descent, painting the sky in hues of pink and orange, their spirits remained high. Their shared day had forged a stronger connection than ever, and they realized that the bond they had created went beyond Sean's impending predicament. They had found in each other a confidant, a source of comfort, and a friend who could stand by their side, no matter the circumstances.

The day culminated with a sense of contentment, a feeling that they had celebrated life, triumphed over challenges, and embraced the beauty of the present moment. The promise of their friendship was like a beacon of hope, a reminder that even in the face of uncertainty, human connections could light up the path ahead.

Their journey to the hotel held an air of mystery and excitement. This unexpected turn would soon unfold into a delightful surprise. As they approached the elegant establishment, Dr. Gabehart couldn't help but feel a flutter of curiosity in her chest. The aura of luxury and sophistication surrounding the hotel's exterior hinted at something special awaiting her inside.

When Sean proposed that they enter together, citing a brief meeting he had to attend, Dr. Gabehart reluctantly agreed. She collected her purse, a small accessory that held her essentials, and handed the keys to their car to the attentive valet. Little did she know that this moment would lead her to a place she had long dreamed of visiting.

As they stepped through the doors, the hotel's opulent interior unfolded, a tapestry of refined aesthetics and timeless beauty. The surroundings exuded an aura of grandeur, a perfect backdrop to the surprise that awaited her. Dr. Gabehart's eyes flickered with curiosity, a combination of anticipation and wonder that danced in her gaze.

Stepping into the hotel lobby, anticipation and excitement hung in the air as if the walls were aware of the impending surprise. Dr. Gabehart and Sean approached the security desk; their presence met with a courteous nod. With grace and confidence, they explained their purpose – to meet a friend, an encounter that promised to turn an ordinary day into a memory to be cherished.

Guided by the security personnel, they embarked on a journey upward, the elevator gently ascending them. Each floor they passed added a layer of intrigue, bringing them closer to the culmination of Sean's thoughtful planning. As the elevator doors slid open on the top floor, revealing the entrance to the renowned French restaurant, Dr. Gabehart's expression transformed into a masterpiece of delight and wonder.

In the heart of the hotel, a culmination of Sean's thoughtful planning came to fruition, a place that had lived in Dr. Gabehart's dreams for years. The ambiance was a symphony of elegance, the soft glow of chandeliers casting a warm embrace over the diners. The very air seemed to carry the promise of exquisite culinary experiences and memories in the making.

The sight that greeted her was nothing short of breathtaking – the city's panorama spread out before them, a tapestry of twinkling lights that merged with the stars above. The top-floor vantage point offered a view that painted the night sky with a touch of magic as if the universe had conspired to add a touch of enchantment to this evening.

Dr. Gabehart's heart swelled with a mixture of awe and gratitude. The reality of Sean's promise had exceeded her expectations, and she found herself at a loss for words. Yet, her actions spoke volumes as she embraced Sean, her genuine appreciation flowing freely in the form of repeated thank yous and heartfelt hugs.

As they stood in such elegance and sophistication, it was as if time had momentarily paused, allowing them to savour the essence of this unforgettable moment. Dr. Gabehart's joy was palpable, radiating from her in waves that seemed to touch every corner of the room. Her laughter echoed in the space, a melody of happiness that resonated with the spirit of the evening.

Amid this ecstasy, she turned to Sean, her eyes gleaming

with admiration. Her words flowed like a river of sincerity, each phrase a testament to her gratitude. She couldn't help but marvel at Sean's ability to turn this day into an extraordinary adventure, a memory she would carry with her for a lifetime.

Dr. Gabehart sealed the sentiment with a gentle peck on Sean's cheek as if moved by a shared emotion. This gesture transcended the ordinary, encapsulating the camaraderie and connection they had developed throughout their journey. Amidst the restaurant's elegance and the city lights' beauty, their bond had deepened, and the memory of this evening would forever remain etched in the mosaic of their lives.

As they were escorted to their table, Dr. Gabehart's heart quickened with realization. The surprise was a testament to the depths of their newfound friendship, a gesture that spoke volumes about the connection they had forged. The restaurant's menu, a symphony of gourmet delights, awaited them, promising a journey of flavours and sensations that would etch this evening into their memories forever.

Surrounded by an atmosphere that blended luxury with intimacy, a sense of gratitude filled the air. The surprise was not just about the restaurant itself; it was a celebration of their journey together, overcoming challenges, supporting one another, and cherishing the beauty of life.

As the aroma of delicacies wafted through the air and the soft hum of conversations intermingled with the clinking of glasses, Dr. Gabehart felt a deep connection – not just with the restaurant's elegance but with the person beside her. Sean's companionship, understanding, and ability to turn an ordinary day into an extraordinary memory were gifts beyond measure.

The evening promised an enchanting feast for the senses.

However, beyond the delectable dishes that would grace their table, what truly nourished their souls was the shared laughter, the meaningful conversations, and the acknowledgment that they had found a source of strength and companionship in each other.

The evening's enchantment continued as Dr. Gabehart and Sean strolled to their table, curiosity bubbling in Dr. Gabehart's heart about the awaited rendezvous. They were led to a corner of the restaurant, where an unexpected scene unfolded before her eyes. Mr. Gladstone sat there, a picture of jubilance and merriment, flanked by two companions, each graced with a radiant smile.

Seated beside the window, with a panoramic view of the serene lake stretching out below, Mr. Gladstone was in his element. His laughter and easy camaraderie with his companions infused the air with an aura of genuine joy. For a man who had known the depths of solitude, this was a moment of exuberance, a celebration of life's vibrant tapestry.

As Sean approached, a warm embrace between mentor and mentee spoke volumes. Mr. Gladstone's happiness was contagious, a light that shone with the brilliance of newfound companionship. He spoke openly of the joy he hadn't experienced in years, a sentiment that echoed with sincerity in his eyes.

Introductions were made in the circle of laughter and shared stories, and Dr. Gabehart was welcomed into the fold. With a gracious smile, she acknowledged Mr. Gladstone's company and met his friends, who radiated the same joy he exuded. Among them was a nurse from AGH who had become a meaningful part of Mr. Gladstone's life over the past weeks. Her presence added a touch of familiarity, a testament to the connections forged within the hospital's walls.

Amidst the restaurant's ambiance and the enchanting city

lights, Dr. Gabehart immersed herself in a tapestry of human connections. The day had been filled with celebration, from the relief of a misdiagnosis dodged to the deepened bonds of friendship. It was a chapter that resonated with the whispers of possibility. As the clock ticked toward the turning of the year, the promise of a new beginning hung in the air.

Seated around the table, the atmosphere buzzed with an easy camaraderie. They engaged in the art of light banter, their voices dancing with humour and a shared sense of connection. Mr. Gladstone, the life of the party, took the teasing in stride, his laughter ringing out like a melody. It was a symphony of jests, each note harmoniously blending into the next, creating an atmosphere where old and new friends could be themselves without hesitation.

Sean bestowed Fiona with the moniker "Malaika," which seemed to infuse her with a touch of mystique. The name brought a smile to her lips, and she embraced it with a twinkle in her eye. As the evening unfolded, she shared stories of her experiences at AGH, offering glimpses into the world she inhabited within the hospital's bustling corridors.

For Dr. Gabehart, this was a unique introduction to someone she had only known in passing. The shared laughter and exchanged anecdotes forged an unexpected connection, a bridge between their professional lives and this unconventional evening of celebration. In this unconventional setting, a fellowship was woven, a bond that extended beyond the confines of the hospital.

The restaurant surrounded them in a world of glee and connection. The city's lights cast a mesmerizing glow, and the conversations flowed like a meandering river, touching upon various topics from aspirations to shared quirks. In this transient pocket of time, they were not doctor and nurse, mentor and mentee, but individuals bound by the fate of the moment.

The atmosphere was electric, with a palpable anticipation for the transition into a new year. Laughter filled the air, momentarily dispelling any lingering worries or concerns. In that shared laughter, a sense of unity emerged, a reminder that moments of joy were to be cherished amidst life's trials.

In the embrace of friendship, the passage of time seemed less daunting. Dr. Gabehart's invitation to the girls was a subtle gesture of companionship, an unspoken assurance that they were all part of this special evening together. As they excused themselves from the table, the girls shared glances of surprise and gratitude. April, the spirited newcomer, seemed particularly eager to embrace the opportunity, her eyes shining with curiosity.

Inside the well-appointed restroom, laughter and conversation flowed as they touched up their makeup and exchanged stories. Dr. Gabehart, with her warm demeanour, encouraged Fiona to relax, assuring her that the evening was meant for enjoyment. April, the wildcard of the group, effortlessly brought a sense of lightheartedness to the conversation, her anecdotes and animated gestures breaking down any lingering barriers.

The girls shared their journeys in the cozy restroom, revealing snippets of their lives outside the hospital walls. Fiona's shyness began to wane, replaced by a growing sense of friendship. Dr. Gabehart's presence, so different from the hospital setting, seemed to inspire a sense of ease, a reminder that they were all, in that moment, simply individuals seeking connection and joy.

As they returned to the table, a subtle transformation was evident. Fiona, though still cautious, had a newfound lightness in her demeanour. Her interactions with Mr. Gladstone took on a more relaxed and comfortable tone. April, for her part, embraced the atmosphere with infectious enthusiasm, making the table come alive with her laughter and animated gestures.

The camaraderie seemed to deepen as if the bonds of friendship were growing stronger with every passing moment. This was a reminder that in the tapestry of life, chance encounters and unexpected connections can shape unforgettable memories.

As the ladies rejoined the table, the atmosphere remained light-hearted yet tinged with a shared intimacy. Sean and Mr. Gladstone's banter continued, weaving a tapestry of humour and camaraderie that had been the hallmark of their interactions throughout Sean's clerkship. The view of the tranquil lake below seemed to mirror the genuine connections being formed around the table.

Dr. Gabehart's return brought a sense of renewal, a reminder that this evening was a celebration not just of Sean's clerkship's end but also of newfound friendships and unexpected moments of joy. The conversations flowed seamlessly, a blend of laughter and sincere exchanges that highlighted the diversity of their experiences and perspectives.

The energy around the table grew more electric. The jokes and jests took on an air of anticipation, a shared excitement for the new year that lay just hours away. In these moments, their bonds seemed to solidify, each person contributing their unique voice to the symphony of celebration.

They engaged in light-hearted banter, finding humour in every topic, ranging from Sean's unconventional choice of bringing Dr. Gabehart on a date that could potentially induce a heart attack in Dr. Plunkett to Mr. Gladstone's hypothetical heart attack during a night of debauchery. The humour was infectious, fuelling a cycle of positive reinforcement.

Amid the laughter and camaraderie, Mr. Gladstone's mention of the possibility of feeling adrift after Sean's departure was a poignant reminder of the connections forged during their time together. The sentiment hung in the air, unspoken yet deeply understood. Sean, attuned to the moment, recognized the depth of those words and found solace in the implicit acknowledgment of their bond.

As the evening unfolded, the conversation transitioned seamlessly from the lighthearted banter to more personal and meaningful topics. The ladies, Dr. Gabehart and her newfound friends Fiona and April, took the lead in steering the discussion toward their respective lives, experiences, and aspirations. The ambiance was one of shared confidences, an atmosphere where walls were lowered, and stories were shared with an openness that belied the relatively short time they had known each other.

The exquisite cuisine that graced the table served as a metaphor for the richness of the connections being formed. Each dish brought a sense of indulgence, a reminder that this evening was not just a celebration of survival or camaraderie but an embrace of life's many pleasures.

As the wine flowed, adding a layer of warmth to the gathering, Sean found himself caught between the camaraderie of the group and his resolve to abstain. Dr. Gabehart's gentle encouragement and playful insistence revealed her concern for his involvement and her keen ability to balance responsibility with enjoyment.

Then there was Mr. Gladstone, the silent observer of the revelry. Due to his medication regimen, he was elevated to be the designated driver. As conversations flowed around him, he watched with fondness and nostalgia, perhaps reflecting on the journey that had led him to this unexpected and memorable night.

The laughter and conversation continued, punctuated by moments of reflection and introspection. The shared stories and experiences served as a reminder that even in the face of life's challenges and uncertainties, there was always room for connection, understanding, and celebration.

As the evening progressed, the group dynamic evolved into a close-knit circle of friends who quickly discovered a shared rapport and a remarkable ability to find joy in each other's company. The banter between the men and the ladies took on a life of its own, a testament to the chemistry that had effortlessly formed among them.

During their dinner, the women swiftly transitioned from teasing Sean for abstaining from alcohol to discussing their willingness to entrust their lives to someone who was dying by assigning Mr. Gladstone as the designated driver.

As the meal progressed, the girls dominated the conversation, cracking more jokes at the expense of the boys. The men were good sports, sometimes even contributing to the humour to enhance the laughter.

In under an hour, five individuals who were barely acquainted just four weeks prior had forged a strong bond and were now becoming the best of friends. They were all making the most of the evening to conclude the year and wished each other a prosperous new year.

With their plates cleared and contented smiles on their faces, the group declined the dessert offer, acknowledging the night that awaited them. Yet, Mr. Gladstone's enthusiasm for the restaurant's culinary creations was unwavering. Eager to share his appreciation for the chef's talents, he summoned the culinary artist to their table, creating an unexpected and delightful encounter.

As the chef joined them, there was an immediate sense of camaraderie, bridging the gap between the world of fine dining and medicine. Mr. Gladstone's introduction revealed Dr. Gabehart's professional role, painting her as a guardian of health in the nearby hospital. The chef's eyes lit up with a mixture of awe and gratitude as he learned that he was in the presence of a medical expert.

Dr. Gabehart exchanged business cards with the chef, a simple gesture that promised future connections and collaboration. Mr. Gladstone, with his characteristic warmth, emphasized that the chef could count on her expertise whenever needed. The chef, deeply appreciative of this newfound connection, extended a heartfelt invitation, welcoming her to the restaurant as a guest of honour, a privilege they reserved for Mr. Gladstone himself.

The exchange between the chef and Dr. Gabehart was a reminder of the unexpected ways in which lives intersect and how relationships can flourish when people from different walks of life come together. Their conversation was a blend of gratitude, respect, and the mutual understanding that each had a unique role in their respective fields.

As the chef departed, Dr. Gabehart felt a renewed appreciation for the connections she had made that evening. The restaurant, once merely a dream for her, had transformed into a place of memorable experiences and meaningful interactions. There was a shared sentiment that this encounter had added another layer of depth to an evening already brimming with laughter, camaraderie, and the promise of new friendships.

As the conversation flowed, Sean's recent completion of

medical school became a focal point of admiration and well-wishing. Aside from April, the group rejoiced in Sean's accomplishment, showering him with genuine congratulations and heartfelt expressions of encouragement for his journey ahead. The camaraderie was palpable as they shared stories of their experiences and aspirations.

The news brought a tinge of sadness to April. She had grown fond of Sean's company and now faced the prospect of parting ways after this special night. Her heartache was evident, though she managed to conceal her feelings.

Recognizing the shift in mood, Sean deftly changed the topic, injecting a light-hearted jest into the atmosphere. His humble demeanour and down-to-earth nature endeared him to the group even more. As he spoke, there was an unspoken agreement to cherish the present moment and focus on the laughter and companionship that filled the air.

With a glance at his watch, Sean reminded everyone that the night held more in store. The upcoming basketball game was a significant part of their plans, and the ticking clock served as a gentle nudge to get the evening's festivities back on track. Aware of the potential traffic woes often accompanying New Year's Eve, Sean's practicality and consideration for everyone's time showcased his thoughtfulness.

With the group now motivated, they rose from their seats, ready to embark on the next chapter of their evening. The camaraderie they had forged throughout this memorable night gave them a sense of unity and shared purpose, a feeling that they were in this together, navigating the challenges of time and traffic as a team.

As the group rose from their seats, a sense of unity and shared purpose permeated the air. Mr. Gladstone, ever the charmer, playfully held his companions close, embodying the joie de vivre of the evening. Meanwhile, a rare moment of vulnerability and personal significance for Dr. Gabehart took centre stage. Her seemingly simple action held deeper meaning as she linked arms with Sean, a gesture that transcended the ordinary.

Walking side by side, their arms interlocked, Sean and Dr. Gabehart exuded a subtle sense of togetherness. Their gesture of friendship, comfort, and solidarity hinted at a connection that had evolved beyond the bounds of a simple relationship. In that moment, the weight of their recent conversations, the laughter shared, and the bond forged seemed encapsulated in this quiet act of companionship.

The elevator's ambiance was electric, with the buzz of shared excitement. The day had unfolded in unexpected ways, shaping the bonds of this diverse group. Laughter, stories, and newfound camaraderie had woven a tapestry of memories that would endure long after the night. As the elevator descended to the lobby, the anticipation for what lay ahead bubbled over.

On their way out, they paused momentarily, awaiting the valet to retrieve their car. Time seemed to stretch, each second tinged with the anticipation of the evening's next chapter. Despite the wait, impatience was replaced by a sense of contentment as the group stood together, surrounded by the echoes of their laughter and shared experiences.

With the car now ready, they headed toward the game, prepared to face the thrills of the event ahead. Their laughter and conversation from the evening echoed in their minds, fostering a sense of shared adventure. As they embarked on this final leg of the evening, they carried with them the bonds of friendship forged on this extraordinary night and the promise of a memorable New Year's Eve to come.

Seated in the car, the group settled in as Mr. Gladstone's storytelling prowess again took centre stage. He was a raconteur par excellence, possessing the rare ability to transform even the most mundane topics into riveting tales. This time, his narrative revolved around his beloved car, a subject that ignited his passion like no other.

As he began recounting how and why he acquired the car, it was as if the vehicle itself came to life. He spoke of it with an enthusiasm that bordered on parental pride, evoking the image of a father discussing his cherished offspring. Each detail of the car's acquisition was meticulously laid out as if he were sketching a masterpiece in the air with his words.

Many might consider the transaction a mere business deal, but it was transformed into an epic saga. Mr. Gladstone weaved the tale of his encounter with the salesman, describing their discussions as if they were diplomatic negotiations between two nations. He delved into the negotiations, capturing the tension, the back-and-forth, and the ultimate triumph of securing what he desired.

But the story didn't end there; it was only the beginning of a narrative that grew more captivating with each passing word. Mr. Gladstone's determination and unwavering commitment to his vision led him to meet with the company's CEO. He vividly portrayed this encounter as a modern-day adventurer journeying through the corporate landscape to secure his prize.

As he spoke, the car's engine hummed with a resonance that seemed to echo his enthusiasm. To Mr. Gladstone, the car was more than a mere vehicle; it embodied his dreams, was a testament to his persistence, and symbolized his unyielding pursuit of excellence. His narrative was an homage to the power of determination, the beauty of craftsmanship, and the satisfaction of realizing a cherished goal.

Listening to his tale, the car's passengers were transported into Mr. Gladstone's world. Each twist and turn of his story elicited admiration, laughter, and shared excitement. It was a reminder that our stories are more than words; they are windows into our souls, glimpses of our passions, and bridges connecting us.

As the car sped toward its destination, the storytelling continued to weave its magic. It wasn't just a car they were riding in; it was a vessel carrying them through time and space, connecting their hearts and minds through the threads of a captivating tale.

The journey continued, marked by the rhythmic purr of the car's engine and the soothing flow of Mr. Gladstone's storytelling. As he waxed poetic about his prized possession, an air of captivation settled over the entire car. Even the ladies, who openly confessed their typical aversion to lengthy discussions about cars, found themselves drawn into the narrative.

With a touch of irony, they acknowledged that Mr. Gladstone's enthusiasm was infectious. As he spoke almost lyrically about his automobile's intricate details and craftsmanship, the ladies exchanged knowing glances. It was as if they had collectively stepped into a realm where the car ceased to be just a machine and transformed into a living, breathing entity.

Sean, attuned to the subtleties of human behaviour, saw a connection between Mr. Gladstone's affection for his possessions and his complex relationship with his family. In some ways, the car manifested the affection and pride he yearned for but couldn't find within his household. Recognizing that this was not the moment for profound revelations, Sean let the conversation flow, understanding that sometimes, listening can be an act of compassion.

Mr. Gladstone's discourse transitioned from the aesthetics to the mechanics of the car, his voice adopting a tone of expertise. He dove into the technical aspects, the horsepower, the torque, and the intricacies of the engineering. As he spoke, it was as if the passengers were embarking on a journey into the heart of the machine itself.

But amidst the discussion of mechanics, the passengers couldn't help but appreciate the luxury that enveloped them. The plush leather seats, the soft hum of the air conditioning, and the refined interior were all a testament to the car's status as a pinnacle of comfort and luxury. As the car glided through the city's streets, it was not just a mode of transportation but a sanctuary of elegance and sophistication.

The car's tale reflected Mr. Gladstone's passion, offered a glimpse into his persona, and invited others to glimpse his world. In that shared journey, the passengers found themselves connected to the car and the man who held it so dearly.

As they arrived at the arena, the excitement of the game and the buzz of the crowd enveloped them. A sea of people had gathered, eager to share in the thrill of the event. The cold air bit at their skin, and they knew they couldn't afford to stand in line for too long without risking the chill becoming unbearable.

Sean, ever the resourceful thinker, tried to assess the situation and find a way around the long line that stretched before them. He scanned the area, hoping to catch sight of a familiar face or someone who could assist. But the crowd was a mix of strangers, and the prospects of a shortcut seemed slim.

However, Mr. Gladstone, with his natural charm and charisma, took a different approach. He excused himself from the group and headed toward one of the security guards stationed nearby. Curious glances followed him as everyone wondered about his intentions.

A brief conversation ensued between Mr. Gladstone and the guard, and their interaction seemed to swing between laughter and seriousness. Their body language spoke of connection and shared sentiments. As they talked, an unexpected emotional exchange appeared to take place. The group, including Sean and the ladies, watched on, intrigued and puzzled by the unfolding scene.

When Mr. Gladstone finally parted ways with the guard, his expression held a mixture of satisfaction and contentment. It seemed that Mr. Gladstone's genuine interaction had touched the guard, leaving an impact that couldn't be measured in material terms.

As Mr. Gladstone walked away from the guard, a small but powerful gesture marked the conclusion of their conversation. The guard looked down at his palm, a smile spreading across his face. The group caught this subtle yet profound exchange and understood that whatever had transpired was deeply meaningful to both of them.

When Mr. Gladstone turned to look back, the guard responded with two thumbs up, an unspoken acknowledgement of the connection that had been forged between them. In that fleeting moment, it was clear that Mr. Gladstone's ability to connect with people transcended societal boundaries and left a lasting impact on those he encountered.

With an air of mystery, Mr. Gladstone beckoned everyone

to join him in the game. Curiosity piqued; those present couldn't help but ask what was happening. However, Mr. Gladstone remained tight-lipped, offering only cryptic responses such as "tricks of the trade." Despite their confusion, the group followed him eagerly, ready to uncover the hidden secrets.

"Whenever you meet anyone in life, there's a good chance you can benefit from them if you play your cards right, and there's also a chance they can benefit from you. In most cases, these benefits come at little cost to either party. If you know what you're doing, you can turn a crisis into opportunity, and opportunity into luck," he advised Sean.

Sean couldn't help but respond with a hearty laugh, acknowledging the depth of Mr. Gladstone's teachings. He realized that these life lessons, wrapped in Mr. Gladstone's unique and candid expressions, held the potential to shape his future in extraordinary ways. With a playful grin, Sean exclaimed that if he managed to remember even half of the wisdom shared, he was bound to lead a remarkable life.

Their laughter resonated in the hallway as they walked, deepening their shared understanding. Their footsteps seemed to echo the rhythm of their newfound connection, the lessons of the evening binding them even further.

The group was inquisitive and couldn't help but ask for more details about what had transpired. Mr. Gladstone's response, however, contained a lesson wrapped in simplicity: the art of human connection and its potential for mutual benefit. His words rang with the essence of the adage, "You scratch my back, and I'll scratch yours."

Mr. Gladstone's philosophy was one of recognizing the inherent potential in every encounter. He believed every interaction, no matter how casual, could yield unexpected benefits if approached with the right attitude and intentions. It was about finding common ground, understanding shared interests, and tapping into the resources that people naturally possessed.

It was a reminder that the web of human connections was intricate and often led to unanticipated opportunities, turning what might seem like obstacles into stepping stones toward success.

As they finally stepped into the arena, an atmosphere of excitement enveloped them. The crowd's energy, the anticipation of the game, and their sense of unity created a vivid backdrop against which their newfound friendship flourished. The lessons they had learned from Mr. Gladstone, the camaraderie among friends, and the promise of a thrilling game ahead all converged in a perfect moment that would be etched in their memories forever.

With Mr. Gladstone leading the way, the mystery of his "tricks of the trade" still lingered. As they walked, the group couldn't help but wonder about the enigmatic encounter with the security guard.

Curiosity got the better of them, and with each questioning glance directed at Mr. Gladstone, he would simply respond with a cryptic smile and his signature phrase, "tricks of the trade." The phrase held a sense of wisdom and mischief, leaving everyone intrigued yet amused by his secrecy.

As Sean looked around at their group of five, he couldn't help but notice that there seemed to be an extra ticket among them. It struck him as odd, given that he knew they had only four tickets. Confused, he turned to Mr. Gladstone, the mastermind behind the entry into the arena, and posed the question that was nagging at him.

"How did we end up with an extra ticket?" Sean inquired, genuinely intrigued by the mystery surrounding everything Mr. Gladstone did.

Mr. Gladstone, ever the enigmatic figure, responded with a sly grin, "Tricks of the trade, son."

Sean chuckled at the response, not entirely surprised by Mr. Gladstone's playful answer. He had come to expect such reactions from him, where more profound wisdom and insight lay behind the humour and mystique. This was a testament to Mr. Gladstone's unique approach to life and the experiences it presented.

Sean's laughter was a blend of amusement and acceptance. He realized that trying to decipher Mr. Gladstone's methods was like chasing after a wisp of smoke – you might catch it momentarily, but it would slip through your fingers before you could fully grasp it. In many ways, this interaction with Mr. Gladstone symbolized their entire time together – a dance of wits, knowledge, and camaraderie.

As they made their way to their seats, the air around them was charged with the excitement of the game about to unfold. The extra ticket remained a subtle reminder of Mr. Gladstone's presence and knack for orchestrating the unexpected. It was a reminder that life often held surprises and opportunities that could be unlocked through unconventional means.

Sean decided to take Mr. Gladstone's response at face value, embracing the magic of the moment rather than seeking an explanation. It was a testament to their unique bond and the unpredictable journey they had embarked on during these four weeks.

With the game about to begin, the anticipation and excitement were palpable. As the crowd erupted in cheers, Sean couldn't help but feel grateful for this extraordinary experience and the lessons he had learned along the way. Like a hidden treasure, the extra ticket symbolized the unexpected joys that life could offer when approached with an open heart and a touch of Mr. Gladstone's trademark "tricks of the trade."

As they strolled through the bustling crowds, Mr. Gladstone's accidental bump into Dr. Gabehart served as a momentary interruption in their laughter and conversation. Immediately recognizing his misstep, Mr. Gladstone offered a swift apology, demonstrating his innate courtesy even in the midst of a lively evening.

However, the incident triggered Mr. Gladstone's memory of the news he had heard earlier in the day – a piece of information about Dr. Gabehart's well-being that piqued his concern. Without missing a beat, he leaned toward her and inquired, "Doc, are you okay? I heard you weren't feeling well this morning."

Dr. Gabehart's response was gentle yet firm, a reflection of her determination to enjoy the evening without dwelling on any potential worries. "I'm okay now, but this isn't the time or place to talk about it. It's Sean's last night with us, so let's make it worth it. I haven't been out like this since I started medical school, so nothing that happens here tonight will ever leave this place, okay?"

Her words conveyed a sense of camaraderie and unity, emphasizing the significance of the present moment and their shared intention to celebrate Sean's departure in a memorable way. Her request for confidentiality underscored the bond they had formed over the past weeks—a bond that transcended professional boundaries.

Mr. Gladstone, always ready to embrace the spirit of the moment, playfully seized the opportunity to uplift the atmosphere. With a boisterous exclamation, he declared, "Alright. The doctor is in the mood to party!" His cheerful response resonated with their collective determination to enjoy themselves and put any concerns aside for the time being.

Fiona chimed in with her sentiments of support. "Yes, doctor, you work yourself too hard, and you deserve to relax and enjoy the small things in life every now and then," she concurred, her words echoing the group's shared sentiment.

The air was filled with a sense of unity and lightheartedness. They were a group of individuals from different walks of life, brought together by circumstances, chance, and the shared desire to make the most of the evening. The bustling energy of the city and the anticipation of the game blended seamlessly with the connections they had formed, creating a tapestry of moments that would be cherished for years to come.

As Sean momentarily excused himself to fetch refreshments for the group, the others settled into their seats, finding comfort and anticipation in the atmosphere of the crowded arena. Seizing a moment to express her gratitude for Sean's unwavering dedication and positive impact on their lives, Dr. Gabehart turned to Mr. Gladstone with a generous proposal.

"O.G., do you mind if I take care of this one? Sean has been great to me and has served the hospital well. I'd like to pick up the bill for this game," Dr. Gabehart suggested, her intention reflecting her deep appreciation for Sean's contributions.

Mr. Gladstone's response was sincere and affectionate, resonating with the depth of their bond. "Then take him out again for dinner and a game another time. This evening is all on me," he countered, his voice reflecting his determination to show his gratitude to Sean in a meaningful way.

He continued, his tone carrying an emotional weight that illuminated Sean's impact on his life. "Sean is my doctor, my brother, and my friend. The last few weeks have been some of the best days of my life, and I've been everywhere and done everything. No words, money, or gifts can show my gratitude for what he gave me. He came at the darkest time in my life and made the world bright again. He gave me hope. Well, for only a few months."

Mr. Gladstone's words painted a poignant picture of Sean's role in his life, underscoring the transformation he experienced through their interactions. He spoke of Sean's remarkable qualities, acknowledging him as an "amazing kid" whose influence extended beyond the confines of medicine.

"I wish him all the best in his life, and may everything and everyone he touches be blessed with good health and happiness," Mr. Gladstone concluded, his warm smile directed towards Dr. Gabehart. His expression embodied a sense of deep gratitude and affection, a testament to the connections they had formed during this unique chapter of their lives.

Dr. Gabehart and Mr. Gladstone's exchange captured the essence of their collective appreciation for Sean's presence. It encapsulated the significance of their journey together and the power of human connections to uplift and inspire even in the face of challenges.

Fiona's heartfelt sentiment added another layer of appreciation to the conversation, underscoring Sean's profound impact not only within the medical realm but also in the lives of the patients he cared for. "Yeah, Sean has been amazing to everyone, and he's truly going to be missed," she affirmed with genuine admiration. Her words painted a vivid picture of Sean's ability to instill hope and inspire positive change even in those facing challenging health situations.

As the conversation continued, April, who had been quietly absorbing the dialogue, suddenly realized that the "miracle doctor" Fiona had been enthusiastically sharing stories about was none other than the Sean she was sitting with now. The revelation struck her, and she couldn't help but express her astonishment. "I thought Fiona was making up those stories. It's amazing realizing that he's real," she exclaimed, her voice reflecting a mix of surprise and awe.

Sean returned to the group at this juncture, his arrival punctuating the conversation with his lighthearted demeanour. He acknowledged the time constraint but remained in the moment, eager to share the excitement of the upcoming game with his friends.

"Too bad we don't have time to keep this nonsense going. The game starts soon, so let's get our groove on," he announced, handing out refreshments to each member of the group. His words carried a blend of anticipation and enthusiasm as they prepared to immerse themselves in the thrill of the game, relishing the shared experience of the evening.

Amid the excitement of the game, the group found themselves fully immersed in the experience, forming a united front despite their differences in age, background, and gender. As the players battled it out, the friends on the sidelines rallied with fervent cheers and boisterous support.

Dr. Gabehart, usually more preoccupied with medical matters than sports, surprised everyone with her shameless enthusiasm. She threw herself into the spirit of the game, raising her voice to a pitch that matched the intensity of the court. Her reactions were so genuine that she took the game's fouls and plays personally, responding as if each move had been a direct affront. Her involvement transcended mere spectatorship, drawing her into the emotional heart of the competition.

The atmosphere was electric as they all channelled their energy into cheering, jumping, and letting their voices resonate throughout the arena. The confines of their ordinary lives faded away, replaced by the exhilarating camaraderie of the game and the shared experience of welcoming in the New Year together. Amid the joyful chaos, their connections deepened, and the memories of this night became a cherished cornerstone of their unique bond.

The fleeting worry about being recognized and facing her husband's wrath briefly crossed Dr. Gabehart's mind. However, she quickly brushed it aside, determined not to let any negativity infiltrate the fantastic evening they had been enjoying. The joyous moments, the shared laughter, and the newfound friendships were far too precious to be overshadowed by fears.

During the game, they refrained from alcohol, using the time to ensure they were sober for the rest of the night's celebrations. This intentional choice allowed them to remain present and fully engaged in the experience, savouring every moment as they eagerly anticipated the festivities ahead.

Although their team suffered a loss on the court, it failed to dampen their spirits. Their enthusiasm and connection to one another were unyielding, transcending the game's outcome. Their shared laughter and lightheartedness remained intact, a testament to the strength of their bond and the resilience of their collective enjoyment.

Exiting the arena, their togetherness was evident in their intertwined actions: Mr. Gladstone with his two companions and

Sean with his arm wrapped around Dr. Gabehart. The physical closeness mirrored the emotional connections they had forged throughout the day. The night was still young, and the best was yet to come as they headed to the next stage of their celebration.

Once outside the arena, an unexpected encounter unfolded. A stranger approached April with visible excitement, exclaiming his admiration for her. "I can't believe this! I've watched your movies, and I think you are amazing. I didn't think I'd ever run into you like this," he gushed, his face lighting up with recognition and enthusiasm. He extended his hands in an open gesture of appreciation.

As the interaction unfolded, Mr. Gladstone's keen sense of propriety kicked in. He couldn't help but feel that the man's approach was disrespectful to April and those around her. It was as if he sensed a line had been crossed, a boundary disregarded in the presence of newfound friends and celebratory camaraderie.

Although the stranger's excitement was understandable, Mr. Gladstone's protective instinct prompted him to react. He might have felt that the atmosphere they had carefully cultivated throughout the day was in danger of being disrupted. His quick assessment of the situation highlighted his commitment to preserving the integrity of the memorable night they were sharing.

In his eyes, each member of their group deserved respect and consideration, regardless of their backgrounds or roles. The way the encounter unfolded reminded him that maintaining the harmony and positivity they had been experiencing required both vigilance and a sense of collective responsibility.

April's past carried certain complexities, and she had confided in Mr. Gladstone about some regrettable choices she had made in difficult times. She had explained that her actions were driven by extreme financial distress, offering context to her past that many might not fully comprehend.

As the man's approach became increasingly disrespectful, Mr. Gladstone's protective instincts went into high gear. His sense of chivalry and respect for everyone compelled him to intervene. He addressed the situation in a firm but polite tone.

"Young man, please excuse us and refrain from addressing a lady in that manner," he said, his gaze unyielding.

Despite the discomfort of the encounter, the group continued walking, wanting to distance themselves from the stranger. However, the man's demeanour took a confrontational turn as he fired a provocative question.

"Oh yeah? Who're you, her sugar daddy?" he taunted, his words laced with a mixture of bravado and insinuation.

The man's response carried a dismissive tone and potentially even a touch of hostility. Mr. Gladstone's intervention to protect April and maintain the decorum of their night was met with defiance. It highlighted the need to defuse the situation with caution and sensitivity, considering the shared camaraderie that had defined their evening thus far.

Amidst the escalating tension, Sean recognized the volatile potential of the situation and attempted to intervene. He tried to lead the guy aside, hoping to defuse the confrontation before it escalated further. However, the man seemed determined to provoke and continue the confrontation.

The man's words took a nastier turn, revealing his derogatory attitude and disdain. He hurled insults at both Mr. Gladstone and April, seemingly uninterested in any form of de-escalation. His words struck a nerve with Mr. Gladstone, who was known for his composed demeanour but was visibly growing angry.

While angered, Mr. Gladstone maintained his desire to resolve the situation without violence. He sternly reminded the guy to show respect and allow them to continue their evening. Yet, the man's arrogance persisted. He challenged Mr. Gladstone's authority, asserting that he would use the legal system to his advantage if physical contact were to occur.

The situation reached a boiling point as the man made a rude gesture and continued his provocations. Mr. Gladstone, his patience tested to its limits, found himself unable to contain his anger any longer. With a few deliberate steps, he closed the distance between himself and the stranger, delivering a powerful punch that rendered the guy unconscious.

The unexpected turn of events left the group momentarily stunned. The confrontation had escalated beyond what anyone had anticipated, leading to Mr. Gladstone's swift and decisive response. As the immediate shock subsided, the group exchanged surprised glances, unsure how to react to this sudden change in the night's trajectory.

After the unexpected turn of events, a mixture of shock and relief hung in the air. The group's initial surprise slowly gave way to a shared understanding that the situation had been resolved, albeit in an unconventional manner. Fiona and April were concerned about Mr. Gladstone's well-being, rushing to his side to ensure he was okay. Besides the typical discomfort that follows such an altercation, Mr. Gladstone reassured them that he was fine.

On the other side, Sean and Dr. Gabehart attended to the young man who had been knocked unconscious. They performed basic checks to ensure his safety, monitoring his breathing, pulse, and responsiveness. Gradually, he regained consciousness and was able to stand on his own. He was disoriented and angered by the situation, making his intentions of taking legal action known to everyone.

As the guy threatened legal action and hastily retreated from the scene, Mr. Gladstone's response captured the moment with a touch of his characteristic wit. "Good luck with that; I'll be dead in a few months."

The evening had taken an unexpected twist, yet Mr. Gladstone's casual remark offered a dose of reality and humour. With his girls by his side, Mr. Gladstone led the group forward, ready to continue enjoying their New Year's Eve despite the brief interruption. The incident further cemented their camaraderie as they walked away with a shared sense of relief and a story to tell.

The group deliberated on the best course of action for the remainder of the evening. April and Fiona suggested returning to the restaurant to continue their celebration in its luxurious ambiance. However, Mr. Gladstone had a different idea. He shared that Sean had a conveniently located apartment nearby and suggested they all head there instead.

Dr. Gabehart expressed her concerns and feelings of conflict about the situation. She was grappling with the sense of potentially betraying her husband by continuing to enjoy the evening. Sean, empathetic to her emotions, provided a perspective that resonated deeply. He reminded her that entering the new year alone or with her husband might lead to regrets. In his gentle and compassionate manner, Sean encouraged her to seize the opportunity to be surrounded by friends and embrace the joy of the moment.

His words resonated with Dr. Gabehart, reminding her

that the evening was about celebrating life and the friendships they had formed. The prospect of entering the new year in the company of newfound friends was an opportunity she didn't want to miss.

Mr. Gladstone playfully teased Dr. Gabehart, highlighting their familiar dynamic. The rest of the group chimed in, gently urging her to embrace the festive spirit and choose a more uplifting way to welcome the new year. With the consensus leaning heavily in favour of continuing the celebration, Dr. Gabehart relented, recognizing that her initial hesitation might lead her to miss out on a memorable experience.

She joined her friends in the car, and they all headed to Sean's apartment, leaving behind any lingering doubts. The journey to the apartment was accompanied by Mr. Gladstone's eclectic playlist, which soon had everyone in high spirits. The lively tunes struck a chord with the group. April and Fiona especially found a few songs that resonated deeply with them, leading to enthusiastic sing-alongs throughout the drive.

As the car pulled into the hotel where Sean's apartment was located, the familiar surroundings and warm reception from the staff indicated that Mr. Gladstone was well-known and respected there. The staff greeted him with genuine excitement, their smiles reflecting the favourable impression he had left on them. Despite his absence due to his hospital stay, Mr. Gladstone's kindness and demeanour had made a lasting impact on the hotel staff, who regarded him as a hero of sorts.

Engaging with the staff, Mr. Gladstone shared his arrangement with Sean regarding the apartment. The staff assured him they would take excellent care of Sean during his stay, understanding the significance of his friendship with Mr. Gladstone. Expressing his gratitude, Mr. Gladstone handed out a few bills to each staff member as a gesture of goodwill and well wishes for the upcoming year, a small but heartfelt way to convey his appreciation for their support and service.

Mr. Gladstone's tradition of treating the hotel staff like his family demonstrated his caring and generosity. His interactions with the staff weren't just transactional; they were infused with a genuine desire to bring smiles and warmth to their lives. The small tokens of money, tasty delights, and occasional precious gifts symbolized his appreciation for their hard work and his commitment to spreading joy wherever he went.

As he continued to the apartment with April, Fiona, and the rest of the group, Mr. Gladstone's playful comment about starting the new year in his bed lightened the mood. His wink to the staff added a touch of humour to the moment, cementing his connection with those around him. The anticipation of the upcoming New Year's celebration was palpable, and the group moved forward with a sense of unity and shared excitement.

Upon arriving at the apartment, Sean noticed a few things out of place and some clutter scattered around. Determined to make a good impression, he quickly tidied up the space, picking up discarded items and straightening any crooked objects. Meanwhile, Dr. Gabehart politely excused herself to refresh herself. April and Fiona followed her lead.

During the preparations, Sean and Mr. Gladstone engaged in a reflective conversation about life's twists and turns. They discussed the unpredictable nature of fate, the surprising friendships that can emerge in unexpected circumstances, and the importance of embracing every moment. Their talk blended wisdom and youthful optimism, two perspectives that beautifully complemented each other.

As they set up drinks and selected songs, the apartment transformed into a festive space, ready to welcome the New Year with open arms. The atmosphere was charged with a mixture of excitement and nostalgia. This feeling often accompanies the transition from one year to the next. As they waited for the ladies to return, they exchanged knowing glances, silently acknowledging the significance of this moment in their journey together.

The ladies emerged from freshening up in a stunning display of beauty and elegance. Sean began playing music and gracefully led Dr. Gabehart onto the dance floor for a passionate display of horizontal hip movements.

The music's rhythm intertwined with their movements, creating an atmosphere of anticipation and uncertainty. Sean and Dr. Gabehart danced with familiarity and a newfound awareness of each other's presence. The music melted away the worries of the past and the uncertainties of the future, leaving only the present moment, the warmth of their connection, and the promise of a new year.

Their steps were synchronized, their bodies moving like they had danced together countless times before. The room was filled with electric energy, a palpable chemistry that hung in the air. The glances they exchanged spoke volumes, revealing unspoken emotions that had been building between them.

As the night wore on and the clock ticked closer to midnight, the tempo of the music gradually shifted, guiding them from passionate movements to slow and tender embraces. The mood became more contemplative, and as they held each other, the world outside seemed to fade away, leaving only the two of them and the shared moment they were about to enter.

They embraced the music, their thoughts, and each other's

company as they awaited the turning of the year. This moment held the promise of new beginnings, fresh opportunities, and the continuation of their unique and unexpected bond.

A bittersweet tension lingered as the melodic notes of "At Last" by Etta James filled the room. The countdown to the New Year commenced, and hearts beat in harmony with the clock's ticking. The atmosphere was charged with excitement, nerves, and the weight of unspoken possibilities.

Mr. Gladstone and his companions shared knowing glances, acknowledging the moment that was about to unfold. Yet, amid the celebration, a quiet hesitation remained between Sean and Dr. Gabehart. Their connection had deepened over the day, and the potential for a different kind of connection hung in the air.

But life isn't a Hollywood script, and the most significant decisions often require careful consideration. Sean's hesitation was born from a place of respect and friendship, a realization that sometimes preserving what's meaningful is more important than indulging in fleeting desires.

As the song played on with only seconds until midnight, they found themselves caught in a delicate dance of emotions. The night had been filled with laughter, camaraderie, and shared experiences. The unspoken remained suspended between them as they gazed into each other's eyes.

Sometimes, the most meaningful moments are the ones that are left unsaid, the paths not taken, and the boundaries preserved. As the music played, they held onto their connection, aware of the intricate tapestry of emotions woven between them over their day and evening together.

In that tender moment, as the clock struck midnight, the

world outside seemed to fade away, leaving only Sean and Dr. Gabehart wrapped in each other's embrace. Their hands intertwined, fingers locked in a testament to their shared connection. With a deep breath, they leaned into each other, their heads touching as they marked the passage into a new year together.

Dr. Gabehart gently pulled back as if guided by an irresistible force, her gaze locked onto Sean's eyes. The unspoken words between them transformed into a powerful surge of emotions. She closed the gap between them without hesitation, sealing the transition from the old year to the new with a passionate kiss.

Everything else seemed to dissolve in this moment—the uncertainties, fears, and complexities. Their lips moved in a dance of longing and unspoken desires, reflecting the shared moments, challenges, and laughter they had experienced together. It was a culmination of a day filled with surprises, a reflection of the undeniable chemistry that had sparked between them.

As Mr. Gladstone and his two companions celebrated in their own way, Sean and Dr. Gabehart were in their world, which momentarily transcended time and space. The kiss acknowledged what had already blossomed between them throughout the previous day. It expressed the bond they had forged—one founded on friendship, respect, and the recognition of something more profound.

For those few minutes that extended into eternity, their lips and tongues were a canvas on which their emotions painted a story of possibility, connection, and the journey ahead. When they finally pulled away, their eyes met once again, a silent promise exchanged in that shared gaze.

The new year had started not only with fireworks and celebrations but also with a kiss that promised adventure, challenges, and perhaps even more. As the music played on, the room was filled with the echoes of their shared connection, now imbued with the tenderness of a New Year's kiss.

When Sean and Dr. Gabehart were finally done, a brief but pregnant pause ensued. It had finally happened - a moment of joy for Mr. Gladstone and a moment of wonder for Fiona and April. In just minutes, Sean and Dr. Gabehart had their most profound conversation without saying a single word. Although some previous developments had hinted at this moment, Sean and Dr. Gabehart were still in disbelief at what had just happened.

The atmosphere in the room was tense for a moment. However, Mr. Gladstone took the initiative to break the silence by expressing his intense passion for music. Courteously, he asked the group if they would be willing to listen to him play a melodious piece. The group, appreciative of his gesture, eagerly agreed to his proposal.

Mr. Gladstone's fingers gently caressed the keys of the piano. As the first notes reverberated through the room, a sense of tranquillity settled over the space. The room seemed to come alive with the melody he produced, his hands dancing with a grace that belied any self-doubt he might have had. The haunting beauty of the music was both enchanting and melancholic, evoking a myriad of emotions.

As the music flowed, Sean found himself lost in the enchantment of Mr. Gladstone's playing. It was a beautiful distraction, a bridge between the unspoken moments that had transpired earlier and the present reality. Dr. Gabehart, too, was captivated by the music, her gaze fixed on Mr. Gladstone as his fingers moved with an elegance that spoke of years of practice.

The gentle melody carried the weight of unspoken stories, reflecting Mr. Gladstone's life experiences, joys, and sorrows. It was as if he were using the piano keys to share a part of himself that words could not convey. The room was filled not only with the resonance of the piano but also with the echoes of emotions that flowed through the air.

With every stroke of the piano keys, Mr. Gladstone's emotions seemed to pour into the room, filling the space with an almost palpable energy. The music became a vessel for his feelings, each note carrying a piece of his soul. The tempo of the melody mirrored the ebb and flow of his emotions, starting slow and gentle, then gradually building in intensity.

The hauntingly beautiful music began to weave a narrative, drawing the listeners into its embrace. It was as if Mr. Gladstone was sharing his life's experiences through the language of music, every chord and melody a chapter of his journey. The room itself seemed to transform, the mundane fading away as the power of the music took hold.

As the tempo shifted, the atmosphere grew more intimate and profound. The notes seemed to caress the heartstrings of everyone present, evoking feelings and memories that had long been dormant. The depth of Mr. Gladstone's emotions was mirrored in the glistening tears that streamed down his cheeks, unashamedly displaying his vulnerability.

The emotions in the room were tangible, a shared connection that transcended words. Each listener became a part of the music, their emotions intertwining with Mr. Gladstone's, creating a symphony of feelings that enveloped them all. It was a moment of raw honesty, a glimpse into the depths of the human experience.

The music continued to swell, the tempo reaching its crescendo. The emotions that had been building throughout the performance now overflowed, spilling over like torrential rain. The room was filled with a sense of catharsis as if the music had unlocked the floodgates of pent-up feelings.

The tears on Mr. Gladstone's cheeks mirrored the emotions of everyone present. The music had transported them to a place of shared vulnerability, deep connection, and the beauty and complexity of being human.

For a moment, time seemed to stand still. The power of the music lingered in the air, a testament to the capacity of art to unite souls and evoke emotions that transcend boundaries. The group was bound together by the beauty of the music, the depth of their feelings, and the promise of a new year filled with endless possibilities.

As the music continued, a sense of unity enveloped the group. The earlier awkwardness seemed to dissipate, replaced by a shared appreciation for the beauty being created at that moment. Each note played was a testament to Mr. Gladstone's determination to share a part of himself and break through the barriers that often separated people.

As the music enveloped them, it was as if the boundaries between individuals melted away, leaving only a shared experience of emotions and connection. The room reverberated with the echoes of Mr. Gladstone's emotions, a symphony of shared feelings that resonated deeply within each listener.

Fiona and April's intertwined gestures reflected the profound impact of the music. Their tears and shared embrace testified to the healing power of art. Sean's arms around Dr. Gabehart not only provided physical support but also symbolized the unity of their emotions in that moment. The music had the remarkable ability to evoke long-buried feelings, granting everyone the space to confront and release what had been kept hidden.

The music's richness and complexity reflected the intricate emotions of human existence. It danced between moments of joy and sorrow, of triumph and introspection. Mr. Gladstone's mastery of the piano allowed him to convey the depth of his emotions through every stroke of the keys, creating a tapestry of sound that resonated with the hearts of his listeners.

The music provided an emotional release, a catharsis that left them all feeling lighter, more connected, and at peace. The room seemed to breathe with them as if it, too, had been swept up in their emotional journey.

In that shared moment of vulnerability, they realized that the power of music transcended language, age, and circumstance. It had the remarkable ability to touch the soul and evoke emotions that words often failed to capture. The group became united by the beauty of the music and the unspoken understanding that they were sharing something genuinely extraordinary.

When the final notes faded into the air, there was a collective sigh as if everyone had been holding their breath throughout the performance. Mr. Gladstone smiled, a mixture of gratitude and humility in his eyes. He had bared a piece of his soul through his music, and in doing so, he had woven a connection that transcended words.

The room was filled with warm and genuine applause, a tribute to Mr. Gladstone's musical talents and the depth of emotions he had shared during his performance. The applause was more than just a show of appreciation for his piano skills; it recognized the connection that had been forged among them all during those magical moments.

As the applause subsided, a collective sense of gratitude was in the air - appreciation for the music that had allowed them to shed their masks and reveal their genuine emotions. Gratitude for the vulnerability they had all embraced brought them closer together than they could have ever imagined.

The bond that had been formed was not just a fleeting moment. It was a profound connection rooted in shared emotions and experiences. The music had acted as a catalyst, breaking down barriers and allowing them to see each other's authentic selves. In that vulnerability, they had found strength, comfort, and a sense of unity that would linger long after the final note had faded.

As they sat there, basking in the afterglow of the music and the emotions it had evoked, they knew this night had been extraordinary. It had been a night of celebration, camaraderie, and finding solace in the company of others. As they welcomed the new year together, they did so with hearts full of gratitude, connection, and the knowledge that they had shared a moment that would stay with them forever.

The music bridged the gaps, creating a sense of camaraderie and unity that no awkwardness or uncertainty could tarnish. The night took unexpected turns, revealing the depth of their connections.

As the music's echoes lingered in the room, the group sat together, reflecting on the journey that had brought them here. The New Year had been ushered in with a kiss, a melody, and a bond that would continue to evolve, promising new adventures and the beauty of shared moments.

"I want to thank all of you for taking the time to listen to my performance. It was truly a moving experience to share my music with you. I appreciate your patience and for allowing me to finish my piece in its entirety. Your support means the world to me, and I am truly grateful for this opportunity to share my music with all of you." Mr. Gladstone said humbly as he rose from his seat.

Dr. Gabehart was visibly emotional, her eyes welling up with tears as she spoke. Despite her struggle to keep them at bay, she composed herself and responded, "No, that was truly amazing. Thank you for sharing such a personal part of yourself with us."

"Thanks, Doc. I wanted to express my gratitude for your presence here today. It may seem like a small gesture, but sharing my music with you and receiving your genuine appreciation has been a gift. I can honestly say it's one of the best moments of my life," he said with a warm chuckle.

He proceeded, "In any case, I am not aware of what the two of you are currently engaged in, but I'm taking my girls to bed. Doc, I promise I'll be at the hospital and in bed by noon tomorrow. Have a pleasant night!"

With Mr. Gladstone's departure, the room was left with a sense of quiet reflection. The music had created a space for deep emotions to surface, and now that the notes had faded, those feelings lingered in the air. Sean and Dr. Gabehart exchanged glances, a silent acknowledgment of the intimacy they had shared earlier. Yet, both seemed unsure of how to proceed.

Sean and Dr. Gabehart were seated on the couch together. However, it wasn't long before Dr. Gabehart stood up and announced that she should be leaving. She graciously thanked Sean for spending the day and evening with her.

"I understand that you want to leave, but O.G. is still a patient—and a high-risk one at that. As you know, only I can properly care for him, and I would appreciate some assistance in case anything goes wrong tonight. This may be the last time he will ever be able to visit his haven of over twenty years. Please help me give him this gift before I leave, and that will be my parting present from you," Sean suggested.

Dr. Gabehart found it difficult to counter Sean's argument, as his apprehensions regarding Mr. Gladstone were also in line with hers. She was unsure of how to defend her position.

Dr. Gabehart hesitated momentarily, torn between her desire to leave and her genuine concern for Mr. Gladstone. She knew Sean was right – Mr. Gladstone's health was fragile, and having someone around could prevent potential medical issues. She sighed, acknowledging the truth of Sean's words.

There was a looming possibility of events taking place upstairs that involved Mr. Gladstone, and there was a chance that they could escalate into an emergency. Sean's concern was shared by Dr. Gabehart, who acknowledged that she could not bear the burden of knowing that something dreadful occurred while she was absent.

"Fine. So, what's there to do here because now I can't sleep with this hanging over my head?" she asked.

Sean reassured her that Mr. Gladstone would be fine, but they must exercise caution and remain vigilant. He offered her another drink and stated, "In my bedroom, there's a massive screen where you can watch a diverse range of content that suits your fancy."

Considering their earlier moment of passion, this invitation led to a humorous exchange about the incident. The two departed from the living room, with Dr. Gabehart playfully promising to subject Sean to a highly feminine movie.

"Please, not that!" Sean exclaimed with a tone of disappointment.

Dr. Gabehart led the way, and Sean followed closely behind, trying to hide his disappointment.

As they entered Sean's bedroom, Dr. Gabehart was struck by the sheer size of the screen. "Wow, you weren't kidding. This is impressive."

Sean grinned. "Yeah, it's one of my favourite things about this place. You can have a mini movie theatre experience right in this room."

Dr. Gabehart chuckled. "Well, I think it's time for that girly movie I promised you." She grabbed the remote control and started scrolling through the options. "Let's see, romantic comedy, musical, drama... Ah, here's one."

Sean raised an eyebrow as he looked at the title on the screen. "Seriously? Are you trying to torture me?"

Dr. Gabehart burst into laughter. "Oh, come on, it can't be that bad. Besides, it's only fair after I gave you your first kiss of the year."

Sean rolled his eyes playfully. "Fine, fine. I guess you make a point."

They settled onto the comfortable bed, and Dr. Gabehart started the movie. As the cheesy plot unfolded on the screen, they both couldn't help but laugh at the over-the-top romantic gestures and predictable storyline.

"You know, I think I'd rather be back at the hospital dealing with emergencies than watching this," Sean quipped.

Dr. Gabehart elbowed him playfully. "Oh, come on, it's not that bad. And who knows, you might enjoy it."

As the movie continued, their laughter and banter created a lighthearted and genuine sense of harmony. The weight of the events from earlier seemed to fade away, replaced by the simple joy of shared company.

After a few hours, a loud knock was at Sean's bedroom door. It was April in full-blown panic mode. Without hesitation, Sean rushed into Mr. Gladstone's bedroom, only to be met with a scene of chaos and despair. Fiona was in a state of panic as she desperately attempted to revive Mr. Gladstone. April's screams, shouts, and cries filled the room as she begged Mr. Gladstone to wake up.

Fiona was evaluating Mr. Gladstone's condition, but this was out of April's comfort zone. April was screaming uncontrollably while pleading with Mr. Gladstone not to die. As Sean entered the room, he noticed the crisis and stepped in to take over from Fiona. He quickly assessed the situation to determine if there was anything he could do to help or if he needed to call for an ambulance and notify Dr. Gabehart.

"Girls, what happened? I thought I told you to take it easy on him," Sean queried, gesturing for Fiona to assist him in gently moving Mr. Gladstone from the bed to the floor.

As Sean and Fiona carefully moved Mr. Gladstone to the floor, April continued to sob and panic. Sean checked Mr. Gladstone's pulse and breathing, his medical training kicking in amid the urgency of the situation.

"Malaika, keep talking to me. April, I need you to calm down. We're going to do everything we can to help him," Sean said with urgency.

Fiona's voice trembled as she spoke. "I don't know. We were having fun, and then suddenly he started gasping for air, and then... this."

Sean continued to assess Mr. Gladstone's condition. His breathing and pulse were absent, and his face had turned pale. Sean's heart raced as he realized that Mr. Gladstone had a massive heart attack and needed immediate medical attention.

Sean instructed Fiona to monitor Mr. Gladstone's vital signs and do her best to keep her composure as he worked to stabilize him as he tried to figure out his next move.

Meanwhile, April's cries continued to fill the room, and Sean looked over to her. "April, I know this is scary, but we're here with him and will do everything possible to help him. He's going to be fine. Stay strong."

Sean tried to focus on providing the best care possible under the circumstances, but the situation was overwhelming.

As if answering a call, Sean promptly made his way to his room, where he returned with an injection, a few pills, and a defibrillator. Fiona assisted him in setting up the machine while April observed with deep apprehension. With the machine now activated, Sean proceeded to administer a shock to Mr. Gladstone with the defibrillator. Regrettably, there was no immediate response.

Fiona and April were getting more anxious, apologizing to Sean that they didn't mean to kill him. Sean ignored them as he injected Mr. Gladstone with a drug, adjusted the machine, and shocked him one more time.

As Mr. Gladstone's body jerked in response to the shock from the defibrillator, a gasp filled the room. His eyes fluttered open as he came back to life. Sean sighed in relief, quickly assessing Mr. Gladstone's responsiveness.

"O.G., can you hear me?" Sean asked, his voice filled with urgency.

Mr. Gladstone blinked a few times but didn't say a word. Sean asked again, and Mr. Gladstone blinked a few more times and then focused on Sean as he replied, "Yeah, yeah, but dude, you need a tic-tac."

They all laughed as the room filled with a massive sense of relief.

Fiona and April were both in a mix of shock and relief, their expressions shifting from fear to amazement. Tears welled up in April's eyes, and Fiona put her arm around her to offer comfort.

"You scared us there, O.G.," Sean said with a hint of a smile, though his relief was palpable.

Mr. Gladstone managed a weak chuckle. "Well, I can't let you all have all the fun, can I?"

Fiona reached for her phone, speaking in a shaky voice. "I'll call the ambulance and update them."

Sean nodded in agreement. "Good call, Fiona. He seems stable now, but we should get him to AGH immediately."

As the tension in the room dissipated, April wiped away her tears and approached Mr. Gladstone with a mix of gratitude and embarrassment. "I'm sorry. I panicked when I thought you were gone. Thank you for coming back to life."

Mr. Gladstone extended a weak hand and patted her arm. "No need to apologize, my dear. I'm the one who should be apologizing for making you panic like that."

Fiona turned to Sean. "I can't believe you knew what to do. That was incredible."

Sean's face flushed with a mixture of modesty and pride. "Well, it comes with the territory."

Mr. Gladstone managed to sit up with Fiona's help, still a bit shaky. "Kid, you've surprised me more times than I can count."

April wiped her eyes, trying to regain her composure. "I can't believe this all happened. It's like a movie."

Sean chuckled softly. "Life has a way of throwing unexpected twists at us."

"Speaking of life's unexpected twist, Sean, that was amazing!" Mr. Gladstone exclaimed as he tried to get up.

"We probably shouldn't do this again. Take these pills, and we'll get you to the hospital as soon as the ambulance arrives," Sean told him.

The girls went on to hug Mr. Gladstone as he took the pills Sean gave him. It seemed like an intoxicating moment for him since he talked to Sean like he didn't understand the gravity of what had just happened. He held the girls passionately and told them not to worry as they had given him the best night of his life.

"Sean, did I tell you how amazing I just felt?" he asked, but Sean wasn't enthused.

"You just scared the living daylights out of these girls,"

Sean said as he got things ready for the ambulance that was on its way.

Mr. Gladstone laughed at this response as he told Sean to relax and not take life too seriously.

Mr. Gladstone's infectious laughter filled the room, though his voice was still slightly shaky. "I guess I might have overdone it a bit, huh?"

April and Fiona were still clinging to him, their expressions a mixture of relief and affection.

"We were so scared. We thought we lost you," April said, her voice quivering.

Fiona nodded in agreement, wiping away a tear. "Yeah, we thought we messed up big time."

Mr. Gladstone patted their backs gently. "You two didn't mess up anything. I'm the one who decided to make a dramatic entrance back into the living world."

Sean had prepared everything necessary for the ambulance's arrival. "O.G., as entertaining as that was, we must get you to the hospital. We need to play it safe after what just happened."

Mr. Gladstone raised an eyebrow playfully. "Oh, come on, Sean. Can't we forget the hospital for a couple of more hours? I've entered the new year with a bang and want to keep going."

Sean replied, his tone firm. "O.G., you scared all of us tonight. You're going to the hospital, no excuses."

He let out a dramatic sigh, leaning back in mock defeat. "Alright, alright. Hospital it is, then. But only if you promise me you won't let this story die with me."

Sean chuckled. "Deal, as long as you promise not to give us another scare like this."

"Can you imagine if I had gone like that? Sean, I'll pay you a million bucks to have that written on my tombstone to tell the world that that's how I headed for the happy hunting ground," Mr. Gladstone said as he laughed.

The group exchanged relieved glances. Despite the unexpected turn of events, they were together and safe, and they had already proven that their bonds were unbreakable. Amidst the chaos, they had found strength, humour, and a renewed appreciation for life. As they waited for the ambulance, they were reminded that even the most unpredictable moments could lead to profound connections and lasting memories.

"Where's Dr. Gabehart?" Fiona asked.

Sean replied, "After that long day, she watched some chick-flick and passed out. We better make sure that everything that happened here tonight stays here. Please help me get Mr. Gladstone back to the hospital safely. The ambulance will be here shortly. Malaika, you'll go with the ambulance and talk to Dr. May. I'll call her right now, and she'll be expecting you. April, are you okay?"

With everything that had just happened, April wasn't sure how she was supposed to feel. One part was terrifying for her, but the other was fascinating. She apologized to Mr. Gladstone, hoping that next time would be a better experience. Sean quickly told her there wouldn't be a next time, and this should be a wake-up call for him because the next heart attack would likely kill him at once.

Fiona nodded in agreement with Sean's instructions. "Don't worry, I'll make sure everything goes smoothly at the hospital. And O.G., please promise us that you'll take better care of yourself from now on."

Mr. Gladstone grinned mischievously. "Oh, come on, darling. Where's the fun in that? Life's too short to be overly cautious."

Still a bit shaken from the incident, April managed a weak smile. "I'm glad you're okay, Mr. Gladstone. But yeah, please take care of yourself."

Sean turned to April. "Are you okay, April?"

She nodded, her voice a bit shaky. "Yeah, just a bit overwhelmed. That was... intense."

Sean put a reassuring hand on her shoulder. "I know, it was a lot to take in. But you handled it well, and Mr. Gladstone will be fine."

April let out a sigh of relief. "I hope so. It's just... I didn't expect all of this when I agreed to go out tonight."

Sean smiled gently. "Life has a way of surprising us sometimes. But remember, these unexpected moments can create some of the most meaningful memories."

Sean and April exchanged a glance filled with relief and gratitude. Amid the chaos, they had shared an experience that would forever bond them and their unlikely group of friends.

"Sean, this was the best moment of my life. Thanks, buddy," Mr. Gladstone said as he lay on the stretcher, ready to be wheeled out by the paramedics as Fiona followed.

"It'd be my pleasure if you don't die on me like this. Let's get you to the hospital so you can rest," Sean replied before telling April that she could spend the rest of the night in the apartment, or he could drive her home.

April appreciated the gesture, but she was okay with taking a cab because Sean looked like he needed to rest.

April smiled warmly. "Thank you, Sean. For everything tonight. It's been... well, it's been a rollercoaster, to say the least."

Sean grinned. "That's one way to put it. But I'm glad you were here with us."

April smiled. "Go get some rest, Sean. You've had quite a day."

Sean gave her a quick hug. "Take care, April. And remember, if you ever need anything, don't hesitate to reach out."

April felt a mix of emotions – relief, gratitude, and a newfound connection with the people with whom she had spent this memorable evening.

With a grateful smile, April left the apartment. As the door closed behind her, Sean took a deep breath and reflected on the night's events. It had been an extraordinary journey filled with unexpected twists, intense emotions, and the forging of strong bonds.

As he turned off the lights and made his way to his room, he felt a sense of fulfillment, knowing that he had positively impacted the lives of those around him.

Last Call

As the hands of the clock serenaded the arrival of a new year, the corridors of AGH were adorned with an air of diligence and compassion. Like a symphony of dedicated healers, the hospital staff orchestrated a harmonious transition into the year ahead.

In the grand tapestry of the hospital's rhythm, some figures stood like steadfast sentinels amidst the ebb and flow of festivities. Among them were Mother, Fiona, and Dr. May, whose dedication was like that of a lighthouse guiding ships through turbulent seas.

While many sought respite during the Christmas season, these brave souls remained at their posts, their commitment unshaken. Mother, with the grace of an angel, embraced double shifts, each a testament to her boundless care and compassion. Like a tireless symphony conductor, she orchestrated the hospital's operations with unwavering determination.

Fiona, a newer addition to the staff, demonstrated a remarkable dedication that shone like a lone star amidst the night sky. Working within the confines of the hospital's overtime policy, she imbued her tasks with diligence that was both admirable and inspiring. With the heart of a warrior, she upheld her responsibilities while others savoured holiday leisure.

Dr. May, a beacon of medical wisdom, was a guardian angel for the hospital during the holiday season. Her commitment transcended the bounds of a typical schedule, and she often took up residence within the hospital's walls for days at a time. Like a sage on a spiritual quest, she embarked on her rounds, tending to the needs of her patients with a determination that knew no rest.

Amidst the festive cheer and the lure of celebration, these three individuals continued to shine with an intensity that was nothing short of remarkable. They carried the weight of their responsibilities with a grace that painted them as heroes within the story of the hospital's holiday season.

As the world donned its holiday attire, these figures remained steadfast in their pursuit of healing and care. Like a sacred fire that burned eternally, their devotion illuminated the hospital's corridors, a silent reminder that the spirit of service transcended the bounds of tradition and merriment.

In the heart of this day, Dr. May stood as a beacon of unwavering commitment. Her unceasing dedication was reminiscent of a marathon runner, pushing through the challenges with a determined stride. For three consecutive days, she had walked the corridors of the hospital, a modern-day vigil for the wellbeing of her patients.

Amid her relentless efforts, Dr. May found solace in brief interludes. A warm, soothing bath served as her sanctuary, a momentary escape from the demands of her noble calling. Yet, even in these precious moments of respite, her mind remained tethered to the hospital, ready to leap into action at a moment's notice.

As the sun arced across the sky, she continued her mission of healing, pausing only for fleeting sustenance and a few precious moments of rest. The hands of the clock may have ticked on, but Dr. May's spirit remained as unyielding as a fortress wall. Her dedication illuminated the corridors like a guiding star, a testament to her unwavering commitment.

In this crucible of time, Dr. May began to absorb the essence of Sean's approach to patient care. His empathy and genuine concern had woven their way into her interactions with patients and colleagues alike. A newfound understanding flourished within her, enabling her to bridge the gap between the clinical and the compassionate, much like a skilled artisan fusing two precious metals into a harmonious whole.

Though the hours stretched long and fatigue whispered at the edges of her consciousness, Dr. May stood resolute. She had become a living embodiment of devotion, a tribute to the noble spirit of medicine that perseveres despite adversity.

The ripples of Dr. May's newfound approach were palpable, akin to the expanding circles on a pond's surface after a stone is cast. Her interactions had transformed from mere exchanges of information to profound connections that resonated with authenticity and empathy.

The currency of respect, which she had earned through her unswerving dedication, had now compounded with the weight of her words. She was becoming more than a physician; she was evolving into a beacon of wisdom and solace for those around her.

Amid this transformation, Mother, a seasoned observer of human nature, couldn't help but notice Dr. May's remarkable change. Her curiosity piqued, and she dared to inquire into the cause behind this positive shift. Dr. May's response was succinct yet enigmatic: "I'm trying to get those two points." The words seemed to dangle in the air, shrouded in mystery.

Confused but content with the positive evolution, Mother

couldn't help but revel in Dr. May's newfound dynamism. It was as if a dormant butterfly had emerged from its chrysalis, embracing the vibrant world with renewed vigour. For Mother, it was a testament to the transformative power that lies within every individual, waiting to be awakened by the gentle touch of motivation and self-discovery.

From the moment Mr. Gladstone was wheeled in by the ambulance, Dr. May's gaze became a steadfast vigil, a watchful guardian attending to his every need. It was as if her dedication and attention had converged into a singular beam of concern, focused entirely on the patient who had become a central figure in her professional life.

In a sincere act of humility, Dr. May confronted her past misjudgments with unwavering honesty. She openly acknowledged her missteps in Mr. Gladstone's treatment, demonstrating exceptional self-awareness and professional integrity. Her confessions were like rain on parched soil, renewing trust and paving the way for a renewed patient-doctor relationship.

It was not just the words she spoke but the sincerity with which she conveyed them that struck a chord in everyone's hearts. Each time she expressed regret for her previous diagnostic errors, it was as if she was offering a heartfelt apology to Mr. Gladstone's very soul. The profundity of her emotions resonated through her voice, eyes, and every gesture.

In those four weeks, Dr. May's repeated apologies to Mr. Gladstone accumulated like drops in a vast ocean, a testament to her unyielding commitment to rectifying her past misjudgments. For every apology, she asked for his forgiveness and pledged her determination to prevent any recurrence of her mistakes.

This ongoing act of contrition was a lesson in humility and

growth. It reflected the adage that it takes a strong character to admit one's faults and a courageous soul to make amends. Dr. May's journey was a reminder that even those who are trusted to heal are, in the end, only human, susceptible to errors but capable of rectifying them with grace and determination.

Amid the gentle tempo of medical equipment and the hushed whispers of the hospital corridors, Dr. May and Mr. Gladstone engaged in conversations that transcended the confines of a hospital room. Like an intricate tapestry woven with shared stories, hopes, and reflections, these dialogues painted a picture of two souls connected by circumstances and a burgeoning bond.

Dr. May's reminders to Mr. Gladstone to take things easy were not merely professional injunctions; they carried the undertone of genuine concern and affection. In her words and demeanour, one could discern the traces of a maternal figure guiding him with a gentle yet firm hand and seeking to ensure his well-being.

Within the context of those fleeting minutes, Mr. Gladstone's heart swelled with a warmth that mirrored paternal pride. He saw in Dr. May a young woman brimming with potential. As her informal mentor, he experienced a sense of fulfillment that seemed to transcend his medical condition. The mentor-mentee relationship blossomed into a heartwarming bond, where his wisdom was shared with genuine care, and her receptiveness was a tribute to her respect for his life's experiences.

Dr. May, in turn, became Mr. Gladstone's reminder of life's preciousness. Her earnest attempts to instill in him a greater appreciation for the fleeting beauty of existence were not just medical advice but a testament to her compassionate spirit. These conversations, often profound and soul-searching, unfolded like a delicate dance between the sage and the seeker, between a seasoned man pondering life's legacy and a dedicated doctor striving to heal his body and spirit.

As their rapport deepened, their familiarity grew to the point that Mr. Gladstone affectionately referred to Dr. May with endearing terms. These simple names spoke volumes about the comfort and trust that had blossomed between them.

In moments of professional fatigue, Dr. May found solace and strength in Mr. Gladstone's company. His words, infused with wisdom garnered over a lifetime, became her anchor, reminding her of the purpose of her work and the resilience that resided within her. Like a lighthouse guiding her through the turbulent seas of stress, his brief pep talks during her long shifts renewed her determination to soldier on.

In the quiet cocoon of their conversations, Dr. May and Mr. Gladstone found a refuge from the clinical routines and medical procedures. Their words became a lifeline, weaving a connection that transcended the barriers of age, illness, and profession. It was a testament to the profound impact human connection can have in even the most challenging circumstances, a beacon of hope amidst the hospital's hustle and bustle.

Around 10 a.m. on New Year's Day, Sean received a frantic call from Dr. May. She exclaimed that Sean had to come to the hospital, a matter of life and death.

Sean's heart raced at the urgency in Dr. May's voice. He knew that "life and death" were not words she used lightly, and his mind raced through what could have gone wrong with Mr. Gladstone.

"O.G. just had another heart attack, and things aren't looking good. He's stable for now, but something is incredibly wrong. You need to be right here, right now," Dr. May said, her voice wavering as she struggled to convey the sudden shift.

Sean rubbed his eyes, fatigue tugging at him as he processed Dr. May's urgent plea. The request transcended professional obligations and spoke to his deep bond with Mr. Gladstone. With a sigh, he swung his legs over the side of the bed and began rousing himself to face yet another crisis.

During his conversation with Dr. May, Sean expressed his helplessness in the situation, stating that his clerkship at the hospital had already ended. He further elaborated that he had concerns regarding potential legal consequences that may arise from Dr. Plunkett.

Dr. May countered, "You don't understand. I'm not asking you to come and do something, but he's asking for you. He needs you. He needs his friend. Please, Sean, don't let me beg, and don't leave your friend hanging."

Dr. May's words lingered in his mind, a testament to the gravity of the situation. She had used the words "he needs you," which struck a chord within Sean. He knew that his presence wasn't just about medical expertise but about supporting a friend in dire need.

"Alright, I'll be there shortly. Keep him stable and keep a close eye on him," Sean said.

She told him she would call Dr. Gabehart immediately to let her know what was going on, as things were beginning to look bleak for Mr. Gladstone.

Sean's mind felt heavy with the weight of his thoughts, like gathering storm clouds on the horizon. He shifted on his bed and turned towards Dr. Gabehart, who calmly inquired about his perceptions of the situation.

"I think these heart attacks were a long way coming. We focused on the heart valve and then his cancer but didn't check his arteries. He's an old guy who loves red meat and whiskey, never ate a salad in his adult life, and smoked himself halfway to death. Of course, his arteries would be mostly blocked," he replied in exhaustion.

"So, an emergency triple bypass? Do you think the General will do it on such short notice?" Dr. Gabehart asked.

Dr. Gabehart's questions reflected the concerns that had been gnawing at him since he received Dr. May's distressing call.

"You're right," he began, his voice carrying the weight of fatigue and concern. "Given his history and lifestyle, emergency triple bypass might be the only viable option. But you know Mr. Gladstone—he's stubborn as a mule when it comes to medical procedures, especially ones that involve surgery."

Dr. Gabehart nodded in agreement, her expression mirroring Sean's solemnity. They both knew convincing Mr. Gladstone to undergo such a procedure would be an uphill battle. His independent spirit and aversion to hospitals often led him to resist medical interventions, even when they were in his best interest.

"I can already hear him saying that he's lived a good life, seen the world, and danced with danger more times than he can count," Dr. Gabehart mused with a half-smile, her eyes reflecting a mix of fondness and frustration. "But we can't just stand by and let him slip away, especially when there's a chance for him to recover."

Sean rubbed his temples, feeling the weight of his responsibilities as a friend and a medical professional. "You're right. We can't give up on him. We have to find a way to make him see the value in this surgery, to make him understand that it's not about giving up his freedom but about giving himself a chance to keep living life on his terms."

Dr. Gabehart's gaze never wavered from Sean's, and their unspoken understanding reminded them of their shared commitment to Mr. Gladstone's well-being. "We've seen him fight through so much already, Sean. Maybe it's time for him to fight for himself, to choose life over pride."

Their conversation hung in the air, a blend of concern, determination, and their unbreakable bond with their enigmatic patient.

"If he says no to surgery, that leaves radical pharmacological intervention as the only option," Dr. Gabehart suggested.

Her words hung in the air; her concern mirrored in Sean's furrowed brow. It was true that radical pharmacological intervention was not without its risks, and considering Mr. Gladstone's complex medical history, they had to tread carefully. But Sean's contemplative pause indicated that he might have been harbouring an idea he wasn't quite ready to voice yet.

However, Dr. Gabehart begged him to stop thinking about any experiments on this poor man's life. She proposed they find a way to make the next couple of months easy for him in the worst-case scenario.

As Sean moved to get ready, Dr. Gabehart watched him with curiosity and anticipation. They had faced countless medical challenges together, always working as a team, their minds melding in pursuit of the best outcomes for their patients. Even when the odds seemed insurmountable, they had found solutions that defied conventional wisdom.

Sean finally spoke, his voice steady but thoughtful. "You know as well as I do that Mr. Gladstone is unlike any patient you or I have encountered. He's not just a medical case; he's a living, breathing paradox. Stubborn as they come, yet his spirit has carried him through the darkest times."

Dr. Gabehart nodded, her expression a mix of understanding and empathy. "He's more than a patient to us. He's family."

Sean's gaze met hers, a hint of a smile tugging at the corner of his lips. "Exactly. And family means fighting for one another, even when the odds are stacked against us."

Dr. Gabehart caught on to the direction of Sean's thoughts, her eyes widening slightly. "You're thinking about...?"

Sean nodded, his eyes determined. "Something unconventional, untested, and might just be the craziest idea we've ever had. But if there's a chance, however small, that it could work and give Mr. Gladstone more time, wouldn't it be worth exploring?"

Dr. Gabehart's lips curved into a smile, a mixture of surprise and admiration. "You're proposing a personalized treatment plan tailored to Mr. Gladstone's unique physiology and circumstances?"

Sean's grin widened. "You got it. It's a long shot, and I have no idea if it'll even be possible, but if anyone can push the boundaries of medical science, it's us."

Their eyes locked in a moment of shared determination,

their camaraderie cemented by weeks of collaboration and trust. They both knew the challenges ahead would be immense, but they were also keenly aware that Mr. Gladstone deserved every chance at life they could offer.

"Let's do it, Sean," Dr. Gabehart said, her voice unwavering. "For him. For us."

Dr. Gabehart, while in bed, told Sean she couldn't go home because it'd take hours before she could make it back to the hospital.

"Can you be a darling and fetch me a couple of things so I can get ready here?" she asked.

"Fine. I'll buy your essentials downstairs, and someone will bring them up for you. I'll get you scrubs from the hospital, and they'll be dropped in the lobby within the next half-hour," Sean replied.

With a thankful smile, Dr. Gabehart expressed her gratitude towards Sean before he left to freshen up with a quick shower, leaving her to bask in the warmth of his affectionate kiss.

In the room's half-light, Sean's promise hung in the air, a testament to their bond that stretched beyond the confines of the hospital walls. Dr. Gabehart watched him move with gratitude, appreciating his willingness to always go the extra mile. His footsteps faded, leaving behind a tranquil moment of solitude that she welcomed.

Sean's mind was a whirlwind of thoughts and plans as the water cascaded over his tired body. The challenge ahead was monumental, the potential risks immense. Yet, as he stood beneath the steady stream of water, he couldn't help but feel a sense of exhilaration. He was driven by the belief that they could make a difference, that their determination could carve a path where others saw only obstacles.

After about 30 minutes, Sean arrived at the hospital. He sent Dr. Gabehart everything he had promised, and she had started getting ready.

Sean sat next to Mr. Gladstone, and they laughed about some events from the previous night. Sean reminded Mr. Gladstone not to laugh too hard and cause another heart attack, which turned into another joke. Mr. Gladstone thanked Sean for the previous night and said it was the best night of his life.

The room was a blend of shared laughter and bated breaths. Sean and Mr. Gladstone, in their unique way, had found a way to turn the gravity of the situation into a light-hearted exchange. Their camaraderie had created a protective shield around them, temporarily shielding them from the harsh realities surrounding them.

"Come on now, O.G. You're supposed to be taking it easy," Sean teased, a playful glint in his eyes.

Mr. Gladstone chuckled, the sound rich and hearty. "Well, you know me, Sean. Always up for a good laugh, even if my heart disagrees."

Their banter was a testament to their bond, the kind of friendship that could find humour even in the face of adversity. Sean's presence was a source of comfort for Mr. Gladstone, a reassuring reminder that he wasn't facing his challenges alone.

"You know, last night wasn't just about the music," Mr. Gladstone began, his tone taking on a more reflective note. "It was about being surrounded by the people who matter most. You, those two wonderful girls, and even Dr. Gorgeous. It felt like...

well, it felt like a glimpse of something beautiful."

Sean nodded in agreement, his expression thoughtful. "You're right, O.G. Those moments when you're surrounded by the people who care about you, they're the ones that make life truly special."

A sense of quiet understanding settled between them, a shared acknowledgment of the power of human connection. In those moments of vulnerability and sincerity, Mr. Gladstone and Sean were able to find solace, even in the face of uncertainty.

Their conversation shifted to lighter topics, and the room was filled with laughter once again. This was a stark contrast to their hospital environment and a testament to their ability to find joy amidst the challenges.

As the late morning sun filtered through the window, Sean felt profound gratitude for his friendship with Mr. Gladstone. Their bond had been tested by time, adversity, and even the threat of loss. Yet, it had emerged stronger, a reminder of the resilience of the human spirit.

Sean's presence by Mr. Gladstone's side was a comforting constant, a reminder that despite uncertainty, there were things worth holding onto.

Sean and Mr. Gladstone continued to share their thoughts and laughter. It was a reminder that amidst the trials of life, there were moments of connection that could light up even the darkest days.

A well-dressed gentleman entered the room as Sean sat with Mr. Gladstone, engaged in a pleasant conversation. Given his ostentatious attire, Sean couldn't help but feel uneasy at the man's presence. However, his apprehension dissipated as the man and

Mr. Gladstone exchanged hearty laughter and warm pleasantries.

"Counsellor. Thanks for coming here on such short notice. Did you bring me my stuff?" Mr. Gladstone asked.

He responded, "Yeah, sure," and handed Mr. Gladstone a bottle of whiskey.

The lawyer's arrival hinted at a larger framework in Mr. Gladstone's life, one that existed beyond the confines of the hospital room. With a friendly smile, Mr. Gladstone introduced Sean to Mr. Greene.

Sean extended his hand in greeting, acknowledging the significance of the man before him. "Pleasure to meet you, Mr. Greene."

"Likewise, Sean," Mr. Greene replied with a nod, his tone carrying an air of professionalism.

As Mr. Gladstone's lawyer, Mr. Greene held a certain gravitas, representing Mr. Gladstone's intricate affairs beyond the hospital walls. This was a reminder that even within friendship and camaraderie, threads of responsibility and practicality needed to be addressed.

The exchange of the bottle of whiskey was both a gesture of familiarity and a testament to Mr. Gladstone's personality – one that enjoyed the finer things in life.

Mr. Greene's presence also brought a touch of formality to the room, juxtaposed against the easy camaraderie between Sean and Mr. Gladstone. It was a reminder that life is a mosaic of connections – some woven through shared experiences, and others through legal, professional, or familial ties.

As they continued their conversation, Sean listened intently to the dynamic between the two men. There was a respect and understanding that only years of association could foster, and it was evident that Mr. Greene was not just a lawyer but a confidant who knew Mr. Gladstone's life intimately.

With the bottle of whiskey in hand, Mr. Gladstone raised an eyebrow at Sean, a mischievous twinkle in his eye. "Care for a toast, Sean?"

Sean was perplexed because his only argument with Mr. Gladstone concerned any potentially harmful activity. It would have been cheeky and discourteous of him to request a bottle of whiskey and consume it in Sean's presence.

"O.G., is there something you want to tell me?" Sean asked.

"Oh, where're my manners? Mr. Greene has been my lawyer for the last thirty years. This guy has handled every business deal I've ever done, including my prenup. The good guy brought me my fifty-year-old bottle of whiskey to enjoy on my last hooray," Mr. Gladstone replied.

Sean's perplexity was evident, for he had not perceived any cues that could have suggested Mr. Gladstone's intentions. With a quizzical look, Sean probed further, "I'm sorry, I don't quite understand. What exactly are you trying to convey?"

Mr. Gladstone told him he was an intelligent guy and should figure it out.

"Are you sure about this?" Sean inquired.

Mr. Gladstone sat straight up on his bed while enduring mild back pain since he hadn't taken his pain medication for a few hours.

He started, "Sean, I was helpless before you came along, and a DNR was my solution until you gave me the greatest gift a human being can give another: hope. You gave me five months to live the rest of my life, which I couldn't control anymore. I've had two heart attacks in the last twelve hours, and you've told me the next one will likely end it once and for all. I've lived all my adult life trying to be in control of everything I touched, and now I'm beginning to feel helpless because the reality is I've lost control of my own life. Do you think I'm wrong for wanting to make the final call on my terms?" He finished talking with his eyes filled with tears.

After Mr. Gladstone's explanation unfolded, Sean's confusion shifted to understanding. The pieces began falling into place, and he realized there was more to the situation than met the eye. The mention of a prenup, business deals spanning decades, and the fifty-year-old bottle of whiskey created a new perspective on Mr. Greene's presence and the significance of the whiskey itself.

Mr. Gladstone's response was sincere and nostalgic. It was as if he were revealing a glimpse of his past, a history that spanned decades and had been interwoven with Mr. Greene's legal expertise. The mention of the prenup hinted at personal aspects of Mr. Gladstone's complex and multifaceted life.

Listening to Mr. Gladstone's explanation, Sean realized that this interaction went beyond a simple hospital visit. It was a testament to the enduring relationships that can be forged over time, whether through legal matters, business endeavours, or personal bonds. Mr. Greene's role was more than that of a lawyer; he was a steward of Mr. Gladstone's life story, entrusted with the legal intricacies that come with it.

As Sean looked from Mr. Greene to Mr. Gladstone, he could see the mutual respect and camaraderie that had evolved over three decades. This was a reminder that life is a tapestry woven with threads of different colours, each representing a facet of our existence. At this moment, Sean was granted a glimpse into a thread woven through legal documents, shared experiences, and perhaps even a bit of old-fashioned storytelling.

"I understand, it hasn't been easy. If you're okay with it, which you seem to be, I'll support you entirely. Now, let me open that baby and let's do this!" Sean responded as he took the bottle of whiskey and poured it into three cups, and the trio started drinking.

He checked the last time Mr. Gladstone had received his pain medication and was keeping an eye on him and how much he was drinking. They drank, talked, and laughed like they were celebrating something special, which, in some twisted way, they were.

With a nod of acknowledgment, Sean raised his glass to Mr. Gladstone. "To the enduring bonds that stand the test of time."

Mr. Gladstone and Mr. Greene smiled, their glasses joining Sean's in a collective gesture of a toast celebrating the present moment and the history and connections that had brought them together. It was a reminder that our interactions enrich life's narrative, the relationships we nurture, and the threads that weave through the fabric of time.

Sean's initial confusion had given way to a profound understanding of Mr. Gladstone's intentions. As the layers of Mr. Gladstone's words unfolded, Sean grasped the gravity of the situation and the significance of the moment they shared. It was a conversation that delved deep into the complexities of life, mortality, and the choices one makes when faced with the realization of limited time.

Mr. Gladstone's vulnerability was evident in his words, and emotions welled in his eyes. He had lived a life characterized by control and determination. Now, facing an uncertain fate, he sought a measure of control even in his final moments. This was a poignant reflection on the human spirit's resilience and the desire to shape one's destiny, even when the circumstances seemed dire.

Sean's response was marked by empathy and compassion. He acknowledged Mr. Gladstone's feelings and validated his desire to make a deeply personal decision. Their connection had evolved beyond doctor and patient; they had become friends who shared not only medical challenges but also the intricate tapestry of life's complexities. Sean's willingness to stand by Mr. Gladstone's side in this choice was a testament to their unique bond.

The pouring of the whiskey and the shared laughter that followed were a poignant contrast to the weightiness of their conversation. They reminded each other that even in the face of challenging moments, there could still be moments of lightness and connection. Their laughter carried an air of camaraderie, a recognition that life, with all its intricacies, could still be celebrated and cherished.

A sense of camaraderie enveloped the room as the cups clinked and the whiskey flowed. Sean, Mr. Gladstone, and Mr. Greene shared a profound moment of understanding, acceptance, and friendship. Each sip saluted the complexities of life and the power of choice. It was a unique kind of celebration, one that acknowledged both the challenges and the beauty of existence.

In that room, as the hours passed and the whiskey flowed, they created a memory, an unforgettable moment that would forever be etched in their hearts. It was a testament to the bonds that can be formed in unexpected places and under unusual circumstances. As they laughed, talked, and clinked their glasses, they embraced life in all its shades, savouring every drop of experience.

Mr. Gladstone then told Sean he had a favour to ask, and if Sean weren't comfortable to do it, he'd understand.

"I've told my lawyer about my plans, and he told me that I need two witnesses to make the whole thing legit before two doctors sign off on it," he told Sean.

Sean thought about it briefly and replied, "O.G., you know you can always count on me. I want you to know that if this was a different time, place, and under different circumstances, I'd have tried everything to give us a couple of more years."

Mr. Gladstone looked at Sean with a mixture of gratitude and understanding. This moment encapsulated their journey, the trust they had developed, and the weight of their decisions. His eyes glistened with tears, reflecting the complex emotions he was experiencing.

"I know, Sean," Mr. Gladstone replied, his voice a blend of sincerity and warmth. "And I appreciate everything you've done for me more than words can express. But this is my choice, and I'm grateful you will stand by me even in this."

The room seemed to hold an unspoken understanding, a shared recognition that life's journey was often filled with twists and turns, challenges and joys, and the moments that defined its essence. Sean's willingness to be there for Mr. Gladstone in this final chapter was a testament to the depth of their friendship and their respect for each other's autonomy.

As minutes passed and the conversation flowed, they discussed the logistics of Mr. Gladstone's wishes, the legal requirements, and the intricacies of the decisions being made. It was a sobering discussion that was laced with the gravity of the situation. Yet, even amid it all, there was a sense of camaraderie, a shared understanding that they were navigating uncharted waters together.

They had found an ally in Mr. Gladstone's lawyer, Mr. Greene, who understood the legalities and recognized the human element at play. His presence reminded them that every facet of life was interconnected, and even legal proceedings could be intertwined with genuine emotions and personal stories.

The room seemed to be filled with solemnity and camaraderie. The shared laughter had given way to a quieter, more contemplative atmosphere. The weight of their decisions hung in the air, a reminder that life's journey was a tapestry woven with moments of joy, sadness, and everything in between.

Through it all, Sean remained steadfast, offering support, understanding, and a listening ear. Their bond had transcended the conventional boundaries of doctor and patient, evolving into a genuine friendship built on trust and shared experiences. In this room, they were united by medical challenges and the intricate threads of their individual stories.

As time passed, their conversation turned to memories, reflections, and the legacy Mr. Gladstone hoped to leave behind. It was a conversation marked by honesty, vulnerability, and a shared understanding of the impermanence of life. In those moments of quiet contemplation, they created a memory that would forever be etched in their hearts, a testament to the power of friendship, the complexities of existence, and the choices that defined their paths.

The atmosphere in the room shifted with Dr. Gabehart's abrupt entrance and the tense energy that followed her. Sean glanced at her, his eyebrows furrowing slightly at her rushed appearance. He had known that her personal life was complex and fraught with difficulties, but this public confrontation was unexpected.

Dr. Plunkett's outburst was unsettling. His voice echoed through the room as he demanded answers: "Answer me, woman! Where were you last night? I resent you for ignoring me like this. Talk to me now!"

His anger and frustration were palpable, starkly contrasting with the otherwise subdued environment in the room. The intensity of his emotions was almost suffocating, and it was clear that this was a profoundly personal matter spilling into the hospital corridors.

Dr. Gabehart's response, or rather, her lack thereof, only added to the tension. Her decision to ignore Dr. Plunkett's outburst seemed calculated, a deliberate act of defiance against his attempts to control and dominate her. Her cheerful demeanour in the face of his anger displayed her newfound strength, a refusal to be intimidated or silenced.

As Sean observed the unfolding scene, he felt a mixture of concern and admiration for Dr. Gabehart. Her courage to stand up for herself in an undoubtedly difficult situation spoke volumes about her resilience and determination. Yet, the fact that such a confrontation occurred within the hospital walls raised questions about the boundaries between their personal and professional lives.

Dr. Plunkett's anger seemed to escalate as he demanded answers, his voice growing louder and more desperate. The other occupants of the room exchanged uneasy glances, unsure of how to navigate this unexpected intrusion of personal conflict into a space that was typically reserved for medical care and support.

Dr. Gabehart's entrance into the room shifted the dynamics. Her remark about the festive atmosphere juxtaposed with the serious nature of Mr. Gladstone's condition highlighted the contrast between the hospital staff's personal lives and their professional responsibilities.

Her words were a mix of concern and disapproval, indicating that the scene before her was unexpected and perhaps inappropriate given the circumstances. Her address to Sean and Mr. Gladstone hinted at a deeper conversation that needed to take place, likely involving the boundaries between personal and professional relationships.

Dr. Plunkett's explosive reaction, however, escalated the situation further. His anger seemed to have grown since they entered the room, and he directed it squarely at Sean. "I told you to get rid of this kid, and now he's getting a patient drunk. Sean, get the hell out of my hospital now, and I'm going to make sure you'll never practice medicine in this life!"

The intensity of his accusations and threats was jarring, sending shockwaves through the room. Though visibly taken aback, Sean maintained his composure as he exchanged a quick, measured glance with Dr. Gabehart.

Amid the chaos of emotions and raised voices, Mr. Gladstone's hospital bed remained the scene's epicentre. His presence seemed almost surreal against the backdrop of the unfolding drama.

It was as if Dr. Plunkett was invisible and inaudible as Mr. Gladstone responded to Dr. Gabehart, "Dr. Gorgeous, I'm glad you're here. There's something important I need to ask you, and I understand if you're uncomfortable."

"What are you talking about, O.G?" she asked.

Once she saw them drinking, she thought she knew what was happening, but she became confused as she looked at the lawyer, Mr. Gladstone, and then Sean.

Sean told her, "It's time, and he wants you to sign off on it. This's his lawyer to ensure everything goes well on the legal side."

"O.G., are you sure that's what you want?" Dr. Gabehart asked.

Mr. Gladstone quickly replied, "I had an amazing farewell last night, but after the second heart attack this morning, I knew five months was a stretch. I've lost control of everything. Please help me determine my fate."

The indifference to the regular medical procedures in cases like this was gut-wrenching for Dr. Plunkett. However, he was still invisible and inaudible in this room even as he turned to Dr. Gabehart, screaming, "This man refused life-saving treatment, and now he's ending his life with no psychiatric evaluation. Don't you dare do it, Gabrielle. I'll make sure you will regret this for the rest of your life if you sign that paper."

The atmosphere turned sombre and contemplative as the weight of Mr. Gladstone's request settled in.

Dr. Gabehart's face reflected compassion and uncertainty as she listened to Mr. Gladstone's plea. The gravity of the situation was palpable, and the room seemed to hold its breath, suspended in a moment of profound introspection. The lawyer's presence underscored the legal formality required for such a decision.

Sean's unwavering support and the presence of Mr. Greene, the lawyer, indicated the seriousness of Mr. Gladstone's intentions. His words expressed acceptance of his reality and a sense of relinquishing control in the face of circumstances he couldn't overcome. They were poignant reminders of the fragility of life and the complexity of personal autonomy.

As Mr. Gladstone and Dr. Gabehart engaged in this delicate conversation, Dr. Plunkett's protestations had been drowned out by the emotional gravity of the situation. Though loud, his voice was overshadowed by the profound decisions being discussed.

The moral dilemma Dr. Gabehart faced was apparent. On one hand, her oath as a medical professional compelled her to preserve life, and Dr. Plunkett's outburst echoed those concerns. On the other hand, she was confronted with a patient who, in full awareness of his prognosis, wished to retain control over the manner of his passing.

Dr. Gabehart's gaze shifted between the lawyer, Mr. Gladstone, and Sean. She saw the weight of their hopes and desires in their eyes, understanding that this was a defining moment for all involved. Her own emotions played out across her features as she grappled with the magnitude of her decision.

Finally, after a prolonged moment of contemplation, Dr. Gabehart spoke softly, addressing Mr. Gladstone, "O.G., I want you to understand the gravity of what you're asking. This decision has profound implications, and I'm here to ensure that your autonomy is respected while also adhering to the ethical principles that guide my profession."

She turned her attention to Sean and the lawyer, her expression earnest, "And to both of you, I want to make it clear that my role is to ensure that Mr. Gladstone's wishes are respected within the bounds of medical and legal ethics."

As she spoke, it was evident that she was approaching the situation with the utmost care and responsibility. She was considering not only Mr. Gladstone's wishes but also the implications of her decision for everyone involved.

The room seemed to hold its breath once more as the weight of her words settled in. The gravity of the situation was unignorable, and everyone present understood the significance of the choices being made at that moment.

Dr. Gabehart went over to Mr. Gladstone and hugged him dearly. She told him, "I understand, O.G. I wish things had turned out differently. It's been a privilege to be part of your final days, and I will miss you. You'll always have a special place in my heart because you changed my life for the better in the brief time we spent together."

Mr. Greene handed the papers to Dr. Gabehart, who signed all of them without hesitation. The moment was poignant and profound as the room echoed with the weight of the decision that had just been made. Dr. Gabehart's words were a poignant acknowledgment of the unique connection she had formed with Mr. Gladstone during his time at the hospital. Her embrace held warmth and sorrow, a testament to Mr. Gladstone's impact on her life.

As the lawyer handed over the necessary documents and the signatures were affixed, the legal proceedings echoed the gravity of the situation. The room had become a nexus of acceptance, compassion, and a shared understanding that life's impermanence would be met with dignity and choice.

She prepared four cups and poured whiskey for herself, Sean, Mr. Green, and Mr. Gladstone.

The glasses were raised, and Dr. Gabehart's toast carried an air of reverence. "To Oscar Gladstone, who'll forever be remembered as O.G. You've left a mark in our hearts that'll never be erased. As we part ways, I want you to know that you are loved very much, now and forever, and you'll be sorely missed. Yes, life is better when it's all about matters of the heart. The spirit of O.G. will always be with us! Here here."

Each sip reflected gratitude and a deep sense of farewell. Dr. Gabehart's eloquent words captured the essence of Mr. Gladstone's character and the indelible mark he had left on those who knew him. The clinking of the glasses felt like a collective acknowledgment of his journey and the bond they had all formed.

Dr. Plunkett's futile protestations seemed to dissolve into the background as the room was united by a shared moment of closure. He was a lone voice against a tide of acceptance and understanding, overshadowed by the overwhelming emotions and camaraderie that had taken hold.

The atmosphere was bittersweet in this shared experience. The whiskey, which flowed as a beverage and a symbol of camaraderie, seemed to embody the essence of Mr. Gladstone's spirit—strong, cherished, and unapologetically himself.

As the room settled into a contemplative stillness, it was as if time paused to honour the journey that had led them all to this point. The heart's capacity for connection, growth, and empathy was on full display, reminding everyone present that life's most profound moments often centred around matters of the heart.

Dr. Plunkett's anger had transformed into something far

more dangerous – a psychotic rage that seemed to override any semblance of reason or decorum. He had seized Dr. Gabehart's arm with an iron grip, his actions driven by an uncontrollable fury. He then dragged her into the bathroom in Mr. Gladstone's room.

In the confined space of the bathroom, a storm of emotions had erupted, leading to a confrontation that was escalating rapidly.

Yet, in a swift turn of events, Dr. Gabehart's rage surged to the surface. The power dynamics shifted as she took control, her strength and resolve emerging as she pressed him against the wall. Her left forearm on Dr. Plunkett's neck and tight grip on his "twin boys" with her right hand were not just physical restraints; they were manifestations of the anger, frustration, and defiance that had been brewing within her.

The bathroom seemed to shrink around them, the walls bearing witness to this intense clash of wills. Dr. Plunkett's attempt to silence her had backfired, as her grip on his marbles effectively robbed him of his voice. The palpable tension in the air was matched only by the desperation in his eyes, and the inability to articulate his thoughts and feelings only fuelled his helplessness.

Dr. Gabehart's action was a stark assertion of her autonomy and a refusal to be silenced or controlled. It was a primal display of strength in the face of adversity, an embodiment of the power she had found within herself. The confrontation was a battle of physical strength and emotions that had long been suppressed, unfolding in a space that held echoes of fear and determination.

The bathroom became a crucible of conflicting emotions as the seconds stretched into moments. The clash between a couple, two medical professionals, once bound by a shared vocation, had given way to a raw and unfiltered display of their inner struggles. The walls seemed to absorb their energy, reflecting the intensity of their emotions.

Dr. Gabehart's grip was unyielding, and Dr. Plunkett's desperate attempts to free himself only amplified his vulnerability. The silence that enveloped them was heavy with unspoken words, each movement and gesture a language of its own.

It was a moment frozen in time, a battle of wills that mirrored the complexities of the human psyche. As their eyes locked, it was as if the bathroom walls held within them the weight of their shared history, their unspoken grievances, and the choices that had led them to this precipice of confrontation.

Her words, laced with anger and resolve, sliced through the tense air of the bathroom. Each syllable carried the weight of her frustration, and her grip on Dr. Plunkett's "family jewels" was a stark testament to the intensity of her emotions. The power dynamic had shifted dramatically, as the one who had once been subjugated was now held captive by her rage.

"If you ever touch me like that again, yell at me, and try to humiliate me like that, I'll end you. Someone has offered to drop a truck engine on your back because of how you treat me. It's enough that I married you to appease my parents. I can deal with your nonsense at home, but don't you dare tell me how to do my job or try to disrespect me in front of my patients or staff," she said with growing anger.

Dr. Gabehart's voice trembled with a potent mix of suppressed emotions, her words dripping with the acidic bitterness that had accumulated over time. Her defiance was palpable, a manifestation of her years of silent endurance.

Her grip tightened as she spoke, and her eyes bore into his, conveying a message beyond mere words. Her anger was not just about the present moment; it was a culmination of years of disrespect, of being belittled and dismissed. The bathroom seemed to shrink even further, the walls almost suffocating under the weight of their confrontation.

Dr. Plunkett's eyes widened with a mixture of fear and realization. He was face-to-face with the consequences of his actions, confronted by the repercussions of his abuse. The woman before him, whom he had thought he could control and manipulate, had become a force to be reckoned with – a manifestation of the strength he had underestimated for far too long.

Dr. Gabehart's words echoed in the confined space, declaring her determination to reclaim her agency and resist the tyranny she had endured. The bathroom had become a battleground of wills, an arena where her suppressed frustrations were finding an outlet, and her desire for self-respect and dignity was finally taking precedence.

The silence that followed her words was heavy with tension. This silence resonated with the unspoken truths and the shifting dynamics between them. Dr. Plunkett's attempt to regain control was met with unwavering resistance, and the power struggle was now a clear testament to the strength that had emerged from the ashes of years of suffering.

In this charged moment, the bathroom walls were silent witnesses to the transformation unfolding within its confines. Dr. Gabehart's grip was a tangible symbol of her newfound strength, a metaphor for the shackles of oppression from which she broke free. As their eyes locked in an intense stare, the bathroom became a canvas upon which their conflict and confrontation were etched, a testament to the resilience of the human spirit when pushed to its limits.

Amid his silent struggles, Dr. Plunkett's eyes darted wildly as if searching for a way out, a lifeline from the vice-like grip that held him captive. His eyes, once a manifestation of his authority, now mirrored his vulnerability and the stark reality that his power had crumbled beneath the weight of his actions.

Dr. Gabehart's voice pierced the air like a blade, her words slicing through his feeble attempts to beg for mercy. Her tone was laced with fury and unwavering resolve, a stark contrast to the cowed figure before her. The grind of her teeth echoed the internal turmoil that had been building up within her for far too long, a crescendo of suppressed anger and pain that had finally found its outlet.

"And yesterday, I didn't have the surgery because I got a second opinion that confirmed I didn't have breast cancer. They were lumps from the bruises you caused all those times you've been hitting me. This is your first and last warning. I'll ruin you if you ever repeat any of that nonsense. Mark my words."

Her revelations were like shards of glass, shattering the illusion of his control and dominance. The truth behind the lumps that had haunted her, the physical manifestations of his abuse, painted a harrowing picture of the darkness that had lurked beneath their seemingly ordinary facade. The revelation was a testament to her courage, a declaration that she would no longer suffer in silence.

Her words carried a warning that reverberated with a chilling intensity as she spoke. Dr. Gabehart's determination was unwavering, and her promise of retribution hung like an unspoken oath. The bathroom had become a confessional of sorts, a space in which the depths of her pain and her newfound strength collided in a fierce symphony of emotion.

Dr. Plunkett's attempts to communicate his remorse were futile, his voice stifled by the grip that confined him. He was forced to confront the consequences of his actions head-on, to witness the pain he had inflicted upon another human being. The helplessness etched across his features was a stark reminder of the power dynamics that had shifted drastically in this moment.

In this battle of wills and emotions, the bathroom had transformed into a battlefield where the past met the present and years of suffering culminated in a cathartic release. Dr. Gabehart's grip was a metaphor for the chains she had broken, the shackles of fear and submission that she had cast aside.

As her final warning hung in the air, it was clear that this encounter was a turning point, a pivotal moment that marked the end of one era and the dawn of another. Once a place of vulnerability and fear, the bathroom had become a sanctuary of empowerment and reclamation. And through it all, the silence that followed her words was a powerful testament to the transformation that had taken place within its walls.

The room's atmosphere was charged with a lingering intensity as Dr. Gabehart emerged from the bathroom, her steps purposeful and her gaze fixed ahead. The release of Dr. Plunkett from her grip had signalled the end of their confrontation and the beginning of a new chapter for her. It was a testament to her strength and her determination to overcome the demons that had plagued her life.

As she approached Mr. Gladstone's bedside, her voice cut through the air with a curious request that drew puzzled looks from both Sean and Mr. Gladstone. Her words were unexpected, a stark departure from the gravity of the situation that had unfolded just moments before.

"Sean, hit me again."

Sean's brow furrowed as he registered her words, confusion and concern mingling on his features.

Dr. Gabehart's actions were as sudden as they were unexpected. Without hesitation, she downed three shots in quick succession, the liquid fire of the alcohol igniting her senses and momentarily drowning out the emotional turmoil that had gripped her moments ago. The sharp intake of breath that followed the fiery liquid was a tangible release, a catharsis in the form of a burning sensation.

Her choice to consume the shots was a paradoxical blend of defiance and liberation. It was as if she sought to reclaim control over her own body, a silent declaration that she would no longer be defined by the pain she had endured. The juxtaposition of the alcohol's sting against the backdrop of the room's emotional tension created an almost surreal scene, a snapshot of a woman reclaiming her power in the face of adversity.

Dr. Gabehart's actions were a visceral embodiment of the resilience that had carried her through years of suffering. In this small act, she conveyed a complex tapestry of emotions, from her recent confrontation with her husband to her unwavering dedication to her patients, including Mr. Gladstone.

The room, which had witnessed confrontation and catharsis, now symbolized transformation and empowerment. A newfound sense of agency marked Dr. Gabehart's path forward, a determination to break free from the chains that had bound her for far too long.

As the room's occupants processed the raw energy of the moment, the silence that followed seemed to express a quiet reverence for the journey that had brought them to this point. This silence spoke volumes, a testament to the resilience of the human spirit and the power of taking one's life into one's own hands.

The mood in the room seemed to lighten as Mr. Gladstone and Sean exchanged knowing glances, sharing an unspoken understanding of the recent bathroom encounter. It was as if they recognized that sometimes, battles waged behind closed doors were battles nonetheless, and their focus remained on making the best of the time they had left.

Mr. Gladstone's casual brush-off of the incident was a testament to his larger-than-life personality and his ability to navigate difficult situations with a mixture of humour and pragmatism. The altercation in the bathroom had been a mere blip in the grand tapestry of moments that had defined his life, and he seemed intent on not letting it overshadow the time he had left.

Mr. Gladstone brushed the incident aside as he asked Sean, "Brother, would you do the owners?"

Sean's response was swift and full of respect. The term "brother" carried a sense of camaraderie built over time, a bond formed through shared experiences and deep conversations. It was an honour that Sean embraced willingly, a reflection of the connection he had formed with Mr. Gladstone.

As Sean left the room and returned with what was about to become Mr. Gladstone's last meal, the moment's significance hung in the air. The simple act of preparing a cocktail for a physician-assisted suicide for Mr. Gladstone was more than just a task; it was a gesture of care and affection. The cocktail held a bittersweet beauty as if it were a farewell feast carefully curated for a friend about to take his final breath.

Amid this poignant moment, Sean's actions took on an air of gravity and tenderness. The injection he held in his hand represented more than just a medical procedure; it symbolized trust, friendship, and the ultimate act of compassion. Dr. Gabehart's approval, conveyed through a simple nod, spoke volumes about their understanding.

As Sean prepared the injection, there was a palpable sense of solemnity in the room. Each movement carried the weight of the decision being made. This decision would alter the course of Mr. Gladstone's fate. The drug, a conduit of both relief and finality, flowed into the syringe, a silent acknowledgment of the complexities of life and death.

Amidst this profound moment, an unexpected interruption shattered the gravity. Dr. Plunkett stormed out of the bathroom as he struggled to walk straight, his rage palpable in his voice and demeanour. His words were a desperate attempt to assert control, a reminder of the power dynamics at play. "Sean! You're not a doctor, and you don't have any privileges in this hospital. Put that down, or I'll get you thrown in jail!"

Dr. Plunkett's threats seemed to bounce off the resilience of those gathered in the room.

Mr. Greene, the lawyer who had been a silent observer until now, stepped into the spotlight with unwavering poise. His assertion of Sean's authority, backed by legal reasoning and Mr. Gladstone's explicit consent, rendered Dr. Plunkett's objections obsolete. It was a moment of validation, where legalities met humanity, and the bond between Sean and Mr. Gladstone was legally recognized.

Dr. Plunkett's departure, marked by frustration, was a realization of defeat in the face of collective determination. Retreating from the room symbolized his acknowledgment that the prevailing sentiment, the shared conviction to honour Mr. Gladstone's wishes, was more potent than any individual opposition.

Then, a new presence entered the room, Dr. May, whose entrance posed a question to the unfolding scene. "What's going on?"

Her inquiry echoed with curiosity and concern as if she had stumbled upon an enigmatic tableau.

"Well, sweetheart. We talked about this a few hours ago, and I've decided to go through with it. You've been especially wonderful to me, and I'm very grateful for your services to me and this hospital. As I've told you repeatedly, great things await if you keep working hard and truthfully. I'm proud of the person you've become over the last four weeks, and I leave this place hoping this is only the beginning for you. Now, get a drink and celebrate with me as I check out," he said as she walked over to him and passionately hugged him.

Mr. Gladstone's words, imbued with gratitude, wisdom, and acceptance, echoed through the room like a bittersweet melody. His decision, rooted in his recognition of life's impermanence, was embraced by those around him. Dr. May's hug, offered in the face of an inevitable farewell, embodied a sense of unity and shared humanity.

Upon receiving her drink, Dr. May momentarily glanced at it before turning her attention to Dr. Gabehart. She gave her a subtle nod of approval, indicating that it was okay to partake in this unconventional party. Satisfied with this confirmation, she took a sip and joined the celebrations of life. Shortly after, Mr. Greene approached her with a stack of documents that required her signature. Without any hint of hesitation, Dr. May promptly reviewed and signed each one with utmost care.

The passing of documents and the legal formalities intertwined with profound personal moments showcased the juxtaposition of institutional protocols and the human connections within them. Dr. May's participation and her swift and willing endorsement reinforced the respect and trust that had developed between her and Mr. Gladstone.

As the glasses were raised in a toast, it was a celebration of life, of the connections that had been forged, and a poignant farewell to a dear friend. The room held an ambiance of melancholy and acceptance, a testament to the complex emotions at life's crossroads. As the drink flowed, it was not only a celebration of the end but a tribute to the journey that had been shared—a journey of friendship, understanding, and the profound experiences that shape us as individuals.

With a warm gaze, Mr. Gladstone offered Sean his final piece of advice: "Many individuals strive to earn titles and have them bestowed upon them as a form of recognition, but only a few work to honour the title itself. Sean, your interactions with patients consistently uphold the noble title of a medical doctor. I must confess, upon observing your interactions with other patients and nurses, I have often thought to myself that I would aspire to be like you in my next life."

Mr. Gladstone and Sean laughed together, wiping away their tears before continuing, "I know you have a fighting spirit, but I want to remind you to choose your battles wisely. Sometimes, showing our strength means allowing others to win and empowering them. Other times, we win by preserving intangible and immeasurable aspects of our livelihood. Before engaging in any opposition, understand the price and cost. As a natural leader, always protect your team, just as the General would tell you. While things may not seem great for you right now, I believe in your intelligence, dedication, and problem-solving skills. Your future is bright, and I have faith in your success. Please take good care of the girls for me. Although I may not leave behind a legacy, I hope to be remembered positively when you share my story."

Mr. Gladstone closed his teary eyes and said, "I'm ready now."

Amidst the melancholy air that now enveloped the room, Mr. Gladstone's words carried a profound wisdom, a culmination of a life lived fully and the insights gained along the journey. The concept of honouring titles, not for ego or recognition but for the sincere service they represent, resonated deeply. His advice to Sean, delivered with warmth and humour, was a testament to the mentorship that had grown between them.

As Sean listened, he absorbed Mr. Gladstone's words like precious gems of guidance. The notion of selectively choosing battles resonated, a reminder that strength lies not only in triumph but also in insight. Mr. Gladstone's words mirrored the complexities of life, where the pursuit of victory sometimes requires relinquishing the immediate battlefield in favour of a greater purpose.

Mr. Gladstone's compliments, tinged with lightheartedness and camaraderie, showcased the mutual respect that had grown between them. Sean's image as a natural leader, his dedication, and his problem-solving mindset spoke of qualities that had been recognized not only by Mr. Gladstone but also by others around him.

The emphasis on preserving and nurturing the people around him, encapsulated in the metaphor of protecting one's troops, demonstrated a holistic view of leadership that extended beyond personal achievements to the well-being and growth of the collective. This view reflected Mr. Gladstone's approach, where his concern for others' comfort and happiness had been a defining trait.

Amid the heavy emotions, there was a flicker of levity as Mr. Gladstone's laughter intertwined with the shared tears. His insight, cloaked in humour, touched upon the intricate dance of life—the harmony of joy, sorrow, laughter, and tears that make up the human experience.

Mr. Gladstone's closing request to care for the girls he cherished echoed with a sense of responsibility and trust. It encapsulated his recognition of Sean's capacity to nurture and protect, a torchbearer of their shared values.

As Mr. Gladstone concluded his words, the room held a collective pause. At this moment, the gravity of the impending departure mingled with the solace of acceptance. Closing his eyes, a final surrender to the journey's end was a quiet, powerful symbol of letting go.

In that room, surrounded by those who had become his confidants and companions, Mr. Gladstone's journey took its final step. His legacy, far from being forgotten, was etched into the hearts of those who had walked alongside him. It was a legacy of camaraderie, wisdom, and a celebration of life itself.

Sean injected the drug into the central line and slowly opened the drip before sitting beside Mr. Gladstone.

As the drip began its measured infusion, a palpable hush settled in the room, a poignant acknowledgment of the threshold that had been crossed. Sean's steadfast and tender presence beside Mr. Gladstone resonated with the depth of their friendship and the unwavering support he had offered. The moments ticked by, each drop of the drug echoing like a poignant heartbeat.

Now watching over the drip, Dr. May embodied the responsibility of this final act—a sacred vigil, a continuation of the care and attention she had provided to Mr. Gladstone during his hospital stay. Her presence and Sean's created a cocoon of empathy and compassion around their departing friend.

As Mr. Gladstone flatlined, a collective sigh reverberated through the room. Sean's tears, glistening like jewels, mirrored the shared emotions of everyone present. His grief was raw and unfiltered, a testament to the depth of the bond they had forged.

Dr. Gabehart's voice, a vessel of solace, pierced through the silence with the haunting notes of "Amazing Grace." The melody carried a sense of reverence, a tribute to the life that had transitioned and a celebration of the grace that had intertwined their paths. The song's words, a reflection on redemption and a longing for divine peace, encapsulated the poignant moment—a soul departing from the earthly realm, finding solace in the arms of grace.

Tears flowed freely as the song continued, a chorus of heartache and honour. In that room, their emotions converged into a collective tribute, an acknowledgment of the journey that had ended and a reflection on the legacy left behind.

Mr. Gladstone's passing, marked by the tender serenade of "Amazing Grace," was a touching reminder of the fragility of life and the interconnectedness of human experiences. As the last notes faded, they were left with the memory of a life well-lived, a friend well-loved, and a legacy that would continue to inspire and resonate in their hearts and actions.

Dr. Gabehart walked over to Dr. May as she couldn't hold herself while watching Mr. Gladstone shuffle off the mortal coil. Despite being drenched in tears, she had tried to be strong through singing.

Dr. Gabehart tried to show strength in the presence of a subordinate. They hugged tightly while Sean was struggling to release Mr. Gladstone's hand, even when he knew Mr. Gladstone had officially cashed in his chips.

In the wake of Mr. Gladstone's departure, a tender sense of loss hung in the air, tangible yet intangible. Once filled with camaraderie and celebration, the room now held the weight of his absence. Dr. Gabehart's embrace of Dr. May was a poignant testament to the shared emotions that transcended hierarchies—a moment of human connection amid profound grief.

As Dr. Gabehart offered her strength, it became apparent that the bonds formed in the crucible of patient care extended beyond professional roles. The tears that flowed were a testament to the humanity that permeated the clinical setting, where compassion and empathy intertwined with medical expertise.

Sean's reluctance to release Mr. Gladstone's hand echoed the lingering presence of their friendship. In those final moments, the touch became a bridge between two worlds—the one that Mr. Gladstone had departed and the one he left behind, forever imprinted on the hearts of those who had walked alongside him.

Amidst the tears and heartache, there was a shared understanding that Mr. Gladstone's passing was not merely an end but a transition—a passage from a life well-lived into the realm of memory and legacy. As they clung to each other, grappling with the complex tapestry of emotions, they embraced the lessons, love, and wisdom Mr. Gladstone had bestowed upon them.

The room, now tinged with the residue of farewell, was also infused with a deep appreciation for the moments shared and the impact that one individual had on the lives of those around him. As the weight of their collective grief settled, they knew that the echoes of Mr. Gladstone's laughter, advice, and spirit would linger on, shaping their lives and the lives of those they touched in the days to come.

When Fiona received the summons to the room, she had no idea what to expect. Her emotions overwhelmed her as soon as she entered, and she fell to the ground, weeping uncontrollably. Dr. Gabehart rushed to her side, offering her support and a comforting embrace. Despite her efforts, Fiona continued to cry for several minutes, unable to contain her emotions.

Fiona's raw emotion was a stark reminder of Mr. Gladstone's impact on everyone around him. Her tears were a testament to the deep connection they had shared. At that moment, the room seemed to hold not just the memory of Mr. Gladstone's departure but also the void he left behind in the lives of those who had known him.

Dr. Gabehart's gesture of embracing Fiona was a balm to the wounded hearts, a silent comfort that spoke volumes. Sometimes, in the face of grief, words fall short, and a simple embrace can convey a depth of understanding that words cannot capture.

As the room gradually quieted and the sheets were pulled over Mr. Gladstone's body, a solemn sense of finality settled in.

Preparing for his departure was a heartbreaking ritual, a way of showing respect and care even in the last moments.

Sean's stillness as he sat captured the mixed emotions swirling within him—memories, regrets, gratitude, and the ache of loss. It was as if he were sitting at the crossroads of the past and the future, contemplating the impact of this man's life on his own journey.

When Mr. Gladstone was wheeled out, it marked the physical departure of a beloved soul, but the essence of his presence lingered on in the memories of those he had touched. Sean's solitude in the room was a moment of reflection, a time to process the reality of the loss and to gather his thoughts.

The room felt emptier with Dr. Gabehart stepping out, yet it was still charged with the echoes of the moments they had shared with Mr. Gladstone. In that quiet space, Sean found himself in the company of Mr. Greene, a fellow witness to the poignant farewell that had just unfolded. Their shared silence spoke volumes, a tribute to the man who had left their lives, leaving an indelible mark on their hearts and minds.

Amid the weight of the recent events, Sean and Mr. Greene found solace in sharing memories of Mr. Gladstone. Their conversation became a tribute to his larger-than-life character, a way to honour the moments of joy, laughter, and wisdom that he had brought into their lives.

As Mr. Greene imparted his insights on death and the process of letting go, it was a reminder that even in sorrow, there's a certain beauty in how life transitions to whatever comes next. The wisdom he shared reflected his years of experience and was a testament that facing mortality can often bring about a deep sense of reflection and perspective.

The stories they exchanged about Mr. Gladstone were like threads that wove together to create a tapestry of his personality. The crazy anecdotes and memorable experiences they recounted showcased the many facets of a man who had lived life fully and unapologetically. These stories became a way of keeping his spirit alive and remembering him as a patient and a vibrant individual who had touched their lives.

However, as Mr. Greene acknowledged the limitations of time and his responsibilities, he decided to address the administrative aspects of Mr. Gladstone's passing. It was a reminder that even in the face of personal loss, there are practical matters that need attention, a testament to the complexities of life that continue even after someone has departed.

Sean received a couple of papers from Mr. Greene, who explained that they were necessary to fulfill some of Mr. Gladstone's final requests. Without hesitation, Sean signed all the parts that required his signature without taking the time to read or consider the contents of the documents.

"Are you sure you don't want to read what you're signing?" questioned Mr. Greene.

Sean reassured Mr. Greene that Mr. Gladstone would not have asked him to sign something that could harm him. He even suggested that there may be a hidden joke in those papers that would make sense, maybe years later.

Mr. Greene informed Sean that Mr. Gladstone wanted him to have his most treasured possessions: his watch, car, and apartment. "He was very clear about wanting you to have them. He mentioned that you're like a son to him, and he wanted to leave you something meaningful."

Sean's expression turned thoughtful as he absorbed Mr. Greene's words. The gravity of the gesture hit him, and he was moved by the depth of Mr. Gladstone's affection for him. "I'm honoured, really. He meant a lot to me, too," Sean replied with a touch of emotion.

Mr. Greene nodded in understanding. "I can see that the feeling was mutual. He held a special place in his heart for you, Sean."

As they conversed, it became evident that Mr. Gladstone's final wishes were practical arrangements and heartfelt expressions of the connections he had formed in his life. Through the watch, the car, and the apartment, he was leaving tangible reminders of his legacy and the relationships he cherished. Even though he was gone, his spirit and impact would continue to live on through the memories and connections he had forged.

Mr. Greene also informed Sean that when he signed his will, Mr. Gladstone's last words were, "Thank him for me for not letting me die with my watch."

"I knew there was a joke in there," Sean responded.

Mr. Greene was a little confused and asked, "I don't get it; what's the joke?"

Sean told him that it was the watch. Even if he had tried to explain the joke, he wouldn't get it because it's all about matters of the heart.

"That's very interesting, and it makes me wonder even more. I've known Mr. Gladstone for a long time and have been his lawyer for over thirty years. I've never seen him give anything to anyone for free like this. I was surprised when he instructed me to give you all this. When I asked him, he said the same thing, that I wouldn't understand because it's about the matters of the heart. Dr. Gabehart toasted to Mr. Gladstone and finished with the same phrase. I still don't get it," Mr. Greene explained, still trying to figure out this phrase that three people kept saying with huge smiles.

"Yeah, you're right, but maybe you'll get it one day," Sean replied.

Sean's cryptic responses only added to the intrigue surrounding this enigmatic phrase. As Sean stood up and prepared to leave, Mr. Greene couldn't help but smile in mild confusion. He watched as Sean walked out of the room, leaving a sense of mystery that seemed to revolve around the deep connections and emotions that had defined Mr. Gladstone's life.

Sometimes, the most profound sentiments can't be easily explained with words. "Matters of the heart" are often complex and multi-layered, defying straightforward explanations. The phrase Mr. Gladstone, Dr. Gabehart, and Sean had used encapsulated a sentiment that transcended the ordinary. This sentiment was woven into the tapestry of their relationships and experiences. It was a sentiment that would continue to resonate, carrying the memory of Mr. Gladstone and the bonds he had formed.

While walking out, Sean accidentally bumped into Fiona. She immediately informed him that Dr. Plunkett Sr. wanted to see him in the other Dr. Plunkett's office. She added that the situation seemed serious as Dr. Gabehart was also present. Fiona was curious to know what it was all about.

Sean told her he had no clue but was going to find out. "Wish me luck!" he said as he walked away.

Fiona watched Sean walk away with a mix of concern and curiosity. She knew that whatever was happening in the Plunketts' office had to be important, considering the gravity of the situation and the fact that Dr. Gabehart was there, too. She couldn't help but feel a slight sense of unease, wondering what could be happening and how it might affect the hospital and its staff.

As Sean entered the office, he found Dr. Plunkett Sr. sitting behind the desk with a stern expression. The atmosphere was tense, and Sean sensed something significant was about to be discussed.

Dr. Plunkett Jr. was standing right next to Dr. Plunkett Sr., leaning on a bookshelf. Dr. Gabehart was sitting right across from Dr. Plunkett Sr.

Dr. Plunkett Sr. offered Sean a seat next to Dr. Gabehart.

"Thank you for coming, Sean," Dr. Plunkett Sr. began, his tone measured. "We have some important matters to discuss and must address them openly and honestly."

Sean nodded, his expression serious. He knew that this meeting was about more than just the events of the past hour; there seemed to be an underlying issue that needed to be addressed.

He introduced himself, "My name is Dr. Plunkett Sr., and I own this hospital."

Sean shook his hand and sat down before Dr. Plunkett Sr. continued, "I understand things have been unusually chaotic in this hospital since you started your cardiology clerkship with Dr. Gabehart. The series of events leading to a patient's passing just moments ago are very troubling, to say the least."

Sean interrupted, "Dr. Plunkett, I'm sorry to interrupt, but

I'll save you the trouble. Dr. Plunkett, your son, has made it clear to me that he'll see to it that I'll never practice medicine simply because of our minor difference in opinion when I started my cardiology clerkship. I've accepted that a negative review such as the one I will get from this hospital will make me untouchable to almost everyone in this country. I know he'll never change his mind, and I've made peace with that. As for the incident with Mr. Gladstone, I take full responsibility, legal or otherwise. Dr. Gabehart should not be held liable for my actions. I regret that, and I offer my full apology to you and the hospital for any inconvenience I've caused in my four weeks here or in the future as a result of my actions today."

Dr. Plunkett Sr. listened attentively as Sean spoke, his expression thoughtful. After Sean finished, there was a brief silence in the room before Dr. Plunkett Sr. leaned back in his chair, his fingers steepled in front of him.

"Sean," he began, his voice measured, "I appreciate your honesty and willingness to take responsibility for your actions. Clearly, you've thought this through and are prepared to face the consequences."

Before Dr. Plunkett Sr. could finish responding to Sean, there was a knock at the door. It was Mr. Greene, and he was allowed into the office.

When Mr. Greene realized the tension in the office, he apologized for disturbing him and told Dr. Plunkett Sr. he could wait until they were done with their meeting.

Dr. Plunkett Sr. replied, "No problem, Sir, I understand you're Mr. Gladstone's lawyer. Do you need help with anything?"

"Nothing big. Mr. Gladstone instructed me to make a few

things clear to the hospital to avoid problems dealing with the circumstances leading to his death. His death was his wish; he knew what he was doing, and I witnessed that together with a few of your staff. With that in mind, you shouldn't worry about a lawsuit from his estate as our firm is also handling that," Mr. Greene informed Dr. Plunkett Sr.

"Thank you, counsellor. Would that be all?" Dr. Plunkett Sr. asked.

"Well, there's one more thing. Mr. Gladstone was under the impression that his assisted suicide might cause some problems for the staff that were involved. I wanted to let you know that he has already paid us handsomely to defend those individuals against any punishment from this hospital's administration, or any other administration for that matter. And that would be all. Good day to you all," Mr. Greene said with a smile before turning round and walking out.

Dr. Plunkett Jr. wasn't impressed by the presentation, but his father quickly returned to addressing Sean. "Well, Sean, I'd like to finish this, and we can discuss your concerns after."

Dr. Plunkett Sr. said to Sean as he opened a letter that was addressed to him before he continued, "This is a letter addressed to me from Dr. Gabehart, and I'd like to read it to you all." He started reading:

Dear Dr. Plunkett Sr.

I am your daughter-in-law and your employee. I hope you will take this letter in the spirit it is intended—that is, in the

fullest capacity of professionalism and nothing personal. I am not pleased with this hospital's leadership, and I would like you to consider this letter my two-week notice if you disagree.

This hospital needs a change in leadership to one that inspires both patients and staff to provide and maintain premium health services. However, the current leadership antagonizes the same people it is supposed to lead and serve to the detriment of medical care and this medical institution's credibility.

Dr. Plunket Jr., my husband, has consistently shown gross incompetence in dealing with patients and staff. I would like to take over his responsibilities as he leaves his current position as the chief administrator of this hospital, effective immediately.

I would also suggest that Dr. May take over the cardiology department, which I will vacate, and hire the soon-to-be Dr. Sodeman as a medical consultant for Autonomy General Hospital.

Most staff and patients would agree with this direction of the hospital. I understand if you disagree, but I would be walking out, and so would some of the most dedicated staff because they are also tired of the current leadership.

Regards

Gabrielle Gabehart, MD

Dr. Plunkett Jr. started laughing hard while clapping his hands as he stood beside his father.

"This is cute. You must be dreaming to think there's any possibility of that happening. All of you kids have no experience, and you don't know how it is to have the responsibility of running a hospital. You treat a few patients and think you can do what I do?" he said as he continued laughing hard.

Dr. Plunkett Sr. looked at Dr. Gabehart as he said, "Well, my son is not completely wrong."

Dr. Gabehart was quick to object, "The same son that told his wife she had cancer, which took an inexperienced medical student to disprove in a few minutes? A few other doctors independently assessed the history and tests, and came to the same conclusion as the medical student."

Dr. Plunkett Sr. raised an eyebrow, clearly intrigued by Dr. Gabehart's statement. He turned his attention back to his son and spoke, "Son, is there any truth to what Dr. Gabehart is saying?"

Dr. Plunkett Jr. seemed taken aback by the question, his laughter fading. "Well, that might have been a small mistake, but everyone makes mistakes, right?" he stammered.

Dr. Plunkett Sr. wasn't impressed, mainly because his response was unprofessional and indifferent to patient care, two things he took seriously.

Dr. Gabehart continued, "It's not just about a single mistake. It's about a pattern of behaviour that affects patient care, staff morale, and the overall reputation of this hospital. Our patients deserve the best care possible, and our staff deserves a leader who inspires and supports them."

Dr. Plunkett Sr. looked down and pondered briefly before asking Dr. Gabehart when she wanted her answer.

"Right now," she replied.

The situation had reached a juncture where the tides of change could no longer be ignored. Dr. Plunkett Sr., accustomed to steering the ship of his hospital with seasoned hands, faced a storm of circumstances that demanded a course correction. The news of his son's professional misstep, so carelessly revealed, struck a chord within him. It shattered his carefully orchestrated harmony like a thunderclap in a clear sky.

With wisdom gleaned from years of experience and the knowledge that leadership was a mirror reflecting the actions of its constituents, Dr. Plunkett Sr. realized he stood at a crossroads. The path he chose would not only define his son's fate but would ripple throughout the fabric of the hospital and potentially tarnish his legacy. An old saying whispered in the chambers of his thoughts: "A father's love should not blind him to his child's faults."

So, he summoned the strength of a ship's captain facing a gathering storm. He knew that the mast of his reputation swayed in the wind of public perception. The situation called for a fair and just remedy, not only for the hospital but also for his honour. The weight of his responsibility lay heavily upon him, much like the burden of a ship laden with precious cargo.

This was pushing things a little too far. Still, Dr. Plunkett Sr. understood that if word got out that he had kept his son as the head of his hospital even after learning about his gross incompetence, that'd likely question his leadership as an owner as well.

"Fine, we'll have a trial run for the next six months if Dr. Sodeman and Dr. May agree with you on this direction," he said. He shook his head in disappointment that things had come to this point where he had to demote his son and promote his daughter-in-law.

"Dr. May and Dr. Sodeman are both on board, and my first task will be to suspend Dr. Plunkett from all his duties while every case he has handled over the last five years will be reviewed," Dr. Gabehart said as her husband started throwing a tantrum.

"You're now the boss, I guess." Dr. Plunkett Sr. replied as he threw his head on the desk in exhaustion.

Sean and Dr. Gabehart got up and walked out of the office with smiles. Sean didn't say a word as he walked before Dr. Gabehart.

When Dr. May ran into Dr. Gabehart to find out what had happened, Dr. Gabehart was trying to talk to Sean. "Sean! When are you going to start?!" she asked.

Sean didn't look back and kept walking with his chest out and head held high as he replied, "I'm going on a vacation, so I'll see you in two weeks to six months."

Dr. May looked at Sean, then at Dr. Gabehart, then at Sean and then at Dr. Gabehart again, wondering what had happened in that office.

Dr. Gabehart explained to Dr. May, "Sean taught me to take control, and today I had the guts to do that. It's a wild world, but sometimes, you need courage to get things done and get what you want. Fighting for someone or something is easy when you truly believe in your actions. I believed in him when I met him; I trusted him when I saw every patient trusting him, but I knew I should treasure him when I saw how he handled Mr. Gladstone's final moments."

Dr. Gabehart held Dr. May's hand as they started walking towards the office to start packing and moving into the new office as the new chief of the hospital.

Dr. Gabehart's words resonated throughout the corridor like the echoes of a bell rung with purpose. The air seemed charged with a newfound energy, a palpable undercurrent of change that surged like a river breaking free from its confines. Her revelation was akin to a guiding star emerging from the darkness, illuminating the path ahead.

Her reference to Sean's influence was like a beacon of wisdom in a world often shrouded in doubt. The concept of seizing control, like a ship's captain taking the helm during a storm, was not lost on those present. It was a reminder that sometimes, amidst chaos, clarity could be found through the power of decisive action.

Her words also conjured the image of a knight, armoured in resolve, bravely riding into the fray for a just cause. It was a testament to her bravery, fortitude, and willingness to stand up for what she believed was right. The corridor felt infused with her conviction, like the air after a thunderstorm, freshly cleansed and invigorated.

Like intertwined branches of a sturdy tree, Dr. Gabehart and Dr. May's bond spoke to their unity and strength. They walked together, hand in hand, like comrades stepping onto the battlefield. The prospect of a new office, a new chapter, symbolized the dawn of a fresh era, much like the rising sun signalling the start of a new day.

The air felt charged with anticipation, like the atmosphere before a grand unveiling. The transformation unfolding before them was like a butterfly emerging from its cocoon. This metamorphosis promised growth, change, and renewal.

The hospital corridors witnessed their journey – a journey that mirrored the odyssey of life itself. From the quiet courage to seize control to the bond that formed between kindred spirits and the ascent towards a new beginning – all these elements intertwined, much like the threads of a tapestry weaving a tale of resilience, hope, and transformation.

"He's a burning fire that'll take an army to put out, and we are fortunate to have him join our ranks," Dr. Gabehart affirmed, her words carrying the weight of admiration and respect.

Dr. May's curiosity was piqued, and she couldn't help but question Dr. Plunkett's sudden change of heart. "Hold on a second," she interjected, puzzled, "Didn't Dr. Plunkett claim he would ensure Sean's expulsion from the medical field? And now he's being hired?"

Dr. Gabehart's smile was enigmatic as she responded, "Life has a way of twisting and turning in the most unexpected directions. Sometimes, what we predict is far from what unfolds."

Her demeanour shifted to one of self-reflection, a rare glimpse into the inner workings of her thoughts. "I've never been as amazed by myself as I am in this very moment. Sean managed to alter the course of my life in just a few hours, and I had the privilege to reciprocate that by altering his path in mere minutes," she mused.

Dr. May's inquisitiveness was unrelenting as she questioned when Sean was expected to start. The two women walked side by side, their steps rhythmic like the rhythm of their camaraderie, bonded by shared goals and aspirations.

Dr. Gabehart's response revealed the profound connection she had forged with Sean. "He said at least two weeks, but I have a strong inkling he'll be here bright and early tomorrow. Thanks to his efforts, I'm about to assume the helm of this hospital, and you, my dear, will ascend to the role of head of the cardiology department. It's a well-earned promotion. Yes, there's still much to learn, but your curiosity and determination will see you through. Sean and I will always be by your side every step of the way," she assured Dr. May, the warmth of mentorship and friendship evident in her words.

A twinge of emotion welled within Dr. May, but Dr. Gabehart's unwavering spirit guided the conversation. "It's remarkable how the simplest gestures we often take for granted can hold immeasurable significance to others. Be it our wisdom, compassion, or even our possessions, we don't always comprehend the extent of their impact on someone else's life. The exchange of knowledge and support is a profound part of our existence," she remarked, her tone as profound as a wellspring of wisdom.

"We're all interconnected, like threads woven into the fabric of existence," Dr. Gabehart continued, her words akin to a soothing melody. "Our hearts, minds, experiences, and dreams are all pieces of a greater puzzle. In this chaotic world, we need each other, leaning on one another to navigate its complexities and extract meaning from our finite time here. Remember, none of us stand alone; we're all islands in the vast ocean of humanity."

Her sentiments culminated in a single sentence: " If I had to sum it all up, I'd say it's all about the matters of the heart."

THE END

9 781068 979842